About the Authors

Avril Tremayne became a writer via careers in shoe-selling, nursing, teaching, and public relations. Along the way, she studied acting, singing, pottery, oil painting, millinery, German, and Arabic (among other things). A committed urbanite, her favourite stories are fast-paced contemporary city stories told with sass and humour. Married with one daughter, Avril lives in Sydney, Australia. When not writing or reading, she's thinking about food, wine, and shoes.

Zara Cox writes contemporary and erotic romance. She lives in the Garden of England aka Kent – with her hubby and two kids. She loves to read and travel. In 2017 she managed to visit her number one bucket list destination – Hawaii – and is now actively pleading with her husband to live there! She loves to hear from her readers; you can get in touch with her via Twitter @zcoxbooks, on Instagram zaracoxwriter, or Facebook zaracoxwriter

Cara Lockwood has written more than thirty novels, including *I Do (But I Don't)*, which was made into a Lifetime Original Movie. She grew up near Dallas, raised by her Japanese-American Dad and Scottish/English mother. Her work has been translated into several languages. Cara lives near Chicago with her husband and five children (two by biology and three by marriage), and their eighty-five-pound Goldendoodle, Theodore.

A Christmas Dare

AVRIL TREMAYNE

ZARA COX

CARA LOCKWOOD

MILLS & BOON

First Published in Great Britain 2023
by Mills & Boon, an imprint of HarperCollins*Publishers* Ltd,
1 London Bridge Street, London, SE1 9GF

www.harpercollins.co.uk

HarperCollins*Publishers*
Macken House, 39/40 Mayor Street Upper,
Dublin 1, D01 C9W8, Ireland

ISBN: 978-0-263-32039-8

MIX
Paper | Supporting
responsible forestry
FSC™ C007454
www.fsc.org

This book is produced from independently certified FSC™ paper
to ensure responsible forest management.

For more information visit: www.harpercollins.co.uk/green

Printed and Bound in the UK using 100% Renewable Electricity
at CPI Group (UK) Ltd, Croydon, CR0 4YY

GETTING NAUGHTY

AVRIL TREMAYNE

This one's for my mother – who may require a strong drink to read past this page!

CHAPTER ONE

TEAGUE STRETCHED HIS arms over his head and sucked in a lungful of summer air as he peered at Frankie's doll-sized cottage, which was situated at the end of a long driveway that ran alongside a squat redbrick apartment building.

It was so small he'd probably have to duck to fit under the lintel.

If she invited him in.

If she even heard him knock, given it was barely eight o'clock on a Sunday morning.

His memory of Frankie's Saturday nights was that they were big and wild, so unless she'd changed drastically in the ten years since he'd last seen her, chances were that at this precise moment she'd be either comatose or contemplating the walk of shame from wherever she'd ended up after work last night.

And it was too bad he chose *now* to remember that instead of thirty minutes ago, when he'd gotten into the taxi at Sydney Airport. At that point, he could have done as his best friend Matt had suggested during those chaotic last moments at Heathrow: gone to his hotel, gotten some sleep, and called Frankie at a civilized hour to arrange a time to meet for the handover.

Handover! Like he was doing some illicit drug deal.

Not that dealers dragged their supplies around with them in wheeled suitcases. Or maybe they did. What did he know? He was a corporate lawyer, not a criminal one.

Whatever. It was too late to change his mind because he'd let the taxi go and stranded himself.

"Oh, for fuck's sake, get it over with," he ordered himself, and trudged up the path, stopping at a ratty-looking welcome mat that announced, You Have Arrived at Your Destination.

"I don't think so, Frankie Lee," he scoffed, stepping up to the door.

He tugged at the collar of his shirt to make sure it was sitting straight, ran a hand over his hair, dragged in another lungful of air and knocked.

Unsurprisingly, there was no answer.

He knocked again, just so he could say he'd really tried.

Waited for proof of life.

Nothing.

Okay, three strikes and you're out a-a-and knock.

Silence.

He looked back down the driveway, picturing Frankie in one of her vintage dresses, black hair disheveled, makeup smeared, humming a satisfied tune and swinging her shoes from one hand as she meandered up the path as though she owned the world and all its contents.

Ha! Walk of shame? Not likely. Swagger of pride was more her style.

But, of course, there'd be no sign of her yet. At eight o'clock she'd still be in bed with…well, whomever she'd gone to bed with.

Teague tried to picture a likely "whomever" but that wasn't so easy to visualize. For all Frankie's brazen sex appeal, Teague could only recall one identifiable boyfriend from that year she'd spent in Washington, DC. Kyle. Big, burly, covered in tattoos. Kyle hadn't been around long enough for Teague to get more of a handle on him than that; Frankie had dumped him within a month of their arrival together in DC, after he'd pitched a fit over her taking a second job.

That second job was as a dancer in a gentlemen's club, so Teague had some sympathy for the guy. Or he would have had, if Kyle hadn't already worked himself into a lather over Frankie working as a server at Flick's, which marked the guy as more proprietary asshole than concerned boyfriend. Because come on, *Flick's*? Seriously?

Flick's was a grungy, student-hangout bar/restaurant. None of its patrons had ever stood a chance with Frankie. Hell, most of them were underage, and Frankie might have only been nineteen, but the rolling confidence of her walk flashed a warning that she'd already seen—and enjoyed—everything life had to offer, so they shouldn't bother approaching her unless they were packing something more interesting than a fake ID. Teague had been under no illusions that he was in the running, despite being two years older than her and probably the only legal drinker in the place. She could fluster him by doing nothing more than breathing in his general direction. The only guy she hadn't flustered had been Matt—but then, those two were like spirit animals.

So, okay, maybe it *wasn't* so hard to envisage the guy whose bed Frankie was in. Someone like Matt.

Teague sighed. He loved Matt like a brother, but sometimes it sucked playing running back to Matt's star quarterback. And after a twenty-three-hour flight Teague decided he was too tired to receive yet another handoff. So enough! The end! There'd be no call to arrange a time with Frankie. Teague would slip the damn thing under her door, then delete the number Matt had punched into his phone and go have his vacation.

He bent low, assessing the size of the gap…heard a faint rustle. What the—? Uh-oh.

Shit!

The door opened before he could move. He heard his name—"Teague?"—and closed his eyes. Fuck. Just fucking *brilliant*, to be caught with his head level with Frankie's crotch.

"Are you coming up anytime soon?" she asked in her sleepily amused Australian drawl, as though a guy bowing down for her on her doorstep was par for the course. Which it probably was.

Slowly he unbent, eyes traveling up the length of a silky cream-colored robe covered in bold red flowers. An outfit deserving of a smokily sinful bordello.

And then his eyes reached her face, and she smiled at him in that how-about-it? way she had, and it killed him that despite the fact he was now thirty-two years old, with a megasuccessful career, property in three countries and billions in the bank, she still had the power to make him feel like a schoolboy with a crush on his teacher. And he didn't even *have* a crush on her. He'd never let himself have one, because she was too—too *much* for him, too dangerous. Hadn't that been the whole damn point of keeping his distance all those years ago?

"Hello, Frankie," he said, blinking a little at her hair, which was hacked off halfway between her ears and her shoulders, the depthless black of it livened up with an inch-wide band of electric blue across the blunt ends. Everything else about her was as he remembered. The gold-tinged skin, the swollen-looking lips that seemed permanently stained a shade of almost red, the pale gray eyes—the left one turned in very slightly, an imperfection that was mystifyingly, profoundly, vulnerably alluring. The haughty black eyebrows that started low over the inner corners of her eyes and ended in a late arch, and heavy black lashes so thick they framed her eyes like eyeliner. She wasn't beautiful but she was so vibrantly alive it had always been an effort not to stare and stare and stare at her.

"Come on in," she said and stepped back.

"My suitcase…"

"A suitcase?" She laughed—a suggestively throaty chuckle. "Does that mean you want to stay with me?"

"No!" *Jesus!* "No, no. No."

"So that's a *no*, then, is it?" She smiled again as she hitched up her slipping robe at one shoulder. "Pity." One beat, two, as she pursed her lips, assessing him like he was a side of meat hanging at the butcher. As she turned away, she added, "Ah, well, bring it in anyway."

By the time Teague stepped over the threshold, she was disappearing through an archway at the end of the room.

He closed the door, then just stood there as a riot of color dueled with his eyes. Red couch, big enough for two people to sit on—or it would have been, if not for a basket taking up one half. The basket was overflowing with wool in too many shades to count and had at least six sets of knitting needles sticking out of it, and it boggled his mind because...*Frankie? Knitting?* There was an exotic rug in reds, browns and indigos taking up most of the wall behind the couch, and the floorboards were covered by a similarly styled rug in variegated creams, ochres and olives. A low coffee table in dark green sat on the rug in front of the couch, and a table at one end of the couch served as a display plinth for a small sculpture—an abstract twist of glass.

There was a doorway at the end of the room, to the right of the arch through which Frankie had disappeared. The door was ajar, so he could see into the room beyond. Rose-pink walls, a section of bed—rumpled white sheets, no coverlet. He pictured Frankie on those sheets—gold, crimson, gray, black, electric blue—and his heart started to thump uncomfortably.

"Teague?" she called. "You like whiskey when you're straight off a flight, don't you? So this is me, offering whiskey if you'll come on through!"

He took a jolting step toward the archway, toward her voice, and then she added, "Or whatever else you want…" and he stopped, waiting, because he knew it was a pause, not an end. "Because all you need to do is name it and it's yours!"

Name it. *Name* it?

And it was there—the answer. *You, I want you.*

His pulse zoomed up so fast, he thought the top of his head was going to fly off. He didn't want her. And even if he did—okay, okay he *did*, he always had, but so what, every guy did—it made no difference. She didn't mean he could have her, that was just—just the way she talked. She'd never meant any of those things she used to say, those things he hadn't had the knack for laughing off because he didn't flirt. Ever.

A hot flash of memory—the first time he'd seen her in Flick's. She'd smiled at Matt, whom she obviously already knew, from across the room, then zeroed in on him—probably having felt his awestruck eyes on her. She'd headed toward them, carrying an overstacked tray of empty beer glasses and conducting an effortless flirtation with at least three separate groups of guys en route. She'd asked him if he liked what he saw. He'd said no, causing her to look at him like he was an alien life-form, and he'd stumbled out something about her being too young—like what the fuck? He'd meant she was too young to be working at Flick's, because of course she wasn't. He was simply trying to impress her with his intelligence and legalese seemed the quickest way—a launching pad to talk to her, since her accent told him she was Australian and he knew licensing laws were different in Australia. And she'd chosen a different interpretation of "too young" and told him she was three years over the age of consent, and if he was interested, to ask Matt for her number.

And the pattern had been set. Frankie giving him the come-on every time she saw him, him fucking up the responses.

How good does a girl have to be to score a date with you, Mr. Perfect? Um, er, huh?

I'd ask you to get the eyelash out of my eye for me, Mr. Perfect, if putting your hands on me wouldn't give you a heart attack—not that I wouldn't enjoy giving you mouth-to-mouth. I, um, huh?

If you decide to get naughty and come watch me dance at Club DeeCee, Mr. Perfect, I'll give you a free lap dance. Er, um, no, *no*! Followed by an actual recoil, during which he'd spilled his beer. He'd rushed on to say it wasn't that he *disapproved*, at which point Matt had stepped in, calmly suggesting Teague leave things there because Frankie didn't need anyone's approval, she needed money or she'd have to fly home. So Teague, smooth operator, had reached for his wallet—like, *fuck*!—and she'd kind of frozen as she'd looked at the wallet in his hand and he'd found himself holding his breath. And then she'd said if she'd wanted to turn tricks, she would have stayed in Sydney, and the next second she was gone.

The invitation to Club DeeCee had not been repeated.

"Hey!" she called out from beyond the arch, bringing him back to the present. "Come on in, Mr. Perfect! I promise not to bite—unless you ask me nicely."

And he felt something snap. Mr. Perfect. He was fucking tired of being Mr. Fucking Perfect.

Mr. Perfect Boyfriend to Romy—*sure, Romy, we'll go as slow as you like*. Mr. Perfect Friend to Matt—*sure, Matt, take the girl I love*. Mr. Perfect Son for his parents—*sure, Mom and Dad, I'll be careful, I won't do that, won't go there, won't take any more risks*.

He wanted to *not* go slow. Wanted to win the girl. Wanted to take a risk again.

Wanted to tell Frankie, *Sure, bring it!* A pity he wasn't staying with her? Then okay, he'd stay, as long as it was in her bed. Wanted to throw her down on those white sheets and lick every inch of her until she screamed for him. Tell her to go ahead and bite him, bite him anywhere she wanted, put her mouth all over him, do whatever she wanted to him. He'd take the damn dare, and *not* think about the consequences for once, and—and *know*, dammit. Know what it was like to be the man she wanted and not some fucking cautious, stuck-up, Victorian-era prig doing things the right way and giving everyone what they wanted except himself.

He took a step—he was so ready for this!—and then "I was joking!" floated out to him. "It's just whiskey waiting in here, I'm not going to molest you!"

And he stopped again.

Just joking. Just whiskey.

He wasn't here for Frankie Lee. He was here for Matt—to hand over whatever the fuck was in the velvet pouch Matt had shoved at him like a guilty secret. And then he'd do what he did every December on his annual three-week vacation: patch up his facade in advance of facing another year of being everyone's Mr. Perfect.

He took a slow breath and forced himself to move through the arch into what seemed to be a kitchen/dining-room combo at the front, with what looked to be a laundry at the back, stretching around to the right, out of sight. The kitchen was the most basic he'd ever seen. A bench against the wall inset with an oven and cooktop, a row of cupboards hanging high above the countertop and a short return from the wall that housed a mini fridge and a set of pantry shelves. There was no island separating the kitchen from a small table that had one low stool shoved underneath it. No other seating area—unless you counted the wrought-iron table with two mismatched chairs outside. The door leading out there was open, so he didn't know if Frankie expected him to go outside, stay indoors, sit or stand—all he could do was hover.

She was facing away from him, doing something at the counter, but the moment she turned the two of them would be close enough to share breaths. And goddammit, that robe had decided to slip off her shoulder after all—far enough this time that he could see her shoulder was bare, and he did not need to see that!

"Don't tell me you had a problem finding your way!" she teased, without turning around.

"No," he said.

He wished he could add something witty, but he couldn't think past her naked shoulder.

Then again, he'd never been garrulous in Frankie's company. It was just more noticeable today because for the first time ever it was only the two of them. No Matt, Romy, Veronica, Rafael or Artie—none of the old DC gang—to act as buffer and make his taciturnity unremarkable.

She turned at last, passing an unopened bottle of whiskey to him. He instantly studied the label intently, praying she'd get that damn robe back into place while his eyes were safely averted.

Barron. He'd never heard of it. Not that he cared. All he cared about was stopping himself from wondering what her skin would feel like, if the blue ends of her hair would burn him if they slid across his chest, his belly, his thighs, how she'd taste the first time he licked between her legs...

First time? No. No, no, no. No times.

Just joking. Just whiskey.

"Matt said you're going to watch the start of the Sydney to Hobart Yacht Race then fly down to Hobart for the finish, so I thought you might like to try a Tasmanian whiskey," she explained, no doubt wondering what the fuck was going on with him to make him stare so long at a bottle. "The Barron distillery is close to where the boats finish. I hear everyone goes to the Customs House Hotel after the race but if—if it bothers you to be there and you feel like getting away from the crowd, you could sneak off for a wee dram."

Teague brought his eyes up from the bottle. "Why would it bother me?"

"Doesn't it?"

"No."

"I've got it wrong, then. I just... I'd heard... I mean,

didn't you crew in the Sydney to Hobart in your last year of law school?"

"Yes. So?"

"So didn't you nearly—?"

"Drown? Yes. So?"

"So-o-o...didn't you give up ocean racing after that?"

"That wasn't the reason," he said.

Several moments passed during which she kept her eyes steady on him, as though she'd extract every last secret from his soul.

"Not going to tell me, huh?" she said at last, and something about the way she was looking at him made him *want* to tell her, just so she'd know he could be as wild as she was, as wild as any of them, that he once *had* been, so she could stop looking at him like that—like she understood he'd lost something and it was killing him. How could she understand? There was nothing stopping her from doing anything the hell she wanted.

"Well, that's okay," she added softly, and he realized she was more dangerous than ever. Like those sirens from Greek mythology perched on their rocks in the sea, only she didn't have to sing to men to lure them to destruction—she could make them sing to *her* as they wrecked their boats on her shore. Otherwise how could it be that he wanted to tell her things he'd never told anyone?

"As it happens, I like strong, silent types," she went on, and the moment was gone. She waved a hand in the direction of the laundry. "The bathroom's around the back there on the right if you want to grab a shower.

Just maybe move the underwear I have hanging over the shower rail."

"I showered on board," he said, way too quickly, because Jesus! He didn't need to see her underwear and he sure as shit didn't need to touch it.

"The joys of first-class travel!" she said blithely.

"Yes." A monosyllable was all he could manage? Seriously?

"And shaved, too, I see."

"Yes." Mon-o-syllable. *Fuck*.

"You know, I don't think I've ever seen you unshaven."

Not even a monosyllable. He didn't know how to interpret that. He suddenly felt as if being clean-shaven was tantamount to being a eunuch.

"I've often wondered what you'd look like," she continued. "Late at night. Or first thing in the morning…"

Nope. He could not speak.

"Which leads me to my next offer. You probably slept on the flight—I hear those first-class suites are something else—but if you didn't, you're welcome to use my bed and take a nap, since I know people can't usually check in to their hotels until the afternoon. You can get to the bedroom via the bathroom or through the living room. I can show you the way if you like…?"

What the hell did she expect him to say to that? "I… No."

"No as in…?"

"As in I booked my hotel room from last night so I…I'm good."

"You're 'good'? Still? After all these years? That's a shame."

"I mean—"

"Because if you *weren't* good, if you were suddenly *bad*, I'd suggest you use my bed for some other purpose."

Ah, Jesus, he was not up to the challenge of this conversation. It sounded so much like she wanted… But she couldn't mean… Could she possibly…? No. Nope. Joking. All she was offering was a glass of whiskey.

"Not today, huh?" she said, and this time her laugh was more like a sigh as she turned back to the counter. "Okay, how about I get you a glass and you can take that whiskey outside and soak up some vitamin D. They say it helps with jet lag. Something about melatonin."

"I don't have jet lag." God, why could he not stop sounding like a robot?

"Then screw that theory and just do it because it's peaceful out there at this time of the morning and there are *two* chairs, so I won't have to sit on your lap," she said, opening one of the cupboards on the wall and stretching up—which required her to lift up onto her toes and hang onto the counter with her free hand.

She let out a tiny snuffle of exertion, and Teague's chivalrous instincts kicked in, jolting him forward to reach over her to get the glass himself.

Fumbling, his fingers on hers… Frankie going completely still.

A heart crack of a moment, as it hit him somewhere in the region of his balls that this was the first time he'd touched her. The scent of gardenias was in his nostrils.

Warmth—*her* warmth—insinuated itself into his bones. The fine tremble in her fingers vibrated through him. He was aware of the pounding of his heart, the insistent ache in his hardening cock—oh, God, please don't let her feel that!

Madness, that she could wreak such physical havoc just by leaving her hand under his. If she knew what was happening to his body, the burn and want and awful need, she'd laugh herself sick. And yet the urge to put his mouth on her naked shoulder and taste her skin was so hard to resist. If only she meant all those things she said, he'd—

Scream. Kettle. Whistling on the hot plate.

He snatched back his hand.

Thank God.

Sanity. Reality.

He stepped back from her, leaving her with the glass.

She switched off the hot plate and turned to him, holding out the tumbler. It was expensive-looking cut crystal, but it had a chip in the rim, and that one tiny flaw twisted something in his chest.

He took the glass and their fingers touched again, and her smile faded.

There were dark smudges under her eyes—he wanted to run his fingertips gently over them. A blush—he wanted to lick the heat of it from her cheekbones. And there was something shimmering in the stillness of the moment that told him she'd let him do both those things. But how did a guy go from an accidental finger graze to such intimacy?

He didn't. He couldn't.

One of her hands came up to press against her cheek, as though to control the flush of blood beneath her skin, and she let out a laugh that was different from usual—disbelieving, a little embarrassed—and he felt that twist in his chest again.

"Go on out to the courtyard," she said, and returned her attention to the counter, picking up a cloth as though preparing to wipe it down, only to knock a spoon onto the floor.

He bent to pick it up for her but she stiffened and said, "Leave it. Please just…leave it. I'm going to make myself a cup of coffee so go on out. Two minutes. Give me two minutes."

He nodded even though he knew she couldn't see it and carried his glass and the bottle of whiskey outside. Looking around, he decided "courtyard" was an optimistic description. It was a small paved rectangle enclosed by a border of potted plants, with a barbecue in one corner, the rickety table with those mismatched chairs in the center and a gaudily painted garden gnome that was missing a hand plonked seemingly at random.

He chose one of the chairs for himself and positioned it to face the apartments, away from where he could see Frankie in the kitchen, and poured a generous finger of whiskey.

A minuscule sip had him sighing in appreciation. It was piney, creamy—wonderful. He wondered how Frankie remembered he liked a whiskey straight off a flight; he couldn't remember ever mentioning it. Hell, he wondered how she knew he liked whiskey, period, given he hadn't been a regular at Flick's. Veronica would have said it was because she was a "booze whisperer." Ha. She'd reminded him of that at Matt and Romy's wedding, where he'd been best man and could have been excused for feeling like crap. Veronica had said something about him being—hello—perfectly behaved.

"Beneath this urbane exterior is a seething mass of violent contradiction, ready to go on an imperfect rampage," Teague had told her.

"It's a shame you never got together with Frankie, in that case."

"Frankie?"

"Frankie—sexy Aussie, Flick's booze whisperer by day, exotic dancer by night."

"Yeah, right!"

"Why not?" Veronica had queried.

"Because… Just because."

A prophecy of sorts—gee, thanks, Veronica!— because here he was, five months later, drinking Frankie's whiskey. He was pretty sure he wasn't about do any rampaging, though.

He screwed his eyes shut, put his elbows on the table, clasped his head in his hands and dug his fingers into his skull. Tried to breathe out some agitation.

"Need some painkillers?" Frankie's voice.

He opened his eyes, gave himself a moment to set his face, then looked over his shoulder to where she was standing, framed in the open doorway.

"You look like you have a headache," she said.

"I don't."

"Do you want a cup of coffee instead of the whiskey?"

"No."

"Tea?"

"Whiskey's fine."

With the shrug of one shoulder—which almost dislodged that damn robe again—she came over to sit opposite him, her back to the block of flats.

He topped up his barely touched whiskey to give himself something to do as Frankie raised her mug and inhaled the steam wafting up from it.

"I'm a philistine, I know," she said, "but that year in the States got me hooked on crappy coffee. *Do not* tell any of my Australian friends—they'll disown me if they discover I drink instant coffee instead of going to a café every morning for a cappuccino-piccolo latte-macchiato-whatever."

"I don't know any of your Australian friends." Stating the fucking obvious as he tried to not anticipate another slinky fall of that robe.

She took a dainty sip of her coffee before answering. "We can rectify that, if you like. Sydney's buzzing with summer parties, there are two and a half weeks until Christmas, and on Christmas day if you're not doing anything there's a thing on Bondi Beach for all the orphans, so—"

"I'm not an orphan." Boorish.

"'Orphans' is more of a state of mind for this gig. What it really means is—is loners, I guess," she said.

"I'm not a loner." *No, I'm a block of fucking wood.*

"I mean people who are in Sydney with no one to spend Christmas with."

Silence.

And then she cocked her head to one side, examining him. "Not a loner?"

"No." Granite. Not wood, granite.

"'Cause you always seemed to like to be alone. Even when you were with the others you were…well, alone."

How to explain that it wasn't that he liked to be alone, he just *was* alone.

Impossible.

Because then he'd have to talk about the grief. He'd have to admit that he'd lost more than a sister when Cassandra died twelve years ago—he'd lost part of himself. And he didn't want anyone else to know that, because they'd want him to find it again, and it was too late to look for it because that wasn't *him* anymore.

Yep, impossible.

And so he raised his glass to take a sip of whiskey and said nothing.

"Or maybe it was that you just did your own thing," she mused. "You never let yourself be pressured into any of Matt's crazier schemes, at least not until n—" She stopped abruptly, but Teague finished the sentence in his head: not until *now*.

Slowly, deliberately, he put his glass on the table. "Am I—are we—in one of Matt's schemes?" he asked. "Is that why I'm here?"

She put down her mug, licked her bottom lip. "You know why you're here, Teague. At least, you know part of it."

He reached into his shirt pocket for the small velvet he'd shoved in there before disembarking from the plane. The bag he'd scrupulously *not* looked into the whole damn flight. He held it out to her.

She watched *him*, not her hands, as she took the bag and unzipped it. It wasn't until her eyes dropped that he let himself look down to see what was so important it had to come with him rather than be sent via a courier.

A ring.

His vision narrowed to the glitter of the platinum band in the sunlight, the cool glow of the emerald center stone, the intense sparkle of surrounding diamonds. But the telling thing was that she'd slipped it onto the third finger of her left hand.

"It's prettier than I remembered," she said.

White-hot rage coursed through him at those words. Prettier than she remembered? How the fuck could she not remember it exactly? God, what had Matt done to him? Why lay the burden of this history on him now, when it was too damn late? He didn't want it. Didn't want to know. But it was there. No going back.

Matt had once proposed to Frankie.

Matt had once been in love with Frankie.

Matt had waited until he and Teague were alone and pressed for time before co-opting Teague into returning the ring to Frankie—which had to mean Romy knew nothing about it.

Teague picked up his glass again, raised it to his mouth and knocked back a gulp of whiskey as the enormity of what it meant almost overwhelmed him. The enormity of what he'd lost.

Romy, he'd lost Romy. No, worse than that—he'd *given* her away. He'd pleaded Matt's case for him when

Romy had been prepared to move on from Matt, because Matt had never loved anyone except her and Matt was *torturing* himself over her. A once-in-a-lifetime love shouldn't be denied—that was how Teague had consoled himself. And now...

Oh, God! *God!* Now to discover Romy *wasn't* Matt's once-in-a-lifetime love? To learn Matt had loved another woman enough to propose to her?

He shot to his feet, knowing he was about to lose his shit.

"Where are you going?" Frankie asked, startled.

Hell—I'm going to hell. "Thanks for the whiskey."

She stayed sitting, giving him a quizzical look. "Why are you brooding at me?"

"I'm not brooding."

"Yes, you are."

"I don't brood. Rafael broods."

"Rafael only ever brooded in Veronica's direction. You brood all over the place, you always did. It's just that you're an iceberg, so it's hidden beneath the surface. It's irresistible, you know. Makes women wonder what lies beneath."

That threw him, so much that it took him a moment to relocate his voice. "I don't brood," he said again—it seemed to be the best he could come up with.

She leaned back in her chair. "Okay, you don't brood, and you're not irresistible. Happy?"

"Yes. No. I don't—" He stopped abruptly, telling his feet to move. Frustrating as hell when they wouldn't.

She sighed gustily. "Taking a wild guess here, but did Matt not explain *any* of the background to the ring?"

"He doesn't have to explain it to me, only to—" He cut himself off again, bit his lip to stop her name from coming out of his mouth.

Her eyes narrowed. "Not to you, but to…Romy?" She sighed. "Romy. Of course. I see."

And because the thought of her "seeing" enraged him when he'd been hiding it for so long, the words "You see what?" snapped out of him like a whip. He was almost vibrating with the need to tell her she was wrong.

"Things you *don't* see, Teague. Things you could never see, things you seem to be unready to see even now, things you might never see even if someone waves them in front of your face before beating you over the head with them." She stood then, too, as though spoiling for a fight. "But you know what? Good for Romy. *Lucky* Romy, to have two men so devoted to her, so in love with her for so damn long their brains turn to mush!"

"I didn't say I'm in love with her," he said, way too loud.

She snorted. "Oh, please, don't *even*. That year I spent in DC there were plenty of women who wanted a piece of you, but they all knew they were wasting their time. The only one who didn't know how you felt about Romy was Romy—and that was willful ignorance, because if she'd let herself see it she'd have had to let you go."

"She *did* let me go. She's married. *They're* married! They have Rose now."

"And Romy made you Rose's godfather—which means, bozo, she's *not* letting you go." She rubbed the heels of her hands over her forehead and made a sound redolent of both frustration and disgust. "And why should she when you won't let *yourself* go?"

"There's nothing left to let go *of*."

"Sure there is. Your propensity to wallow in misery over what you can't have! How many years have you chalked up pining for her? Eleven? And it was hardly the love story of the century—only two measly months, and nobody ever saw you hold hands, let alone kiss! So perfectly discreet, so completely *passionless*! Yet you hung in there and let no one take her place with you. And now to find you're *still* hanging in there?" She laughed, but there was a jeer in it. "All I can say is you must *enjoy* being miserable."

"I don't enjoy it!"

"No? Then get over it, the way the rest of us do. 'Cause I can tell you, lots of us want people who don't have the good sense to want us back."

"If you're talking about Matt—"

"I'm not talking about Matt. *God!* I'm not interested in Matt and I never have been—not like that. And he's never been interested in me that way."

"How can you say that when he bought you an engagement ring?"

"I can say it because *he* wasn't my fiancé—*you* were."

CHAPTER TWO

WHAT THE FUCK am I doing? was the thought uppermost in Frankie's mind as she let those words settle.

Making an idiot of herself over Teague Hamilton seemed the best answer. It's what she'd done that whole year in DC—lusting, very obviously, for a man who was hung up on someone else.

She thought back over that harried phone call from Matt, the to-and-fro about the ring, about Teague, Matt's slight hesitation before he'd said that last thing and disconnected: *You're a smart girl, Frankie, figure it out, will you?*

Since it was obvious Teague remained hung up on Romy—and damn if she didn't find that infuriatingly stubborn loyalty as attractive as everything else about him—Frankie wasn't sure what there was to figure out. Did she want to waste any more time? Because even a normal ménage à trois was overrated, if you asked her; one where the third participant was purely a fantasy in the thick head of one of the active players had to be straight out masochism.

If only he didn't look so delicious, standing there all frosty-fronted and buttoned-up.

If only she wasn't so sure she could defrost and un-button him if he gave her a chance!

If only he'd give her even *half* a chance…

He sat again, reached for the whiskey, poured out an-other nip and wrapped his fingers around the glass with-out lifting it. She marveled at that magical something he had that could make anything near him transform into something whole and lovely—even that crappy chipped glass.

Oh, God, she had to have him. Had to try one last time. Maybe if she tamped down the femme fatale, parceled out the offer of sex in digestible chunks, she might not scare him off this time.

He raised the glass to his mouth at last and took a sip.

"Better?" she asked, taking her seat again.

All he did was look at her.

"*Not* better," she said. "Want me to explain?"

He flicked a vague hand on the tabletop as though he'd reached the end of his stamina, which she inter-preted as an invitation to proceed.

"Remember Kyle?" she asked, starting easy.

"Big, muscles, tats. Badass."

"More ass*hole* than badass," she said, and sucked in a quick breath. "Well, a year after I came home, he turned up in Sydney, engaged to an Aussie. He clearly has a thing for the accent—not that I'm throwing stones, seeing I'm partial to American ones." She paused to give him a chance to register that he, himself, had an American accent. But…nope. Blank.

"A-a-anyway," she went on, "Laura—the fiancée—understandably wanted to get married here in Sydney, where her family is, and because Kyle really *is* an asshole, he decided it'd be fun to invite me to the wedding. I was on the verge of sending back a thanks-but-I'm-pairing-my-odd-socks-that-day reply—" she had to pause there, because she needed a moment to rein in the fury that Kyle would dare expect her to turn up, after what he'd done to her "—until a week before the wedding, when he came to King's Castle, the club where I work, with an entourage of drunks, presumably an early bucks night. At that point, I figured I'd go to his goddamn wedding and take the hottest date I could get."

"And you chose Matt."

"Well, not exact—"

"Because Kyle was always jealous of him," Teague interrupted, pouring himself more whiskey. "I remember Matt and Romy talking about it."

"As I was about to say, not exactly."

He frowned at her. "But they told me—"

"Yes, they flew in for the wedding, but Kyle wasn't jealous of *Matt*!" Frankie said, watching to see if he noticed the slight emphasis—but he obviously still didn't have a clue, so she swallowed a sigh and continued. "And I wasn't intending Matt to be my date. It's just that I mentioned the wedding in passing on the phone, and he wanted the job because, well, why not? Which tends to be the way Matt and I operate. Why not?"

She laughed, because looking back, it was insane. "By the time he and Romy landed, he'd upped the drama quotient and decided we needed to be fake-engaged. *Romy*, however, insisted Kyle wouldn't buy a relationship between me and Matt because we had too much of a brother-sister vibe. Go figure, huh?" Pause. "Brother-sister? Because we're so much alike? And people who are too much alike…?" Pause. Surely he knew what she was saying? Surely he could work out she was alluding to him and Romy? Mr. and Ms. Perfect—a doomed combination, 'cause everyone knew opposites attracted. Bu-u-ut, nope. Not even a blink. "So I guess I'll cut to the chase. Fact is, Romy said if we wanted to mess with Kyle's head, *you'd* make a better fiancé." Another pause, to see if that sank in.

But all she got was a confused question. "Why would that mess with his head?"

"Huh?"

"I've never spoken to him."

Dear God, men could be obtuse! "No, you've never spoken to him, but he saw you at Flick's. He saw you… and me…? Watched me serve you…?"

He was shaking his head, still not getting it. Seriously, did lawyers not need to be smart?

"What possible reason could you give for you living here and me in the States?" he asked, missing every damn point.

"That we were still deciding where we'd ultimately settle—here or in New York."

"I'd never live apart from my fiancée."

"No, you wouldn't, would you, Mr. Perfect? But Kyle

bought it—probably because he's Mr. *Asshole*!" she said. "And let's face it, everyone back in those DC days knew your family was rusted onto the Upper East Side and you'd be rusting on right along with them in due course. Plus I'd made it crystal clear to Kyle during our ill-fated, short-lived romance that it would take a miracle to budge me from Australia, so yeah, you and I had big decisions to make."

"Then why did we decide to get married?"

"Er, because we were in love?"

He shoved a hand through his hair. "If I loved you so much I'd consider leaving New York for you, why couldn't I be bothered to come with you to your ex-boyfriend's wedding?"

"Ah, well, you see, your father was receiving some big law prize, so you sent Matt to represent you and to—to protect me."

"Protect you from what?"

"Unwanted advances."

"Whose?"

"Kyle's, of course. You see, he didn't just visit the club, he expected me to dance for him."

"He what?"

And damn if he didn't look as though he was going to punch something—a look she remembered from the time Kyle had come into Flick's to rant at her after that hideous night at Club DeeCee, and Matt had had to restrain Teague to stop him intervening. "Of course, I didn't dance for him, and he left…relatively peacefully," she said. But Teague was still looking thrillingly on the edge of violence, so she moved right on.

"So, anyway, Matt, Romy, law prize, yada yada. The thing is, we built up the story until it was so convincing, I almost believed our impending nuptials were a done deal. Frankie's wedding—that's what we called it. A weekend of utter insanity, looking back."

"And none of you thought it would be of interest to me to know I'd suddenly acquired a fiancée?" he asked, supercarefully.

"No-o-o, because—technical point—you *hadn't* acquired one. And they probably didn't tell you because…" She trailed off there because somehow, without changing his expression, he looked more ominous than he had over Kyle being a dick.

"Because?" he breathed out.

Swallow. Pull off the bandage fast now. "Because we knew you'd hate it."

"And how did you know that?"

"Because you weren't, you aren't… I mean you're not… That is, you're…you…?"

A moment, during which he blinked once, and then he said, "I see."

His face was completely expressionless now, and that made Frankie so nervous—and, face it, way too turned on—she couldn't immediately think how to proceed.

"Go on," Teague said, his voice as smooth as dark blue silk.

"I guess the thing that made it work was that Kyle was never going to see you again, because he's not in your circle *or* your league, and he and Laura were going to live in Chicago, which meant *I* was never going to see *them* again, so…"

"So?"

"Well, so what was the harm in it?"

He blinked at her again. Blink. Blink. *Banked fury* is how she'd describe it. Hot as *fuck*! "And the ring?" he said.

"We knew it needed to be a good one, because everyone knows you're filthy rich. No, not *filthy*. *Never* filthy. Clean. Clean-cut. I mean—" Stop. Babbling. She cleared her throat, got herself together. "So, anyway, the three of us went shopping, and we chose this one—" she waggled the fingers of her left hand "—because it looked like the kind of ring that would come out of a rich family's vault."

"It's nothing like the rings in our family vault!"

"Well, *Kyle* didn't know that. And you have to admit it looks expensive. Because it *was* expensive."

"And Matt bought it for you—even though he could have borrowed one from my *actual* family vault if he'd bothered to ask me."

"But they thought… They never would have expected, um…"

"I get it. Believe me, I get it. I was not—not…"

"Not *insane*," she said, because surely that was a compliment, but he blinked again, like it was some strange, startling, unwelcome news being broken to him. "And, anyway, the ring was a last-minute plot embellishment so there wouldn't have been time to ask you for a ring, even if we'd dared, and…and…and what difference does it make? Matt was on the way to being seriously wealthy, and you know how generous he is and—"

"So why didn't you keep it, if he could so easily spare the money?"

"Because I don't do that. I don't accept unearned gifts from men. Matt knows that. The plan was for him to sell it and donate the money to charity."

"Charity."

"Charity. But I guess… Well, it wasn't important to him, the—the ring…after it served its purpose. So he—he forgot about it."

"Forgot."

"Forgot. Until…" She paused to take a deep breath. "Until a week ago, which is where things get tricky."

"Tricky?"

"Or *interesting*, depending on your point of view."

"Interesting."

"The fact you keep repeating me makes me think you may need to pour yourself some more whiskey."

"I don't need any more whiskey."

"Then pour it and put it in the middle of the table in case *I* need it."

He said nothing, just grimly poured the whiskey then pushed the glass dead center.

"So," she continued, "think about what happened a week ago."

"Can we not play guessing games?"

"I need to do this gradually."

"A week ago…" he prompted.

"Rose's christening" she said. "Matt called to thank me for the gift I'd sent."

"The silver rattle with the coral teething handle."

"Oh!" she said, surprised. "You saw it?"

He shrugged, looking grumpily awkward, as though he'd been caught doing something embarrassing. "They showed me all the gifts."

"Did you like it?"

Another awkward shrug. "It's very…you. The vintage thing."

"So you *didn't* like it?"

"What? Yes. No. I mean— What? I liked it, okay? I *do* like it."

"So you like me?"

"I, er… What?"

"You say the rattle is very me, and you like it, which has to mean you like me. Don't look so freaked out! It's not a crime to like me. Lots of people do."

"Yes, all right, I like you. Now can we move on?"

"Okay, okay!" she said. "Sorry to discompose you."

"I'm not discomposed."

Except that he was, she could tell.

"I like you, too," she said, just to push it.

"Frankie, for the love of—"

"Fine, fine, keep your shirt on…or not. Sorry! Okay, I'll get on with it. The thing is, the fact the rattle is vintage reminded Matt he still had the ring, which is art deco, of course, and we—we did a deal and…" She stopped there, reaching for words. "Hmm. This is harder than I thought it'd be."

He multitasked by giving her a what-the-fuck? look while shaking his head and throwing his hands in the air, and she had to fight hard to resist raising her hand to her hot cheek again. Blushing was so *obvious*—no wonder she never did it! But she had to continue, blush or not, because she could almost *see* her window of opportunity closing and she knew once it closed it wasn't going to open again. It was now or never.

"In for a penny, right?" she said, and scraped her chair back from the table as though the extra foot she'd put between them would help her breathe. "The ring... I told you, I didn't want it."

He looked pointedly at her finger.

"Yes, I know, I've ended up with it anyway," she said, and removed the ring, put it back in the pouch and tugged the zipper closed. "But what if I were to tell you the only reason I let Matt send it was because he promised me you'd bring it?"

"I'd say he and Romy could have told me over scones and tea anytime this past week instead of making me think there was some dark betrayal going on with all the cloak-and-dagger crap he went through at the airport."

"You're really not getting it, are you?" She covered her face with her hands. "Am I not making it obvious or does he just not want to know?" she said into them.

"If I'm the 'he' you're talking about," Teague said dryly, "I can assure you 'he' would *love* to know what's going on!"

She took in a deep breath, then removed her hands. "A dark betrayal—that's exactly what was going on. Nothing to do with him and me, nothing to do with you and Romy. To do with you and me."

"Yes, with me as your unwitting fiancé, I got that."

"Not that." She licked her lips. She'd always prided herself on her straightforwardness but *God*, this was difficult. "The thing is, I've thought about you... I mean, you're so... It's just that—" She broke off with an inarticulate exclamation of disgust. "Okay, I'm just going to say it."

"Well, thank God for that!"

"It wasn't the ring Matt was sending me. He was sending me...you."

Tick, tock, tick, tock.

And then he frowned like he really *did not get it*!

"Teague!" she cried. "Seriously!"

He looked behind him, as though he thought she must be talking to someone else even though she'd just addressed him by his damn name.

"Teague!" Trying again. "I'm talking about you having a fling while you're here."

"I don't have flings."

"Oh, I *know* that, Teague! I tried hard enough to get you to have a fling with me the whole time I was in DC! But now... Well, now you're here, and I never thought you would be, so I'm making one more attempt. And you can say no, but I hope you don't, because I think I can help you not be miserable, or at least give you a respite from it while—while you're here. In Sydney. So. That's all."

Silence. Stillness.

A rush of heartbeats later, with her words hanging in the air, he shook his head. "No," he said.

"Well!" She blushed again, brought both hands up to her face. "This is embarrassing."

"No, I mean—" He made a sound—like a cross between a sigh and a huff. "You said something about meeting your friends, so I thought you must mean I should have fling with one of... But—" Slight head shake. "Do you mean a fling with you? No. You can't mean that."

"That's funny, Teague, because I'm pretty sure what I'm doing right at this moment, sitting here at some godawful hour of the morning when I'm far from at my best, is offering myself to you straight up, since you've never been able to take a fucking hint."

He looked over his shoulder again. God, did he really have no idea how insanely hot he was? He was frowning as he brought his eyes back to her. "But... I don't... Huh?"

"I see I need to spell it out, so here goes—I want you, Teague Ingram Spencer Hamilton. I want every perfect inch of you, and I have since the moment I saw you. Which would make *you* the man Kyle was jealous of and *therefore* the perfect fake fiancé. But I can see we need to take baby steps here, so I propose that I come over there and kiss you. If you like that, we can talk about going further. If you don't...? Well, I guess we're no worse off, are we, since it's just a kiss between consenting adults?"

"Okay," he said.

"Okay?" she asked, cautious now, because that seemed way too easy a capitulation after the agony she'd just been through.

"Why not, right?" he said, and bit at his top lip. "That's the catchphrase? Why not?"

Why not? Not exactly enthusiastic consent, but her somersaulting heart urged her to go for it anyway, so she was already bracing to get up out of the chair...

But, no. No, dammit. Because it was him, she needed it spelled out. "You mean I can kiss you?"

"Yes."

"Is that the whiskey talking?"

He shook his head. "Yes," he said.

"Oh."

He nodded then. "I mean no."

"Er…"

"I mean it's not the whiskey. I mean yes, I want you to kiss me."

Done. Frankie got to her feet, no more dancing around, no more fencing. She was going to kiss him until his toes curled and his hair caught on fire. And if it came to nothing, she'd be glad she'd been given the chance to know what it was like to be with a man like him, a man who did nothing without care and thought and respect and decency, even if it only lasted for a kiss.

Slowly, she came around to stand beside him, every move cautious, like she was stalking skittish prey. "So…" she said, gesturing to his lap. "May I?"

He nodded, opening his arms to unfetter the access, and she lowered herself carefully onto his lap. His arms closed then, coming around her. She drew a shaky breath because it felt so good to be held by him. She looked into his eyes and lost herself for a moment in the bright, clear blue of them. A blue so pure she could almost believe he belonged nowhere else, only here, under a cloudless Sydney sky.

How long did they stare at each other? She didn't know. She didn't even know she'd laid her palm against his cheek until she felt a twitch beneath it—just a tiny tic.

She lowered her eyes to his mouth and found that its perfection was marred by a small white scar at the outer right edge of his top lip. Scars. Everyone had them, but she, of all people, knew you sometimes had to look close, or deep, or even all the way through a person, to see them. He'd bitten at that mark, when he'd agreed to let her kiss him, and that already told her something: that being not quite perfect bothered him. And because of that, the almost undetectable scar made him more perfect to her, more perfect *for* her.

The rest of him was immaculate. Chiseled jaw, straight nose, symmetrical features. His hair was expertly cut, thick and neat, dark blond streaked with wheat. His eyebrows and lashes were a burnished deep gold. He was delicious summer to her—the beach colors of him, the heady promise of warmth and sun-touched skin and luminous light. So dazzlingly handsome, she was slow to become aware of other things about his body that had nothing to do with bright days, but everything of urgent nights. The leashed power in his arms, the rock-hard strength of his tensed thighs beneath her bottom, the implacable erection against her hip...

She'd never been more conscious of her near-nakedness—which was saying something since she danced in her underwear for an audience four nights a week—and the thought of him touching her skin made her more excited than she could ever remember being. She had to do this right. *Had* to. She didn't care what it was that had wedged open a chink in his armor—rebound, jealousy, pique, a need to prove something or to be someone else—but she knew this moment was vital. "Ready?" she asked.

"Yes," he breathed out, and she slowly, slowly brought her face close and rested her mouth on his. She closed her eyes, waiting through the first thrill, savoring the moment—not just the feel of his firm lips but the way his arms tightened around her. She tried to catalog all the sensations swirling inside her, wanting the memory to be embedded deep. The air still with the heavy warmth that foretold a slide from pleasantness to heat within the next few hours. The faint green scent of her plant border mingling with the tang of salt in the air and his understated vetiver aftershave—earthy, grassy, smoky. The occasional squawk of a seagull and faint whooshing of waves hitting the sand at nearby Bondi Beach. His heart, beating fast like hers. His cock, straining in his jeans, the presence of it getting her from damp to wet with astonishing ease.

Oh, Teague, she said in her head, because she needed to hear his name *somewhere* in this moment and she dared not say it aloud in case he came to his senses, and his lips parted as though accepting it from her.

She tasted whiskey as he licked at her lips, and the world swung like a flickering lantern in a storm. Men liked her mouth—the shape, the pout—but from Teague she wanted more. *Teague* she needed to actively lust for it, so although she wanted to take her own pleasure, she forced herself to stay pliant for him, letting him take and test and do what he wanted.

His arms were tightening, then loosening, then tightening as he shifted beneath her, like he was searching for control. She knew what he was going through—but she also knew the cure was to be found in going further than a kiss. His hands went to her hair, gripping tight to hold her still as he moved from licking to sucking at her mouth, even as he continued to move restlessly beneath her. She wished she could take him inside her right that second, because she could *feel* how good it would be.

And then suddenly, she was straddling him, but she had no idea how he'd repositioned her without disconnecting his mouth from hers. Magic again. A magic that spoke of experience as unexpected as the size of his cock, which was obvious now her legs were on either side of him. She could feel herself swelling for him, her clitoris pulsing so insistently she wanted to put her fingers there to relieve the pressure. She loved the restraint that kept him from rushing onward, craved it, even…and yet the challenge was there: to make him lose it. But hadn't that always been the lure of Teague?

Slowly, she opened her mouth—an invitation to enter. He neither hesitated nor plunged, simply fitted his mouth to hers and let himself take what she offered. Thrilling, to both control the action and be with someone who had such control over himself. Even as one of his hands left her hair to slide the robe off one of her shoulders, he moved slowly and deliberately, kissing more deeply. She felt her breast come free of the silk, and then his hand was cupping her, his thumb rubbing back and forth over her hard nipple. God, how did he know the exact level of pressure to make the pleasure so wickedly intense?

Lick me there, she begged, but only in her head because this was no time for spoken words, only for what he would do unasked. *Please, Teague, please.*

Again, he seemed to hear that silent plea, because his mouth left hers and he trailed his lips, his tongue, over her chin, down her neck, across to her breast, all the way to the tip, where he licked…and kept licking.

She looked down, wanting to see his hand holding her breast, his head where she'd imagined it so many times, his tongue rasping over her. A whimper escaped, then another. She couldn't seem to stop her hips from moving back and forth, urging him on. Not that she wanted to divert him from what he was doing—she wanted whatever was happening to unravel at whatever pace he set. She'd been waiting for this man for so, so long, and he was so *good* at this, at making her wild and keeping her leashed.

She felt a tug at her robe again, the other shoulder, and then her robe slid down in a silken fall around her waist, held in place by a ribbon tie she wished would spontaneously break so he could see all of her.

But he was wholly preoccupied with touch and taste as he cradled her breasts in his hands, alternating his licking tongue with one tapping fingertip over her nipples. So methodical—the soft tap, the steady lap. Better than she'd dreamed. Because of what he was doing or because it was *him* doing it? She didn't know. And she didn't care, as long as he kept going.

She pulled her arms free of the robe, raising her hands to his head, his hair, not to pull him closer but to just…touch. She imagined removing his clothes with the same patience he was lavishing on her breasts. Unbuttoning his shirt, sliding down the zipper of his jeans, stringing out the reveal. The thought of seeing him naked, of touching his skin, of tasting him, made her want to beg him to let her at him. His name trembled on her lips, but just as she would have said it, he changed the pressure of his tongue and her breath caught hard.

Oh, God! Dear *God*! Everything inside her was going haywire, crackling and surging. Her breathing was suddenly chaotic. Shallow pants and gasps. She was trembling, her hands tightening in his hair, and— Oh! Oh, oh, oh! She wanted to catch it, whatever it was that was spiraling inside her. But she couldn't. It was fast, like quicksilver, elusive, but building, expanding. It couldn't be, it couldn't. But it was, the spiral expanding to a whirlwind, faster, faster, stronger, God, God, God.

"Ahhhh!" The sound burst out of her as the vibration of her orgasm rocked her from her nipples all the way down to the core of her jammed over his cock. "Teague!" she cried, and it was somehow shocking to hear her voice, his name vibrating in the air, and realize that everything that had happened since she'd sat on his lap had happened in silence. Shocking…and so sexy.

His hands tightened on her breasts—the only sign that he'd heard that impassioned plea of hers—but the pressure of his tongue remained constant, over, over, over, feasting on her as she rocked on his lap and keened out his name again, and at last she slumped, her limbs loose, her head flung back, her hands slipping from his hair.

Did he realize what he'd just done to her? It had never, ever happened like this before. She wouldn't have believed it was possible to orgasm from a man doing nothing more than using his fingers and tongue on her nipples while she sat on his lap. And now she wanted more, because if he could do that to her so effortlessly, what would happen when he brought that exquisite patience into play between her legs? When he eased into her, when he took her? Oh, God, how she wanted him to take her.

She let out a little groan and pushed herself hard against his cock—*take a hint, Teague.* And he took the hint, all right—he stopped dead.

Hold, hold, hold, as his breaths huffed out of his nostrils, and then his hands released her to grip the tabletop on either side of her.

The next second he was turning his head, averting then closing his eyes, closing her out, closing himself in.

Oh, no. *No!*

A darting look down displayed Teague's impressive erection—*surely* this wasn't over?

But try as she did to convince herself he wasn't rejecting her, she knew that he was. And the fact that it was a conscious decision, an intellectual decision—because it sure as hell wasn't a physical one—cut deep. He might want her—he clearly *did* want her—but he didn't *want* to want her.

And that just wasn't good enough. She wasn't going to be anyone's runner-up gift certificate, the consolation prize you accepted half-heartedly when you didn't win—she was the first-place *trophy*, goddammit, or nothing!

She dragged her robe up, thrust her arms through

the sleeves. "Safe to look now," she said, aiming for amusement, not quite hitting it.

He brought his eyes back to her, and she cocked her head at one of those lean, strong arms of his that were still caging her in.

He dropped his arms—release—and she eased herself off his lap and stood, tightening the sash of her robe. She took a step back, readying a condescending do-you-*really*-think-I-care? eye roll for the gentlemanly apology she felt sure was about to come. Would it be for what he'd done to her? Or for not wanting her after all?

He opened his mouth—but before he could enlighten her, the cry of a baby drew his startled attention.

Frankie knew the source of the cry: there was a new baby in apartment 3B. She also knew, as Teague's eyes fixated on the back of the apartment building, that it wasn't the baby per se that was making the blood drain out of Teague's face. The problem was all those windows— five stories of them—looking down on her courtyard. Putting on a sex show probably ranked somewhere after two trillion on Teague Hamilton's bucket list—right after getting a lap dance at a gentleman's club.

She felt the dumbass blush start up and did her best to battle it back. Fact was, she hadn't intended a peep show for the neighbors, but Teague would probably think it was all in a day's work for her. He probably also thought it was normal for her to go from a kiss to an orgasm in… what? Three minutes flat? Hell, he probably thought she had an orgasm every time she gave a guy a lap dance.

"I guess I'd better go," he said, standing as he brought his eyes back to her.

She got the eye roll in after all. "Guess you'd better."

"I'm sor—"

"Don't say it," she said, cutting him off. "I already know."

"That's not… It's just… I mean, it's not you, it's m—"

"Jesus," she said, cutting him off again. "*Definitely* don't say *that*!" She produced a laugh from some hidden well of pride. "I'm not the kind of girl to resent a quick orgasm on a Sunday morning, so let's just leave it at that. I'm fine, you're fine, I'm pretty sure the baby wasn't watching, and if anyone else in those apartments saw us, at least they don't know who you are, and since I won't breathe a word to anyone you know, your reputation will remain stain-free."

She stepped back from him. "So, moving on. I'll go throw on a dress while you call yourself a taxi. If you like, you can call Joe, my regular driver—his number's on the fridge. He works the godforsaken hours between two and nine in the morning, so if you're lucky you'll scrape in as one of his last jobs. And he knows to come all the way up the driveway, almost to the door, so no need to do the walk of shame down to the street with who-knows-who watching." She stretched her mouth into a no-hard-feelings smile. "By the time Joe's here, I'll be ready to say goodbye like any old friend and wish you happy holidays or whatever you Yanks call the season to be jolly."

She swiped her almost-full mug off the table, and as she walked toward the house, tried not to care that it was still warm to the touch.

"Frankie!" he said, just as she stepped inside.

She stopped but didn't turn around.

"I don't want…to be miserable," he said. "Just—just so you know."

She looked at him over her shoulder. "You don't *want* to be, but you are, aren't you? I'm sorry I'm not the one to help you with that after all."

And then she forced herself to walk unhurriedly to her bedroom, as though she was perfectly, absolutely fine, thank you, because *she* wasn't miserable, even if she'd just thrown herself at a guy who *did not want her* for the three-thousandth time!

She closed her bedroom door supersoftly, then leaned against it and slapped a hand over her mouth to trap the moan that was fighting to get out.

Fuck! Fuck, fuck, *fuck*!

Failure. Utter, abject failure.

Well, what had she expected? A half-naked lap dancer who had the indecency to come faster than a speeding bullet wasn't exactly the woman Prince Charming would set his sights on. And all before the clock ticked over to 9:00 a.m.—giving new meaning to the question "will he still respect me in the morning?"

Well, fuck that. She respected *herself.*

If Teague wanted to be hung up on a woman with whom he'd never had sex and never would, he was welcome to go on being miserable for the rest of his fucking life. Ha! As if Romy was being all princessy and virginal, anyway, married to Matt, of all men. Maybe Teague needed to think about that before he sloughed off an offer of hot, dirty sex with *a woman who actually wanted him*!

Well, not her problem. She had plenty of clients at King's Castle who didn't judge her for a damn thing! They'd cry with joy if she let them touch her the way she'd let Teague Hamilton touch her! She had one regular who was a billionaire, just like Teague, and he'd begged her a hundred times just for a kiss.

Okay, truthfully, Banjo Snow was a billionaire but he was *not* "just like Teague." Banjo was…sleazy. Married, with a mistress on the side, as well as propositioning Frankie every chance he got.

She had other clients, though. Geoff Rhodes, for example. A nice guy who liked her in her clothes as well as out of them, and who happened to be one of the best real estate agents in Bondi so was scouting out premises for the shop she planned to open.

Her shop. That was what she should be thinking about, not some fantasy that was past retirement age. She had a storage locker full of treasures she'd been lovingly collecting for years, she had Matt's ring to launch the store via a charity auction, and the only reason she didn't have a boyfriend was because a man was in her top ten list of good things to have but not in the top three or five or even eight! There would be time for men once she knew her business had a chance of making it.

Perspective. That's what it was all about. A fling with the man of her dreams would have been nice, but it wasn't essential to her happiness.

She took off her robe and hung it on the clothes rack she used in place of a wardrobe, then flicked through the hangers and chose a cheerful 1950s sundress, printed all over with cherries on a pale blue background. An innocent, nonthreatening dress. She took a few minutes in the bathroom to brush her hair and slap on some makeup, then she came back through the bedroom, opened the door and stepped into the living room with a chirpy "Right, then," to announce herself to Teague.

But there was no Teague. And his suitcase was gone.

Almost before her brain accepted that he'd left the house, she heard voices outside. She went to the door, concluding that Joe had arrived and Teague must have gone out to put his bag in the trunk. She reached for the handle…and then pulled her hand back. If Teague had intended to come back in and say goodbye, he wouldn't have closed the door, would he?

Unless he hadn't realized the door automatically locked itself. In which case, she could save him the effort of knocking for readmittance and just go out to him.

Again her hand went to the door handle, but before she could touch it she heard a car door open and close. A moment, two…the sound of the taxi reversing.

So. It was over.

For the longest moment she stayed perfectly still, hand held out, listening to her breathing. In. Out. In. Out. And then… "You're fine," she said out loud. "You're working tonight, you've got a dollar target to hit, you've got the ring, you've had an unexpected orgasm and you got it from *him*. What more do you need?"

But talking common sense didn't work. She needed to touch something solid. But there was only the door, so she gripped that handle after all, and leaned in, so that her forehead was against the wood. Breathing again. In. Out. In. Out.

It would pass, this weakness. But just for a minute she needed to do some of that wallowing she'd accused Teague of doing. Because he'd been here, alone with her, in her house. She'd had a once-only opportunity, and she'd grabbed it, she'd offered herself to him, and he'd said yes. He'd said *yes*, dammit—but she wasn't who he wanted, and what she had to offer him, he didn't want *enough*.

And there was nothing she could do about it.

Not one damn thing.

CHAPTER THREE

TEAGUE HAD NEVER been in a gentleman's club, but he thought he knew what to expect: overpriced drinks, scantily clad women, men stuffing money down bras and in thongs.

He'd stacked his pockets with cash because there was apparently something called "make it rain" you were supposed to do, which involved throwing money on the stage to show your appreciation of the dancers. The thought of actually doing that had been giving him some unpleasant moments since he'd arrived outside the double set of heavy metal doors proudly emblazoned with the club name, King's Castle; he was fairly certain he was going to look like a dick flicking five-dollar bills around.

He could see endless opportunities for embarrassment. Giving too much money, not giving enough money, drooling on the stage where Frankie was dancing and forgetting to throw any money at all. Looking like he didn't belong, looking like he *did* belong. Having everyone notice the seemingly uncontrollable erection he was already sporting. Not knowing how to request

a lap dance, or when to pay for it, or how to act when
he was getting it. Doing everything so wrong he'd be
thrown out on his ass by a bruising bouncer.

Yep. Endless possibilities. Especially given Frankie
had always had a genius for making him feel both over-
stimulated and underseasoned.

Oh, God, he really, truly, did not belong here. He
had to leave.

He turned on his heel just as group of desultorily
chatting men sauntered into the dimly lit alley and
headed for the club. With barely a flicker of an eyelid in Teague's direction, one of them swung open the
doors and they entered as a group, clearly not agonizing about making it rain.

He realized, suddenly, that he had bigger things to
worry about than his inexperience with gentleman's
clubs—like not being the only one inside who'd be making it rain for Frankie. It was two in the morning, for
Christ's sake. For all he knew, a thousand men had already drooled over her tonight—men who knew what
the fuck they were doing.

Which added one more problem to his plate: he had
no idea how he'd react to witnessing other men lusting
after her. Because by slow degrees, during the day and
into the night, it had become fixed in his mind that he
was going to have that fling with Frankie—no matter
what he had to do to make up for the shambles of this
morning—and that meant she was going to belong to
him and only him for the next two and a half weeks.

Okay, maybe it hadn't been so much by slow degrees
as by a series of jolts to his system.

The first was during the drive to his hotel.

He'd taken his suitcase out so that when Frankie came out of her bedroom she'd know he wasn't intending to hang around like a sex pest, and had accidentally locked himself out of the house. His automatic reaction had been to knock on the door, but he'd realized that if she'd been ready to say goodbye, she'd have been in the living room before he let himself out of the house—and so of course he hadn't knocked, because no way did he want her to think he was deliberately summoning her in a half-dressed state!

It was a short step from there to convince himself that her taking so long in the bedroom was a deliberate tactic to avoid seeing him again, and that her comment about saying goodbye "like any old friend" was supposed to be ironic. They'd never been *new* friends—how could they be old ones? She clearly hadn't wanted to say goodbye, she'd just wanted him gone.

So when Joe had arrived a minute later, he'd put his bag in the trunk and gotten in the car. He'd given Joe the name of his hotel, made a comment about the weather and buckled his seat belt extra firmly as Joe reversed down the driveway as a kind of symbolic dead bolt.

But by the time the taxi had been halfway to the city, he'd made another logic leap and determined that Frankie had faked that orgasm just to get him to stop what he was doing. In his experience, a woman didn't come like she was dissolving when a guy had done almost nothing to get her there—and certainly not a woman like Frankie Lee, who knew every sexual rope in the universe and had probably tied up a helluva lot of men with each and every one of them.

He'd been torn between a need to get to his hotel and raid the minibar and a desire to have Joe take him back to Frankie's so he could beg her to let him show her he could do better.

He'd closed his eyes at that point, wanting to block out the world, but she'd been there behind his eyelids. *God*, she was sexy. Just the memory of the voluptuous not-quite-give of her lips as he'd kissed her had had him hard and aching all over again. He'd almost been able to hear the telltale hitch of her breath as she hovered on the edge of coming, and the frantic way she'd moaned his name made him want to hear her say it a million more times. Teague—an uptight, preppy-boy name, but coming from Frankie it was an aphrodisiac. He'd licked his lips, almost tasting her hard nipples, feeling the heat of her against his cock—damp heat, he'd seen the evidence on his jeans and wanted to feel it against his skin.

And that was when it had hit him, in a back-the-fuck-up moment, and he'd opened his eyes. He'd caught Joe looking at him a little warily in the rearview mirror and known he'd said, "Back the fuck up," out loud but he just did not care because damp heat, hard nipples, the anxious "Teague" all meant Frankie hadn't been faking it. She'd wanted him to go further.

And goddammit, he'd stopped, and locked himself out of her house, and given up!

Yep, jolt number one, delivered with a metaphorical smack to the head.

Jolt number two had come when he'd seen the size of his hotel suite. Two bedrooms, a large sitting room, a private outdoor terrace, a full kitchen, a dining area with a table that seated eight, a lavish bathroom with a massive spa bath and a huge shower with a marble bench set against a wall just in case you needed a rest after being pounded by four separate water jets! The suite was at least twice the size of Frankie's entire home, and appeared even bigger because it was all white and beige and cream and—and just, ugh! It suddenly seemed preposterous to have booked such a place knowing he'd be alone in it every damn day and every damn night.

And in had crept the insidious thought that maybe he wouldn't have been alone if he'd gotten out of the damn taxi and knocked on Frankie's damn door!

The third jolt had happened after he'd dragged on some boxers and a T-shirt, closed the black-out drapes and gotten into bed for the catch-up sleep he should have had before seeing Frankie, and the smell of gardenias had had him bolting upright in bed. He'd fumbled with the remote control that managed every setting in the suite, turning on the bedroom lights and searching the room for a flower arrangement. But there'd been no such arrangement.

He'd leaped out of bed and walked through the suite clutching the remote in his hand like it was a revolver, turning on lights as he went, looking for the source of the smell. He'd found nothing, which meant what he could smell was her on his skin.

He'd showered then, but when he'd gotten back into

bed and closed his eyes, he'd still been able to smell her. And he'd tossed and turned, and tossed and cursed, and turned and groaned. And at the end of all that, he could see her as well as smell her, lying in her rumpled white bedsheets. Gold skin, gray eyes, black-and-blue hair, crimson mouth, telling him to try again and she'd consider having that fling, even though he didn't deserve it after running away like a damn coward.

Back out of bed, stabbing at the remote as he strode over to the drapes, forcing himself not to manually wrench them off the rails, but to wait, wait, wait, as the view opened to him slice by slice. Stepping onto the suite's private terrace, hoping the sunlight would burn off the mist in his brain and bring him back to reality.

He'd forgotten how beautifully, brightly blue Sydney was, and he had the best of it in his sights—not only the water, but also the Opera House, the distinctive coat-hanger-shaped bridge linking north and south. The yachts on the harbor... Oh, God, the *ache* of those yachts.

He'd rubbed his hands over this face, wondering if everyone thought what Frankie did: that he'd given up sailing because his near-drowning experience had scared him off.

Probably.

But the truth was, that race was the first time he'd unshackled himself since Cassandra's death. It had been exhilarating, like he was fighting back instead of accepting. Dark skies. Gale force winds. Sea whipped into a foaming frenzy. Keeping himself alert until his teammates could locate him, and return for him. They'd dragged him back into the boat and just kept going because he was no more important than the rest of the crew, and he'd felt invincibly alive and...and real.

And that was when jolt number four had hit. The truth of his existence: that he was only half-alive, and that drowning was more than a threat, it was his reality. His *life* was drowning him—washing over him in waves that held him down but never seemed to break.

Teague Ingram Spencer Hamilton. Dignified, understated, even-keeled. Family scion—too important to risk. In a job he was good at but didn't especially enjoy. Expert lover of women he never managed to actually love. Good women, kind women, successful women, women who'd sometimes fallen in love with him—except that they hadn't; it had been his alter ego they loved, Mr. Perfect. Even Romy had seen only half of him, the half he'd turned himself into for her when she'd found the spark was missing—the stalwart friend, playing it safe by not asking for more. And he'd lost her anyway, to a man who didn't know the meaning of the word *safe*. And ever since then, he'd been...

Well, what had he been ever since?

Miserable, according to Frankie. Wallowing in it. How could she see that so clearly when he hadn't seen it himself? He'd always thought of himself as simply playing the cards he'd been dealt. But as he'd looked at the yachts in Sydney Harbour, he'd known it wasn't really called playing when you held the cards so close to your chest you never let one touch the table. It couldn't even be called Solitaire, what he'd been playing, because he didn't dare look at the cards himself. And so the race of his life had been going on without him. There'd been no one to drag him back into the boat if he made a mistake, so he didn't *make* any mistakes.

Mr. Perfect. Everyone he knew described him in some term or another that meant the same thing. Perfect looks, perfect manners, perfect friend/student/son. But all it really meant was that nobody could see inside him.

Except that Frankie *had*. She knew he was miserable.

And hello jolt number five. Like a spear right between the eyes. He wanted someone to see inside and know exactly who he was, even if they ended up hating his guts. He wanted to fall out of the fucking boat and flail in stormy seas, and have someone know he was in trouble and drag him in, and if there was no one there to pull him into the boat, he'd save him-fucking-self! And if he couldn't save himself? Well, at least it would have been fun while it lasted.

Which had brought him—after a day of fits and starts, and troubled sleeps, and half-eaten meals and endless soul-searching—to this dark alley, ready to knock on Frankie's door again. Freshly showered and shaved, dressed in what he thought were appropriate clothes for an elegant club—dark pants and a long-sleeved upmarket T-shirt in pale blue made of cotton so thin and fine it clung to him like cool silk. Understated, but a little bit sexy. He burst out laughing. Jesus! Was he seriously saying he looked sexy? He really was losing it.

Okay, time to get his ass in the club. How hard could it be to walk in and order a whiskey? It wasn't like Frankie was a serial killer, waiting in there with a chain saw—she was going to be practically naked, no room for concealed weapons.

No, no *concealed* weapons—they were going to be on glorious display. To everyone in the whole damn place.

"Right," he said, and headed grimly for the entrance.

CHAPTER FOUR

THE MUSIC WAS muted enough to hear a hum of conversation but loud enough to mask actual words and individual voices. Good. Teague didn't want to be yelling at Frankie; nor did he want to be overheard.

The decor had a richly exclusive look about it. Maybe it was the color palette—black, charcoal, chocolate and cream. Or maybe it was the lighting—subdued, but with occasional searching shafts picking out a glint of skin, a sequin, flashes of glass and metal.

An impressively stocked bar filled one wall. Each man occupying a stool there seemed to be alone, except for one who was chatting to a dancer. The opposite wall contained a series of recessed nooks, closed off with beaded curtains. The remainder of the place looked like an upscale dining room, with well-spaced tables, only half of which were occupied. Waitstaff circulated throughout, unobtrusive.

The main game was the pole-studded circular platform in the middle of the room, atop which four girls were dancing—not completely naked, Teague was relieved to note. Men seated around the platform had their eyes glued to the performers, occasionally tipping by placing money on the stage. One question answered— not that Teague could see himself sitting close enough to the stage to tip that easily.

Frankie wasn't anywhere to be seen. Teague figured he'd give one last careful glance around to get his bearings, then he'd head over to the bar, order a drink and ask the bartender if she was working tonight. If it turned out she wasn't, then he'd—

Whoa!

Whoa, whoa, *whoa*!

There she was. Emerging from one of those recessed rooms with the beaded curtains.

She stepped into the path of one of the brighter lights and her hand came up, shielding her face. Just a brief moment, then her hand came down and he saw something in her face beyond tiredness. A pained exhaustion that made him hate himself for waking her that morning.

He remembered she'd once quipped that dancing for six hours in seven-inch heels wasn't a job for weaklings, and he looked down, hoping the seven inches was an exaggeration—but his eyes never made it past her teeny tiny black…what? Shorts? Panties? Something he thought a 1930s chorus girl might wear. *Whatever* they were, they had his heart bypassing his throat and leaping all the way into his skull, where it pounded like a hammer. She wasn't wearing less than the other women in the club—if anything she was wearing more, because those shorts came all the way up to her waist. The problem was that they were sheer, and through them he could see crystals. Like diamonds. On her skin. Right down *there*.

Ho-o-o-oly shit. The hottest thing he'd seen in his whole fucking life. She had to earn a fortune every time she walked past a guy. They'd be clamoring to shove money down there.

But if so, where was the money? Not inside her underwear or he'd see it. So...

There! A black band of lace around her perfectly tanned, perfectly toned, perfectly perfect right thigh. He couldn't see any bills poking out, but there was a small bulge beneath the lace on her outer leg. Good to know where to put it.

Now get your eyes up, pervert, he ordered himself... only for his hot gaze to snag on her black lacy bra. Not as sheer as the shorts but he could make out her areolae. To his shame, the first thought in his head was how her naked breasts had looked that morning. Two firm, flawless, pale gold handfuls. Upturned pink-bronze nipples, hard as cherries against his lapping tongue. Jesus H. Christ, he had to get his eyes up, *up*, before he went to her, grabbed her hand and dragged her back to his hotel so he could do it again.

He forced his eyes to her face, saw her paste on a smile, straighten her shoulders, toss back her hair. She was midstep, casting a speculative look around the club, when her eyes landed on him.

Arrested moment, her lips parting in surprise—and then she came directly for him, right up to him.

"So?" she said, and there was a challenge in that word.

"So is the offer still open?" Challenge accepted.

"It is."

And somehow he wasn't surprised that it was that easy. Because it was Frankie Lee, and she didn't have to play games to get what she wanted. "Then…what happens next?" he asked.

She glanced at the wall behind him. He looked over his shoulder. A clock.

"Forty-five minutes until we close, so come over to the bar and grab a stool next to Len—Len's Cyn's boyfriend. Cyn's the glamorous blonde on the stage. And Len's a nurse, if you want the lowdown on surgical procedures for getting the stick out of your ass. I'll let Jase, our bartender, know you're with me so no one bothers you." A pause, as she slanted a look at him from beneath false lashes. "Unless you *want* to be bothered? In which case I'd recommend Bella."

What the—? Who the—? "Bella?"

"A friend of mine. Or there's Xanthe, or—"

"But that's not— I mean, I'm here for you, Frankie."

"Yes, but I'm working until three, so if you want to see what a lap dance is all about, Bella's the best. She's saving for a holiday in Thailand so she could use the money."

His eyes went to those wall recesses, just as a nondescript-looking guy came out of one, adjusting his pants as though he was in some pain. "Is that what you were—?"

"Yes," she said, and arched one eyebrow as though daring him to make something of it.

"Will you do it again?"

"I hope so. Bella's not the only one who needs money."

He looked around the room. Saw the group of men that had come in ahead of him. One of them was openly ogling Frankie. Okay, time to extract the stick from his ass. "Then I'm asking you for a dance," he said.

A split second was all it took for her face to blank, as though a shutter had come down.

"Of course, I'll pay you," he added quickly. "I'll pay you for the rest of the night."

"Pay me?"

"You need money, and I… Well, you know I can afford it, Frankie, I could afford to buy every dance every night from you for the next two weeks if you…" He trailed off there, knowing he'd committed some epic kind of faux pas—exactly what he didn't want to do—even though he wasn't sure what the faux pas was.

Frankie spun on her heel, and he thought it was all over until she flung a "This way" over her shoulder at him.

With some trepidation, he followed her.

CHAPTER FIVE

"FRANKIE," TEAGUE SAID, coming up behind her. "Wait, just...wait."

But she pretended not to hear him and kept going, skirting around the dance platform and heading toward the VIP rooms, eyeing the discreet lights set in the ceiling above each space that would tell her which was available.

Stupid to feel demeaned by his buying a dance from her. Stupid. Stupid. Stupid!

Hadn't she offered him a freebie once upon a time?

And it wasn't as though she was ashamed of what she did. She liked men, she liked flirting, she liked the sensuality of dancing for an audience, she liked that the job kept her fit.

Most importantly, dancing had given her dignity. She'd fought hard for every scrap of dignity she'd scraped off the streets of Sydney since she'd been tossed out to fend for herself at sixteen. She'd *earned* every scrap, on her fucking uncomfortable high heels, with a smile on her face and a twirl in her hips.

There was power in what she did. She'd felt it ever

since that Saturday night a million years ago when she'd had to drop out of university and had danced for the first time to buy her way into what she'd thought would be a different kind of life in America. And when that life had turned out to be not so different after all, she'd come home and kept dancing, using the money she made to finish her business degree and set her up for whatever future she chose. She knew the way she earned her money was by selling a fantasy—but it was a fantasy she controlled, and there was not one ounce of shame in her for taking that control.

Only now, with Teague…

Dammit, she didn't feel in control. That was the problem. She felt dangerously *out* of control, because when she'd seen him in the club, visions of something wistfully, scarily romantic had popped into her head. Like some dumbass scene in a Hollywood movie. Being swept into his arms, carried out the door, whisked away in a white limousine to a happily-ever-after.

"Let me buy a lap dance off you" didn't quite cut it by comparison.

Ugh. Maybe the lap dance was a good thing. Being put in the right box from the start—a woman for hire— would stop any romantic-fantasy infiltration and make it strictly business.

She stopped outside her room of choice to take a steadying breath—and that was when Teague grabbed her hand and sent her heart skittering as though she hadn't just given herself that snap-out-of-it talking-to. Such a simple thing, yet it made her want to turn and beg him not to come past the beaded curtain.

A sound to her right drew her attention. Xanthe, approaching a different room with one of her regulars; she gave Frankie a subtle thumbs-up—a sign she thought Frankie had scored the jackpot. And, of course, Frankie had. Teague was the best-looking man ever to have come into the club. Probably the wealthiest. But in reality, neither of those things meant squat. In here, he was no different from the man Xanthe had in tow; as long as they paid they were equally welcome.

She pulled her hand free and gave Teague a playful *tsk-tsk* as she swiveled toward him, her back against the beads. "No touching allowed," she said.

He looked suitably confused. "What?"

"House rules. No touching or Gus will kick you out."

More confusion. "Gus?"

"Also known as The Mountain. Our biggest, baddest bouncer. He's standing at the bar watching you right now and he'll keep watching."

"So…there are cameras?"

"Of course," she said, knowing he'd hate that, and left him to locate the scowling Gus while she brushed aside the beads and stepped into the room. She let the displaced curtain clack back into place, then paused to compose herself for the ordeal ahead.

A heartbeat, two—that was as long as it took for the beads to click again, telling her Teague was behind her.

She turned to face him. "You've never been in a place like this before, have you?" she asked, and then laughed. "Why am I asking? *Of course* you haven't."

He frowned, quick and hard. "What does that mean?"

"That this is too naughty for you, Mr. Perfect. But

hey, we'll give it a go. See if I can take some of the shine off your halo." She inclined her head toward the upright chair in the center—no couch in this room, no tables to hold drinks, all the better to circle him. Panther and prey. And she was going to stalk him, by God. "Sit and relax—that's all you have to do. I'll do the rest."

He sat, but he was not relaxed. She found it oddly endearing that he should be so uncomfortable. So endearing, she had to steel herself against telling him to get up, get out, go back to his hotel and forget all about her. But steel herself she did, because she still wanted him more than she'd ever wanted anyone in her misbegotten life, and she *knew* how to make men want her when she danced for them.

"Don't worry," she said, "I won't go further than I'm allowed to go."

"Allowed?" He frowned. "But you're allowed to do anything you want."

A thought that made her heart skip a beat. But… "Not at work, not on the job," she said.

"Job…"

"You know, like your job is to be a lawyer?" she responded.

More confusion…and then she saw him breathe in slowly. "I get it, okay," he said, and nodded, like he was girding his loins for battle.

She studied him, sitting there, way out of his comfort zone, and wondered if he knew how lonely he seemed, waiting for something to happen.

He really should have chosen Bella. Bella would have made this new experience something he could smile about. But Frankie couldn't professionally charm him. What small talk could she offer when what she wanted to do was take away the sadness? What fantasy could she offer when he was *her* fantasy? When she wanted to be different with him from what she was with her clients? Different *for* him...

Arrgh! Too much introspection for a thirty-minute dance. Maybe he *was* her fantasy, but what he was paying for was for her to be his. Time to get to work.

While she waited for a new song to start, she assessed the way Teague was sitting, then approached him to make some adjustments, all business. A fleeting touch on each shoulder: "Just shift forward a little...good." A brief squeeze of his knees. "Spread your legs... That's it." A tap on his clenched fists. "Keep these on the chair either side of you—hold on to the base next to your hips if you like."

"To make sure I don't touch you?" he asked.

She only smiled at that. No time to speak because she read the imminent change in the music. She stepped well back, keeping her eyes on his, counting down, knowing the next song was cued and ready, a-a-and... "Tick tock, your time...starts...now," she said, as the song started playing.

She kept her body still and her legs together—a simple column to focus his eyes. Only when she knew his attention was riveted on her did she move. Just her head. A leisurely roll, first in one direction, then the other. The goal, *her* goal, was always the same at this stage: to move so s-l-o-w-l-y the client was entranced. Like a

snake charmer, luring the captive out of the basket—
only the power was the snake's.

She had it all mapped out, every progression defined—
the same for every private dance. Keeping her distance,
letting the view of her body whet the appetite, making
the client long for her to come closer. Body language told
her the tipping point—that moment when the client went
from enjoying the anticipation to needing more.

But within forty seconds of the song starting, Frankie
knew this dance wasn't going to traverse the usual route,
because Teague hadn't even flicked a glance down at
her body.

It was a foreign experience, to have a guy deliberately keep his eyes only on her face; she was going to
have to go off script to earn her money.

She raised her arms at her sides, keeping them
slightly bent, her fingers delicately posed ballerina-
style. Again, she rolled her head—one way, then back.
Moved her shoulders—one at a time. Brought her hips
into play. She envisaged herself as a shifting, changing
sea as she let the music take her over, swelling within
her...

But she may as well have been a nun, in a habit,
*boing*ing on a pogo stick for all the impact she was having. What the hell? The only one of them who seemed
to be getting aroused by what she was doing was her!
And that *never* happened!

Oh, God, *God*! She was going to have to shift her feet
and open her legs, because her clitoris was a too-tight
knot. She needed something hard against it to ease the

throb—preferably his cock, which meant she had to get to the lap part of the dance fast and grind the knot loose.

What would happen if she came when she did that, like she had so effortlessly this morning?

No. No, she couldn't. She'd be furious if a client did that to her so she *could not* do it to a client! She had to have more control than the client—that was the way it was supposed to work. *Teague* was supposed to be the one in the grip of rising lust, not her.

Maybe she could pry those gripping hands of his from the chair and put them on her breasts—a reminder of what he'd done to her that morning. Then she could draw his hands down her body to her hips, then her thighs...

Ah, God, she was getting seriously wet at the thought—and yet there he was, still as a statue, eyes glued to her face, giving nothing away. Well, she'd just have to *make* him give something away.

As she walked slowly toward him, she sensed him brace. There was a tension in his thighs, like he was preparing for her to move between them. Which, of course, was exactly where she'd been heading, but she suddenly decided she would *not*, and without so much as a hitch in her step, she detoured around him, coming to a stop behind his chair.

She let the moment stretch out, hoping she was making him wonder what she was going to do as the music enveloped them. She had to close her eyes for a moment, working that out herself, because there was something about the smell of his aftershave that was making her a little crazy. He was so delectable, how could she not want to send her hands down his chest and into his—?

No! She opened her eyes—safer.

Her hands would go no farther than his chest. She raised them, willing them not to shake as his shoulders tensed the way his thighs had. Hair, she decided. Safest option. Hairdressers touched hair all the time without molesting their clients.

But as she slid her hands into the squeaky clean strands, and felt the breath he held, it was as though she was absorbing him through her fingertips. This was impossible. She forced her hands down to his shoulders and as he released that pent-up breath her body seemed to sigh along with it. She kept her hands on his shoulders and leaned in close, her hair brushing his cheek. "If you don't want me to touch you, say so now."

"I want you to touch me, Frankie," he said.

"Okay," she breathed out, and couldn't resist a tiny, kittenish lick at his earlobe. "But stop me at any time."

And, figuring that was enough warning, she slid her hands down to his chest and rubbed them firmly over his pecs. God, he felt good. Lean and hard under that miraculous top, which was so slinky-thin she could feel the faint crunch of his chest hair through it. His nipples were hard points—the best sign. She wanted to see them, feel them against her palms, wanted to lick them, suck them into her mouth.

Oka-a-ay, time to move again.

Keeping one hand on him, she glided around the chair so she was standing in the space between his spread thighs, then leaned forward to grip the back of the chair on either side of his head, caging him in the way he'd caged her between the chair and the table this morning.

She swayed, side to side, hoping he'd drop his eyes to see what she was doing, but not once did he look at anything other than her face. Man of steel. Too, too perfect. She was going to have to force it, make him see what he seemed so determined not to.

She found the right beat of music to release the chair and turned her back to him. Slowly she lowered herself into a squat between his knees, and then even more slowly unrolled her body, keeping hold of her ankles and waving her backside at him. She'd been told many a time her ass was her best feature, and tonight it was packed in some mighty flirtatious vintage-style underwear she'd had made specially for the shop—black mesh with a froth of baby blue frills crowding the back.

And at last he was actively struggling with his breathing. She shifted her legs slightly apart, hoping he'd see that the crotch was wet and know that it was for him. She wanted him to slide his hands in there and feel it. Wanted to sit on his lap and release his cock and take it into her until he begged for more. She knew where the cameras were; knew she could position herself just so to avoid them... But she knew, also, Teague would freak out all the way down to his conservative soul if she went there. A beaded curtain was an even flimsier barrier than the row of potted plants separating her courtyard from that cock-blocking apartment building. Illusory privacy, not real. So she was just going to have to deal with the sex scenes in her head, stop herself from imagining what it would be like to scrape off a layer of his clean and get him to talk dirty to her.

Her breath shortened at the thought of him telling her what he wanted to do to her, that he was going to fuck her, but she suspected that even if they were sealed in a bank vault ten floors below the surface of the earth with Armageddon on approach and no hope of rescue he still wouldn't say such things to her!

What she needed was 3:00 a.m. to roll around so she could get him away from here and say those things herself. Take him the way she should have taken him this morning—aggressively but in private. Give him the fuck of the century.

She wanted to look between her legs at his lap to see if she was having a measurable physical impact on him, but didn't trust what she might do if he had a hard-on. She was going to have to work out how he was feeling from what his face told her. She looked over one shoulder, then over the other. A rigid jaw, flared nostrils, the flicker of an eyelid. Those things were indicative but not conclusive. She might be imagining them or projecting her own desire onto him.

Time to face him and get closer.

With a last swish of her bottom, she twirled, a full body roll bringing her into a position where she was leaning close, her hands on his shoulders, her nose almost touching his.

Long, intense moment, during which she forgot to breathe and he gave nothing away.

Iceberg. She was seeing the opaque white ten percent. She needed what was underneath, the hidden glassy blue. And she was willing to risk a torn hull from what was below the surface if she couldn't find a way to tip that iceberg upside down...

Ah, the song was ending.

No matter. Twenty-two minutes to go, and Dazey, the club DJ, would make the changeover to a new song seamless. She didn't even have to ask Teague if he wanted another dance; since he'd signed on for thirty minutes, all she had to do was stay exactly as she was and carry on.

She felt his hands on hers, and for a moment thought he meant to use them to tug her down onto his lap, but instead he lifted her hands from his shoulders, using his hold on them to steady her as he stood.

He released her the moment he was out of the chair and raised his hands, surrender-style. "Sorry," he said. "I had to touch you, but I'll stop now."

"What's wrong?" she asked and hated the telltale plaintive breathiness of her voice.

"Nothing," he said. "Just...nothing."

She licked her lips as she watched his unmoved face, automatically searching for a way to please him, then reached behind her back for the clasp of her bra. "I can take this off...?"

"No."

"Yes! I can! It's my choice to do it or not."

"No!" he said again. "You've done enough, Frankie. I told you I get it, and I do."

"Enough?" she said, not quite believing the most important lap dance of her life was ending like this. "But you wanted half an hour."

He dug into his pants pocket and removed a wad of cash that had her staring. "I'll still pay for the time."

Slap!

He peeled off ten notes—*hundred-dollar notes*—and then another five, and held them out, and when she just stared at them, he counted out more, and said, "Tell me when—"

"Stop!" she said immediately. "That's crazy. I barely did anything, and you didn't enjoy what I did do."

"Didn't I?" he asked, and when she said nothing, he took a step closer. "Since I'm not allowed to touch you, I'll have to ask you to touch me."

"Wh-what?"

He touched a fingertip to his neck. "Feel here. My pulse."

"Your pulse?"

"Do it. You'll see."

She lifted her hand, put two fingertips where his had been and felt the thrum of fast, urgent blood.

And then he stepped back so that her hand dropped. "Take the money, Frankie."

Her throat all but closed as she took the notes from him, peeled off a single note and handed back the rest. "That's enough. I'm not a charity case."

"Matt said he sometimes paid you to sit out a dance. And I...I'm sure you're tired since I woke you so early today. If you take all the money, you can sit out the rest, can't you?"

"I just said I'm not a charity case."

"But Matt—"

"Fuck Matt! You're *not* Matt!" And wasn't that the

truth! Matt knew the life, knew the way a person with pride coped to function *outside* the life. "So if you're so eager to part with your money, go to the bar and buy a bottle of champagne. Or ask Jase for a glass of his best cognac—it's superb, worth the cost."

"Frankie—"

"Stop, Teague. Just…stop, okay?" She dragged in a breath. "I need a few minutes to freshen up. I've got one more roster out on the stage before we close."

"But—"

"I need to take my turn, Teague. It's the system. If I'm not in here, I have to do it."

"Oh. I—I see." He cleared his throat. "So I guess I'll see you outside when you're finished."

"Yep," she said, and stopped only to flick the light switch to advise the room was now available, before she made her way through the curtains and out to the dressing room. Not that she needed to freshen up—what she needed was to get herself into the right headspace for performing in public knowing the intensely private Teague would disapprove of every move she made.

But as it turned out, she didn't have to worry about Teague's disapproval, because when she made it back to the club a few minutes later, he was nowhere to be seen.

"Way to go, Frankie," she murmured. "Lose the same guy twice in one day."

She checked the clock, then strode confidently to the platform, flashing her trademark come-one-come-all smile.

CHAPTER SIX

THE ALLEY IN which King's Castle was situated didn't allow for cars, so it was Frankie's usual practice to wait inside at the bar with Gus and Jase until Joe texted her to let her know he was at the corner. She'd never had any frightening experiences leaving the club, but she took precautions because you never knew when a guy was going to decide to be a dick.

Tonight, she was later than usual. It had struck her that three in the morning was the most depressing time of any day—the time it hit you that your life was nothing like a romantic Hollywood movie—so she'd reset her pickup time, taken longer than usual to wash off her makeup, and bought the guys a drink.

Not that 3:40 a.m. was any better than three o'clock, but hey, listening to Jase and Gus talk about their plans for the next three nights, when the club would be closed, was better than what was on offer at home.

On which subject—she hoped Teague wasn't planning on changing his mind again and dropping into King's Castle tomorrow night. Not that he was likely to. He'd been inside for sixteen minutes by her reckoning; according to Jase, he hadn't even stopped to buy a drink after that abortive lap dance. He'd come, he'd seen, he'd decided "yeah...nah," she *definitely* wasn't for him, and he'd left.

Her phone beeped with an incoming text, and it annoyed her that she hoped for a moment...

But it was Joe, of course.

"That's me gone," she said to the guys, and hopped off the bar stool.

She twitched the circular skirt of her bright yellow frock into place, grabbed her handbag off the bar and slung it over her shoulder, then scooped out her keys and positioned the longest, sharpest one between her index and middle fingers—instant weapon.

As usual, Gus offered to carry her work bag out to the taxi, and as usual she refused the offer and hoisted the thing off the floor herself. Both it and her way-too-big handbag got heavier by the week, but their heft made them good back-up weapons.

She headed across the floor, opened the door and stepped outside, into what felt like a wall.

"Oof," she said, and heard a corresponding "Ouch."

Not a wall. She was staring at a pale blue chest.

Teague.

Teague?

"Um, maybe you could move that key a fraction to the right...?" he said.

She looked down, saw where her swinging, key-clenching fist had hit him, and burst out laughing. "Sorry," she said.

He laughed, too, but there was a decided wince in

it. "I dress to the left, just so you know for future reference."

"Future reference?"

"Should I get out of line and you want to make it count."

Her synapses didn't seem to be firing. "Future, as in…?"

"As in…two weeks and three days, right?" he said, and in one smooth move she found herself swung around so that she was tucked under his arm, her heavy bag now in his hand, not hers.

As with this morning's chair straddle, she had no idea how he'd accomplished that and was bedazzled by it—which explained her inane comment: "You left ages ago."

"An hour and ten minutes," he said, "and yes, it felt like ages. When I told you I'd wait for you outside, I didn't expect you to take so long."

"Oh!" Lights going on in her mashed-up brain. "Outside! I thought you meant outside as in outside the room, outside in the *club*, at the bar, or at the stage, or something like…that?"

He stopped, looked down at her. "Was I wrong to wait for you, Frankie? Say, if so."

"I don't…think so."

"You don't *think* so?" He lifted his arm from around her and angled her to face him. "That's not enough for me."

"Then—then what will be enough?"

"You tell me. I'm the one who made the mistake."

"Mistake?"

"Asking you to dance for me."

"That's kind of what guys do in there—ask girls for a dance."

"But you didn't *want* to do it, and I should have…I don't know—read your signals or something. When you suggested Bella or whatever her name is, it should have been obvious, but I thought— Look, it doesn't matter what I thought, does it? I was wrong to ask you and I won't do it again. And in any case…" He winced again, and this time she noticed his nose wrinkled when he did it, and it was flat-out adorable!

"In any case?" she prompted.

"There doesn't seem much point in a lap dance if I can't touch you."

"But I didn't get to the good part."

"There's a good part?" He huffed out a laugh. "I hope that club has resuscitation equipment in that case."

"The thing is, I—I might have let you touch me. Some of the girls allow it. Touching. If you come back in and that's what you want…" Trailing off again. What the fuck was she doing? She felt like jabbing that key of hers in her goddamn eye, because she *did not dance for people she knew* and she *did not allow touching*!

"I'll keep that in mind next time and—and I'll let you choose for me. I mean, choose one of the others."

"Great," she said, but in her head, she was thinking maybe she should be jamming her key into *his* eye. Into *both* his eyes, so he didn't see a *damn thing* next time he came to the club. "You'll have to wait, though. The club is only open Thursday to Sunday. I would have told you but…well, I guess I have told you now! And it wouldn't have mattered if I didn't tell you because you weren't likely to turn up tomorrow night." Babbling, she was babbling. "Although if you had planned on turning up, and you weren't waiting out here, I have no idea how I would have told you." *Shut up, Frankie.* "Because I don't know where you're staying and I don't have your phone number." *Shut up!* "But I guess it doesn't matter because I know it's not your scene. Which is—is… cool."

"So maybe give me your phone," he said, and put her bag down.

She blinked at him.

"Is that a problem?" he asked. "'Cause I thought people having a fling probably needed each other's cellphone numbers."

"Yes—yes, they do," she said, strangely breathless as she swapped the keys in her hand for the mobile phone in her bag. She unlocked the phone and held it out to him.

A minute later he handed the phone back to her and said, "Call me and make sure it works."

"I trust you. And I could just call Matt if you made a mistake inputting the—"

"Call me, Frankie, and let's leave Matt—and Romy, for that matter—out of the whole deal, since this is between you and me."

"Okay," she said, because that was basically music to her freaking ears, and called him. "There, it's ringing, so—"

He answered the call before she could hang up. "Hello?" he said.

"Er, hel-lo," she responded.

"So since you were wondering where I'm staying, I thought we could go there for the night instead of all the way out to Bondi. Is that okay with you?"

She started laughing. "Yes—so is this where we discuss what we've been up to today and what our plans are for tomorrow, or do we do that when we next see each other?"

He laughed, too, as he disconnected the call and shoved his phone back in his pocket. And then he picked up her bag as though it weighed approximately nothing. "You sure my hotel's okay? It's just that it's closer, so on your work nights, it makes sense to me that we stay there. We could do your off nights in Bondi. If…" Shrug. "I mean if you're intending we spend every night together. No pressure if that's not how flings work."

Dear God, she was breathless. "I'm sure about the hotel, I like your plan, and that *is* how flings work—or at least, how this one's going to."

And under the streetlight in that dingy lane, he smiled at her, and she saw that his smile—a *real* smile—was both slow to bloom and lopsided, because the side of his mouth with the scar didn't lift the same as the other. And then he raised his hand and touched a finger to the damaged side, like he was self-conscious about it, and her heart lurched in her chest.

"So we're all set?" she said from her mouth, while her heart screamed: *kiss me!*

And when he leaned down as though he'd heard that scream in her head, only to put the kiss on her damn cheek, she had to clutch his sexy-as-fucking-hell T-shirt because her knees went weak.

"We're all set," he said, and when he took her back under his arm, Frankie's heart lurched again, and she knew in that moment, she just *knew*, this fling was going to get a little too Hollywood romance for comfort unless she was very, very careful.

CHAPTER SEVEN

FRANKIE HADN'T SAID one word to him since they'd gotten into the taxi. She hadn't looked at him, either. She'd just stared at the back of Joe's seat.

Teague didn't blame her for zoning out. She had to be ready to drop with fatigue.

Which was fine. Okay, it wasn't fine, because he'd been a dick for waking her at eight in the morning. What *was* fine was if she wanted to delay starting their fling until she'd had a good night's sleep. He'd simply pretend he hadn't been in a state of blistering arousal all day. If anyone knew how to keep his hands off a girl, Teague was that man! He'd done it for two months with Romy without suffering undue frustration.

Romy. Who he hadn't thought of ever since he'd left Frankie's house.

What would she think of him going to a gentleman's club?

What would she think about him taking Frankie back to his hotel?

What would she think of his fling with Frankie?

He tested those questions in his head but was too

impatient to focus on them. The answers didn't matter, anyway. What Frankie was thinking was what mattered, and she was such a mix of come-get-me and approach-only-so-far, it was hard to read her.

How could it be that she could control every man within a mile of her with one look from her mesmerizing eyes, the raise of an eyebrow, a saucy smile…and yet tremble like a leaf just because his fingers touched hers on a whiskey glass?

How could she tell him in the morning she wanted to have a fling with him and yet resent him asking for a simple dance from her that night…and then brush aside his apology, as though he hadn't done anything wrong after all?

How could she make him think of midnight at eight in the morning because of the way she moved in a sinfully silky robe…and yet look like a burst of midday sun in the dark of night in her yellow dress?

And how could a simple roll of her head have him death-gripping a chair to stop himself from dragging her onto his lap…and yet the sight of baby blue ruffles on her bottom give him the power to rein in the savage need to crush her against him?

She was like a roguish kitten with the heart of a prowling leopard, daring you to come closer if you were bold enough, but only willing to show you half of who she was.

Kitten, leopard, vixen, siren. Whatever she was, in whichever combination, he wanted her.

He slanted a look at her as they approached the hotel, just as she closed her eyes. A moment later, and only a moment, she opened them and reset her face, much as she'd done when she'd emerged from behind those beaded curtains almost two hours ago.

Yes, he wanted her, but he could wait.

Joe pulled to a stop outside the hotel and Teague automatically reached for his wallet.

Frankie stopped him by gripping his wrist. "No," she said. "This is on my account, already paid."

He held up his hands—backing off—and wondered how many times in the next two and a half weeks he was going to be giving in. He got out of the cab, intending to go around to her side and open the door for her, but Joe beat him to it.

Teague waited, her bag in hand, watching as Frankie dug a parcel wrapped in Christmas paper from the depths of her purse. She handed the parcel to Joe, then kissed his cheek, and Joe hugged her like she was a favorite daughter. She whispered something in his ear that made Joe laugh, and then he released her and got back into the taxi and drove off.

"Christmas present," she explained, joining Teague under the hotel awning.

"So I guessed."

"He made out like it was a big deal but it's just something I knitted, and I'm not even a good knitter!"

"You've sure got a lot of wool in that case."

"I've got a lot of presents to make."

"What did you make him?"

"A beanie."

"In summer?"

"As it happens, he's off to Canada tomorrow with his

wife and kids for the Christmas holidays—skiing. And, anyway, aside from scarves, beanies are all I know how to knit. Which means everyone's getting beanies this year because they got scarves last year."

"Everyone?"

"Not *everyone* everyone, just the people I like. They can be trusted to ignore the fact that I'm still dropping as many stitches as ever."

"Joe didn't look like he cared about a dropped stitch or two."

"There are more than one or two, believe me! But that's what happens when you do something in a hurry—imperfection. Not that you'd know, would you? You're the patient, measured, sensible type."

"So you're about to have a fling with a hundred-and-ten-year-old accountant?"

"What? Oh!" She laughed. "As it happens, I like the slow, steady type, closely related to the strong, silent type. Kind of…perfect."

"I'm not perfect, Frankie."

"For two and a half weeks you don't have to be, Teague—you only have to be perfect for me. Opposites attract, you know? Yin and yang?" Pause, as she looked searchingly up at him. "So are you ready? Are we going in?"

"We're going in," he said, and took her hand in his. Her fingers stiffened, but only for a second, and then she relaxed and nodded, as though saying silently, "I'll allow it," and let him lead her inside.

"Nice hotel," she said, as they reached the elevator.

"Glad you like it," he replied, and pushed the up button.

"High-class. I hope the staff don't think I'm a prostitute and turf me out."

"I don't care what they think," he said, and when she pulled her hand free after all, he looked down at her. "What is it?"

"Elevator's here," she announced, and barely waited for the doors to fully open before stepping inside.

Teague followed her in and swiped his keycard before hitting the button for his floor. He wondered why it was a bad thing that he didn't care what the hotel staff thought about him.

Or maybe that wasn't what was bothering her. Maybe it was something simpler. Tiredness, obviously—easy fix there, as she could go straight to bed. Hungry? She could order something from the room-service menu. Maybe she unwound after a hard night's work with a drink. Well, the bar in his room was at her disposal.

"I'll need a shower," she said, as the elevator doors opened onto his floor. "Wash the club off me."

"If that's what you want," he said cautiously, because there was a warning glitter in her eyes.

"No, that's what *you* want," she said.

Oka-a-ay, he'd definitely made another faux pas somewhere between getting out of the taxi and arriving on this floor. "Am I supposed to care if you have a shower or not, Frankie? Because I don't."

"If you don't care, you can take me the way I am."

"As long as you take me the way I am, we're good," he said, and opened the door.

"Yeah, but you're nice and clean and I'm—"

"Please don't finish that sentence," he said. "Just go in."

He stood back for her to enter, came in after her and listened for the snick of the door closing. Uncertain how to proceed, he hefted her bag in his hand and tried a smile. "How about I put your things in the bedroom and we—oof!"

He hit the door, his arms full of Frankie, her bag ending up who-the-fuck-cared-where because she was kissing him, claiming him with a fast, hot whirl of tongue.

But as suddenly as the kiss had begun, it ended, and she pulled back. "I want you to know what you're getting," she said.

"I know what I'm getting," he said.

"I don't think you do, I don't think you have any idea, so I'm going to tell you. I'm not Romy. I'm not warm and nice and sweet. I'm not going to hold you at arm's length and be your friend and wait for one of us to figure out it's not going to work. I'm just going to take what I want."

"I know who you are, and I want you *exactly* as you are. I don't want to be kept at arm's length, I've got enough friends who treat me nice, I'm sick of waiting and this only has to 'work' until Christmas, so take whatever you want until then."

"Then let's ink a deal," she said. "You wanted to pay me to dance for you in the club, you wanted to pay for the taxi, you don't care if the hotel staff think I'm a prostitute—"

"That's not what I said, Frankie."

"That's exactly what you said."

"Then it's not what I meant, and you know it, so what's this really about?"

"It's about keeping our heads screwed on straight. Being clear what we're getting. So here's the deal, Teague. You want to pay, you pay. You've got yourself your own personal prostitute."

"Frankie, that's not—"

"So, the fee," she said, cutting him off. "Let's see. For two and a half weeks, I'd estimate my time at… twenty thousand dollars."

And because she clearly thought he was going to balk at that, he went with a counteroffer: "Fifty thousand."

A pulse of silence, and then she said, "You're insane."

He rolled the word *insane* around in his head and liked it. "Call it the equivalent of the engagement ring nobody asked me to get out of the family vault for you."

"You know you could swipe-date the hell out of Sydney and pay nothing, right?" she asked, in her usual amused drawl, but this time it didn't fool him—he'd shocked her, and that gave him a savage kind of thrill.

"A different woman every night isn't what I want," he said.

"What do you want? What are you expecting? Be specific. That's a lot of money you're offering but it won't get you 'access all areas.' I'll be charging extra for butt plugs, hot wax and nipple clamps, and whips are definitely out no matter how much you offer."

He swallowed a laugh—God, she was outrageous, and it was fucking exhilarating! "If that's what you're used to, I'm going to be a disappointment," he said. "I'm new to insanity—you might have to show me a few things."

"I'll show you mine if you show me yours," she said, tipping up her chin, defiant. But one of her hands had formed a fist—not to punch, but to keep her steady—and that tugged at something in his chest so that his urge to laugh evaporated.

This was no joke. The bravado, the chin, the fist—he wanted all of that. Her body, yes. Sex, absolutely. The way she laughed and teased and cut and parried and thrust. Everything. "What I want is more complicated," he said.

He saw the swallow she took—and he wanted that, too. "As long as it doesn't involve any electrical stimulation or rigging a pulley system, I'm sure we can work something out."

"Even if what I want is a variation of 'access all areas'?"

"You're starting to scare me."

"I'm starting to scare myself."

"Now you're *really* starting to scare me."

"I want you, Frankie."

"I think we've already established you're going to get me."

"I want you night *and* day."

That silent pulse again, then her mouth twisted. "Why? Do you think I'll sneak off and fuck someone else while you're not looking? Because for the kind of money you're offering, I'll sign a fidelity pledge in my own blood."

"That's not what I think, and you don't need to sign a damn thing."

"Then I don't understand what you want me to do."

"I want you to stay with me, not just for sex, until Christmas."

She darted a look around the room. "You mean stay here, right?"

He tapped his chest. "I mean stay here, whether it's your house or this suite."

She licked her lips—and God, he wanted to be the one doing that. "It sounds... It really does sound like you—you want...a girlfriend."

"Yeah, it does, doesn't it? Well, hell, I was your fake fiancé, wasn't I? So *why not*, right?"

"Because I work."

"You work at night. And, anyway, who says girl-friends can't work?"

"I dance for other men."

"I know."

"I—I *knit* in my downtime. It's boring."

"And I watch sports on TV. More boring. Do we have a deal?"

She blinked, her fist finally unclenching, and then came a long moment of suspense while she stared at him in a way that suggested he'd reacquired his alien-life-form status of old. When at last she nodded, his heart went fucking crazy.

And then she laughed—like something inside her was going crazy, too. "Clearly I'm going to have to teach you how to negotiate, though," she said. "Because I would have done it for ten thousand."

He grinned at her. "And I would have paid a hundred thousand."

She shook her head at him. "It's a good thing you didn't let Bella dance for you tonight. She would have had half your fortune off you within fifteen minutes and you wouldn't have been let out of the room until her plane departed for Bangkok."

He took a step closer. "I didn't want Bella, Frankie," he said, and when she started to raise her hand again to her still-pink cheek, he took it and laid it flat against his pounding heart.

"So we're bypassing the carotid artery this time?" she asked, and gave a breathless little huff as she twisted her hand beneath his, and brought his fingers to her left breast. For a moment, she let his hand rest over her heart, but then she curled it so the back of his knuckles rubbed over her nipple. "Two for one—you should be able to feel my heartbeat, 'cause it's banging like a drum, but also feel how hard my nipple is."

"Yes," he breathed.

"Or how about you test how much I want you here…" She took his other hand and brought it down to those brilliant crystals. "Or perhaps a little farther…" She opened her legs, guiding his hand between them, and he thought he was on the verge of an excitement-induced coronary. "But let's get things straight, Teague. Daytime is yours, nighttime is mine. And in these night hours, what I want is not for you to make love to me, but to *fuck* me."

He lost it, then, dragging her in, kissing her hard, harder, reefing up her dress, hands on the ruffles covering her ass. He lifted her, rubbed her against the front of his pants, gasping against her mouth when she wrapped her legs around his waist.

No words, as he strode with her to the bedroom. He had some half-formed intention of laying her down and stripping her, but he couldn't—just could not—let her go, couldn't stop kissing her. Her mouth, Jesus God, her mouth was everything.

But in the end, she was the one to drag her mouth from his. "I want to see you. Let me go so I can take your clothes off."

"No, no, can't," he said, and kissed her again, and she seemed to give up then, tightening her arms around his neck and rubbing her core hard over his cock. "Oh, God, what you do to me," he moaned against her mouth, and she took over the kiss, her tongue twirling inside his mouth as though she'd scald him all the way to hell with it.

He thrust his hips against her because he just had to, and she received the jut of him with one of those lap-dance undulations and he was gone, stumbling back, hitting the foot of the bed, landing on his back on the mattress with her on top of him. Perfect, fucking *perfect*. She raised herself until she was sitting low on his belly, her knees on either side of him.

Keeping her eyes locked to his, she lifted herself just far enough to drag up his T-shirt, then lowered herself again. "I want you to feel me on your naked skin," she said, panting. "Feel what you're doing to me. I've been like this all day for you. Waiting all day. For you."

He lay there, panting right along with her as she

pushed his T-shirt farther up, up, off him. His hands went to her hips to pull her down hard on his belly, because yes, he could feel what he was doing to her and he fucking loved it. Wet. She really was wet. And hot. Sticky heat, seeping through her underwear. He wished he could press Pause and keep her exactly like that all night. But almost before he caught that thought, his mind was racing ahead to what it would be like when he entered her for the first time. His blood stopped pumping in favor of surging, flooding him with a need so huge he started to shake. He wished he'd let her strip him after all, wished he was naked with a condom magicked onto his dick so he could slam his insane lust straight into her, all the way.

Words, he had to find words. "Condom," he said. "Nightstand." And then… "Don't."

Not exactly comprehensible, but those three words, coupled with his hands practically crushing her hips to keep her hard against him, seemed to filter into her brain in a way that made sense to her, because without lifting herself off him, she reached over to the nightstand, where he'd left a handful of condoms, swiped one up and put it on the bed beside her knee.

"Reach your hands around me to your pants and undo them," she said, then swallowed hard. "Now, Teague. Right. Now! I want your cock out and you're going to have to find a way to do it without disconnecting me because I'm not moving off you until I have to."

And so he reached around her, undid his belt, then his pants, shoved them down as far as he could but not nearly far enough to suit him. Next, his underwear, and as he eased that down, Frankie upped the torture quotient by sliding her hands up his chest and palming his nipples. "Oh, Teague," she whispered, "I like you like this, with nothing and no one in my way. I want you inside me so much I'm throbbing for it. I'm going to fuck you so good tonight, make you so happy you said yes."

"I'm already happy, and I'll say yes to anything you want—ask me for anything, tell me what you want."

His reward was for her to lean forward and down so she could lick his mouth. "Do you like my mouth?" she asked.

"I love your mouth, *love* it—kiss me."

"Yes, I'll kiss you, and that way we'll be connected as I get into position for what I want to do with my mouth next."

She braced her hands on the bed on either side of his face and moved in for a sucking, licking drag against his mouth, and as he strained up to take more—*more*, dammit—she raised herself on hands and knees, her lips still clinging to his, and scooted back. She smiled against his mouth—success—then used her hands to push herself upright so she was sitting on top of his thighs.

A long, hot look at him, a fingertip running up the length of his cock then swirling around the tip. "I knew you'd be as beautiful here as you are everywhere else," she said, and then smiled as she retrieved the condom.

"I'll do it," he said, reaching for the packet. "I'll be faster."

She pulled it back out of his reach. "Now, what would

be the fun in that?" she said. "I think I'd like your hands up pushing against the headboard—safety first."

Safety? What the fuck?

"Trust me," she said, and they stared at each other for a long, long moment. "You can, you know."

"I know," he told her, and amazingly, he knew it was true. He could trust her. He *did* trust her. He trusted her to say what she wanted and what she didn't, to give and take equally, to be with him by choice, not for the money—and Frankie's *choice* was important, which meant so was he.

He would find a way to show her she could trust him, too—and that it had not one thing to do with what he was paying her. For now, the only way he could show her was to reach his hands over the top of his head and push them against the headboard exactly as she'd asked. And if he watched her like a hawk, it had nothing to do with safety—it was because he didn't want to miss a moment of this first time with her.

She looked so innocent, even though she held a condom packet in her hand—the bright yellow of her dress fanned out from her hips on either side of her on the bed like a sunflower. And then she smiled, tilting her head so she was looking at him from beneath her lashes, and she transformed instantly into pure, hot sex. That red-and-ready mouth, the glittery triumph in the silvery gray of her eyes. She knew she held him in the palm of her hand, just as she held that condom packet, which she was now rubbing between her fingertips like she was imagining stretching it over his cock.

She raised the packet to her lips and tore it open

with her teeth, and just that was enough to ratchet up his breathing because it signaled that soon, very soon, he'd be inside her. He hoped he'd last more than one thrust before he came. He wouldn't unless he got himself under rigid control. He had to think of something else, something…boring. Like the merger he'd finished working on last month. All that endless crap about disclosure obligations, securities laws, securities exchange listing standards, fiduciary duties. Or what about documents? Contracts, agreements, forms, statements. Documents were boring. Documents made him want to go out into the middle of an ocean, where nobody could hear him scream and—

Jesus! She was easing the condom from the packet, and not with her fingers but her lips. Oh, God, the condom was in her mouth. In her *mouth*! A tiny flash of tongue—what the hell was she doing?—and then she formed her lips into an O shape and he saw the ring of the condom was in front of her teeth, and he was sure he was going to die of excessive, unadulterated lust.

Hands. Her hands, holding the base of him, as he thrust up in a suck-me maneuver he couldn't control. And now he understood why she'd made him push against the headboard, because he was racked by tremors and he didn't trust himself to let go.

She edged back, unhurried and seemingly unconcerned that he might be about to do something brutal to her. And then she lowered her head, and before he was ready—how could he ever, ever be ready?—her mouth was over the tip of his cock. He felt a slight pressure there, as though the tip of her tongue was squeezing him, and he gasped, and gasped again, and groaned, and slowly her lips were moving, pushing the latex over the head, rolling it down the length of him until, miraculously, he was fully sheathed. Her lips were still there, though, moving first up and then down, smoothing along his cock as though testing the fit of the condom.

"Frankie, I'm dying!" he blurted out.

But she kept going, relentless.

"Frankie, you're driving me out of my mind. I won't be able to stop!"

She licked him, then said, "I don't want you to stop," her voice all husky and gorgeous.

"I mean I won't be able to stop myself from—from… Arrggh."

"Coming?" One more lick, and then she replaced her mouth with her fingers, and ran them up and down. "That's the aim, for you to come, for you to come *hard*," she said, and he was thrilled to hear the tremble in her voice that told him she was as turned on as he was.

Up came her arms, reaching over her shoulders. A twist and the bodice of her dress loosened. Next, her hands went to her side, a zipper came down. She reached for the hem of her skirt and with a fluid sweep the dress was up and off, discarded, and her hands returned to his dick. He swallowed, and blinked, and shook his head in a fruitless attempt to clear it of lust fog. Had she really just put a condom on him with her mouth?

Yes.

And now she was sitting on his thighs, and her nipples looked like they were about to poke holes through her bra, and those provocative crystals were sparkling through her transparent underwear. It really was a miracle he hadn't dropped dead. It would be a small price to pay, death—but he'd prefer to do it after they had sex. That way he could die happy.

"I want to see the crystals," he croaked.

"Do you, now?" she teased.

"I do."

"Then you're going to have to tears these panties off me, because I'm not moving more than an inch away from you until I've fucked you."

"Wh-what?"

"You heard me," she said, and ran her fingers over his cock again. "Get your hands off that headboard and rip them off me."

Would he do it?

Frankie hoped so, because she needed the violence of that to match the way she wanted to take him—a claiming fuck, rough and wild. And she meant it, too, when she said she wasn't going be more than an inch away from him—not for the rest of the night if she could help it. She was more intensely excited than she'd ever been in her life and she wanted to go all the way with it. Wanted to know what it would be like to be his woman—no matter that it wasn't real. And she didn't care that he was paying her. She didn't. She wouldn't. She'd *use* it, as a license to be as wanton and wicked as she wanted to be. Because she could be, with him. She could tell from the way his upper lip was clenched between his teeth as he concentrated, from the dampness at his hairline, the rigid muscles in his arms, that whatever the effort to hold back cost him, he *would* hold back—a woman could trust a man like that to not hurt her.

And then came the flare of untamed heat in his eyes as he let go of the headboard. He looked ready to rip that gossamer silk not just off her, but to shreds. "You're turning me into a barbarian," he said, bringing his hands to the waistband of her panties.

"I want you that way. I want you *all* ways," she said. As his hands moved down, fingers tracing the diamantés through the fabric, she added, "Do you like them?"

Short, hard laugh. "Yes."

"Then I'll wear them every day for you." And then she stiffened as he nudged a finger farther down so that it settled into that little notch just below where the crystals ended. "Go a little lower, if you like," she said, and as she shifted slightly to make it easier for him, he did go lower, his touch featherlight, grazing her clitoris. "Rip your way in," she said.

"They're too pretty."

"I have a dozen pairs."

He shook his head, and she saw it was final, and she exulted in his absolute control. "Then fuck me while I'm wearing them," she said, and reached down herself, dragging the crotch aside. A shivery moan, as his seeking fingers slid fully against her ready-to-come clit. She had a lightning-fast decision to make: let him keep stroking there or take him inside.

But now, this time, she knew what she needed—to be completely connected to him, filled with him. And so she took his seeking hand and brought it to her breast, and as he plucked restlessly at her nipple, she eased up onto her knees again, then impaled herself on him in one feral swoop.

"Ga-a-ahhhh," she cried, and even though she'd already seen that he was big, the size of him nevertheless jolted her. He pinched her nipple hard, as though he was having his own convulsive reaction to being held so tightly inside her.

"Fuck!" she gasped. "Fuck, I didn't expect... *Fuck!*" She raised herself off him, then lowered herself back down, over, over, over, going a little bit wild as she increased the speed. He was so hard, so stiff, so snug in there, she didn't have to guide him and she didn't have to hold back. She grabbed his hand, the one gripping her hip, and slapped it over her unattended breast. "Pinch me again, do it, both of them, go, go, go, go-o-o, oooh, God!" Circling her hips. "You feel good in there."

"Don't I know it," he groaned back at her, and rocked himself inside her, kept rocking.

She closed her eyes, wanting to absorb the shocks—his cock, his fingers. Her nipples were aching so badly, she wished he could suck them, but she didn't want to lean forward in case she disturbed the rhythm of his thrusts. He was hitting her exactly where she needed to be hit, and her climax was roaring at her, and she didn't want to stop it, did not, did not, did not— "Oh, God!" she cried as it grabbed her, as it shook her. She tried to stop it; she couldn't come, *could not*, because he hadn't come yet—but there was no way to hold it back.

"Frankie," he said, going full-on fierce himself now.

He released her nipples, hands going to her hips, holding her tight against him so he could shove himself in her hard, hard, hard, and then, again, "Frankie!" as all of him stiffened.

One, two, three, four more thrusts, then his hands slipped from her hips and she collapsed forward on his chest. She wasn't breathing so much as sucking in oxygen, her heart throbbing out the blood, her skin tingling, muscles trembling.

And to think she had two and a half whole weeks of this, two and a half weeks of him.

It was a lifetime, if you looked at it the right way.

Except that it wasn't a lifetime. It was two and a half week, bought and paid for.

Harlot for hire.

Funny that she'd been running from such a fate ever since she'd turned sixteen, only to run headlong into it all by herself fourteen years later. No one was coercing her into it, no one had forced it on her—it was all her.

Ha. It was a relief, almost, to have fulfilled her aunt's prophecy. No more waiting for the ax to fall, because it had already bitten into her flesh. No blood, either—how could there be, when she'd done the deal with a man she'd been waiting eleven years to have.

Yep, a relief.

And yet, when Teague threaded a hand into her hair to keep her cheek pressed to his chest, tears pooled in her eyes and she had to jam her lids shut to make sure the moisture didn't seep out onto his chest. Because if he knew she was crying, he'd do something dangerous. He'd jump the gun on daytime and go into full boyfriend mode. He'd hug her, or stroke her hair, or kiss her cheek, because that was the kind of man he was.

She didn't need that kind of man. Didn't want to delude herself that there'd be a white limo to drive her off into a Technicolor sunset at the end of this fantasy. What there'd be was fifty thousand dollars and a goodbye, and that was fine by her. Just fucking fine. Because Teague might be the one paying, but she was the one in control of the—the *value*. It was her body, and she could sell it if she wished. Hell, if she gave the money to charity, she could even feel virtuous about it. Yeah, she'd do that. Donate the money. Bung it in with the proceeds from the auction of Matt's ring at the official opening of LeeF Vintage.

She forced her eyes open, blinked until the tears were gone, then licked one of his nipples, kept licking until she knew she had him exactly on the precipice of where she wanted him.

Then she lifted her head to look at him and smiled. "How about we get naked for the next round?"

CHAPTER EIGHT

FRANKIE WOKE TO an empty bed and checked the time on the clock on the bedside table. Eleven o'clock! Late for her—but then, it had been more active a night than usual.

In Frankie's experience, reality rarely lived up to expectations. But every torrid fantasy she'd had about Teague Hamilton since that first time she'd caught him staring at her in Flick's—as though he wanted to simultaneously fuck her and give her his jacket to cover herself—had been eclipsed by the real thing.

Last night had been manic. And erotic. And…elegant. Elegant! Now there was a word not often associated with sex! And yet it was true because, of course, it was Teague. He'd made her come frequently, powerfully, but also effortlessly. No rough edges or awkward angles, no pulled muscles, no sudden aches and cramps, no bruising grips or careless fumbles or savage love bites.

Even in that first frenetic coupling, when he'd accused her of turning him into a barbarian, there'd been no rip and tear, and he'd made sure of her pleasure before letting himself go. And from then on, with the edge taken off the first rush of lust? Whew! He seemed to know every erogenous zone the human body possessed, and he'd certainly been intent on proving that to Frankie by searching out every last one of hers. Who'd have thought patience would be such a turn-on?

Frankie knew lots of women got off on having a guy go for them like he couldn't wait. She used to be one of those women—flattered that a man couldn't keep his hands off her. But she'd learned that such men usually brought little to the encounter except a need to get their own rocks off fast, so they rushed to get to the good bits. Whereas Teague...

Well, for Teague, *she* was the good bit. He'd been attentive to her every gasp, every twitch, every sigh. *Do you like this? Can I try that? Is it working for you? You feel so wonderful/smell so delicious/look so good. I love the sounds you make/the way you do that/how you taste/the way you touch me.* The words had turned her on, but so had the sound of his voice, the reverent touches, the skill and strength of him—all devoted to her!

He'd passed up a blow job, for goodness' sake, because he'd preferred exploring her more thoroughly! If that wasn't a miracle she didn't know what was.

Usually when she offered a blow job—and it was a rarity these days!—the guy had his dick in her mouth before she'd finished speaking and the whole shebang ended three minutes later with her hair grabbed in a too-tight fist and her head bobbing up and down until she was choking on semen, whether she was ready or not! Unedifying, to say the least. But yep, that was what it was like with most men.

Most men…

Not all men.

She laughed out loud at that and had to jam Teague's pillow over her face to smother it. *Not all men!* She had a feeling such a lazy, pathetic, hackneyed defense had never escaped Teague Hamilton's lips. And an even stronger feeling that giving him a blow job would be something wonderful because *he* was something wonderful.

She breathed in the scent of him from the pillow, trying to catch his essence—but it was only his vetiver scent she could smell, and although that was delicious, it wasn't him. Teague was more than a scent, more than physical beauty. He was a strange combination of sexy and straitlaced, strong and sweet, guarded and giving, and she honestly didn't know which of all those parts of him she liked best.

But maybe—maybe it was the part of him that wanted her to pretend to be his girlfriend. The part that made him tap his chest when he told her where he wanted her to be. That glimpse of need under the tip of the iceberg.

She'd wanted to take a peek under there, but now she wasn't so sure it was a good idea, because in that heart-tap moment she'd seen something that reminded her of herself.

Yesterday morning, she'd told Teague he always seemed to be alone, even when he was with others. But last night she'd had to face the truth—that *she* was the one who was alone. She had friends, she had clients, she'd had way too many lovers, but she was alone on the inside. She'd been alone for so long she'd forgotten what it was like not to be. And all it had taken to make her remember was a man trying so hard not to touch her in that VIP room at King's Castle, and waiting for her outside of her work, and taking her bag for her, and tucking her under his arm as they walked to a taxi whose door he opened for her, and holding her hand as they entered a hotel she could never afford to stay in as though she belonged at his side.

She'd wanted to know what it would feel like to be with Teague—a man who did nothing without care and thought and respect and decency—and now she knew: it was devastating. It made her yearn to be more than what she'd made herself into, more than what she was, more than what she could ever be because she could never be his.

And so, of course, she'd sabotaged what was supposed to be a straightforward fling by making herself a prostitute—a way to make sure she didn't get any wayward ideas.

She moved Teague's pillow down to her chest and closed her eyes, breathing out the mind-clouding vetiver, trying to recapture the kiss-my-ass mood she'd talked herself into last night, but her breaths didn't seem to belong to her. Her lungs were like balloons, inflating, then deflating, but she didn't own them anymore. She'd sold them, along with the rest of her body.

And to think she'd started the night feeling demeaned by giving him a lap dance, which at least was her damn job!

She threw Teague's pillow back onto his side of the

bed, and as though it had hit a sound button, she heard the door to the suite open, followed by a low murmur of voices.

Room service, she guessed.

Other doors opening. *Sliding* doors. Breakfast on the terrace, maybe…?

The terrace. Jesus! Teague had opened the curtains after that last time to show her the gobsmacking view. Part of the suite tour when he'd given her a key.

Oh, God, he'd given her a fucking *key*. She'd prostituted herself to make sure she kept her head screwed on straight, only to end up as his fucking girlfriend! Next thing you knew, he'd be sending her to a boutique with his credit card, taking her out to dinner with his business associates and buying tickets to the opera. Hello Hollywood!

She grabbed that pillow again, shoved it over her face and screamed into it—and then threw it right off the bed.

Well, fuck it! He was about to find out that when she said she wasn't a Romy substitute, she meant it. This relationship was going to get back on track. Hold the warm and nice and sweet and bring on the brash and bold and—and *prostitutional*. And she wouldn't be giving that money to charity! Nope. She'd use it to go on a damn cruise, or to buy a damn car, or to pay for a damn tantric sex course, or—or *something*.

On that thought she swung herself out of bed. She tried to sneer as she heard Teague murmuring something at the suite door, because he was probably over-tipping given his propensity to throw cash at people, but couldn't manage anything except a twisted smile. God, this was bad.

Even badder was seeing that her handbag had been placed on an armchair and her club bag was sitting upright on the floor beside the chair. The thought of him bringing her stuff in like he was her own personal valet sent something swooping inside. But she was not going to get all weepy over it. Nope. Just...no. His internal clock was off after the flight from London, that was all, so he'd gotten up too early and had time on his hands. A one-off thing. No big deal.

She strode over to the chair and rifled through her handbag, grabbed her comb and hurried toward the bathroom. With breakfast already delivered all she had time to do was detangle her hair. Maybe splash some water on her disturbingly blush-happy face and blob some of Teague's toothpaste on her finger for a make-do teeth clean.

But as she reached the vanity, she saw that a toothbrush in the hotel's packaging had been set out for her on the countertop beside the basin, and that gesture threw her enough that her comb went clattering to the floor. She picked up the toothbrush box, but her hands were shaking so much she tore the cardboard as she opened it. Un-fucking-believably, that brought tears to her eyes.

Furiously, she blinked them away. What the hell was there to cry over? It was a *disposable toothbrush*. It wasn't as though she could press the damn box between the pages of a book as a keepsake!

Tossing the box into the bin with unnecessary vehemence, she quickly brushed her teeth, then swooped her comb off the floor and tugged it ruthlessly through her hair, did the whole water-splashing caper and felt happy that all she had to wear was her crumpled yellow sundress, wherever the hell that was—probably pressed and hanging in the damn closet. If he thought he was getting a high-class call girl, all designer clothes and makeup, he was about to be disabused of that notion. He'd ordered the "girlfriend" package and this was about as glamorous as it got for her in the daytime.

She turned to leave the bathroom only to do a double take at the sight of two fluffy beige bathrobes hanging side by side on hooks behind the door. Like, *two*! One large, one small. Those disgusting tears pricked at her eyes again. Enraging! So what if there was a robe for her? Hotels always had guest robes.

But… Well, it hadn't been there last night—only his had been there, which meant he'd made a conscious decision to hang one there for her, right next to his.

Still, so what? Maybe she should go out onto the terrace buck naked just to prove to him she didn't need the hearts and flowers crap!

Ah, damn, no. She wanted to wear the robe. She blinked—blinked hard—as she took it off the hanger and slipped it on. Not sexy. In fact, the best that could be said for it was that it was snuggly. But when she looked at herself in the mirror, damn if she didn't feel like a fucking princess.

"Except princesses probably don't say 'fucking' on a regular basis," she told her reflection. "So don't confuse who you are or what you're doing with Prince

Charming, okay? And while you're at it, stop getting carried away over mundane bathroom items and get the—the *fuck* out there. There, take that, Cinderella! Fuck you."

Cinderella! As if! At least the thought of wearing seven-inch-high glass slippers to slink around King's Castle got her laughing, and she was still laughing as she went back into the bedroom and opened the drapes.

Teague was out there, staring at the harbor, but he turned the moment she opened the doors and gave her that slow, crooked smile she desperately wished he didn't own.

"Wow," she said, too brightly, as she stepped out. "It's even better in daylight."

And so, of course, was he. The poster boy for cool, rich American dude, despite the fact he was barefoot and wearing nothing more special than jeans and a white T-shirt with its long sleeves shoved up to his elbows. His hair was slightly damp, indicative of his having showered, probably in the en suite bathroom of the other bedroom, and he'd shaved—of course. He had the physique of a tennis player. Fit and fine and just fucking perfect.

She joined him at the balcony, looking out at the water. Her fingers twitched with the need to touch him. Just his tanned forearm would do, because those dark gold hairs glinting in the sunlight were drawing her like a magnet. But she carefully kept her hands to herself. She wasn't going to buy into the girlfriend fantasy for the simple reason she *wasn't* his girlfriend—a distinction Teague seemed not to care about, because he put his arm around her and pulled her in a little closer.

She controlled a reactive shiver—barely—and figured she'd have to allow him to do that kind of stuff, given he was paying for it. She'd just draw a metaphorical line down the middle of her own fritzing brain and separate the way she allowed herself to touch him from the way she allowed him to touch her. She'd limit herself to sexual overtures; he would be allowed carte blanche. And maybe—ma-a-aybe it was okay for her to enjoy it when he touched her, as long as she didn't get carried away and didn't let him see she liked it. She'd simply focus on something else, like what it was out in the harbor that was keeping him spellbound.

She followed his line of sight and saw it was a yacht. A beautiful, sleek dream of a yacht, gliding effortlessly across the water. Well, that made sense.

"You miss it," she said.

His arm tightened fractionally around her, and then he breathed out, long and slow. "I do, I really do."

She glanced up at his face, about to ask why the hell he didn't sail, in that case, but he looked so wistful, sad almost, she couldn't bring herself to ask. And somehow, before she knew it, her arm was around his waist, and she was leaning her head against his shoulder and—

Oh, fuck!

If her body was already ignoring her head, where would she be in two weeks and two days' time when he left?

She eased her head off his shoulder, but her arm wouldn't budge. Okay, she was going to have to go in with that question, and if he didn't like it, all the better. "So, if almost drowning wasn't what stopped you, what did?"

"It's complicated. My sister…my parents. Long story."

"Well, we've got three whole days."

"Yeah, but if I start enthralling you with tales of my derring-do sea adventures, you might drop a stitch and ruin someone's beanie," he said.

"Smart-ass."

He turned his head and smiled down at her, but the smile seemed forced. "Truthfully, Frankie? I fucked up years before that race, and I've been doing penance ever since. The race was just an indulgence. A misguided one."

"Ah, so now you're a man of mystery as well as everything else."

He grinned, and the mood lifted. "Do you like men of mystery?"

"Why, yes, I believe I do."

"Then come and eat breakfast," he said, walking her to the table. "Plenty of mystery available under those metal covers because I had no idea what you normally eat so ordered everything I could think of."

"I *usually* have cereal," she said as he pulled her chair out for her.

"Of course you do!" he said, taking his own seat. "'Cause that's the one thing I didn't order."

"Oops," she said. "Well, lucky for you I'm making an exception today because I'm hungry. Like, for actual food, not just for your body."

And dear God, he did that thing where he looked over his shoulder as though he couldn't believe she was talking to him, and when he came back to her, his fingers were brushing against the scar on his lip, and her heart did a slow somersault.

He picked up the coffeepot, poured her a cup. "If you prefer tea, just say so," he said, offering the cup to her. "Or juice—there's freshly squeezed OJ, or something pink, which I think might be grapefruit?" He grimaced at her. "Because, sorry, but the coffee's good!"

"Ah, you *say* the coffee's good, but you're American," she replied. "You guys are very easy to impress." She took a sip. "It's *just* passable—in other words, for me, it's excellent, so thank you!"

She looked at the spread of food. Pastries, cold meats, who-knew-what under those covered dishes.

"So," he said, and cleared his throat, "do you have to be somewhere today?"

She put down her coffee cup. "Yes, home. The shower I never got around to last night, beanies to make, swims to take, neighbors to titillate by doing naughty things with my boyfriend in the courtyard. So I guess we just go downstairs and the cabs are waiting outside…?"

"I have a car. I mean, a car service. I can take you."

"A car service? So you mean your *driver* can take me."

"Technically, yes."

"Aha."

"What? Am I losing macho points by not driving the car myself?"

"You are if you're scared of driving on the correct side of the road!"

"Oh, please! Try driving in Manhattan and then talk to me about fear. It's just easier with a service. Pickups, drop-offs, no parking problems. And you can use it to get to and from work, since Joe's on a ski slope somewhere wearing a half-stitched beanie."

"Hmm, now what can I offer you in exchange for putting a driver at my disposal?"

"Nothing. It's called being a good boyfriend."

"Oh, I know," she said as though he hadn't spoken. "But it'll depend. Does the car have a privacy screen?"

"Is that important?"

"It is if I want to fuck you in the back of the car."

He startled, his coffee cup clattering back into its saucer.

She bit a quivering lip as she removed a cover from one of the plates, and then she looked over at him. "Want some?"

"Huh?"

"Eggs."

"Oh. Oh, no. No."

"Then how about sex in the back of the car? Do you want that?"

"Um…"

She helped herself to the eggs. "Because if you do, I'll shower here before we leave." She raised the lid of another dish. "Bacon—fabulous!" She transferred three rashers to her plate. "But if you *don't*—and I'm guessing that's where you're heading, Mr. Perfectly Behaved in Public—we can let the driver go when we get to my place, and I'll change into my swimsuit, and we can go to the beach, and afterward, when we get home, I'll finally get my shower, and *then* I can fuck you. What do you say?"

He got abruptly to his feet. "I'll get my gear and call for the car."

Teague tried not to think about sex as the car—which didn't have a privacy screen, thank God—pulled smoothly away from the hotel, but it wasn't easy with Frankie's voice saying "I want to fuck you in the back of the car" thundering in his brain.

Even *with* a privacy screen, that wouldn't be happening.

No, no, no.

But he hoped the water at Bondi Beach was cold, because he needed a little shrinkage if he was to be in public with her without the whole beach taking notice of his gargantuan dick.

And after the beach…

Oh, God, she said she'd shower, and that instantly raised the prospect of him joining her in there, sliding his hands all over her soapy body, turning her to the wall so he wouldn't be distracted by those fuck-me crystals, spreading her legs, dropping to his knees, licking into her from behind and making her come so hard she'd never look at another man again.

And whoa!

Whoa! Wake-up call.

They had two weeks and two days together, and that was it. She could look at any man she wanted to look at after that, none of his business.

The car turned a corner and he sucked in a sharp breath as she put her hand on his thigh to steady herself. On purpose, of course—she had a seat belt on and didn't need help stabilizing. But even knowing she was toying with him, the muscles beneath her hand tensed as he waited for her to move it.

A second later she did move it—to his inner thigh, then up, so the side of her hand was grazing his balls.

Ahhhh. God *help* him. He had never, ever been so hot for a woman. Like, *never.*

And whoa!

Whoa!

Never? What about Romy?

Yesterday morning, Frankie had described his relationship with Romy as passionless. Now, searching for memories that would disprove that, he had to face the truth: what he'd felt for Romy wasn't the urgent lust he was currently battling to control, it was more a sense of…well, calm. He'd met Romy a year after Cassandra's death and Romy had fit, somehow, with the way he was living his life. She was the boat that didn't rock, a safe harbor. Even their breakup had been smooth sailing—an easy segue into friendship. Even though friendship hadn't been what he'd wanted, he'd accepted it without losing his cool, playing those cards he'd been dealt.

Whereas now, with Frankie...? Jesus, he sure didn't feel calm or cool. Frankie wasn't a safe harbor, she was the turbulent sea. He couldn't imagine an easy segue to anything in two weeks and two days when they parted—it would just...be over. It would have to be over, because she'd be here in Sydney and he'd be in New York.

Oh, God, he couldn't breathe thinking about that. What the fuck had he done to himself? Stupid question. He knew what he'd done. He hadn't waited to be dealt any fucking cards, that's what. He'd rigged the deck to get exactly what he wanted—her, night and day. It was like that long-ago Sydney to Hobart race, when he'd taken a chance to remember who he once was. But returning to his Mr. Perfect reality after that race had half-killed him, and he should have learned his lesson. He wasn't that man anymore.

Okay, he had to stop this. No! Please no, he couldn't stop it. But...but he could slow it down. Anticipate the end, control the path so he could get that easy segue.

He gritted his teeth and reached for her hand, lifting it away from his leg and placing it on the seat between them.

She looked across at him, then down at her hand, and smiled, like she knew what was going through his head and thought he was amusing, and then turned to look out the window.

A minute, he lasted, before he put his hand flat on the seat a quarter of an inch from hers. That much he could allow.

But when they turned another corner, and her hand slid fractionally toward his and their pinky fingers touched, he couldn't bring himself to move his hand away.

It was just somehow easier to breathe when he was touching her.

CHAPTER NINE

No.

Teague said it to her in a lot of different ways. From the gentle, physical *no*, as he lifted her hand from his leg in the car, to avoidance, when he refused to look at her from the neck down once she'd changed into her red gingham one-piece, to the direct, vocal *no*, when she offered to put sunblock on his back.

The fact that she got only a semi *no* when she asked him to put some on her own back should have felt like a victory, but he slopped it on her so fast she had to disabuse herself of any notion that he'd enjoyed it.

Clearly Teague's definition of "girlfriend"—the type of woman he would throw a casual arm around while on the private terrace of a hotel suite—was going through some kind of metamorphosis. In fact, she would have said he was retreating.

Considering where she'd got to in her morning deliberations, that should have been good news. She *wanted* him to retreat, didn't she? If he retreated all the way, he could keep his money and she could pretend he'd never knocked on her door yesterday.

So she wasn't quite sure why she made the snap decision to embark on Operation Beach Babe—unless it was because she was a shallow sex maniac who couldn't resist a guy who looked like an aviator-sunglasses-wearing golden Adonis. And then, of course, there was the fact he looked adorably disconcerted at the raging erection that his muted blue swim trunks did absolutely nothing to hide.

She had to give it to him—he *tried*. Using an assortment of beach-related items, including a towel, a water bottle and even, at one point, Frankie's straw carryall. And by God, she wanted him—both for the erection and the adorableness.

Frankie had been to the beach with a lot of men over the years; she knew how to engineer an accidental-on-purpose bump against a guy in the Bondi surf to get him randy as a bonobo ape, so she figured ten minutes, tops, before Teague would be dragging her out of the water and up the hill to her house for a comprehensive ravishing. But when she tried a gentle bump, he shifted away from her.

A slightly less gentle bump had him steadying her with his hands…before he shifted away from her.

Her third attempt was more strategic, involving the identification of a suitably large "scary" wave, squeal-jumping at Teague, then wrapping her legs around his waist—a move that got him looking at her like she was a great white shark.

Daunting.

Or it would have been, if she hadn't first caught him darting a look at her breasts and then seen him bite at his top lip right over that delectable scar, and then *she'd* cast a quick glance of her own at his dick, only to ascertain he wasn't exhibiting any visible signs of shrinkage.

It was inconceivable to her that a man could so obviously want a woman and yet not touch her when she was making it ridiculously obvious he could fuck her six ways from Sunday and she'd be back for six different ways within an hour of him finishing.

So…time to ram the iceberg!

On the short walk back to her house, she mentally rehearsed and discarded a full dozen "girlfriend" openings for the discussion they had to have, but when Teague stopped outside the door instead of following her in, and said, "So I guess I should call for the car," all she could find to say was "Huh?"

He cleared his throat. "I should get out of your hair, go back to the hotel."

Drastic action required. "Negative," she said.

"Negative?"

"As in the opposite of affirmative. As in, I thought we agreed we were going to have sex."

"I didn't…want to presume."

"Then I'd better warn you that I'm *going* to presume unless you tell me right now, right this second, you never want to see me again. I'd actually prefer that to interpreting all your mixed messages. You arrive, and you leave. You don't want a fling, then you do, then you want more than sex, you want a girlfriend. You put your arm around me on the terrace at your hotel, then won't let me touch you on a crowded beach. So I really need you to decide. Come in, and we continue doing *something*, or don't come in, and we stop every-thing. Your choice!"

She held her breath, not knowing which way he'd go, not sure which way she *wanted* him to go…

And then he stepped over the threshold and closed the door, and she released that held breath slowly. "That's the first hurdle cleared," she said. "Now let's get over the second one, so listen up, Teague—titillating though the idea of us playing reverse caveman is, with me beating you over the head with a club and dragging you by your hair to my lair, it's going to get old real fast. I already spent a year chasing you. Don't you think you could take a turn? Here, I'll even start you off. So—step one…" She whipped off the loose kaftan she'd thrown on over her swimsuit. "And now, step two…" She started to peel down her swimsuit, then stopped. "Oh! Would you look at that?" She removed a condom packet that she'd tucked into the top.

"Jesus, Frankie!"

She pressed the condom into his hand, swallowing a laugh at his startled expression. "If you want a religious experience, you've come to the wrong place."

"You don't understand. It's not you, it's—"

"I swear if you finish that, I'm going to punch you."

"But it *is* me. Because I realized today that I want you more than I ever…more than… Ah, God!"

"More than Romy?" She sighed. "I admire your loyalty, but if you can't see that's it's actually a good thing to want a woman you can have more than a woman you can't, there's no hope for you in the realm of mortals. And I'm mere-mortal enough to be glad she didn't want you the way I do, because I swear if you'd slept with her, she'd have chained you to the bed rather than lose you so you'd be married to her now and I'd still be having wet dreams about you."

And, of course, he looked behind him, and then came back to her warily, his fingers tracing that scar.

"Oh, my God," Frankie marveled. "You don't know how good you are in bed, do you? I'm sorry, but that's taking humility to the outer level of stupidity. You. Are. Good. At. Sex. Got it? In fact, you are *phenomenal* at sex. I've never had a better lover."

He looked at her like she may have lost her mind. "But…wet dreams? You? Me?"

"Well, not now I've got the real thing," she said, and when he just stood there, she gave up. She peeled her swimsuit down her body, then kicked it off. "Come here and I'll prove it to you."

"Huh?"

"Okay, don't come here," she said. "Cave girl, it is." And she walked up to him, took his hand, brought it between her legs. "Here's a hint—that's not all seawater."

A heartbeat, two, as he stared into her eyes as though he could find the truth there, before he eased his fingers into her. It was too intense, that look, too searching, so she kissed him, hungry and demanding, and she read her success in the rhythmic thrusting of his fingers. She kept kissing him as her fingers went to the drawstring of his swim trunks, untying it so she could reach inside and take him in her hand.

She pulled her mouth free. "How are your fingers, Teague? Wet?"

"Yes," he breathed.

"Believe this, then," she said, dragging down his trunks. "I've been wet for you ever since you knocked on my door and I'll be wet for you until you leave, so fuck me a million times, anytime you want, any way you want, as long as you fuck. Me. *Now!*"

Surrender—she saw it in his eyes, felt it in the way he jerked his fingers out of her, clumsy for once. He grabbed her hand, took a step toward her bedroom.

"No," she said, and pulled him back, her voice like a fever. "Here, now." She sank to the floor, pulled him down to his knees with her. She wasn't going to give him even as long as it took to get to her bedroom in case he changed his mind. Before she even knew what she was doing, she'd positioned herself on her hands and knees. The shock of that had her stiffening, because the memory was there in a flash. Kyle, forcing her to her knees in the VIP room at Club DeeCee, tearing at her underwear, pushing himself inside her.

No! She wouldn't let that memory stop her. This was Teague, and he would never hurt her. A test. This was a test, and she was going to pass it, goddammit. She forced herself to relax. "Take me like this," she said.

She heard the tear of the condom packet, the fumble as he kicked free of his trunks, the exhalation as he paused. He was looking at her, she knew he was, and part of her wanted that—but that buried part, the darkest part of her, didn't want him to see in case he guessed. Irrational. The scars weren't *there*, they were in her head, and she would heal them, she would.

Teague put his hands on her hips and she thought, she really did, that she was going to get over this stupid weakness at last; it was so *him* to hold and stroke where he could have gripped and wrenched, to pause when he could have shoved, to lean over her back, and nudge the hair away from her neck, and kiss her there as he slowly, slowly entered her. And then she choked on a cry so small he shouldn't have heard it, and yet he stopped, held still. Oh, God! Please don't let him know.

"Are you all right, heartling?"

She squeezed her eyes shut, forcing back yet more unexpected tears. "Yes," she said, and she *was* okay, because he was asking, and because he'd called her *heartling*, an endearment she'd never heard before but loved, and because…it was him.

Apparently, however, that *yes* didn't convince him, because he pulled out of her, and somehow got her to her feet in that effortlessly graceful way he had, and kissed her mouth, and hugged her not too hard, but not too soft, and said, "Let's go to bed, hmm?"

"No! No, I'm okay like this, I am."

"But I'm not."

She searched his face, saw a wince. "What is it?"

"Knee injury," he said. "College football."

"You played football?"

He grinned suddenly. "Running back."

"I don't know what that is."

"A guy who gets handed the ball from the quarterback," he said, his lips twisting. "The thing is, I've taken a few knocks, and now my knee hurts like hell in that position."

She thumped him in the chest, laughing. "You're a shocking liar. Has anyone ever told you that?"

"Well…no, actually, Mr. Perfect doesn't lie," he said. "So…bed?"

And she put her arms around him, and smiled mistily up at him, and he kissed her—cheek, cheek, forehead, mouth.

And she tumbled headfirst into love. Do not pass Go. Do not collect fifty thousand dollars.

CHAPTER TEN

As MONDAY BECAME Tuesday became Wednesday and then Thursday, the night-day dichotomy went out the window and so did Teague's plan to keep his distance.

Seriously, when you were wrapped around a woman most of the night and actually inside her between two and five times in each twenty-four-hour period, it was bordering on ludicrous to try. Anyway, in a house the size of Frankie's, constant touching was basically mandatory, and the more he touched her, the more natural it became.

They ate breakfast, lunch and dinner at home, took twice-daily beach swims, spent quiet nights on the couch, with Frankie knitting something that looked like an instrument of torture and peppering the air with frequent curses over dropped stitches, and Teague watching her way-too-small, kind-of-crappy TV.

By Thursday, he'd offered to pay for streaming ahead of their next Bondi stint, pleading to be rescued from endless coverage of the incomprehensible game called cricket. But all she'd done was tell him to suck it up and get some cultural appreciation into him because cricket was better than baseball.

When he'd suggested buying an old-fashioned DVD player as a second option and she'd rebuffed that by handing him a stack of ancient-looking whodunits to read, he suspected money was the issue—a point that was rammed home when tentatively suggested paying her their agreed fifty thousand up front if she wanted to buy a new TV herself, only for her to look as though he'd slapped her.

It drove him a little bit crazy to have enough money for fifty lifetimes and know she wouldn't let him spend it on her while he was living in her house. And he couldn't work out how it could be that she could earn a hundred bucks with one brief lap dance, and yet live an almost painfully frugal existence. The whiskey she'd offered him on arrival had been a brand-new bottle, obviously bought for him because it was the only luxury item in the house. Her battered pots and pans looked like they'd been rattling around since the nineteenth century; her plates and flatware, mugs and glasses were mismatched; her furniture looked like it had fallen off the back of a truck; and the glass statue she obviously prized had been repaired.

She hadn't traveled anywhere since she'd gotten back from America, and he'd found out the reason she hadn't been at Matt and Romy's wedding was because she couldn't afford the airfare and had refused to let Matt pay for it—the confession of which had embarrassed her.

Her clothes were all vintage, her shoes were also secondhand, and her nonclub underwear was cheap. She touched up the blue in her hair herself, and the paraphernalia in the bathroom told her she did her own waxing—ouch—and applied her own crystals…and how she bent down to do it was a mystery, although there was no doubt her flexibility was impressive.

Teague was desperate to help her, but he knew spending money on her had to be done by stealth.

He started with whiskey, buying three bottles of Barron's, using the excuse that if he was going to be hanging around her house three days a week, guilt would otherwise force him to ration himself and hey, he was on vacation, why should he ration! She'd looked at him narrow-eyed but accepted that argument. Next, he'd sneaked in a bottle of expensive cognac, because she'd mentioned something about cognac at the club. That had gotten him a sharply indrawn breath but no outright rebuke, which prompted him to go further and buy wine—a dozen whites, a dozen reds and a dozen bottles of champagne.

The wine proved to be a step too far; when she'd caught him at the front door signing for the delivery, she'd jammed her hands on her hips, fixed him with a steely eye and demanded to know what the fuck he thought he was doing.

"I don't just drink whiskey and cognac, you know," he said. "I like wine, too."

She wasn't buying it. "You're telling me you're going to drink twenty-four bottles of wine, twelve bottles of champagne, three bottles of whiskey and the cognac all in two weeks? I think I'd better book you into rehab."

"Hey, it's Christmas!"

"Bad. Liar."

"I don't want to drink crap booze, that's all."

"I know what you're doing, Teague."

"Awww, Frankie," he'd cajoled.

"Oh, you—you bastard!" she'd said, and laughed. "Fine! But you're going to have to find somewhere to put it. This isn't a palatial hotel suite, you know."

"So I'll store it in my palatial hotel suite—we'll need some stuff there, anyway—and bring it here bottle by bottle as we need it. And I thought I could, you know, buy some groceries. So I don't feel like I'm eating you out of house and home."

She'd whirled away then, covering her face with her hands.

He'd come up behind her. "It's nothing, Frankie."

"It's not nothing to me."

But she'd let him turn her gently back to him and take down her hands. "Let me, hmm?" he'd said, and raised one of her hands to kiss.

"I can't...do that. I can't let you."

"I'll trade you. Food and booze for a beanie."

"You know my knitting sucks."

"Yep."

She'd burst out laughing again then, and thumped him in the chest, and he'd dragged her in and kissed her, and that was the end of it—except that buying things for her was now officially off the agenda. All he could do was hope she'd let him treat her to lunch and dinner when they moved to his suite in the city.

Dropping her off at work with a swift, easy kiss that Thursday, en route to the hotel, felt so routine he might have been doing it for years. It was only as he watched her walk down the alley that it struck him he'd basically just given her up for other men to ogle. As the driver continued on to the hotel, he reminded himself that her work was none of his damn business and their relationship was temporary, but that didn't make him more sanguine about it.

He was even less sanguine when he brought her stuff up to the suite and put her knitting basket on the couch, because the whole place felt different. The perfect size. Not so...well, beige. Just right, somehow. Right enough to have him walking through the suite, assessing it from an investment perspective, and contemplating what kind of place would suit him should he add to his property portfolio by buying a Sydney apartment. A view of the harbor seemed mandatory, for example...

He went out onto the terrace, wondering idly what the view would be like from Hornby Lighthouse at South Head, near Watsons Bay—the vantage point from which he'd be watching the start of the Sydney to Hobart on Boxing Day. You were supposed to be able to see Sydney Harbor to the west, Middle Head and North Head to the north, and to the east, the Pacific Ocean.

Pacific Ocean...

In two and a half weeks his fling with Frankie would have been four days over, and he'd be flying over that ocean on his way to America.

Of course, he could eke out one more day with Frankie if she had nothing else to do on Boxing Day and felt like watching the start of the race with him. They could come back to the suite for one last night together, and the car could drop her at home the next morning before taking him to the airport for his flight to Hobart.

Hmm. If she watched the start of the race, she might also like to see the first boats—the supermaxis—sail across the finish line, in which case she could fly to Hobart with him. He'd have to check what nights she was working after Christmas. His heart quailed a little at what her reaction might be if he suggested he could buy her airfare, but surely he could wangle something.

Well, he had two weeks to figure it out. Two weeks to convince Frankie she belonged with him, belonged *to* him, whether he was in Sydney or Hobart, or even… New York? Well, why not New York? Why. Not.

"Holy shit," he breathed out, as he assimilated the thought of her coming with him to New York. He had a vague notion that he should block it before it took hold—but he didn't want to block it.

And as he stared out across the water, the world seemed to stop spinning, and he knew in that moment he belonged to her.

CHAPTER ELEVEN

FRANKIE SAW TEAGUE the moment he entered the club at two o'clock and did a double take when he waved at her and headed for the bar, hoisting himself onto the stool next to Cyn's boyfriend, Len.

Why go to such pains to ensure the driver would be waiting on foot outside the club from 2:45 a.m. *on pain of death*—Teague's actual words to the poor guy—if he'd intended to turn up himself?

When she finally got a moment to sneak over for a quick word, he told her he'd missed her, and decided Len had the right idea coming in to keep an eye on Cyn—but if he was cramping her style, he'd stay away the next night.

"It's not about cramping my style, you idiot," she said. "You *know* you hate this place."

"Then I'll stay home tomorrow night and unravel your wool while I watch the cricket—it's growing on me, you know," he said.

And she laughed and called him an idiot again, but her heart soared so high, she danced her way into an outrageous tip in the VIP room and felt pretty damn happy with herself.

* * *

For the next three nights Teague tried not to turn up at King's Castle.

His routine was to take Frankie out for dinner, then walk her to the car, kiss her goodbye and return to the suite, where he told himself he had plenty of things to keep him occupied.

He'd watch cricket—it really *was* growing on him— spend some time managing his investments, research Sydney real estate and sit on the terrace breathing in summer air as he read one of Frankie's whodunits. He had a stack of sailing magazines as well, and was re-searching the Sydney to Hobart contenders—in fact, he'd discovered that Flip Green, an old teammate from his Sydney to Hobart foray, was skippering *Pink Diamond* in this year's race, and had managed to catch up for drinks with him on one of the nights.

But whatever he did, always at the back of his mind was a vision of Frankie dancing—on the stage or in one of the private rooms, with men lusting after her— and a sense of disquiet would start building, so that by the time midnight rolled around he was so on edge he figured he may as well be on edge *with* her in King's Castle as without her at home.

The first night she'd been surprised to see him, but he thought he'd been appropriately casual, giving her no clue how desperate he was to be near her.

The second night, she'd rolled her eyes at him as though to say "I'm all right, stop worrying," which had to mean he was looking the way he felt—like he was going to whip off his shirt and put it on her! But notwithstanding the overly dramatic eye roll, he knew she'd been pleased to see him; he could tell by the way she sashayed her perfect ass as she turned her back on him, and then flung him a cheeky smile over her shoulder as she'd walked away.

The third night, she'd been stationed at the bar. Ostensibly she'd been chatting to Len, but as Teague took his usual seat, she oh-so-discreetly stroked his cock through his pants. God, it had been difficult not to haul her in and kiss the sauciness out of her. He'd felt like he was going to burst with lust, burst with pride. Which probably meant he was a sexual deviant, to be proud of a woman going for his genitals in public, but he couldn't help it. She was just so…*there*. Alive, in charge, mischievous and captivating—and his, only his.

He thought the fourth night would go pretty much the same way. Kind of hoped she'd be waiting by his seat again. He'd even left off his underwear—astounding!—just to give her a surprise should she decide on the same maneuver.

So, of course, that was the night things went completely off the rails.

CHAPTER TWELVE

T<small>EAGUE AND</small> F<small>RANKIE</small> started the night the way they'd started the previous three nights, with dinner in one of the hotel's restaurants. Teague chose the best restaurant, because they'd be decamping to Bondi tomorrow and they'd be back to noodles at home, fish-and-chip lunches surrounded by greedy bastard seagulls on the grass above Bondi Beach, and pizza if he was lucky.

As their meals were served, Frankie spied a promotional menu on a stand on the next table and swiped it to compare it to what they'd ordered.

"Well?" Teague said, spearing a piece of salmon. "Have we been dudded?"

She laughed. "You're starting to sound like an Aussie. No, we have not been *dudded*—or screwed or tricked or swindled, whatever you Americans say. This is a special Christmas menu, only being served on the twenty-fifth. Listen, it's seriously good: blue swimmer crab lasagna with Moreton Bay bug and crab bisque sauce, merlot-glazed leg ham, barramundi with citrus and fennel salad and a champagne butter sauce, and... Oh! Oh!" She beamed at him. "You're going to love this! Burnt butter, raisin and whiskey trifle. Whiskey! As in, *whiskey*!"

He smiled at her. "So do you want to have Christmas lunch here, Frankie?"

"I thought I told you, we're going to the beach." She forked up a mouthful of spaghetti and ate it, then slowly lowered her fork and frowned at him. "Are you not coming to the beach? I mean, I know you're not an orphan but—"

"I thought you said I *was* an orphan for the purposes of Christmas at Bondi."

"Yes, but you said you weren't a loner."

"Well, strictly speaking I'm not at the moment. I have you."

"Yes," she said, a little flustered. "But I'm a real orphan, whereas you… Well, you have parents. I mean, you do still, right?"

"Yes," he said, and shifted in his seat.

She ate another mouthful, then put down her fork again and waited for him to say something else…

And God, he just *had* to say it, had to get it out. "My eighteenth birthday present to my sister was a skydive, and she died."

"O-o-oooh," she breathed out, and reached across for his hand, held it tightly. That was it. No meaningless "I'm sorry" or "How awful"—just the comfort of touch, and it was so perfect he felt the back of his nose sting.

"My fault," he went on, compelled to lay himself bare for her.

"No," she said. "No, Teague!"

"Yes. It was my thing, not hers, to do stupid shit like

that. I was the wild one—hard though that might be to believe. Cassandra was timid, reserved, cautious. Special, she was special, and it had always been my job to protect her, so I don't know what I thought I was doing. Trying to make her more like me, maybe. I had to talk her into it, and even when I knew she was doing it for me, not because she wanted to, I kept going. I pep-talked her, and hugged her, and told her I was proud of her, and then…then— Fuck."

"Ah, Jesus, Teague, you were there?"

"Yeah," he said, and took a deep breath. "Yeah, I was, and I still am, even though it was a long time ago. Twelve years, and it feels like yesterday."

"Twelve years is a long time to be doing penance," she said. "That's how you described it, right?"

He squeezed then released her hand. "But look what happened when I took a break from the hair shirt—I almost got myself killed, too."

"The derring-do sea adventure."

"My first and last rebellion."

"Until now, huh? With me."

"Oh, you're definitely killing me, Frankie. Every night."

She grinned at him. "Flatterer." But then her smile fell away. "But the racing… You said fear of death isn't the reason you gave up."

"To tell the truth, it is, in a way. It's just that it wasn't my fear, it was my parents'. After Cassandra, losing me…" He shook his head. "It wasn't an option."

"So they wanted you to play it safe."

"I played it safe so relentlessly, it became a part

of me, as though it had always been there. I had to do it, Frankie, not because I wanted to, but because I love them. And because they never blamed me, not once. And because I…I'd crushed both their children, I guess."

"I think I understand," she said. "You became Cassandra as well as yourself for them, but not fully either."

He tried out a laugh. "What are you, a psychologist?"

"Hey, you'd be surprised what people tell us dancers in those private rooms."

"No, I don't think I would, since I've just spilled my guts for you all over the table. Anyway, there you have it. Am I eligible for orphan status for Christmas on the beach?"

"I will confer such status on you, yes," she said. "And I'll go one further and spill my own guts to prove I've earned my right to ride the Christmas waves wearing a Santa hat, so get ready for my tragic past."

She did one of her dramatic eye rolls that was no doubt meant to make light of what was to come but didn't quite work. "My parents and brother died in a car accident when I was thirteen." A laugh—which also didn't quite work. "What a pair we are, you and I!" She stopped to eat a bite of her pasta, and followed that with a sip of wine. "Anyway, I was thrust upon my only living relative, poor Aunt Luisa, who'd just had a baby and wasn't coping. It's an understatement to say she and I were not *sympatico*, but to give her her due, she tried. I was the one who didn't give things a chance. I was rebellious and obnoxious, and wild, and—"

"Grieving?" he suggested, wishing he could take her on his lap and kiss her.

"I was going to say I was a pain in the ass, but yeah, that'll do. It's true after all. I was grieving. I still am. You know better than anyone, don't you, that we grieve forever when we lose the people we love. But back then, I hid it…differently."

"You were a child, Frankie."

"Yes, but a precocious one. Too smart, too stubborn, way too much trouble. And Aunt Luisa had her hands full looking after not only little Toby but her husband— a man I refuse to call my uncle because he's a total prick who never lifted a finger to help her. Long story short, I got mixed up with a bad crowd—how unoriginal! Sex and drugs and booze and rock and roll and you name it, I did it, and that's not what you need in the house when you have a baby. And that 'phase I was going through' lasted until I was sixteen, when my long-suffering aunt kicked me out." She shrugged a shoulder, twirled more spaghetti. "Her parting words to me were that I'd end up a prostitute, and you know, I'm glad she said it, because it made me determined not to be one. And, not to dwell on my sordid past, but it was touch-and-go there for a while. My first true love did his best to get me to turn tricks for him."

"Jesus, Frankie!" he said, horrified.

"No need to freak out. As it happens, he was an amateur. I've had far better men try to pimp me out since. And seriously? I owe him a debt of gratitude, because I started dancing just to throw that suggestion in his face, and paid my way into my first year at university and then all the way to America, and lo and behold, there you were and here we are, you and I…" She smiled at him, but it wobbled. "Fourteen years later, and at last I'm fulfilling that destiny Aunt Luisa predicted, and loving it!"

"Don't say that, Frankie."

"It's not an insult to be a prostitute, especially if it's what you choose to do of your own free will. I may not be proud of everything I've done, but I'm not going to waste my time being ashamed, either. Life happens, you have to go with the flow of it and try to love it. Carpe diem and all that shit. But my perspective is a little skewed, I guess. I've lived fast and hard, Teague. You don't want to know some of the things I've done, some of the things that have been done to me."

"And what if I do want to know?"

"I won't tell you. Because I like you exactly the way you are—a little saintly, kinda conservative, cautious, responsible, reliable, dependable, protective. A guy who's so loyal to an old girlfriend, he feels guilty for not wanting her anymore even though she's married. The kind of man who loves his parents enough to change for them, and when he can't quite manage it all the way through to the bone marrow keeps trying and trying. And I…" Her breath hitched. "I don't want to change the way you look at me, as though I'm something fine, because it makes me feel as though I… As though I'm not alone after all." Another hitched breath. "When you're gone, I want to remember you looking at me exactly the way you're looking at me now, and hope that when you think of me, that look will still be there."

He thought just then he'd go to hell happily if Frankie would always look at him the way *she* was looking at him now. It felt like he'd been waiting forever for someone to look at him exactly like that. "Nothing will change the way I feel about you, Frankie," he said.

"I believe you. At least I believe you mean that now." She blew out a breath. "Whew! Well, that's enough sentimentality, right? A week and three days to go—let's sail through our time together and make a determined effort not to run aground on debris—how's that for nautical talk?" She picked up her fork again. "Now, can we please eat? Or maybe give up on eating and go upstairs and fuck each other's brains out? I have a specific dollar target to meet tonight, and I don't want to be late."

Their conversation, not surprisingly, kept running through Teague's head once Frankie had left for the club, and it kept playing and playing, like a recording, until the usual niggling disquiet in his head, which always started as soon as she was out of his sight, developed into full-on dread.

You don't want to know some of the things I've done, some of the things that have been done to me...

Done to her. *Done* to her!

And the memory was suddenly there, fully formed. The night Kyle came into Flick's frothing at the mouth, grabbing Frankie like she was his property. Matt stopping him from intervening, telling him she wouldn't want him, of all people, involved.

"Why not?" he'd asked.

Matt, deflecting. "Just chill the fuck out. She's safe.

I've made sure he knows if he puts her on her knees again, he's a dead man."

If he puts her on her knees again.

Frankie on her knees in the house in Bondi.

Fuck! *Fuck!*

He called for the car and stormed out of the suite every bit as wildly as Kyle had stormed into Flick's once upon a fucking time believing he owned her—and the irony of that wasn't lost on him.

CHAPTER THIRTEEN

OF ALL THE nights for her not to be instantly visible as he walked in!

His eyes flicked to the wall clock. Okay, that explained it: he was an hour earlier than usual; she wouldn't have been expecting him.

Agitated, he snagged his regular seat next to Len, who took one look at his face and said, "Lap dance."

"Shit."

"Drink?" Len asked, and without waiting for a response, signaled to Jase for their usual.

Teague waited until he'd dashed the whole nip of whiskey down his throat and been given another before asking Len, "Who is it?"

"New guy."

Teague managed—just—to not thump his fist on the top of the bar. "How do we know he's okay?"

"We'll know soon enough if he's not. Look at Gus."

Teague looked at Gus, who was watching the monitor in an alcove at one end of the bar.

He sighed, feeling useless, hamstrung. "Doesn't it bother you, Len?"

Len looked at him. "What do you think?"

"Yeah. I just… Yeah."

"I get you're new to the game here," Len said, "so let me tell you, there aren't too many pros to dating a stripper."

"They're not strippers. Frankie doesn't strip."

Len put a sympathetic hand on Teague's shoulder. "Mate, I can see through Frankie's underwear to those crystals she wears."

Okay, the guy had a point. "So tell me, how do you deal with it? Other men seeing Cyn, wanting to touch her, being alone with her where you can't see what's going on?" He raised a helpless hand, then let it drop. "Why do you stay with her?"

Len laughed softly. "Because I love her, mate. The woman, not the job. When she leaves here at night, I'm getting the woman. All these other guys? They get the job. There's a difference. Get one of the girls to dance for you and you'll see it, I guarantee."

"What do you do when you're on a night shift at the hospital and you can't be here?"

"Tell myself I trust her, that Gus has it all under control. And I remind myself that usually there's no trouble."

Teague felt his blood pressure mount. *"Usually?"*

"Look, sometimes a fuckwit needs to be managed, but it's rare."

"Have you seen it happen?"

Len swiveled fully to face him. "You really want to know, ask Frankie about last night."

A frozen moment, then the blood pounded into

Teague's head. "The bruise on her arm," he said. "The fucking bruise. She told me she knocked it getting out of the car."

"Don't know about any bruise, but I know a guy tried it on with her in one of the rooms and landed on his ass outside." He shot a look at Teague. "You're going to have to calm the fuck down, mate, or you're not going to last."

Silence. Long. And then Teague had to know. "So, Len, have you had a lap dance from Frankie?"

Len gave him a cautious look. "Depends."

"On what?"

"If you're going to go postal on me."

"That's a yes, then."

Len winced. "Only because Cyn wanted me to do it. Not just Frankie, all the girls she was close to. Best way to prove the difference between a professional job and what she does for me at home."

"You don't get the others to dance for you anymore?"

"Not my thing, mate."

"So it wouldn't bother you if Cyn danced for me?"

"Sure it would—it always bothers me when she goes past those beads and she's out of my sight. But I'd rather she was in there with you than some of the other pricks in this place." He paused there. "Another whiskey?"

And so Teague drank one more whiskey, very slowly, as he timed how long Frankie had been out of sight, flicking glances between the discreetly positioned mirrors around the club and Gus, who was watching the monitors.

At the thirty-two-minute mark, he saw Gus tense.

His eyes went to the mirror. There she was, coming out from behind the beaded curtain. Checking the clock, brief close of her eyes, looking to Gus. A raise of her eyebrows. A nod from Gus.

Teague spun on his seat, taking in the sight of her, saw she was holding on to the strap of her bra and his heartbeat went off. Fuck! Her bra strap was torn! Like… torn off! Rage tumbled incoherently through him, immobilizing him. He tried to rein himself in, but a twitch of the beads behind Frankie revealed a huge tower of a guy behind her and before he knew it, before he even felt his muscles clench, he was off the stool, running.

A leap onto the stage, dancers scrambling out of his way, another leap off the other side. Gus was charging around the edge of the platform, whether for The Mountain or for Teague himself, he didn't know and didn't care—he just needed to kill that fucking bastard who'd ripped her fucking bra and was taking a step toward her!

"Frankie!" he yelled, and she turned toward him. Her hand came up to her cheek—that meant she was blushing—and then the guy was on her.

A roar—Teague didn't know if it was in his head or coming out of his mouth as he vaulted over a table to get to her. It took only as split second for him to land, but the asswipe who'd dared to touch her was already lying crumpled at her feet.

Teague snatched her into his arms, held on tight, felt the full-body tremble that gripped her—or maybe he was the one trembling.

"See?" she said shakily. "I don't need my keys to damage a guy's balls." And then she wrapped her arms around him and held on and on and on. "Don't worry, don't worry, darling, please don't, I'm fine."

Teague was dimly aware of Gus dragging the guy off the floor, marching him away. The threat had passed, but he didn't want to let her go, couldn't let her go. "I'll take you to the dressing room to get your things and then we're leaving, Frankie."

She leaned into him but he wasn't fooled; he knew the lean was a sweet-talk move—the resolve beneath it was impenetrable, unshakable.

"I can't, Teague," she said. "I have a budget to meet. Come with me to the dressing room by all means if it makes you feel better, but all I need to do is change my bra."

"Please, Frankie! I'll give you the money!" Mistake, he knew it instantly.

"I'll make you a deal," she said, the words nice and slow and even. "You don't give me the money, and I won't do any private dances for the rest of the night."

"That's *this* night, Frankie, but what about next week?"

She pulled free. "And what about the week after next, when you're in New York?"

He opened his mouth, closed it. There was nothing to say to that.

She drew in a deep breath and slowly released it. "Okay, how about I go by *myself* to the dressing room, and you go back to the bar and glower at all my would-be suitors for the rest of the night so they're too scared to ask me for a dance?"

"But—"

She put her fingers over his mouth to stop him. "I

promise you, everything is under control. Everything *was* under control. But for you, I'll be extra careful so you don't have to worry."

Frankie had the dressing room to herself, which was just as well, because she was more upset by that episode than she wanted anyone to know and smiling was a little difficult after you'd been mauled by a huge fucking bear.

She sat on one of the stools at the wall-length vanity and checked her makeup in the mirror. How odd to find it still perfect. But, of course, that asshole hadn't been interested in her face.

She closed her eyes, remembering dancing for Teague in that same space. How he'd gripped the chair, not daring to touch her, not looking anywhere except at her face. And tonight, doing the equivalent of leaping tall buildings in a single bound to save her. Was it any wonder she'd fallen in love with him?

Oh, God, why had he come early, tonight of all nights? Why did he have to see her in that situation? A damsel in distress?

She could smile at that, at least. Were you still considered a damsel in distress when you incapacitated a guy by kneeing him in the balls?

And then her smile faded as she saw the club the way Teague had probably seen it in that moment. A sleazy den where men paid too much for everything and women were sex objects.

"Well, hell, it's true, isn't it?" she said to her reflection, and then she sighed. She wasn't going to get all moral about it, given it was the way she'd offered herself to Teague—as a sex object. And he was *certainly* paying too much. Nope, there was no moral high ground to take here. Just people with needs. Adults who could make up their own minds about what they paid and how they worked.

But maybe she was getting too old for this. She'd turned thirty last month, and even when you kept yourself in excellent shape, the physical toll was high. Especially when dickheads decided you were fair game just because they were paying you a hundred bucks.

She stood, heaved her bag off the floor and onto the stool. Time to organize herself. Money first. Out came her lockbox. As she transferred the cash from the zippered compartment inside the lace band around her thigh, she calculated how many more nights she needed to work to reach her target. She was hoping to make enough to allow her to take a few days off after Christmas. She'd be nursing a badly broken heart, so she doubted she'd be in the mood to dance.

"Oh, boo-hoo," she said out loud. "If you want time off, get over yourself, get changed and get back out there, 'cause you're going to have to shake it half off to make budget tonight without any private dances."

She stripped off her bra and the frilly knickers that fuckhead had thought he'd take off her, then paused to look at her body in the full-length mirror. She still looked good, the scorching blue crystals she'd applied in Teague's bathroom before dinner intact. It'd take more than that pig of a man to ruin her artistry. Teague had managed to keep her last lot relatively intact for days—only one top-up required.

She credited vajazzling with giving her an edge. She didn't work the pole like Bella, she wasn't as beautiful as Cyn, she had no special talent like the double-jointed Xanthe and she never went topless like Jess, so she needed a different trademark, and the crystals seemed to work.

They'd certainly worked on Teague—enough that she'd kept them on during her off-work days for him, which she didn't usually do. Maybe one day before he left she'd remove them and see how he liked her au naturel. Or as au naturel as it got with a full Brazilian.

But not tonight. Tonight, she figured he needed the picture of her life reinforced. They'd been getting a bit too romantic. Time to pull things back a little.

She rifled through her bag until she found a bra and matching panties in pale yellow lace, and once she'd put them on, checked herself in the mirror again. Teague colors: blue and gold. Perfect.

And then she took a deep breath, pasted on her smile and returned to the club…and to the absence of Teague.

Oddly enough, his defection this time made her smile, because she had him worked out by now. He ran when something was tempting him to throw that hard-won caution of his to the winds. Which meant it wasn't her he was running from, but himself.

The first and second times he'd bolted—from her house that first morning, and from the club that first night—she would have let him go. But not this time.

It wasn't every day a girl fell in love, and she wasn't done with it.

She had a week and a half left with Teague Ingram Spencer Hamilton and she was going to suck the life out of every damn minute of it, because that was the way she rolled.

Carpe diem.

CHAPTER FOURTEEN

IT WAS FOUR in the morning when Teague, out on the balcony searching for calm, heard Frankie enter the suite.

He closed his eyes and said a fervent prayer of thanks. He didn't care that she'd obviously kept him waiting just to mess with his head. Didn't care that she hadn't answered his calls or his texts. The call to the car service to find out what was happening, the call to Len, to Gus, sounding like a fucking idiot…? Didn't care.

He only cared that come Boxing Day she'd be out of his reach, and the thoughts of what could happen in the club when he was gone were driving him out of his freaking mind.

But it wasn't Boxing Day yet. And right now she was here, and she was safe, and the fear could recede…

So why wasn't it receding? Why was it reforming, amalgamating with rage and frustration and utter helplessness? Stupid question. He knew it was more than any of those things, what he was feeling. He knew what the tangled knot in his chest was—he *knew*. It was loss. It was grief. And whether he wanted to face it yet or not, it was there, waiting for him.

Life happens, you have to go with the flow of it and try to love it. That's what Frankie had said. But she was an optimist—that courtyard, the beanies, the glued-together sculpture and the chipped glass and the lap dancing and the *everything* of her. And he…well, he had no idea what he was, but he knew he was on the verge of finding himself again when he was with her. And he didn't want to seize any day she wasn't in. And God, time was passing. What the fuck was he going to do?

He tore his hands through his hair. No idea.

So for now, he had no choice but to carpe diem and take his cue from her. Did she want to speak to him or give him the silent treatment? Did she want an argument? Did she want to punch him? He'd let her do any of those things.

She'd let him know what she wanted. And she'd know where to find him—here on the terrace, where he came to think. Maybe she'd rub his back in that way she had and just *be* there and it would settle him, and then they'd laugh at what a fool he'd made of himself at the club and he wouldn't care because she was next to him, with him still, and they had time, they still had time.

He listened carefully, only to hear her doing something in the bedroom. So she wasn't going to come to him?

More sounds. Muted but definable. Now she was in the bathroom…

What the—? He was standing out on the terrace, agonizing over her, and she decided to have a fucking shower?

No. Nope. Not happening. He had things to tell her.

Like that the next motherfucker who touched her was going to get his throat ripped out. He was going to tell her he was going to sit on that motherfucking bar stool from the moment she started work from now on, and he didn't want to hear any crap about him having no say in her life once he was back in New York or he…he'd hire her a bodyguard to take his place on the mother-fucking bar stool once he'd gone! And he was going to go through her precious budget with her and spend the next three days teaching her about investing so she had different ways to make money, and he didn't want any pushback, goddammit!

Right.

He strode inside, through the bedroom, into the bathroom…and stopped at the sight of her through the glass, standing under the spray looking like a water nymph, eyes closed, head thrown back.

He didn't want to move a muscle, didn't want to so much as blink. He never wanted to close his eyes in her presence again, didn't want to miss a split second of being near her, wanted to hoard as many memories as he could.

She opened her eyes suddenly, stepped forward out of the spray. "Oh, there you are," she said, grabbing the soap and running it over her breasts.

He didn't bother responding because it was obvious she'd known he'd come to her and how he'd be feeling once he saw her. Clearly, he wouldn't be talking to her about financial planning for her imminent retire-ment tonight.

She gasped as she soaped her tight, hard nipples.

"Tender," she said, "from the way you sucked them last night."

She rolled one nipple between her thumb and forefinger, moaning delectably. There was a soap bubble caught on the upturned tip of the other nipple and just that one dot of white was as good as a full-length erotic movie, according to his cock.

"Do you want to suck them again?" she asked, all throaty.

"I want…" Swallow. "I want…" Swallow. "Yes."

"Good."

"But I want all of you. My hands and my mouth all over you."

"Even better." She flicked a look up and down his body. "But I hope you're going to do it naked."

He looked down, surprised his pants hadn't melted off him, then at her face again. Her wet hair was plastered to her head, her face completely bare of makeup. She was all cheekbones and dark rose lips and knowing eyes.

"I shouldn't have left the club," he said. So clear, so simple, that truth. Because why was he running from even one moment with her, when the moments left to him were finite?

"Then make it up to me."

"I will," he promised.

She gestured to the shower walls. "So are you coming?"

"I will be very soon, I think," he said, and stepped into the shower, fully clothed. Insane! At last he was fully, completely insane. And it was all for her.

How long did it take to get naked when you were soaking wet? He was destined never to know, because he lost all sense of time and place as she helped him strip.

It was a chaos of flying fingers, bodies twisting and bending, pushing and pulling, his grunts and groans mixing with Frankie's delighted laughter. Shoes being unlaced then toed off, socks tugged off as he hopped. His belt whipped through its anchoring loops, the button on his pants torn off, the zipper yanked down. His shirt buttons went flying, his underwear was shoved down.

He smacked his elbow into the glass and was only vaguely aware that it hurt. Frankie banged her head on his chin but didn't seem to notice, and they both narrowly avoided an ignominious tumble to the tiled floor when he slipped on the soap and Frankie grabbed him to keep him upright.

They ended up plastered together, her arms around him, his face nuzzled into the place between her neck and shoulder. They were both laughing, albeit breathlessly.

Laughing, laughing…

And then no more laughter. Just heat, and steam, and wet skin and need.

There was a bead of water on her top lip and he lowered his head to lick it from her. Just a lick, one lick, to taste. But he couldn't stop, he had no willpower left. She opened her mouth for him and as his tongue slipped inside, the kiss turned from a taste to a feast. Wild, long, deep and hot. Her hands were on his hips, pulling him in—nothing coy about her, nothing equivocal; it was all there, laid out for him. Irresistible, to be wanted this way; shattering to know it still wasn't enough.

He could feel her nipples against his chest and when she broke the kiss to breathe he looked down, needing to see where they touched him, then needing more. He lowered his head, licked first one nipple, then the other.

"Suck them," she said.

"You said they were tender."

"They are—throbbing for you."

And, of course, he couldn't resist that, and so he put his mouth over one, just the tip, and pulled gently with his lips—a series of sweet, soft, concentrated kisses, until she was panting. By the time he switched to the other nipple, her hands were twisted in his hair and she was making desperate pleading sounds he wanted to hear forever.

Another series of sucking kisses, broken only to take in air. "You are the sexiest thing I've ever seen," he said, before returning his mouth to nipples harder and redder.

"You make me want to be the sexiest thing you've ever had," she said, arching for him. "And the sexiest thing you ever will."

"Open your legs for me," he said against her breast, and when she did, he put one hand between her thighs. "Oh, God, you are so! Hot!"

"I am. Hot and wet and ready to fuck you."

He kissed the words from her mouth, sucked them from her, and as his fingers plundered, her arms reached up, her hands at the back of his head pulling him in to deepen the kiss, begging that he not stop, that he never stop.

"I want you in my mouth when you come," he said, and she bolted against him as though the words alone would get her there.

"Yes, yes," she said. "I'm yours, handle me any way you want."

He dropped to his knees, ran his fingers then his tongue over the blue crystals. He knew why she wore them to the club—because they enticed, but they also hid her. He'd told her he loved them, and he did—he loved the eroticism of them and the playfulness. But not tonight, when he wanted nothing of the club, only her.

He stood, turned her to face away from him, nudged her toward the shower wall. "Against that," he said, and she obeyed without hesitation, pressing herself flat against it with her hands up and her legs spread wide.

Again he went down on his knees, put his hands low on the cheeks of her ass to spread her completely open to him and, without any preliminary stroking, put his hungry mouth to work. A lick all the way along her sex. Then another, while she stiffened and shivered and thrust herself at him.

"You taste so good," he said, and licked again. "I love doing this to you."

"Teague, please, I need it harder."

"Like this?" he asked, and eased his tongue slowly but firmly inside her, then out.

"Yes!" she groaned.

"Or like this?" He slid it up and down her opening.

"Yes!" she moaned.

"Or maybe like this?" he said, and rubbed his tongue across her clitoris.

She collapsed against the wall, her hips jerking as he settled in to make her come, alternating between rubs and flicks, gradually increasing the pressure until her clit was in his mouth and he was softly but steadily suckling as his tongue twirled.

"Oh, God, Teague. Teague! You are so good at this, so good, so good, oh, o-o-ooh!"

But he wasn't breaking to talk now, he just wanted her to come, because that was when she didn't think, couldn't think—when he wasn't Mr. Perfect but just hers, exactly the way he was. His tongue was moving in time with the throbs of his pulse, the twitch of his desperate cock. A minute passed, two, as he felt the steady build in her. The tremor in her thighs, the laboring, ragged breaths. Wanting all of her in his mouth, every taste and twitch, he covered her, sucking as his tongue stabbed at her clit, a moment, two, three, and she actually screamed.

He didn't want to stop, and so he didn't. He kept up the tonguing, sucking pressure until she started to slide down the wall, and then he was up, on his feet, pulling her against his chest. His hips surged forward, his cock hard enough to bore a hole in her back. His body was consumed with the need to fuck her fast, but he couldn't do that, not here, not now. Just one taste, though, he had to, *had* to. Just…one.

He thrust into her from behind, and she pushed her bottom back to welcome him. The pleasure of having his cock buried in her was almost blinding in its intensity. Long, long moment, *aching* moment, perfect moment, and then, excruciatingly, he drew out again.

His body bowed, head resting on her shoulder, as he tried desperately to get himself under control.

"Don't stop!" she said.

But he pulled back, released her. "Have to."

She turned around.

He spun her back to face the wall. "No! I'll lose it if I see your face. And I can't lose it. I don't have a condom. And even if I did have one, it wouldn't work in the shower."

"Oh, shit!" she said.

"Oh, shit!" he agreed, and laughed—out of desperation, because the situation was not fucking funny.

"Well, as it turns out, I don't need a condom," she said, and turned to face him again.

"Frankie!"

She brought her hand up, her fingers pressing against his lips to stop him. "I only need your cock, my hands and my mouth."

And for all the water in the shower, his mouth went dry. It was a reflex action to suck her wet fingers into his mouth, drink the water from them.

She moved her other hand, wrapped it around his cock. "I want to make you come with my mouth. For years, I've dreamed of doing this to you. I wanted to do it in that room at the club when I was dancing for you the first night, I've wanted to do it every day and every night since, I've thought of it all day long." She slid her fingers from his mouth, trailed them down his chest until she had both hands on his cock, one holding him at the base, the other sliding up and down the shaft. "Do I shock you, Teague?"

"No, you thrill me, always."

"So can I do it?"

He squeezed his eyes shut. Oh, God it was hard to turn her down. But he got it together, shook his head, opened his eyes and said it. "No."

Her eyes went wide. "No?"

"I *have* to say no!"

"This is cruel, what you're doing to me."

"Frankie, it's not that I—"

"You said you'd make it up to me, for leaving the club."

"Frankie—Frankie, stop," he said, and took her face in his hands. He rested his forehead on hers, closed his eyes again as he tried to manage the lust. "Just—just listen, okay?"

"No." Her arms went around his waist. "Teague, I want this. I'll beg you on my knees."

He released her face, pulled her in, hugged her tight. "That's the problem, heartling," he said. "I don't want you on your knees. Never, ever, on your knees for me. Never."

She stilled in his arms. "You know," she said. "You know what he did."

"Yes."

He felt the shiver run through her, though the water was warm. And then she stepped back, breaking their embrace, and took his hands in hers. "Then not on my knees," she said.

She drew him with her toward the marble bench set against the wall, settled like a queen and pulled him between her legs before releasing his hands and taking his cock between her palms. A mischievous look up at him. "And so you know, Teague, I'm good at this."

"God!" he cried out, hips thrusting before he could stop them.

"I haven't even started yet," she said, chuckling.

"If you keep touching me, it's going to be all over before you do," he said on a groan.

"Why?" she asked.

"Because I'm so close to coming it's not funny."

"When you come, I want it to be in my mouth," she said.

"Oh, God," he groaned, "just to hear you say that is— Ahhhh."

She kept her hands on him, rubbing him softly between her palms. "Smooth and hard and big," she said. She moved her hands so that one wrapped around his shaft, the other went between his legs to cup his balls. She squeezed both hands in a gentle rhythm, enjoying the way his hips flexed and his breaths struggled.

She looked up and smiled to see his eyes so intent on what her hands were doing, and then closed her mouth over the tip of his cock, swirling her tongue around it.

"Jesus, Mary and Joseph," he cried.

She wanted to laugh—but she wanted, more, to please him, so she flicked her tongue again, and again, and then eased him farther into her mouth and went to work, holding the base of him to keep him where she wanted him while her other hand continued to press and release his balls. She gave one suck that was harder than the others—loss of control—and released him.

"Was that too much?" she asked, rubbing him up and down with her hands again, keeping him close to the edge without letting him spill over.

"No, not too much, never," he said. His eyes blazed down at her, his breaths coming hard and fast from his nostrils. "I wish I could tell you what it's doing to me to see your mouth like—like that," he said.

"So tell me. I want you to tell me. I want you to be like me this one time."

"I don't unders—"

"Dirty."

"But you're not—"

"Talk dirty to me. I want you to. I want you to boss me around like I belong to you, your possession. I think when you do, only you, it's going to drive me fucking wild."

His eyes closed, opened. "I like seeing your mouth near my cock."

"Ahhh," she breathed out as a thrill shot through her. He was going to play.

"I want to see your tongue, want to watch it lick me. Tell me you're going to do it."

"I am, I'm going to lick you," she promised.

"Then fucking do it, do it now."

Instantly she obeyed, first stiffening her tongue to lick thoroughly around the tip of his cock, then loosening it to lick up and down the shaft.

"Oh, God, Frankie, oh, G-o-o-ood. Put your hands on my hips."

Obedient, she moved her hands from his dick to his

hips, pulled him in so his dick brushed against her lips. A promise.

"That's not enough," he growled.

"Then what? Order me to do what you want."

"Take me in. Take my cock in your mouth."

Well into the game, now, she took him in, just an inch.

He was panting, thrusting, but trying not to. "Take me deeper," he said, and then an "Oh, God, *God*!" burst out of him. "Keep going, keep sucking until I come."

She took him, teasingly, just deep enough, eyes lifting to his face, loving the way he looked at that moment, an eagle about to fly.

"I want you to swallow my cum," he said. "I want to see you do it, I want to know you're tasting it, I want…" His Adam's apple bobbed almost painfully. "I want you to know what you do to me, I want you to know how it feels when you touch me, I want you to know that I can't control this, I want you to know that I—" He stopped, then cupped the back of her head with his hand, and the way he gazed down at her made her feel like she was everything in the world. "Please, heartling, take pity on me, it's hard for me to talk to you this way when I want to say other things."

Her heart bursting like the sun in her chest, she took him further, sliding her mouth all the way over him, holding him hard with those hands he'd told her to put on his hips, because she knew he wasn't going to let her swallow no matter what he'd said when he was pretending to talk dirty to her, and she was going to make damn sure she did it anyway. His hips were still thrusting helplessly, and she just kept taking and taking him, moving her mouth up and down, until he was breathing in torn-up huffs.

"I'm going to come," he said. "Stop. Stop! You don't have to do this."

She shook her head—she wasn't going to stop—and when he tried to move back she dug her fingernails into him and held him still, taking him deeper, all the way. Both his hands were in her hair, but they weren't urging her, they were just...there, connecting them.

Too much to contain. The taste of him, his hands tightening in her hair, her heart beating and breaking, his muscles tensing, the rapid-fire of his breaths, the staccato jerks of his hips, and then, the agonized scream of her name, "Frankie!" and yes! He was hers!

She kept him there, her mouth surrounding him, until his muscles relaxed. His hands were under her arms then, pulling her to her feet, against his strong, broad chest, mouth buried in her wet hair.

It's hard for me to talk to you this way when I want to say other things.

As Frankie enclosed him in her arms, Teague let himself say those other things in his heart, releasing them so that they flooded him. That he loved her. That he couldn't imagine a time when he wouldn't want to be with her. That he was scared of what would happen when he left her. That he was already grieving the loss of her and wanted to find a way to stop time so he wouldn't lose her. That she had to come with him, please, please, please.

It was frightening, to want a woman this much and

know he had only ten days to make her want him the same way, make her love him. She'd said it would take a miracle to get her out of Australia, but miracles happened, didn't they? If she loved him, she wouldn't let him leave her behind. A sense of urgency was consuming him. A need to entice her by making slow, sweet love to her, but also to fuck her fast and furious and claim her as his.

Fast and furious, slow and sweet, all the in-betweens. He would have to make every way unforgettable. "Come to bed with me," he said, and wondered if she could hear the longing in his voice.

"Of course," she said, and turned off the taps. "But can I make a request?"

"You can ask for whatever you want and I'll give it to you."

"You might regret that!"

"No."

"Don't say you weren't warned."

"Give it your best shot."

"It's a…a fantasy I have. A white limo, red roses, romantic movie kind of thing."

"Er…you know what time it is, right? Where am I going to get roses?"

She gurgled out a laugh. "Hey, use your imagination. You could, say, pick me up in your arms and carry me to bed."

"Okay, got it! Do you want me to towel you dry first?"

"Nah! I've resigned myself to being wet in one way or another for another ten days."

CHAPTER FIFTEEN

FRANKIE WOKE AT NOON—and this time, she *did* have a few aches and pains. She'd also lost half of her vajazzling and would need a quick repair at some stage today.

She looked over at Teague; he was still sound asleep, which was a first. He was usually up before her—showered, shaved, dressed and ordering breakfast.

She got out of bed and dug in her bag for her phone to check her messages.

The twelve texts from Teague from last night were all there—she was never going to delete those! The four voice-mail messages would exist in perpetuity, too. There was a text from Cyn checking up on her after last night's melee. Another from Gus checking up on Teague—male bonding at its finest! And a voice mail from Geoff Rhodes, who had news about the perfect premises for her shop and wanted her to stop by an apartment he was inspecting in North Bondi at one o'clock to talk things through.

She went to Teague's side of the bed and leaned down to kiss his forehead.

He blinked, blinked, focused...and his heart-stopping,

crooked smile bloomed. "Hey," he said, and she went weak at the knees because the combination of his unshaved face and that raspy morning voice was almost too much for her heart to take.

"Good morning, Mr. Perfect," she said. "We have an appointment at one, so drag your butt out of bed."

He turned into his pillow and muttered something unintelligible.

Frankie had to laugh. "How about if I let you buy me lunch at Bondi's most expensive restaurant afterward? Least I can do after you exceeded all my expectations last night."

He sat straight up then, swung his legs out of bed and pulled her onto his lap. "Ha! I'm wearing you down! I'll get that fifty thousand up to a hundred by Christmas."

"You're not *that* good in bed," she said, and then she kissed the side of his neck. "Actually, you are, but don't push your luck on the bucks." She got off his lap and waved a hurry-up hand at him. "Today, all will be revealed and you'll see I really don't need your money."

"Can't you reveal all now?"

"I need props."

"Props?" He got to his feet and stretched his arms over his head. "Hopefully not knitted ones."

"Oh, you!" she said, laughing. "Just get into the bathroom and do your ablutions."

"Want to come and ablute with me?"

"No! Well, yes, but no. We don't have time to muck around."

"Hard-ass. Will you call the car while I shave?"

"Yes—but just so you know, when we get to my house, we're switching to *my* preferred mode of transport."

"Which is…?"

"Like I said, all will be revealed."

Teague couldn't believe his eyes when Frankie, her massive purse slung across her chest and hanging at her hip, puttered out of the parking garage under the apartment block astride a vintage Vespa in an unlikely shade of aqua.

She came to a stop beside him and thrust a helmet at him. "Put that on and get aboard."

"A scooter?"

She grinned. "Fun, huh?"

"Er, no…?" he said but climbed on behind her.

"Pretend it's a yacht," she said. "Only one where the vibrations between your legs and a hot body plastered to your back with an impressive erection bring on a whomping great orgasm!"

"All right for you—but when's my turn?"

She started down the driveway. "The restaurant has great restrooms," she yelled over her shoulder, "so play your cards right and who knows?"

"You're corrupting me," he yelled back.

"Good!"

"We're looking at apartments?" Teague asked, hanging his helmet off one handlebar and looking at the For Sale sign on the outside of the building Frankie was gazing at. "Are you wanting to sell your house? I thought you loved it there."

"Love it? No. Sell it? No—I don't own it, I rent it." She removed her helmet and placed it on the seat. "Would I like to move? Sure! Can I afford this place? No. I love this spot, though. North Bondi is a little more 'local' than the main stretch of beach. Oh, dear, I sound like a wanker saying that! Any minute now I'll be drinking a piccolo latte made with single-origin coffee beans harvested from the Congo and water imported from a Patagonian lagoon."

"Wanker?"

"Aussie talk for... Never mind, I've corrupted you quite enough already!" And then she laughed. "Anyway, hopefully this apartment will be ghastly inside, so I don't get a case of home envy. But regardless, we're not here as prospective buyers, we're here because it's convenient for my real estate agent, who's got the listing for this place. Now, let's go in before he gives up on me."

The realtor opened the door, his phone stuck to his ear, and one-arm-hugged Frankie before gesturing for them to look around while he finished his call.

Frankie went straight for the view, and as Teague joined her, said from the side of her mouth, "How fantastic is that? We're practically on the beach!"

Teague was impressed. Full-height glass doors had been folded completely back, effectively merging the open plan living/dining/kitchen with the balcony area outside. The whole place was spectacular, not just the view. Good size, quality finishes. Bright and light and breezy.

When the realtor said, "Frankie!" from behind them, they turned as one. This time Frankie got a two-armed hug and it made Teague uncomfortable—like a cave-man caught without his spear. He murmured something about checking out the bedrooms and bathrooms and made himself scarce before he could give in to the urge to tell the guy to keep it clean. He was p-r-e-t-t-y sure Frankie wouldn't appreciate that.

When he returned ten minutes later, it was to find Frankie holding out a Christmas-paper-wrapped package, presumably unearthed from that monstrous purse of hers. Beanie, he thought, and grinned as she got another hug from the realtor, his jealousy somehow evaporating.

And then the guy released her, and the two of them shook hands: a deal had apparently been done.

"I thought you weren't moving," he said to Frankie as they made their way back to the Vespa.

Her eyes lit. "I'm not. I'm taking out a lease on a shop."

"Shop?"

"We'll go past there now. I know the place—it's on a street that runs off the main beach road. Great size, but in need of some serious zhushing. I wish I could show you inside, but alas, not today—it's boarded up!"

She beamed at him so beguilingly when they reached the shop, he had to kiss her. He could almost feel the buzz coming off her, so even though they could see nothing through the boards, he praised the place to the extravagant heavens, and got a thump arm to the arm for his trouble.

"You are *such* a bad liar," and he fucking loved it. "But come on, I'll show you something absolutely fantastic. My storage unit."

"A storage unit? Wow!" That scored him another thump.

It wasn't until she opened the unit with a flourish that he understood. And he knew then she wouldn't be coming with him to New York—not in ten days' time, not ever.

The usual feeling of satisfaction descended on Frankie as she looked around at her precious stock, which was laid out pretty much like the actual shop would be. Racks of clothes, shelves full of shoes, handbags and hats. Baskets overflowing with scarves and wraps and gloves. There was a glass display case with strands of beads, ropes of faux pearls, earrings and brooches and hatpins and bangles. Magazine racks full of old fashion journals, boxes of patterns for home sewers. Her one personal extravagance, her art deco desk, was in there, along with a couple of armchairs, a smattering of lamps, framed prints. Oddities, eccentricities and curiosities. LeeF Vintage. Her, in a storage unit.

"You're opening a vintage shop," he said.

"Give the man a cigar!" she said and did a giddy twirl. "What do you think?"

He took his time, walking around and looking at everything closely and carefully. And then he turned to her. "I remember now. You were doing a business degree."

"Yes, but I… Well, I had to do it in dribs and drabs and only finished it two years ago. I had—" she stopped, self-conscious, then forced a laugh and finished the sentence "—money issues, of course!"

"Hence King's Castle," he said.

She conceded the point with an inclination of her head. "It pays well, but I'm also good at it and I—I like it, Teague. Most of the time it's a great place to work. They look after their staff, and most of the clients are decent."

"Except for the ones who are deadshits."

She laughed again—not forced! "That's a very Aussie word—old-school, too. Impressive."

"Len's rubbing off on me." He smiled, but Frankie could tell something was wrong. "It's a good word for those…er…wankers who can't keep their hands to themselves."

Her sense of satisfaction started to slip away. "What do you want me to say, Teague?"

"That you'll let me give you the money," he said, then grimaced like he knew that was the wrong thing to say.

She took a deep breath. "I'm going to short-circuit this argument by telling you I've been saving for ten years, and my retirement date is pretty well set. By mid-January, I'll have enough money to support myself and keep the shop afloat for three years—that's the point where you generally know if you're going to survive. So if thoughts of me dancing in the club keep you awake when you're back in New York, try and remember that it'll be all over in a month."

"And if you make an assessment in three years that the shop won't survive? What then?"

"Then I'll move on to something else."

"I don't want you to need money, Frankie."

"Well, I *do* need money, Teague, and by that I don't

mean I need your money. I'm already taking plenty of yours. Not to mention letting you buy me extravagant meals and keep me in wine and…and indulge my Hollywood Cinderella fantasies as I float around that palatial hotel suite of yours."

"It's peanuts, what you're letting me spend on you."

"Then let me give you the real argument. It means something to me to earn my way. I've been supporting myself since I was sixteen, and I'm proud of it. Letting you support me would strip the pride from me, Teague. Don't do that, don't ask me to let you, because in a moment of weakness I might say yes, and that'll be an important part of me gone. And you of all people know how it feels to lose who you are. I know you don't approve of the way I'm earning my living, but it's not illegal."

"I don't…disapprove."

"Yes, you do."

"I just want… Dammit, Frankie, I want you to *not* be hurt."

"There are lots of ways to be hurt—we both know that."

"If I could pay you to dance for me—"

"I don't dance for men I know."

"Then let me pay you to sit down."

"No."

"Why *not*? You let Matt do it!"

"You're not Matt! It's…different with you!"

"I don't understand why. Tell me why."

The words trembled on her lips. *Because I love you. Because I want you to love me. Because I want you to see me exactly as I am and love me for who I am, not in spite of it.* But how could she say all that when in ten days he'd be gone? All she could do was shake her head, helpless, hopeless.

He shoved both hands in his hair. "Fuck, Frankie! Give me something! I need to know!"

"You don't want to know."

"I do!"

"Okay!" she cried. "Okay. Because whether you believe it or not, you *do* disapprove of what I do, and you also want to save me from it. And, Teague, I've been with men who disapprove and/or want to save me and it doesn't *work*. What they really want to do is own me. And I won't be owned, I will *not*."

"That's not what I want. I just want—" He broke off, scrubbing his hands over his face. "Fuck, yes I do! I *do* want to own you. I do, God help me!"

She burst out laughing despite herself. "Only you would be man enough to admit that up front. So I guess I can be woman enough to admit there's a bigger problem here, which is that I kind of like the way you want to own me—not the principle, but because it's you." She raised her hands. "The way you came running for me last night…? I wanted you to be *exactly* like that. Angry and protective and vengeful. I could have swooned for you—I did swoon for you, a little, in the dressing room." Down came her hands. "But I can't afford to swoon, Teague. I need to look after myself, because you won't always be here to do it. We both know that, no matter what Christmas fantasy we're spinning."

She hesitated there, but decided the point needed to

be driven home hard. A dose of reality. "So I guess I can bare a little more of my soul for you, since we've come this far, and give you the hands-and-knees story."

"I know all I need to know, Frankie."

"You think you do, but you don't. And I…I need to tell you. Let me, please."

"Ah, Frankie—"

"Please, Teague!"

He nodded. "Okay, okay, tell me. And maybe point me to something I'm allowed to break."

"You break it, you buy it," she said, and then laughed. "And no, that isn't an invitation to destroy all my stock and pay me some exorbitant amount of compensation money!" She looked around, picked up a small paperweight and handed it to him. "Here—think of it as a stress ball. In fact—" picking up another for herself "—I may need one, too. So here goes nuthin'. Fasten your seat belt."

She sat in one of the armchairs, waving a hand at one of the others and waiting for him to take a seat. "First thing is, it's an old story from DC, so the wound's scabbed over—it's not like I'm crying into my pillow every night, okay?"

"Just so you know, you're scaring the shit out of me. You sure there's nothing I can break?"

My heart—she almost said it, only just caught herself. "Next time you're in Chicago, go ahead and break one of his bones with my blessing." She took a bracing breath. "So! I was working at Flick's and it was fun, but the pay sucked—let's just say not everyone's as generous a tipper as you. That's why I started at Club

DeeCee. Kyle had a meltdown over it, and we broke up. At least, I thought we'd broken up—he seemed to think otherwise, because he started coming into the club, insisting I dance for him or he'd report me for dancing in a strip club and get my J-1 visa revoked. Such an asshole.

"Of course, he soon decided dancing for him wasn't enough, he needed the optional extra—code for sex in that place, which I never, ever offered anyone, just to be clear. His rationale was that it was no big deal since I used to sleep with him. When I refused, he…well, that part you've got figured out, so I won't dwell on it except to say it involved me on my hands and knees and him behind me, and—" She broke off, staring at the paperweight in her hand, which she was gripping so hard, her fingers had turned white.

She forced herself to loosen her hold, and then looked over at Teague, who had a pretty tight grip on his own paperweight. "The thing is, Teague, it wasn't about sex, it was about power. He thought I belonged to him, and he blamed my job for the breakup, and he hated that other men were seeing what he thought of as his. If I could go back in time, I'd kill him for doing that to me. But that's the woman I am now talking. The girl I was then… Well, she wasn't as tough as she seemed. I ended up blubbing to Matt, and Matt dragged on his superhero cape and took to spending a lot of time at the club watching over me—a bit like you want to do now."

"I wish I'd known."

"I couldn't have borne that. Not you. You were…I don't know…an ideal. Clean and nice and perfect. In love with someone just as clean and nice and perfect. And then there was me…"

"And Matt," he said.

"Matt knows the life, Teague."

"And I don't," he said. And then he performed one of his special seamless maneuvers that ended with her on his lap, cradled in his arms, paperweights miraculously gone. "Then I guess I'd better learn the life, too, so I can get off your case about it and concentrate on more important things."

"More important things like what?"

He looked at her for a long moment. He seemed on the verge of saying something… But instead he kissed her, long and lingering, and then said, "Like lunch—and we're ordering the most expensive stuff on the menu. Lobster, caviar, shit like that. No arguments, okay?"

CHAPTER SIXTEEN

IT FELT WEIRD having Teague come into the club with her like a regular boyfriend from the start of her shift. Weird to come out from the dressing room and see him already sitting at the bar with Len. Weird to have the girls cast her knowing looks.

But it was Xanthe, putting on her makeup beside Frankie at the vanity in the changing room, who kicked the weirdness into overdrive.

"You got dibs on that streak of golden American gorgeousness?" Xanthe asked her, adding a faint smear of liquid glitter to her impossibly high cheekbones.

"Dibs?" Frankie said, and then laughed—a false, too-high laugh. "Um…no!"

Xanthe made eye contact with her via the mirror, "You sure? 'Cause he looked a lot like Sir Galahad riding to the rescue of his lady the other night."

"He's just like that. A gentleman. Always has been."

"Always? I thought you'd only just met him. How long have you known him?"

Known him? Frankie would have said she hadn't known him at all before he'd arrived on her doorstep.

She'd have said she'd been attracted to him, intrigued by him, wary of her own fascination with him, but that none of those things counted as knowing him. She was bemused to suddenly realize she *had* known him—enough to mark him as hers from the start.

"Hello! Frankie!"

"Oh!" she said, snapping back. "We met when I was working in the States."

"You two date back then?"

"No. He was hung up on someone else."

"So you're just friends?" Xanthe persisted.

"Just friends."

Up went Xanthe's cynical eyebrows.

"Okay, friends with benefits." Pause. Think. "Benefits for now."

"Benefits for *now*?"

"He's only here until Christmas."

"Ah. So…are those benefits exclusive?"

"*Yes*, they're exclusive. Jesus, Xanthe!"

"Okay, sorry! I was going to offer him a dance, is all."

Frankie opened her mouth to say something along the lines of "over my dead body" but bit the words back. With only a week to go, it was time to start reminding herself she wasn't really Teague's girlfriend; he could accept a dance from anyone he liked. "Sure, ask him," she said. "Don't expect him to say yes, though. He's not into lap dancing."

"Well, you know what they say—you don't ask you don't get."

Ten minutes later, from the vantage point of the stage, Frankie saw Teague get off his bar stool and follow Xanthe to one of the private rooms, and a shaft of white-hot jealousy brought her to a sudden stop. He turned as they got there, looked directly at her and smiled, and she wanted to march over there and punch him.

Which, of course, would be pathetic. What she should be doing was showing him she didn't care—perhaps by dancing herself into a two-hundred-dollar tip!

She looked around the edge of the stage, chose the best-looking guy, undulated in his direction, and tried to appreciate the way he extravagantly tipped her for the next half hour—like, half a freaking *hour*!—which was when Teague and Xanthe finally emerged from behind that tacky-as-hell beaded curtain, laughing as though they were the best of friends.

Xanthe headed straight for the dressing room, which Frankie knew meant she'd been well-paid and wanted to put her cash away. Making a snap decision, she abandoned Mr. Big Tipper and followed Xanthe into the dressing room to try some subtle pumping.

Fifteen minutes later, she was forced to admit defeat, no wiser as to what had gone down in that private room. She kept telling herself Xanthe was no different from her—dancing for the money, not to boyfriend-steal—but the urge to punch Teague had escalated to the point where she knew she had to stay the hell away from him for the rest of the night.

It was still there when she and Teague got in the car, along with a burning need to demonstrate that she was every bit as good a dancer as Xanthe, goddammit.

"I made a lot of money tonight," was her opener, as the car pulled away from the curb.

"That's good," Teague said, but he seemed distracted.

"One guy tipped me three hundred dollars."

"Great. So you're on track."

"On track?"

"For a mid-January retirement?"

"Oh. Yeah. I guess." Pause. "Did you see him? The guy who looked a bit like Justin Trudeau?"

"Who? Sorry!"

"Justin Trudeau! You know, hot Canadian prime minister."

"Oh. Oh, yeah, I know who Justin Trudeau is."

"Well, the guy who tipped me three hundred bucks looks a lot like…" She trailed off, because Teague had closed his eyes and his lips were moving as though he were singing under his breath. "Oh, never mind!" she said grumpily.

And then she realized the words he was mouthing were the lyrics to the song she herself had danced to for him that first night. "That must have been some dance Xanthe gave you," she said, so ver-y care-ful-ly.

"It was…instructive," Teague said, and chuckled, and her hand curled into a fist so tight she practically stopped the blood supply to her fingers and wondered if she'd be shaking at least two of them out of her palm by the time they got to his hotel.

"Instructive," she said. "As in good?"

"Yeah, she was good. Great!"

Well, fuck! "Did she do her trick?"

"Trick?"

"Where she does a handstand between your legs."

Teague looked a little appalled. "Um, no. Is that usual?"

"We each have our thing."

"It's important to have your 'thing,' is it?" he said and closed his eyes again. "Hmm."

"Are you tired?" she asked.

"What?"

"Are you *tired*?"

He snapped his eyes open. "Oh." Looking guilty. "Yeah, I guess."

She said nothing else until they got into the suite. And then she turned to him, and said, "Well, I guess if you're tired, we should just—just sleep tonight, right?"

"Okay," he said easily.

Okay? "Then I'll use the other bathroom. Quicker, you know."

"Sure."

Sure? "So I'll be back soon. When I'm done. I'll try not to wake you if you're asleep."

"Fine," he said.

Fine? She hovered, trying to find something else to say—because dammit, this whole *thing* was supposed to be about sex, and she wanted to have sex with him, and if he wasn't going to give her that, what the hell was she doing here?

He headed for the main bedroom, humming something to himself.

"I haven't got anything to sleep in," she said—it was all she could come up with to pause him.

He turned, said, "Give me a second," and then kept going.

Humming again, he returned to the living room and handed her one of his T-shirts. "Will that do?" he asked.

Torn between a crazy desire to wear his T-shirt and taking umbrage that he hadn't told her he'd prefer her to be naked, all she could do was nod.

And then he was gone, and she was standing in the living room with nothing to do except what she'd told him she was going to do: shower in the other bathroom and let him get into bed without her.

She hefted her dance bag in her hand. Goddamn, she'd forgotten how heavy it was, with Teague carting it everywhere for her—and that was going to have to stop forthwith! She headed to the second bedroom. "Maybe I'll just sleep in here," she muttered to herself. "What would you say to that, Teague Hamilton?"

But as she made her way into the bathroom, she decided she knew what he'd say to that: *If that's what you want.* That was what he'd say.

She stripped off and turned on the shower.

That was the problem with gentlemanly guys. They never pressured you. They reeled you in by stealth. Underhanded, was what it was.

She tested the water, waited until it was warm, then got under the spray and grabbed the soap.

Carrying your bag and opening doors for you. Getting their car to deliver you to and from work. Buying you breakfasts and lunches and dinners and wine and whiskey and cognac and champagne. Telling you how good you looked every damn day, and how amazing you smelled every damn night. Defending your honor at work even though they knew full well you could do it for yourself, knew you *preferred* to do it for yourself, because that's the way it had always been done—by you, on your own! Obeying you when you told them not to ask you for a lap dance. Being phenomenally good in bed when you'd have been happy enough with "adequate." Actually *enjoying* going down on you to the point of doing it every damn night. Accepting you at your damn word when you said you were tired and needed to sleep. Having pure gold hair and pure blue eyes and a perfect mouth that—that sent your brain haywire when it smiled at you, and had you convinced that if you didn't see it twenty times a day for the rest of your fucking life you were going to die of malnourishment. And how with all of that, and a million other small things, from the way they looked over their shoulder not believing you were talking to them, to touching their fucking perfect scar, not to mention the way they said your name like a prayer when they came, they snuck up on you and wrestled your common sense into a coma, so that before you knew it, you were in love with them and would do anything for them—even make yourself miserable by letting them go in seven fucking days' time!

She got out of the shower, toweled herself viciously and contemplated staying naked. But she couldn't resist the lure of wearing Teague's T-shirt so she dragged it on over her head, telling herself it could be easily discarded when the right moment arose.

She walked purposefully back to the main bedroom, but hesitated as she entered, seeing the shape of him under the covers. How the hell was she going to keep her hands off him? She considered going out to the living room and working on the scarf she was knitting him, but she'd left it a fraction too late to move because he raised himself on his elbow, peeled back the covers to reveal boxer shorts—damn!—and said, "Coming?"

She padded over to the bed, slid in beside him, and closed her eyes the better to soak up the feeling of Teague tucking the covers back over her, and then tensed as she tried to anticipate what he'd do next.

But all he did was pull her close, so that she was cushioned against his shoulder, kiss her temple and run his hand through her hair. "Good night, heartling," he said.

Heartling. Good night. That was it. No sex. They really were just going to sleep.

For a long, long time she lay there, stunned.

And then she turned her head, kissed his collarbone. "'Night, Teague," she whispered into the dark.

CHAPTER SEVENTEEN

AN ARDENT LOVEMAKING session with Teague on Friday morning managed to convince Frankie she'd overreacted to his lap-dancing escapades with Xanthe the night before.

Clearly, he'd come to the club too early and had done it to stave off boredom—nothing more to it than that. So she was relieved when Teague made no move to get in the car with her after dinner that evening.

Her sense of relief vanished two hours later, when she emerged from behind the irritatingly clacky beaded curtain with one of her most irritatingly persistent regulars and crossed paths with Cyn, who had Teague by the hand—by the fucking *hand*!—and was leading him into the space Frankie had just vacated.

She spun to Len, found him smiling benignly as his girlfriend disappeared with his new best mate, and wondered what the ever-loving fuck was going on. One hasty step…and stop. She wasn't going to ask Len what was happening with her own damn boyfriend.

No! Not boyfriend! Not *real* boyfriend! Lover, she could accept! Make that *temporary* lover! And whatever he was, she was not going to ask Len about him, and she wasn't going to ask Teague why he'd come to the club, either. She was going to be breezy and sophisticated and mature and amused.

So when Cyn came over to her an hour later—a full *hour*!—all starry-eyed and babbling about how lovely Teague was, how well-behaved, handsome, funny, sweet, generous and *shut the fuck up, Cyn!!!*—she maintained her composure even though it required such a rigid jaw-clamp she almost cracked a tooth.

Thank God, he didn't buy any more dances after that, even though he made up for it by watching every girl who took to the stage. And to think she'd been pleased when he'd said he'd have to learn the business!

At one stage, she caught him handing over a huge wad of money to Jase and saw a bit of a pantomime between them that led her to believe the money was to be shared equally among all the staff. Another pantomime, for her, when he caught her watching him—a tap of his watch, a point to the clock on the wall, hands on an imaginary steering wheel. And then a clap on Len's shoulder, a nod to Dazey in the DJ booth and he was heading out the door.

She wasn't sure how to act with him when she left the club just after three and found him waiting for her, even though the routine felt normal now—him taking her bag, kissing her temple, slinging his arm around her shoulders and walking her toward the car.

But when she saw the usual town car had been replaced by a white limo, she came to a juddering stop.

"What the hell is this?" she asked him as he opened the door for her.

"Um…a white limo? One of those romantic movie things. So are you going to get in or am I supposed to pick you up in my arms first?"

"Huh?"

"Maybe just get in, Frankie. If you accidentally hit me in the head with your purse and give me a concussion, it might ruin the moment."

She got in, and he slid in beside her, saying, "Please take note of the privacy screen."

The minute the car started moving, he pulled her in for a long, wet kiss.

"How private are those screens, really?" she asked, when he released her and told her to buckle up.

"How would I know?"

"You've been in limos before—I haven't."

"I've been in limos before but never with someone I'm lusting after, so I guess the short answer the way I'm currently feeling is I don't care. As long as the driver takes twenty minutes as I requested, we're good."

"But he'll guess!" she said, even though her body was telling her to shut up.

"Hey, either we're going to get naughty or we aren't."

"Get naughty?"

"Get naughty. Yes or no?"

"Yes," she said.

"Well, thank God for that—the car upgrade was expensive!"

She choked on a laugh—this was unbelievable! "But

I don't trust that screen, so there'll be no moans and sighs. I'm not going to make a sound, just in case."

"Ah, a challenge—excellent!" Teague said, and then added, "Stay in your seat, but take off your panties."

"I hope you know what you're doing, Teague," she said, wriggling out of her underwear.

"No idea," he said, taking her panties from her, "so *shhh* and let me concentrate and get my dirty talk straight in my head."

"Your *what*?"

"Shhh," he said, and then he raised her panties to his face and breathed in as his hand went to her knee and started inching up under her dress. "I like everything about your pussy—the way it looks, the way it feels, the way it smells, and especially the way it tastes," he said, soft and low, for her ears only. "Now open your legs so I can get at you."

She didn't need to be told twice, she was already on fire.

"Ahhhh," he breathed out, as he got all the way up her inner thigh. He stayed there, teasing her with light strokes that grazed her labia.

She shifted, trying to get him to touch her properly.

"No!" he said and withdrew his hand.

"Teague!"

"Do as I say," he said. "Don't move. Stay still and let me finger you."

"Jesus," she hissed out, and suddenly, he speared one finger into her.

"Hot and tight and fucking perfect," he said. "Now don't move or I'll take it out."

Excruciatingly excited, Frankie forced her body to be still, but she had to clench every muscle to stop herself from thrusting against his finger and clench her teeth to stop the moans escaping.

Slowly, slowly he extracted his finger, spreading her moisture, then dipped into her again for more, over and over as he whispered to her, "This is what I wanted to do to you in the car that first morning, my fingers in your pussy, making you squirm and pant for me. Keep still!" More moisture—he was coating her with it. "I love your clit, the way it gets hard like a sweet little pearl…" And his index finger was there, circling it, and she started to shake.

"Teague," she begged.

"Thought you weren't going to make a sound? Want me to stop?"

She shook her head. "Want…more," she moaned, then bit her lip as he pinched her clit.

"When we're in the surf, I want to touch you like this, too," he went on. "I want to push my fingers under the crotch of your swimsuit and feel you. I want to make you come, just like I'm going to do in the back of this limo, where you have to pretend nothing's happening." Two fingers now, sawing across her, harder and faster. "If I could, I'd have my fingers in you every time I'm with you, no matter who could see. And then I'd follow with my tongue. That's what I'm going to do to you tonight—I'm not even going to take off your dress. Maybe I'll do it in the elevator, get onto my knees and lift your dress and lick your clit."

"Teague," she breathed, "Teague, let me come."

"And then I'm going to get you into the room, and I'm going to rip that dress off you, and suck your nipples through your bra as I stick my cock in you and—"

"Teague!" she cried out loud, because—bang!—she was coming and coming, coming so hard she thought she was going to explode. Her back arched, her whole body convulsed, and his mouth was on hers and he was kissing her, biting at her lips, his tongue going wild, panting into her mouth as his free hand found her breast, squeezed it hard.

Long, long, long moment, and then he pulled free. His face was flushed, she could tell it even in the car's dark interior. Slowly he eased his hand out from beneath her dress.

"Jeeeezus," he said, "I hope this car gets to the hotel soon, because I swear I'm going to lose it if I don't fuck you within the next five minutes." He kissed her again. "And I think I should warn you, I'm not feeling like a cautious, responsible, reliable, dependable, boring gentlemanly type of guy. In fact, I may well be on a rampage."

CHAPTER EIGHTEEN

AFTER THE LIMOUSINE LUST, Frankie thought she could cope with anything Teague did at the club the next night, but when he arrived at ten o'clock, only to disappear almost immediately with Jess, it was almost enough to blow her brain out of her ears because everyone knew Jess took off her damn top in those rooms!

Thankfully, Jess seemed to be a step too far for Teague, who was out of there pretty damn quick looking like he'd seen a ghost. He contented himself with watching the stage and letting the girls come to chat with him after that—which was annoying, but better than having one of them sit on him!

The next night, which would be his last night in the club, Frankie was so on edge waiting for him to arrive at ten o'clock she could barely twirl a hip, and she decided enough was enough. Despite all her rules about not dancing for people she knew, she was going to dance for him!

She was wearing her favorite underwear—flesh-colored mesh—and had rouged her nipples. So obvious, but she didn't care as long as she turned him on! She'd also gone Christmas down below, with new bloodred vajazzling and dark green frills on her backside. If Teague looked away from her for even a heartbeat in this getup, she was going to throw a major-league tantrum in the middle of the club, grab him by the hair and drag him out to the back alley to fuck him.

She timed her dances to make sure she was free at ten o'clock—his usual arrival time. But ten o'clock came and went, and then eleven o'clock, and she had to get up on the stage!

So, of course, he arrived midsong, and she had to watch as Bella, the pole-dancing wonder, sauntered in his direction.

One thing about Bella was that she had massive boobs, so, of course, Frankie had to look down at her own pitifully fake-red areolae, at which point she wished she could jump off the damn stage and break both her legs just to cause a distraction.

An hour and fifteen minutes later, he came out looking very pleased with himself, and Frankie's night was ruined, to the point where she earned almost no tips— and seriously, who would want to tip a girl who danced like crap, looked surly as hell and had such weird-looking nipples?

She didn't speak to Teague until they were in the suite, and then she could not hold it in one more second! "Must have been quite a lap dance—you were grinning like a carnival clown for so long afterward," she snarled.

"Well, I certainly understand it's a job. And a tough one."

She threw her handbag on the couch. "I'm so glad Xanthe and Cyn and Jess and Bella could convince you of something I apparently could not. Maybe now you'll be okay with me dancing my ass off."

"Hey, I said I understood, that's all. Honestly? I don't think I'll ever be okay with you dancing for other men."

"Oh! And I suppose I'm supposed to be happy that I shared you this week with four different women, am I?"

"What are you talking about?"

"Nothing."

Silence, during which he didn't take his eyes off her face.

"And stop looking at me!" she snapped.

"Whoa!" he said. "What happened tonight?"

"I didn't make budget tonight, that's all." And then as he opened his mouth, she said, "And don't offer to make up the shortfall! You've done enough damage already."

"How is it my fault?"

"You distracted me!"

"I *what*?"

"An hour and fifteen minutes!"

Her blinked at her. "You *timed* me?"

"Only because I needed to use the room!"

"You *timed* me!" he said, and his slow smile spread, until she wanted to slap it off his face.

"I thought you didn't approve of lap dances," she raged at him.

"You're deflecting. You didn't approve of me *getting* them—that's what this is about."

"You could have gotten one from me."

"You didn't want to dance for me—remember?"

"Yeah, well, I thought you weren't a douche so I was willing to try again!"

"So I'm a douche because Bella danced for me to-night?"

"Yes!"

"Frankie, you *wanted* me to let the other girls dance for me. You tried to push Bella onto me that first night."

"That was because I didn't see, I didn't realize…" She spun away from him, screaming into her hands.

"Ha!" he crowed. "You're jealous!"

"Yes! All right!" She whirled back to him. "Yes! I'm jealous, okay? I'm jealous! I don't want anyone else dancing for you. I don't want any of them to touch you, I don't want you touching them."

He laughed.

She stamped her foot and hated herself for doing it. "It's not funny, Teague! What do I care if those girls dance for you? What do I care if you prefer them to me? I don't care!" She shoved him in the chest. "Except that I want to kill you!"

He hooted out another laugh.

"It's not *funny*, Teague!"

"Sure it is. If you knew what I've done…"

"What do you mean?"

He grinned. "I guess I'll show you. I'd better, in the interests of world peace. Even if it means giving you your Christmas present three days early."

"Wh-what?"

"I'm giving you your Christmas present now, tonight, in approximately two minutes, if you'll stop haranguing me."

"My present? You got me a present?"

"I got you two presents, but this is the main one. So—" he pushed the couch to one side "—give me a minute—" he walked out of the room, then returned with one of the dining chairs "—to put this—" positioning the chair where the couch had been "—here."

"What the hell are you—?"

But he cut her off by simply taking her by the shoulders and walking her to the chair. "Sit," he ordered, and pushed her gently down before picking up one of the ever-present remotes and dimming the lights. "Mood lighting, almost as good as King's Castle's."

"Huh?"

He removed his phone from his pocket, fiddled with it, placed it on the coffee table. "This is Dazey's contribution," he said.

"Dazey?"

His answer was to remove his shoes and socks and kick them out of the way.

"Teague? What the hell is going on?"

And then he tapped his phone and a song started playing—that song, from the first night—and it all came together.

"Oh, my God," she breathed out.

"Just two more things." He hurried over to the couch, dug into her knitting basket and tugged a truly awful green beanie—her first-ever beanie, not good enough to gift—onto his head. "One—this is my 'thing.'"

"Your thing," she choked out.

"Well, I'm not vajazzling myself, I can promise you that," he said. "And two—" he whipped his shirt over his head "—in Club Hamilton touching is actively encouraged."

CHAPTER NINETEEN

ONE THING TEAGUE knew he was good at was the full body roll. Xanthe, Cyn, Jess—dear God, Jess!—and Bella had all praised him for it, so it was what he led with.

Not that it seemed to make much of an impact on Frankie, who was sitting there trying not to dissolve into hysterics.

"No good?" he asked and took a side-to-side sway of a step toward her. "Because that's my signature move so if you don't like it I may be in trouble."

And out came a snorting laugh. "You are seriously, *seriously*, going to give me a lap dance?"

"What do you mean 'going to'—I've already begun," he said, and smiled when she laughed again. "Okay, I'll try one more…" And this time when he did his body roll, she gave him a small clap.

"That's more like it," he said, and glided all the way around the chair before coming to a stop in front of her. He tried out a hip twirl and had to admit he hadn't improved despite three days practicing—it still felt like he was cocking his hips one after the other rather than fluidly rolling them. To distract her from his incompetence, he placed his hands high on his chest, then ran them down, down, sucking in his breath to get enough concavity going to enable him to dip his hands just under the waistband of his pants.

"Are you going to take those off?" she asked with an exaggerated leer, "or is that against the rules?"

"Oh, Frankie, there *are* no rules tonight," he said, and undid his belt buckle.

One flick, and the belt was through the loops on his pants and flung behind him. His fingers went to work on the button, then his zipper, before he slowly eased his pants down his legs. He was a little disconcerted to note she'd raised her eyes and was therefore missing all the sensuousness going on with his lower half, but consoled himself with the thought that there was time for that. Dazey had mixed him enough music to last fifteen minutes.

A kick. And his pants were off and away—and he was back in action with a roll of his hips that was much easier in only his boxers. He considered it a minor miracle that he had a raging hard-on, because giving a lap dance had to rank pretty high on his list of the most embarrassing moments in his entire life. But there was no doubt about it: he was hugely turned on dancing for her, knowing it was going to end with him and Frankie having sex.

The thought of sex was worth putting a little extra zing into the dance. He leaned down, the way she'd leaned down for him that first night. Hands on her shoulders, cocooning her, closer, closer, so that he was staring into her eyes. His hips were swaying, side to side, he could feel the music pumping through him like hot blood, hear her breaths come fast and shallow. Before he knew it, his mouth was on hers and he was kissing her. It was strange, so strange, to have his lips cling so sweetly while his body burned like the devil for her. Cling, cling, and then he pulled away. Hands off the chair, taking a step back, unable to tear his eyes from her. She was sitting there in her flouncy green dress—this one even had a frothy white petticoat peeking out from beneath the hem—and she looked so beautiful it made his heart ache.

Breathless now, he turned his back, needing a moment to recover his wits. Dancing, he was supposed to be dancing for her. An apology for the way he'd once made her feel about her job. A bit of fun. An excuse to come to the club and keep an eye on her the way Len did with Cyn—a way to forget that in a few days he'd lose that right, because no way could he ask her to leave Sydney.

She was tough and independent and proud and smart and ambitious and resourceful and creative and his. She was his. No, he didn't own her, and he never would, and that was part and parcel of loving her, but she *did* belong to him. And he thanked God for the first time in eleven years that Romy had never loved him, because Frankie was the one he was supposed to belong to.

God, he had to say something, something cute to get the lump out of his throat. "That's a kind of a white-guys-can't-twerk move, in case you're wondering," he said, expecting her to laugh.

He heard a sound, like a choke, and smiled.

"Humor is not appreciated at these delicate moments," he chastised, as he poked his ass our farther and waggled it.

Another choke…and he stopped, straightened, turned.

Frankie wasn't laughing, she was crying.

"Hey!" he said, drawing her up off the chair and into his arms.

She buried her face against his chest and sobbed.

"That bad, huh?" he said, trying to make her laugh, but she only sobbed harder. "Frankie, heartling, tell me what's wrong so I can fix it, hmm?"

"You c-can't f-fix time. You c-can't s-stop it. It j-just passes. And Christmas… It's almost here."

And as he stroked her hair, the knot of grief in his chest tightened until his heart ached. "But it's not here yet, Frankie, okay?" he said.

She nodded, and he felt her start to gather herself together, ready to pull free of his arms, but he wouldn't—he couldn't—let her go.

She read him, she *knew,* and wrapped her arms around his waist, and whispered into his chest, "And so you know, this is what I call a swoon, which means you're probably going to have to scoop me up and carry me again."

"I can do that," he said, and as he swung her up into his arms and kissed her, the scent of gardenia flooded him, and the blue ends of her hair burned him—oh, God, they really did—and the salt of her tears melted all the way through to his heart, he knew he couldn't let her go, which meant he had to find a way to keep her.

CHAPTER TWENTY

WHEN TEAGUE GOT a call from Flip the next day, sounding him out about participating in the Sydney to Hobart instead of watching it, the temptation to do a Frankie and say, "Why not?" was so great, the words almost popped out before he could catch them.

But he *did* catch them, because for all the internal change he'd been through in Sydney, the situation with his parents remained static. Yachting around Sydney Harbor he could get away with. Ocean racing through Bass Strait? No way.

Still, whereas last year he would have said a flat-out "no can do" to Flip, this year he prevaricated, merely suggesting it would be difficult for him to commit, so Flip should try and find someone else.

He figured he wouldn't hear from Flip again despite that open-ended answer, and that made him both relieved and depressed—which, of course, Frankie picked up on that night when he was barbecuing steak for their dinner in her dismal little courtyard.

She brought a beer over to him and wound her arms

around him from behind, rubbing her cheek on his shoulder blade. "What happened today?"

"How do you know something happened?"

"Because you've been doing that brooding thing all day—you know, the thing that makes you irresistible?"

He laughed. "Oh, that thing." And then he sighed. "A friend called me. He's the skipper on a Sydney to Hobart boat, *Pink Diamond*."

She said nothing.

"One of his crewmen has had to bow out, and he—he asked me if I wanted in."

"And do you?"

"You know I do."

"But you said no."

"Not exactly. I said he should try to find someone else." Silence.

And then she released him, and came to stand beside him, took his beer bottle off him, sipped, then handed it back. "At least the boat has a pretty name."

"Puh-lease!"

"There's nothing not to like about a pink diamond! Very Australian, you know. Rare, too. From a mine in the Kimberley."

"I don't think that's what Flip—the skipper—is thinking about. It's not his boat. It belongs to some rich-ass jeweler."

"If he sells pink diamonds I'm not surprised he's rich." Pause. "But it doesn't matter what the boat's called, does it? As long as it's well-crewed and makes it to Hobart without drowning its most heartthrobby sailor."

He gave her the beer bottle, so he had a free arm to put around her. "It doesn't matter that I *won't* drown, only that I *might*."

"Well, Teague, I'm not going to feed you any platitudes about you being more likely to get killed by a car, or a lightning strike, or by cardiac arrest when I try out something new on you later tonight—"

"I like door number three."

"—all I'm going to say is that when you gaze at the boats on the harbor, I want to physically throw you on one of them and tell you to hoist a jib or something. It seems such a simple thing for you to do again, here in Sydney, where it's at your fingertips."

"Frankie, you *know* the problem."

"I do. But I think you could find a way to make your parents understand that their son needs to be just himself every now and then. They love you, after all. So if your skipper friend calls you again, maybe this time don't ask yourself what your parents would expect of you—show them who you still are, hmm?"

Christmas Eve.

Time was almost up, so it seemed wretched to Frankie that she and Teague should spend so much of the day apart—but he had some money crisis he had to take care of on this last business day, so she was left to her own devices, delivering beanies, cleaning the house, preparing picnic things for the beach tomorrow…and practicing her a-happy-happy-bon-voyage face in the mirror.

Unsurprisingly, the happy face was defeating her—

she could almost feel her heart was cracking, as though in preparation for the full-on break that would come when Teague left on Boxing Day—but she kept trying. She wanted their final hours together to be a celebration, not a wake. She'd seized the day, and found love; surely that had to be worth what she'd endure when he left?

She thought she was holding it together quite well when they put up her fake three-foot Christmas tree and decorated it with her motley collection of thrift-store decorations. Through dinner, too—wonderful seafood, bought by Teague because he insisted on the full Sydney Christmas experience. But afterward, when he sat on the couch with her on his lap and held her without saying a word, she started crying again.

"It'll be all right, Frankie, I promise," he said, and he looked so determined at that moment, Frankie almost believed him.

Almost…

CHAPTER TWENTY-ONE

TEAGUE WOKE EARLY on Christmas morning, with a strange churning in his gut he recognized as excitement—and not of the sexual kind. Way more important than that!

He showered, shaved, got dressed and went out to the kitchen to make himself a cup of coffee and rehearse his lines for when she opened the present he'd left for her under the tree, and tried out a few variations for when she found the one he'd hung *on* the tree.

When Frankie joined him in the kitchen, she was wearing the robe with the red flowers; he took that robe as a good omen.

"Shall I give you your first Christmas present now?" she asked, sounding uncharacteristically shy.

"Is it under the tree?"

"Hmm, no," she said. "Wouldn't fit under there. It's here…" And she opened her robe to flash him, and he saw that every crystal was gone. "This is me. I hope you like it."

"I love it."

"For that, my good man, you're going to get laid after breakfast!"

"I'm salivating here! Why not now?"

"Because I want to see if you like your other present. I did it in a hurry, so I'm a little embarrassed at the quality—or lack thereof."

"Uh-oh!" he said, but he was ready to burst with excitement over his beanie, too, wondering what color it was and just how much of an abomination it was going to be.

"Hey! It's not easy keeping your knitting a secret when the man you're doing it for is constantly attached to your body!"

"You make a good point," he said. "Okay, living room it is. Go find the present I got you while I make your coffee, and then I'm going to reattach myself."

By the time Teague had her coffee on the table, Frankie was sitting on the couch, holding the plain white envelope across which he'd scribbled her name.

She frowned slightly as she looked at him. "If you've been unimaginative enough to buy me a gift voucher—"

"It's not a voucher," he interrupted, and as he sat beside her, he tapped a finger to the scar on his lip, which sent a prickle of apprehension down Frankie's spine. "Open it, Frankie."

Breathing nice and quiet and slow, she opened the envelope and pulled out a sheaf of papers. "But what...?" She looked at him. "Is this a contract?"

"Yes."

"For what?"

"An apartment."

He said the word but it didn't seem to go past her ears and into her head, so she just sat there.

He cleared his throat. "I bought you an apartment," he said.

It still wasn't making sense. "An apartment?"

"That apartment we looked at."

She shook her head. "We didn't look at an apartment."

"North Bondi. Geoff Rhodes. Views of the beach. You said you wanted to move, that you liked the place, but couldn't afford it."

And at last it sank in. "And I still can't afford it."

"I can."

Heartbeat, two, three, as she stared at him. "I thought you knew me, Teague," she said, and her voice shook.

"I don't— Wh-what?" he asked.

"I thought I'd explained that I didn't want to be owned."

"I don't want to own you, I want to marry you."

"So you're moving to Sydney?"

"No, but—"

She cut him off by simply getting to her feet and moving to the other side of the coffee table. She faced him across it. "You're not moving to Sydney, but you want me to move into your apartment—"

"It's *your* apartment."

"—move into an apartment *you own*, and wait for you to have an occasional trip here? How often are you planning on visiting? Once a month? For how long? One day, two?"

"I don't have all the details worked out, but—"

"Then come and see me when you do."

He jumped to his feet then. "So, you have no problem letting Matt buy you an engagement ring—"

"It wasn't real!"

"—and you jump headfirst into some crack-brained engagement scheme of his that you make up as you go along just to get back at your lowlife ex—"

"It wasn't *real*!"

"—but here I am offering you an *actual* marriage, and I have to have every last detail written in triplicate before you'll even hear me out?"

"Yes! Because that's how *you* do things! You told me you'd never live on a different continent from your fiancée. Why is it okay to do that when it's me?"

"I can't help it that I live in New York and you live in Sydney!"

"We knew that before we started! Hence the two-and-a-half-week fling, for which I'm already being *amply* compensated."

"I want more!"

"What you want is a mistress, or a…a prostitute! And I…I trusted you not to turn me into one—not a real one."

"That's not fair, Frankie! I've never treated you like a mistress or a prostitute—you're the one obsessed with getting paid!"

"You're treating me like one now. You're making me one, but giving it a…a veneer to make me more acceptable. And let me tell you, if I wanted to be a billionaire's mistress, I'd already be one, and I'd be getting a damn sight more out of it than a few days a year. So if that's your fantasy—"

"That's *not* my fantasy!"

"Then tell me what is and I'll give it to you, god-dammit! Today, tonight, tomorrow morning, as many times as you want before you leave."

He strode around the table, grabbed her by her upper arms, glared down at her. "My fantasy is you, Frankie. It always was."

"I sell fantasies, Teague, but I am not a fantasy. You bought two and a half weeks from me, you don't get to buy my entire life by shacking me up and visiting every December. I fucking know you wouldn't do it to Romy!"

"I don't want Romy!"

"You wanted her for eleven years!"

"Not like this, not ever like this. It—it scares me, how much I want you, so much it's like I can't…breathe, unless I'm touching you, and I— I have to breathe, Frankie. If I bought two and a half weeks, it's because that was what you were selling, but I…I'll take what-ever you'll give me and give you whatever you want in return."

"I've offered myself to you every way I know how, and apparently it's still not enough, *I'm* not enough. I'm a vacation, not a life and that's not enough for me, damn you!" She wrenched free of him, went to the tree, reefed his present out from under it and threw it at him.

"Merry Christmas," she said, and strode to the front door, where she paused and spoke to the wood. "I'll be back in ten minutes. Please do your usual trick while I'm gone and run away."

* * *

Teague spent most of the day sitting on the terrace because inside the suite seemed to have reverted to a space that was too fucking big and too damn bland.

Housekeeping had done a thorough job. There wasn't a trace of Frankie anywhere—not a single vajazzled crystal or a tiny scrap of wool. All he had of her was the Christmas present she'd thrown at him, with its cheery card telling him she wished she could keep him warm in New York.

But obviously she didn't really wish that or she'd marry him and come with him.

Okay, unfair. Unfair. But he missed her already, and he didn't want to be fair. No, she wasn't Romy—Romy he'd given up without a fight; Frankie he could not bear to give up.

He got to his feet, and went inside for a bottle of Barron whiskey and an unchipped glass—both of which items increased his depression—then sat on the couch and picked up his present. He was scared to open it, because the fact that it was a fucking knitted eyesore wouldn't matter. What would matter was that she only knitted for people she liked, people she trusted, and she didn't trust him anymore. And he knew he was going to wear it, and every time he did, he was going to love her more.

"Fuck this!" he said and ripped open the paper.

And out it tumbled. Not a beanie, but a scarf—of course it was a scarf, he hadn't earned his beanie yet. It had her trademark scattering of dropped stitches, and it was perfect because it was black, with electric blue bands across each end, just like her hair, and it smelled like gardenia.

His breath caught, jammed in his throat, the back of his nose stung, his ribs felt bruised from his swollen heart. He couldn't bear that he was having to accept a scarf that was a facsimile of Frankie's hair, spritzed in her perfume when what he needed was the scent of her skin.

Talk about wallowing in misery over what he couldn't have!

Frankie wouldn't be wallowing.

Life happens, you have to go with the flow of it and try to love it.

That's what she'd be doing. Living her life without him. While he went back to being everyone's Mr. Perfect, his life racing by without him on board.

His phone rang, and instantly his bruised heart kicked, but the caller ID told him it wasn't Frankie.

Flip. Had to mean the *Pink Diamond* still needed crew.

His finger hovered, about to reject the call, but he heard Frankie, so clearly in his head. *It seems such a simple thing for you to do again, here in Sydney, where it's at your fingertips... I think you could find a way to make your parents understand that their son maybe needs to be just himself... If your skipper friend calls you again, maybe this time don't ask yourself what your parents would expect of you—show them who you still are...*

A burst of energy filled him and he hit the accept button. "Flip! I'm assuming you're still looking…? Ah, well, as it happens, my plans fell through, so sure, count me in."

CHAPTER TWENTY-TWO

AFTER ALL HER talk about the orphans Christmas, Frankie didn't have the heart to go to Bondi Beach on Christmas day.

All she seemed able to do was read the apartment contract over and over and replay that disastrous last conversation with Teague in her head.

And every time she replayed it, she got stuck on that one stinging accusation: *I've never treated you like a mistress or a prostitute—you're the one obsessed with getting paid!*

The reason she got stuck, of course, was because he was right!

He'd offered her a Hollywood happy ending, and she'd reacted like he was Kyle forcing her onto her hands and knees! She deserved to be miserable. She deserved to cry for the rest of her life—and she probably would. Talk about wallowing in misery!

When she woke up on Boxing Day, she cried some more, and as she watched the start of the Sydney to Hobart on TV, she positively wailed because she knew Teague would be going back to the hotel, packing his things ready to leave for Hobart.

Merry fucking Christmas, Frankie!

She glared at her Christmas tree, contemplated picking it up and throwing it across the room, then thought that was the last thing Teague would do and settled for ripping the decorations off it.

Which was when she found the ring—a pink diamond ring hanging next to a two-dollar elf, which seemed to perfectly sum up her fling with Teague.

She stared at it for what felt like an eternity, then slipped it onto the third finger of her left hand…and started crying again.

When her phone rang, her heart went crazy, and she hit the accept button without even looking to see who it was, hoping, hoping…

But when she heard "Merry Christmas, Francesca," her blood boiled.

Matt! Architect of this fucking mess.

"You're a day late, Matthew!" she said. "And don't Francesca me because I already want to kill you."

He started laughing. "Kill me?"

"You sent him here!"

"We had to! Because you were a pain in the ass and didn't come to our wedding."

"I don't— Wait! What?"

"Our wedding, where he was supposed to take one look at you and remember you were the one who always turned him into a blithering idiot and fall in love with you and get his life together. And it seems to have worked, because he's out of his rut and on *Pink Diamond*, so well done you!"

She looked at her ring. "How do you know about the

pink—? Hang on. What pink diamond are you talking about?"

"Um…the boat?"

She slid onto the couch, boneless. "He's on *Pink Diamond*?"

"Isn't that what I just said?"

"I thought you meant my engagement ring."

"Engagement ring? Whoooeee! That is fucking fantastic! Oops—don't tell Romy that 'fucking' slipped out or she'll— Uh-oh, she heard me, gotta go."

"Matt! Wait! Tell me what to do!"

"Well, Frankie, what do you want to do?"

"It doesn't matter what I want to do! I'm not right for him!"

"No? 'Cause I seem to recall you doing a reasonable line in blithering idiot back in the day, too. All those over-the-top come-ons."

"Yes, but he never took the hint!"

"Er, blithering idiot? Thought he was in love with my wife when all he was doing was playing it safe?"

"Playing it safe," she repeated, and then, more slowly, "And I'm not safe."

"Fuck no! Aw, shit! Now that's two fucks—I've really got to go."

And Frankie was left holding the phone to her ear as she stared at that wall for what felt like a thousand years. And then… "I'm the Sydney to Hobart," she said.

And she smiled.

Four hours on deck, four hours' rest in the uncomfortable bunks below, shoveling down rehydrated meals, adding and removing layers of clothing according to heat, cold, wind, rain—but always, always the black-and-blue scarf.

As *Pink Diamond* passed through Bass Strait and the wind picked up to forty knots, Teague had been swamped by seawater, knocked off his feet and pounded into poles, ending up bruised and more than a little battered. He knew he should have found it exhilarating, but only half his heart was in it. The other half was being tossed around at Bondi Beach.

Which was probably why coming up the Derwent River into Constitution Dock was anticlimactic, despite the thousands of spectators cheering, the crew high-fiving and backslapping each other, and the party buzz in the air.

His eyes were peeled for a glimpse of Frankie, even though he knew she wasn't there. This felt like that first morning, when she'd told him he always seemed to be alone, even when he was surrounded by others. He felt it even more keenly when the rest of the disembarking crew were greeted by family and friends, so that even as he allowed himself to be carried along with the crew to Customs House for the obligatory rum, he was rudderless, adrift.

As he drank his rum, all he could think about was Frankie telling him to sneak off for a wee dram if he felt like getting away from the crowd. How prickly he'd been, but now it was exactly what he wanted to do—get away from the crowd…and think about her.

And so he did the Aussie thing and shouted the next round of drinks, but as soon as he finished, he made his excuses and went in search of the distillery.

When he saw the sign—Barron—he smiled. The memory of that morning was so vivid. The first touch on that chipped glass, her telling him to pour some whiskey and put it in the middle of the table in that poor excuse for a courtyard with the out-of-place garden gnome.

Out of place…and yet it had become his place, because it was hers. It was hers…and he was hers…and dammit, she was his! And he was going to drink that dram, just so he could tell Frankie he'd done it when he flew back to Sydney on the next fucking flight without stopping for a shower and shave or to wash his crunchy seawater hair because he was not Mr. Fucking Perfect anymore!

Outside the distillery doors. Heart jumping. Almost feeling her! Knocking on her door—that's what it felt like. One more time.

He opened the door, entered. Concrete floor, barrels lining the walls, the smell of whiskey, and he could have sworn of gardenia, too.

He looked around for a seat, and his heart stopped, because there she was, sitting on a bar stool at a tall table made out of a barrel.

Slowly, he started walking toward her.

CHAPTER TWENTY-THREE

FRANKIE WAS READY to melt, and he'd only taken two steps toward her. It wasn't easy to stay where she was and let him set the pace, but there was too much at stake to rush things.

He came to a stop at the table. "What are you doing here, Frankie?"

Which would have been an inauspicious beginning, except for the glow in his eyes…and the fact he had the scarf she'd knitted hanging around his neck on a warm day. "Waiting to claim my lost property."

He looked behind him—the way he'd done that first morning, as though making sure she wasn't talking to someone else—and it was too much. She was off the stool and flinging herself into his arms and kissing him.

When she drew back, she was breathing hard. "For some hotshot billionaire lawyer, Teague, how can you be such a fuckwit?"

He kissed her, and then grinned as he drew back. "I'm not sure that's the way to talk to a man you owe fifty thousand dollars to!" he said.

"Hey, you got value for money, so don't complain."

"You dudded me."

"Again with the Aussie slang!"

"Well, I'm going to have to speak the lingo, aren't I, since I'm moving here. I mean, come on, do you really think I'm the kind of man who'd live on different continent from his wife?"

Her smile wobbled. "You're the one who put it out there."

"I told you I hadn't worked out the details. I'm new to insanity, but I'm going to get there, I promise."

"And if I said I wanted to move to New York?"

"Then all you have to say to me is 'I want to move to New York.' Remember when I said I'll take whatever you'll give me and give you whatever you want? I meant it. So you want to vajazzle yourself, go right ahead. You want to vajazzle me? Have at it—but perhaps some local anesthetic for the waxing. Want to lap dance the entire male population of Sydney, be my guest. But for now, let's just agree that you like your job and you're about to start a business, whereas I'm so-so about my job, and I want to see how your business turns out." He shrugged. "And I also have a thing for women with Australian accents, and I want to learn how to play cricket, and I want to be a wanker about coffee, and I want hot Christmases and blistering New Years and Sydney weather and Bondi beach, but if you don't want the apartment—"

"But I do want it," she said.

"Hmm. I can see you're going to be a royal pain in the ass. Fickle."

"I mean, I want it if you come with it. And I want… I want this," she said, holding out her left hand. "Which is a hint, just FYI."

"Oh, a hint. As in, will you marry me?"

"I think you're supposed to get down on your knee."

"What about my football injury?"

"You are *such* a liar!"

He gave an exaggerated sigh. "Okay," he said, and got down one knee. "Right. Here goes. Prepare yourself for a bit of a speech, because I want to make sure you know what you're getting. Not that I'm so sure myself, but I'm closer to knowing who I am when I'm with you. You made me new, and I want to be new with you, for you, which is why I didn't open the family vault for your ring—but I will, if you want me to. I'll give you everything I have, everything I am, anything you want, and I know I'm babbling but I love you, I love you so much, and I'm sorry you didn't like it when I said you're my fantasy, but you are. My fantasy, and my reality. So please, Frankie, please marry me."

The tears were there, of course, and also the blush because the whole place had gone quiet, listening. "Just one thing," she said.

"Anything."

"I do know what I'm getting. I always knew. Mr. Perfect."

"I'm not perfect, Frankie."

"Yes, Teague, you are—perfect for me. And that's about as much perfect as I can take."

"Um," he said, "this is the part where you tell me you love me, so I can get up."

"I love you. Please get up."

"Doh! Not thinking straight. Answer first."

"Yes, I'll marry you."

"Now say the love thing again."

"Have you been drinking rum at Customs House? Am I booking you into rehab?"

"Aww, Frankie!"

She burst out laughing. "Fine! Although it's obvious to me that I'm marrying you because I love you. Now please get up and kiss me."

And as everyone in the room applauded, Teague got to his feet and turned to take a bow, then swung back to her, dragged her into his arms and kissed her.

"What happens next?" she asked, when he released her.

"Hmm. We go find a hotel room, and I will have a shower and shave, and maybe, if you're lucky, I'll finish off that lap dance."

"Bring it on!" she said, and went to take his arm.

"Er, no," he said.

"No?"

"You're spoiling the romance."

"What?"

"I feel a movie moment coming on, Frankie," he said, and cracked his knuckles. "So despite my very real fear that your purse weights a ton and will somehow maim me, prepare to be lifted and carried off into the sunset."

* * * * *

DRIVING HIM WILD

ZARA COX

CHAPTER ONE

THERE WERE CERTAIN markers I'd come to rely on over the years. Markers that signified what sort of day was in store for me.

Opening my eyes exactly sixty seconds before my alarm went off was a good starter sign. My assistant getting my coffee at ninety-one point seven degrees, not the scalding one hundred degrees most people thought was the ideal temperature for the perfect cup of java? Wonderful.

Progression from car to lift to corner office without a single one of my three hundred plus staff interrupting my seven hundred and fifty-seven steps? Utter perfection.

Precision and order equalled harmony.

There was nothing precise or orderly or harmonious about the deep rumbling voice firing off questions at my hapless crew fifty feet from where I stood, perfect coffee rapidly cooling in my hand.

No one had approached me...yet, because I'd taught my people to handle problems well.

And also, I knew deep down to my very bones, because I was who I was.

Graciela Mortimer. The woman who went by many monikers.

Billionaire heiress.

Goddess of Charity.

Queen of Cash.

Or the most frequently used—and the one I hated the most—Bitch Ice Princess.

There was some sort of irony in remembering that here, standing underneath the distant shadow of the ice-covered Alaskan Range, on a frozen lake scant miles from the Arctic Circle while surrounded by minions poised to obey my every word. But wasn't my life one giant fucked-up expression of the term? Prime example—hadn't I, in my feverish attempt to not draw attention to myself, inadvertently become the public face of a global conglomerate? That in fervently wishing to be ordinary, remove myself from the harsh spotlight of being a Mortimer, I'd somehow achieved extraordinary status, earning myself, not one or two, but *three* prestigious magazine cover appearances and a mantel full of accolades?

Nevertheless, if the frenzied media coverage over the last year were an indication, my achievements paled significantly in comparison to the man who'd arrived twenty minutes ago in a flurry of a dozen husky-pulled sleds, sleek but weathered in all-white winter gear and reflective sunglasses, and a whole hour late.

Jensen Scott.

World famous adventure photographer.

Half-English, half-Danish on his mother's side. And according to Elsa, my mostly efficient if sometimes too day-dreamy assistant, possessor of killer jawline, fuck-me hair, body and eyes.

In short, six foot five of extremely fuckable man.

From where I stood, I could confirm the six-foot-five stature.

I could also confirm that the man possessed a certain intangible...*presence*, the kind that tweaked even my jaded senses. The kind that *compelled* and intrigued.

With the ever-present threat of a snowstorm and precious few hours of remaining daylight, everyone had pressing tasks to be getting on with. Yet even those scouts tasked with looking out for unfavourable visits from curious polar bears and other Arctic wildlife were distracted by our latecomer.

That straying from procedure grew increasingly unacceptable, sparking my uncustomary *temper*. The kind normally tightly controlled and unleashed on the very deserving. Like certain members of my family.

Incomparable talent or not, right this moment, the man dressing down my project manager without so much as raising his voice higher than the cold, frozen landscape around us was jumping on my last but one nerve. Not quite the last because that was reserved. For what exactly? I wasn't sure. But the instinct I'd learned to heed told me save that last nerve.

Because I'd be needing it sooner rather than later?

Shame I didn't listen to that caution twenty-odd years

ago, back when I'd needed it most. If I had, my life would've been oh, so different than it was now.

You sure about that? You think escaping your destiny would've been that easy?

I ignored the cynical voice in my head that sounded eerily like my mother's and narrowed my eyes at the small gathering.

Larry, my normally unflappable project manager, was positively quaking. And it had nothing to do with the freezing wind blowing off the frozen Alaskan lake we currently stood on.

I discarded my coffee and forced my limbs to move, swearing for the umpteenth time to fire my stylist the moment I returned to London. Despite the five-thousand-dollar insulated winter gear she'd sworn high and low would keep me warm and toasty, I was freezing. And I was most definitely not in a mood for temperamental Nordic men whose broad shoulders looked as though they'd been hewn from the very glacier I stood on.

'Problem?' I asked as I approached.

Jensen Scott turned.

And every single one of Elsa's proclamations zinged off in my brain.

Fuck-me eyes. Tick.

I was hit with a set of eyes so glacial and blue and transparent, the hard kick to my gut took me by surprise.

Killer jawline. Tick.

His square jaw looked sharp and solid and chiselled

enough to cut diamonds, despite being covered in a dusting of dark blond stubble and snow flecks.

Fuck-me body. Tick.

Even under several layers of insulation, the Viking-god build of the man was unmistakeable. His shoulders went on for ever, as did his rangy torso and tree-trunk legs.

The *fuck-me hair* I couldn't verify on account of the snow-white beanie covering him from forehead to nape. Not many guys managed to pull off a beanie. Jensen Scott managed to pull it off with extra aplomb.

Suck-me lips.

My own addendum to Elsa's list.

Tick.

A thinner upper and slightly overfull lower, his mouth was the perfect ingredient for wet-making sex fantasies. The kind you could imagined latched onto your clit for hours while his tongue went to work.

A flash of heat blazed through me, welcome only because of its life-saving purposes. The rest of it— that sweet sting to my clit, that plumping of my labia, the slow slide of hot liquid I hadn't felt in a while and almost convinced myself had become unimportant—I intended to ignore the same way I'd been ignoring the demands of my libido for the better part of a year. It wasn't worth it any longer to go against what I'd denied for the better part of a decade. What I now knew went deeper than a mere proclivity—my utter and unapologetic need for complete control. A hunger I'd attempted to feed with the wrong men and the wrong choices until I'd decided, no more.

Those eyes that looked as if they were sparked with sky and snow narrowed at me. 'And you are?'

I chose not to be offended. Hell, I was even a little glad to not be instantly recognised. 'I'm in charge here,' I stated.

To his credit, he didn't do that subtle double-take some men did when confronted with a woman in charge. Nor did he look to Larry for verification. He simply accepted my word, even while his nostrils flared with his displeasure.

'The problem is that Larry here has been less than candid with me, haven't you, sir?' he accused. His deep, low voice held the faintest Scandinavian accent, probably from his Danish motherland. The kind that made my ears prickle with a need to hear him speak more, just so I could hear the inflexions in that beautifully modulated accent.

Or perhaps it was that *sir*?

I kicked myself into touch, tightened my hold on control before even the mere *idea* of indulging in scandalous thoughts strayed into my consciousness.

'How exactly have you been deceived?' I pressed.

I trusted Larry implicitly. He'd been with me almost from the beginning of what had been a throwaway job cobbled together by my family to shut me up. A project they'd hoped would occupy my time and stop me demanding an active seat in the boardroom. Little had they known that I would breathe my very life into it until it was an equal force in its own right on the Mortimer Group business radar.

That the award-winning charitable foundation *Fortune 500* companies clamoured to be a part of and the associated *Mortimer Quarterly* magazine named the number one for three years running would become an integral part of the family company.

These days I turned away more requests from family members eager to promote their own sectors of the family business almost as much as I turned away other public business requests.

In content and advertisement alone, the magazine was scheduled almost twelve months in advance. Which was why nothing could be allowed to get in the way of its smooth running.

Not even the man lauded as a genius with a camera. The man currently casting a disdainful eye over the assembled crew, the two heavy-duty glacier helicopters standing two hundred feet away waiting to transport us away from this beautiful-but-deadly frozen tundra once we were done, and the half-dozen tents set up around the camp, before meeting mine.

His eyes lingered a second or two longer, a touch of sensual awareness stealing into his face when his gaze dropped to my mouth. And stayed.

Two of the huskies began yapping at each other. A sharp whistle from Jensen silenced them immediately. He blinked and shifted his gaze, and that tight little frisson of awareness dissipated. 'This isn't what I signed up for.'

'Let me get this straight. You turn up an hour late only to inform me that you won't be doing the job you've been contracted to do?'

Everyone around us grew still.

'I despise subterfuge, Miss…what did you say your name was?'

'I'm Graciela Mortimer.' I held out my hand.

Recognition finally dawned as he slowly tugged off his thick glove. His gaze left my face, travelled down my body to my feet before rising again. His large hand engulfed mine and his expression heated up by a degree or two. Not the kind of instant appreciation I was used to but even that sent another spark of awareness through me. Drew my attention back to those lips. To everything I would've let myself imagine they could do. If I were interested.

Which I most definitely was not, I told myself, ignoring the slight surge of disappointment when he dropped my hand and tugged his glove back on.

'Miss Mortimer. I wasn't aware you would be here.' His tone suggested what most did. That the Ice Princess of Charity only got involved with her work when it was time to throw another gala to raise money for her various causes. That, like most, he also believed not every project I put my name to was mine from inception to execution. That I merely *dabbled* until boredom led me elsewhere.

I glanced at Larry, who was writhing in discomfort. 'I know you've been dealing with Larry, but I'd appreciate you explaining to me what exactly is going on here. What exactly were you told?'

'I was led to believe this would be a *wildlife* shoot.'

His emphasis didn't go unnoticed.

'And that's exactly what it is.'

His eyes narrowed. 'Excuse me, but if that's the case, why do I see two helicopters and supermodels and stylists all around me? I'm not sure what your definition of wildlife is, but it's certainly not supermodels in the wild.'

That untamed urge rose, the one I'd been fighting to tamp down or ignore for most of my life. The need to put him in his place in a way he would never forget. To have him on his knees. To *dominate…*

I chose a different route. 'Like it or not, beauty sells, Mr Scott. Each of those models you object to is attached to a company and an article in my magazine that seeks to promote awareness of global warming. And while you might find it distasteful, together with the Mortimer Group, we're raising almost a billion dollars for the cause. Surely the ultimate goal is what matters in the end?'

'No, it's not. Because all this—' he cast a wide, irate arm at the crew '—does nothing but disturb the very wildlife you claim you're here to protect.'

Irritation swelled to annoyance. 'My people did their research and chose the course that would have minimal impact on this location. Had you turned up when you were supposed to an hour ago—'

'It wouldn't have changed a thing. Bears. Seals. Melting glaciers. The occasional bald or golden eagle if you're lucky. That's what Larry hired me to photograph. And I was late because the huskies needed a rest. Four of them are in training, a process which requires patience and time. Not unlike the very wildlife you're here for. Turning up an hour ago wouldn't have been a guarantee of a wildlife sighting. Especially not with the kind of commotion you and your crew are creating.'

Again, my gaze flicked to Larry. He avoided my gaze, confirming that something had gone seriously wrong, somewhere.

'Excuse me, Mr Scott. I need a word with my PM.'

Jensen Scott held my gaze for several seconds, then he nodded and strode several steps away. Again, that urge fizzled, alerting me to the fact that it was merely dormant, not dead. I pushed it away and focused on Larry.

'I'm sorry, Gracie,' he blurted before I could speak. 'All the guys I interviewed either didn't come close to what we wanted or were booked months in advance. I heard on the grapevine that Scott had a very rare cancellation and I—'

'You thought you'd lie your way into signing him?'

He grimaced. 'I didn't think he'd object this strongly. After all, he did the thing with the Danish royal family and a few high-profile people recently—'

'We've known each other for almost ten years, Larry. That's the only reason I'm not firing you on the spot. Pull another stunt like this and it'll be your last. Are we clear?'

He paled further, then nodded gruffly before glancing over to where Jensen was petting one of his huskies.

He murmured to the dog and the creature responded with rapt adoration. The few words that drifted over in the chilled breeze didn't sound like English.

'Do you think he'll stay?' Larry asked. 'Do you want me to—?'

'No.' My objection emerged much stronger than I'd anticipated. 'I'll deal with Mr Scott. Just alert the crew that there might be a change of plans.'

He nodded immediately, his certainty that I'd get what I wanted infusing me with confidence as I approached Jensen.

Sensing my approach, he straightened and speared me with those glacial eyes. 'Well?'

I shrugged. 'It does appear a few…liberties were assumed about your hiring.'

His lips firmed, but he didn't reply.

'So, what will it take for you to stay?'

Something glinted in his eyes. Something that tugged at a vicious need inside me. Then he shook his head. 'Nothing. I would never have signed up for this.'

I swallowed a swell of irritation. 'Seriously? You're that opposed to what I'm doing?'

'Not what you're doing. Just the way you're going about it.'

Patience. Don't lose your shit on him.

'There are sixteen-wheelers trundling along the highways of this state every hour of every day of the year so deeper mines can be excavated and more oil can be drilled. Amongst other things. And you have a problem with a twenty-four-hour shoot over a small area to bring more awareness to a growing problem? A shoot that you've delayed by turning up late, I might add.'

He shrugged, his lips twitching as if he wanted to smile before he grew serious. 'I have a problem with those trucks too. And the mining and drilling, if that makes you feel better.'

'Let's talk hypothetically. Or better… I'll give you one minute to pitch me your version of how this would go if you were in charge.'

Perhaps it was a trick of the light. Perhaps I was imagining it. Or perhaps that lance of searing aware-ness that tunnelled through me was really a result of that look I'd caught on his face. The look that tugged at that desperate need again. The one that said were I to put him on his knees, Jensen Scott wouldn't mind. That perhaps he would even…welcome it?

My heart leapt, even as I tried to throttle down its wild sprint. What if my instinct was wrong? It wouldn't be the first time I'd misjudged a potential suitor. Wouldn't be the first time I'd wholeheartedly trusted my instinct only to end up with ashes.

Still… I stared at him. Watched his face tighten with rejection. But not before I caught a look that treacher-ously resembled…*longing*.

Perhaps longing he resented me for?

He turned away, breaking eye contact to lean down to pet the nearest husky. 'I'd pick one person to be the face of your campaign. Find a way to feature every-one else in another capacity. Your cause might mean something to every one of your crew, but they don't all need to be here to make it count. One person can represent a million.'

For some reason his sound argument made my mouth dry, my heart beat just a touch faster. 'And who would you pick—again, if you were in charge?'

This time I saw a tangible reaction to my deliberate choice of words. His jaw clenched, his nostrils thinning. 'You want to make an impact. Pick the person who has the biggest voice.' He stared at me in that direct and pointed way that left me in no doubt *who* he meant.

'Me.'

He shrugged. 'You decide.' Glacial eyes met mine. 'I'm not in charge.' *You are.*

It was a silent gauntlet thrown at my feet. A brief relinquishing of his control as his eyes deliberately dropped.

Was this a *test*? Would he dare?

Something heavy and profound unfurled inside me, threatening to unleash that forbidden yearning I'd kept in chains. Again, he turned away, this time to check the reins attached to his sled.

Look at me when I'm talking to you.

I bit back the words, took a steadying breath. 'I've spent a considerable amount of time and money to make this shoot happen. Leaving empty-handed would make me very unhappy.'

He tensed for a moment, but he didn't look up.

My heart beat faster. 'Do you want me to be disappointed, Mr Scott?'

'Jensen,' he offered with a low but distinct rasp, still without looking at me. 'Call me Jensen.'

A surge of blood roaring in my ears made me dizzy for a moment. Then a peculiar elation rushed through my veins. One I desperately wanted to deny but found I wasn't quite ready to. Not just yet. Not until I was absolutely sure this man who effortlessly blended into this landscape as if born to it was what...*who* my instincts were screaming him to be.

A submissive.

'Here's what I'm going to do. I'm going to send everyone but the most essential crew away. And you're going to stay and deliver the shoot you promised me.'

He stopped toying with the reins and turned around. When his gaze met mine, his face was carefully neutral, making me doubt my instinct. 'You don't have the right equipment to travel over long distances and different terrain. Your PM was very vague with my agent—now I know why. I came here to find out more about what you need from me...from this project before I started. Even with what you deem an essential crew, you'll have to wait for more sleds to arrive from Utqiagvik. That'll take the better part of half a day.'

I raised my eyebrows as, for whatever reason, my heart banged even harder against my ribs. 'So you're suggesting no crew at all?'

'At the most, I can make room for one more on the sled. Any more means more weight on the sleds and more weight for huskies to pull.'

Just you and me... 'You want me to stay here on my own. With you?'

His eyes glinted before they blinked back into careful neutrality. 'Have you been keeping an eye on the weather reports?'

Someone on my crew had. 'Of course.'

He looked sceptical. 'Then you'll know that in less than three days' time the sun will set for the next couple of months. Today and tomorrow are your only chances to get the variety of photographs you want.' He waited a couple of beats, no doubt for his words to sink in. Then he took a breath. 'What's it to be, Miss Mortimer?'

Call me Graciela.

It was an automatic invitation to new acquaintances and potential donors. *Call me Graciela* was so I wouldn't be reminded that I was a Mortimer. That the blood of an unfeeling, dysfunctional dynasty ran through my veins. It reminded me of the many times I'd attempted to correct that dysfunction, when I thought I knew better, believed I was different. A misguided, cruelly awakening time I would wipe my brain clean of if I could.

The words hovered on my lips but never emerged.

Because I wanted clear, definitive boundaries between myself and this man.

Boundaries I was curious to see whether he would breach. Whether he would prove me wrong.

Or...*right*.

Dangerous, forbidden boundaries. The kind that had

the power to wreck my sleep, turn my daydreams inside out with dark yearning.

'Larry,' I called out without taking my eyes off Jensen. His gaze stayed on my face, dropped to my mouth for a charged moment before returning to mine.

I heard Larry hurry over. 'Gracie?'

'Tell the crew to pack up.'

'We're leaving?' The disappointment in Larry's voice was distinct.

I gave a single shake of my head. 'Everyone else is. I'm staying.'

'Oh? For how long?'

'As long as it takes. What will I need, Mr Scott?'

He didn't correct me this time or invite me to use his given name. 'I have a satellite phone, but if you wish to keep yours, two is better than one. A couple of changes of clothes, in case you get wet.'

'Food? Water?'

He shook his head. 'I have enough to get us through the day.' A hint of hard smile tilted the corners of his lips. 'Be warned, it's more utilitarian than gourmet.'

I let the mild insult bounce off me. If my instinct was correct, he'd learn his lesson soon enough. 'I can rough it for a day or two without expiring from the horror of it all.' I looked past him to the covered trailer attached to his sled. 'Speaking of roughing it, where will I be sleeping?' Thoughts of my warm hotel suite back in Anchorage filled me with longing for a short moment before I pushed them away.

Did he just swallow? 'I have a tent if we decide to

stop for the night. Or my cabin is a couple of hours' sled ride away.'

Larry cleared his throat. I glanced at him to find him frowning. 'Are you…you're really staying here on your own?'

The veiled *'Are you mad?'* in his tone drew equal amounts of irritation and amusement. But more than that, it drew intrigue and possibilities directed at the man standing tall and delicious in front of me. Twin emotions I hadn't allowed myself to experience in a long time. Because inevitably both had led to painful disappointment.

'There's a chance to salvage something from this debacle. Or would you rather I scrap it and call it a failure?' I asked Larry.

'Of course not. I just meant…' He paused, casting a dark glance at Jensen.

'I think your PM is worried about your safety,' Jensen said with a trace of amusement.

I didn't smile back. I was a Mortimer after all. And as with most individuals with nine or more zeros attached to their bank balances, I'd been at the receiving end of a few security scares. I couldn't afford to be blasé about it, even in an icy wilderness like Alaska. 'Should he be?' I tossed at him.

Every trace of humour vanished. 'I won't let any harm come to you. You have my word.'

For a taut stretch our gazes locked, unspoken words arcing between us. 'Instruct the crew,' I told Larry without taking my eyes off Jensen. 'No need to freeze here if you don't have to. Tell Elsa to pack me a change of clothes and get going. I'll check in tonight.'

He knew better than to argue with me. Barely ten minutes later the small camp was all packed up and aboard the helicopters.

The apprehension I should've felt at being alone with this…captivating stranger was curiously absent as I watched my crew leave. Behind me, Jensen stashed my bag under the tarp covering the trailer then approached. I didn't look his way as he stopped next to me.

'I spotted a mother bear and her cubs feeding about half an hour from here near a broken ice floe. We can start there if you want?'

I shifted my gaze from watching the choppers turn into dark specks in the sky. 'You've had that information since you got here and chose not to share it?'

He shrugged, drawing my attention to one broad shoulder. 'It wouldn't have helped if you hadn't been inclined to see things my way. In the time it would've taken to gather your crew to get there, they'd have been gone.'

Neat answer while delivering the punch he no doubt intended to. 'You don't think very highly of me, do you?' There was a distinct sting to that knowledge, one quite different from the dull throb of pain I'd experienced over decades of holding my emotions inside.

'I don't know you. I'm only going on what I've seen so far.'

'Are you? Then why do I get the impression you've already made up your mind about me? Is it perhaps because you believe you *know* me despite us having only just met?'

'Are you accusing me of something, Miss Mortimer?'

I studied the profile he insisted on presenting to me. There was a tightness around his mouth and jaw that spoke to more than the face-value conversation taking place. 'Yes, I am.'

His delicious lips pursed for a second. Then he exhaled. 'The dogs are rested; we can probably make it in time if we leave now.'

'Aren't you going to ask me what I'm accusing you of?'

His gaze finally turned my way, and the endless depth of icy emotion swimming within nearly made me sway. 'No. My statement goes both ways. You don't know me either, so whatever you think of me is most likely flawed.'

'Ah. So that's how we're going to proceed, is it?' I asked softly. But he caught the steel I hadn't disguised. 'First, we skirt each other warily, assessing weaknesses before we land the first punch?'

This time his lips twisted in a cynical twitch. 'I'm sure you have far better things to do than to waste time delving into what makes me tick.'

His tone suggested he applied a very heavy vice versa to his statement. And despite the icy weather, my blood heated up. I reined in sweet, exhilarating control with a subtle clench of my fingers.

'You're right. But I wouldn't have needed the time anyway. I know exactly who you are, Mr Scott.' This time the gleam in his eyes was fairly mocking. But before he could tailor words to that look, I added, 'And I also know exactly *what* you are.'

The gleam faded as if extinguished, his face settling into an inscrutable mask. And even though his gaze stayed on mine, everything about him bristled with restlessness. An almost visceral need to...*deny*.

Except he couldn't. Not without denying a vital part of himself. Not without perhaps...letting himself down? But he strained against exposing his true self to me until his struggle was as real as the snow beneath his feet.

God, what had happened to him?

An equally visceral need to know attacked me, punching right through my defences to that secret vault I'd sealed shut once and for all.

Five seconds ticked by. Ten.

After twenty, his head snapped forward, his jaw jutting out with aggression that spoke of his turmoil. An aggression I wanted to wield beneath my fingers. To test and twist and mould into something sublime.

My breath shuddered out, astonishment at my train of thought nearly overwhelming me.

'The day needn't be wasted. Or we can waste time and your money on a hypothesis that leads nowhere.'

I allowed myself a small laugh, saw a slight tensing of a different kind in his frame as he heard it. 'My hypothesis is definitely leading somewhere. Otherwise why else would you be so wound up? But by all means let's change the subject.' I waved a hand at the vast white tundra. 'Take me to your mama bear, Mr Scott.'

CHAPTER TWO

SHE WAS A SPOILT, overindulged princess.

The kind who watched a few episodes of a reality show about surviving in the wilds of Alaska and suddenly decided they wanted to *dabble in nature*. The type who got it into their heads that stroking a seal or two and posting a selfie with the Arctic wildlife or atop the odd ice floe automatically granted them environmental activist status.

I didn't need to look back at where she was perched on the sled behind me to visualise her clutching her collar, grimacing at the intensifying wind. I was surprised she hadn't whipped out her sleek satellite phone and ordered her chopper to come pick her up.

The bear family might have moved in the time she'd been ordering her staff about.

The time she'd spent *analysing* me with those stunning hazel eyes, deciding whether to toy with me or not.

Muscles jumped in my stomach. As hard as I tried to ignore the sensation, what I'd seen in her hooded, sultry eyes still sent fresh waves of apprehension through me. Not the kind that had anything to do with the work she'd hired me for. That I could do with one hand tied behind my back and one eye closed.

No, the kind of sensation that look had elicited… that fucking *craving*.

I shook my head, partly to clear it, partly in denial. *Dammit, she'd seen it. Then she'd spotted my efforts at denial…*

I gritted my teeth and unnecessarily flicked the reins attached to the dogs. The huskies were highly trained, would respond to the softest whistle or voice command, which made the reins largely superfluous.

Or, hell, was that particular symbolism for me? Was I so hard up, I was now expressing myself through my bloody dogs?

Dammit.

I didn't need this. I should've left Graciela Mortimer's little ice circus the moment I confirmed her project manager had lied to my agent in order to secure my services.

More than any other flaw, *I hated lies*. And the people who told them.

Large. Medium. Tiny white lies. Every single one of them came with wrecking balls that altered lives, changed the dynamics of relationships, no matter how much we fooled ourselves into believing otherwise.

How many had my mother told my sister and me in order to avoid facing the glaring truth?

I'm all right. It doesn't hurt. He'll change. And the worst lie of them all: *he loves us.*

Even before my fifth birthday, I'd known that statement for a lie. And for the decade after that, that fabrication had been exposed time and again until, like poisonous acid, it'd begun to erode my relationship with my mother.

Of course, I knew now it'd been her way of coping, the delusion her own form of security blanket. Hadn't I risked falling into that same pattern of delusion until I'd wised up as a grown man? Hadn't I made allowances for Stephanie's lies just to hang on to what I thought was a solid relationship, all the while knowing that trust, once broken with lies, never—

'How close are we, Mr Scott?'

Of course her voice would have to melt my insides. Visions of heated honey…no, more like the anticipation of watching melted wax in the moment before it hit my skin. The sharp burn before the breathless, sizzling warmth.

That was what Graciela Mortimer's voice had evoked the moment she'd spoken the words *I'm in charge*.

Lort!

I should've left after imparting my thoughts on what she was proposing to do. Which would've been easy considering I hadn't wanted to do this gig anyway. Regardless of the fact that my own company had been driving me insane. Regardless of the fact that I hated myself a little for not being able to stay the course of what was left of my month-long self-imposed hermitage.

I should've left.

Instead, here I was, secretly yearning to hear that

voice again. To do that, though, I'd have to engage her in conversation.

'Ten more minutes. Give or take,' I threw over my shoulder. The GPS co-ordinates I'd noted on my watch would see us there in less time, but I'd learned to make allowances on unknown terrain.

Silence greeted me. Against my will, I looked over my shoulder.

Despite the stylish shades covering her eyes, I felt her gaze boring into mine with unapologetic direct-ness that tunnelled lightning straight into my veins. It singed me into life, making me aware of every inch of my skin, and especially the rush of blood to my groin.

This was why I hadn't walked away.

Yet.

'Give or take what?' she asked with a slight arch of a silky eyebrow.

Good question. My sanity? Another sign that my screaming instincts were right? That she wasn't merely toying with me?

But fuck, where the hell did I get off trusting my in-stincts when they'd let me down spectacularly so very recently with Stephanie?

'Mr Scott, while I have a thing for the strong, silent type…on occasion, this isn't one of them. I will need you to actually engage with me here.'

The dry amusement in her tone should've raised my hackles further. And yet it drew a wry smile. And what was it with that *Mr Scott* when I'd invited her to use my first name?

Perhaps because she didn't need invitation. *She commands it.*

My senses jumped, dark need clamouring through me so hard every inch of my body tightened with anticipation.

Futile anticipation. I had no intention of even probing possibilities. Not after the fucking fiasco with Stephanie.

There was a reason I'd retreated to my remote cabin in Alaska. A reason I'd welcomed the last-minute cancellation to my tight work schedule. When it came right down to it, the need to escape my thoughts and immerse myself in my work were the reason I'd grudgingly accepted what I thought would be a solo assignment.

Which was why I should've left Graciela Mortimer where I found her.

'We're here.' I tugged on the reins with a sharp whistle and the dogs immediately slowed to a stop.

The mother and her three cubs were still on the large floe about a quarter of a mile away, finishing off the last of a fish meal. One of the dogs barked and the mother bear raised her head warily, eyeing us from across the distance.

I sensed Graciela approach, felt her invasive presence when she stopped next to me. The very fact that my every sense clamoured to look into those hazel eyes once more made me avoid her gaze.

'Are they… We're not disturbing them too much, are we?'

The question was soft enough to have fooled me had

I not witnessed the circus I'd convinced her to dispatch. 'Do you care?'

Stephanie would've inhaled sharply at such a blunt question, then, depending on whether she was in her false role or not, would've delivered icy condemnation or tears on command.

Graciela met my question with another imperious lift of her brow and a steady regard when I flicked a glance her way. 'You really don't like me, do you?'

There was another hint of a smile in the question, a suggestion that she didn't care either way. It should've confirmed every impression I'd had of her. Instead, it disconcerted me. Did my opinion of her count so very little?

'You don't care whether I do or not so why bother asking?' I countered.

Her sigh was long and exaggerated, another indication that she found me…vastly amusing. That she could grind me underneath those expensive snow boots she was wearing without a second thought.

Just as Stephanie had believed she could.

Another spoilt little rich girl, this one with a few billion to play with, who believed she could buy anything and anyone in sight.

More than a little vexed that I couldn't detach as easily as I'd hoped from the events of the past few months, I headed for the sled, pulled back the tarp and lifted out my treasured camera and slotted a fifty-millimetre lens to it to capture the close-ups I wanted to start off with.

'You want shots for the print magazine and videos for the digital version, correct?'

'If it's not too much to ask, yes.' Again she sounded amused.

And I couldn't help it. I paused in the process of unscrewing the lens cap and looked her way to find her glasses sitting on top of her head and her stunning eyes fixed on me.

Not a single picture I'd seen of the heiress had done her justice. She had a face that just begged to be photographed. As for her body, despite being under wraps from neck to toe, I'd seen enough pictures of her in the glossy rags Steph used to devour to know just what was beneath the outfit.

Graciela was taller than average for a woman but even though she only reached my shoulder she seemed...taller.

Larger than life.

But while I wanted to believe it was mostly entitlement—because, let's face it, that shone from her eyes and bristled from every pore—there was more. Which again made sense, since she was the very definition of a wild child and went out of her way to prove it with her various antics.

Skydiving in nothing but a string bikini over Rio.

A three-day sex party with a premier league soccer team in a hotel in Mali.

The rumours that she kept a string of lovers across the globe...

The icy wilderness landscape of Alaska was the last

place I'd expected her to turn up, thinking she, like Steph, was the kind to leave all the hard work she'd later take credit for to her minions.

I finished adjusting the exposure to compensate for the darkening sky and took an initial short burst of photos of the polar bear family. Then I swapped the lens for a sixteen-millimetre, for wide-angle shots, and took another burst.

Surprisingly, she remained quiet throughout, didn't fill the silence with mindless chatter, which I appreciated.

'Can the cubs swim at their age?' she asked when I lowered the camera after five minutes.

'If they're more than a few months old, yes, for short periods. But with more distances between icy landscapes some bears have been seen swimming with their young on their backs.'

She nodded, her gaze on the ice floe. 'Is it dangerous for them?' she asked.

'Danger comes from all angles in this environment. This is a slow-moving floe and surrounded by frozen land on three sides. The mother would be on the lookout to ensure they don't drift too far.'

'That's great, but it's moving...towards us.'

I curbed a smile as I swapped cameras and grabbed a tripod to set up more stills. 'We'll be gone before it gets to us.'

She nodded again, but her gaze grew speculative, shifting from the bears to the other floes. They varied in size from a few metres to ones the size of football fields, all broken away from the mass that would normally have stayed solid well into the new year.

'Can I get a short video of the floes, too?'

'Sure.'

She didn't interrupt or badger me with questions once I got into the flow of things. Hell, she even took herself off a short distance away, taking out her phone to take pictures of the distant Alaskan Range and the beginning of the spectacular orange on white sunsets that graced this stunning part of the world.

She returned in time to witness the bears' floe touch another one and the mother supervising her cubs jumping from their floating platform onto a larger one.

With one last warning look over her shoulder, the mother bear escorted her cubs away towards a jagged mountain peak.

'How long before they go into hibernation?'

'Another two or three weeks.'

She frowned. 'They don't look nearly padded up enough.'

I shrugged. 'Probably because they have to travel farther distances to feed.'

As if on cue, a loud, sharp crack sounded. Camera poised, I swung around in time to capture the towering wall of ice break away from a glacier to crash into the lake.

The sound seemed to echo for ever, bouncing off the icy landscape in perfect surround sound. Beside me, Graciela gave a soft gasp. 'God. That's…'

I lowered the camera and glanced at her. 'It's breathtaking and awe-inspiring until you remember that it shouldn't be happening?'

Her face shuttered, her brows creasing in a frown.

I wasn't sure whether she didn't like that being pointed out or whether she didn't want to admit she was affected by what was unfolding before her eyes. Wasn't she here after all because money had been thrown at her charity by people who could afford to contribute ten times more?

'Do you want to be included in the video?' I asked.

She remained silent for several seconds, then shook her head. 'I'll let the environment speak for itself.'

I throttled back my surprise. She'd just passed up the perfect opportunity to get in front of the camera. A camera manned by me. According to my agent, her PM hadn't shied away from tossing his boss's name into their phone conversations at every opportunity in an attempt to sway me. While I knew now he'd bent the truth to suit his purposes, I also knew most people wouldn't pass up an opportunity to be photographed by Jensen Scott.

I came within a whisker of being impressed before I reminded myself this was just the beginning. Women like Graciela Mortimer wouldn't overplay their hand with over-eagerness. If anything, she'd expect *me* to talk her into it.

She'd be waiting a long time for that. I ignored her, shooting a three-minute video in sharp focus, the white landscape capturing the stark story.

'Are you ready to go?' I asked once the echoes had receded and the equipment was packed away.

She nodded. 'Where to next?' she asked briskly.

'Depends. Do you want to show all the gloom or is your piece aimed towards reminding people of the glory too?'

'The aim is for more shock than awe but I'd like to use the time efficiently. So whatever's closest.'

'How about we kill two birds with one stone, so to speak?'

'As figures of speech go, I wouldn't have reached for that one. And for some reason I think you wouldn't have either. Now I'm totally convinced you're trying to get a rise out of me, Mr Scott.'

I was, and a small part of me cringed at the pettiness. 'It's Jensen.'

Again, one corner of her mouth tilted, drawing my gaze to the overfull lower lip. Its juicy plumpness and far too lickable curve. Almost in slow, torturous motion, a perfect picture slid into my brain of those lips wrapped around my cock, drawing sweet torment with every suck. I didn't have a single doubt that Graciela would know just how to suck me off. She was far too confident in her femininity not to be an expert in all things coitus.

'Is it?' she taunted in answer to my offer.

I might have been attempting to rile her, but she was having a ball reciprocating.

'Is there a reason you refuse to use my first name?'

'I think we both know why.'

Why the hell was this friction turning me on? This wasn't the type of interaction that got me off. 'Look, I think we got off on the wrong foot—'

'No. I think we got off on the exact right foot. I remind you of the baggage you're attempting to shed by running off and hiding in the icy wilderness next to the Arctic Circle, and you don't like it.'

Anger fired up inside me, even while I was thrown by her near-accuracy. 'I'm not running anywhere,' I bit out.

'Aren't you? Sorry, my bad.'

I snapped the tarp over the equipment with more force than necessary. 'You don't sound sorry at all.'

She shrugged. 'I'll work on my sincerity while we head for wherever you're taking me next. Shall we?'

We stared each other down, with the friction and tension increasing with every moment that ticked by.

I'd had enough of that with Stephanie, each moment with her spent on the uncertain edge of judging a mood that could veer from icy indifference to volcanic.

Walk away.

The faster I completed this assignment, the quicker I could be rid of Graciela and the unsettling emotions she evoked.

Slowly, as if she'd read my intentions, her expression changed to one of steady assessment tinged with boredom.

Absurdly, that only riled me further, the need to ruffle feathers she'd effectively smoothed with a dismissive thought firing through me.

'You get a kick out of being contrary?'

She shrugged. 'Maybe. Or perhaps you simply don't like the truth pointed out to you. Either way, we can still talk while we...sled. Is that what you call it?' She gestured at the animals.

'You know exactly what it's called,' I replied, noting absently that my heart was beating faster, my senses more fired up than they had been in weeks. 'Pretending you're less intelligent than you actually are may be a turn-on for other men. Not me.'

'And you think that's what I'm trying to achieve here? To turn you on?'

God, the way she said that, with the exact cadence engineered to stroke my cock. Did she practise it to get that perfect degree of hotness and craving?

I had a feeling she knew the exact effect she and her voice were having on me.

'I don't think you utter a single word or make a move without calculating the exact effect you wish to achieve.'

Like a switch her expression grew icy, her eyes dimming to a dull brown before she blinked and cast a disdainful glance at a spot over my shoulder.

I'd struck a nerve. For a moment I wanted to take back my words, but then I wanted to know just what I'd done. To explore that nerve, get to know it better. So I might know this woman better?

She's only here for another day. You don't move in the same circles so if you don't want to, you won't need to see her ever again.

That thought...dissatisfied. I wanted to know Graciela. If for nothing else, to satisfy myself that my instincts weren't wrong about her. That my craving was misplaced. That she was another wannabe, unworthy of the name...

Dominant.

My senses jumped. Harder than before, my gaze falling once more to those biteable lips. To her clothes and what lay beneath. To how it would feel to receive her command to unwrap her, lay my hands on her bare skin, feel her silky pulse jump beneath my touch. Hear her voice hitch with arousal as she revelled in controlling my every desire.

Even if it was a matter of losing myself in a woman just for the hell of it, with no agenda or deeper meaning, I was up for that.

'I don't believe I'm paying you to stand around and work out my IQ, Mr Scott.'

Keep your money. This one's on the house.

I swallowed the words. I was richer than I'd be able to spend in one lifetime, courtesy of a life-changing photograph taken on a faraway continent. I'd been doing well before the photo that had propelled me to fame and fortune had set me up for life. I didn't need her money, true. But I suspected a gesture like that would impress her even less. Not that I was out to impress her. And really, why the hell would I want to cut my nose to spite my face?

More axioms, Jensen?

I cursed the mocking voice and gestured at her to get back on the sled.

Disdain and designer sunglasses firmly in place, she hopped back into her seat.

The next destination was forty minutes' sled ride away and, save for a quick stop to water the dogs, we completed it in silence.

Killik Falls was a natural waterfall cascading from a tiny blue lake cradled in one of the many glaciers situated between Prudhoe Bay and Utqiagvik. The sight of the blue water bursting through a wall of ice was a stunning phenomenon, a fact evidenced by Graciela's gasp when I pulled the sled to a stop near a flat plateau on one of the glaciers.

'Wow, that's breathtaking.'

I let out a relieved breath, noting annoyingly that I'd hoped the sight would please her as much as it'd pleased me the first time I saw it. 'Yeah.'

She stepped off the sled, sliding off her shades to get a closer look. When she glanced at me there was only curiosity in her eyes. 'It all looks great. So why here?'

'It should've frozen over two months ago.'

Her face cleared, leaving behind a solemn look. 'Ah. I see.' She took in the snow-dusted fauna around the lake while I took out my equipment. 'How long has that been happening?'

'Steadily for the past ten years.'

Her lips tightened, but she didn't answer, her gaze flitting over the landscape to pause thoughtfully on the waterfall. 'That's…disturbing.'

Suddenly, I didn't want to film the waterfall. I wanted

to capture her reaction, the way the failing light teased shadows and light over her features.

She would be an interesting subject to photograph. My fingers clenched around the camera, the insane urge to aim my lens at her, zoom in close and catch every emotion, swelling higher with each moment. It grew strong enough to zap alarm through me.

'Perhaps we should get on with it?'

I didn't reply. Wasn't sure I wanted to interact with her while in the throes of…whatever this was. Instead, I went to work, getting a vast array of shots so I didn't miss a thing. When I was satisfied, I put my equipment away and glanced at my watch.

'Gloom or glory?' I asked. I had a site for either in mind I could squeeze in tonight, and her brief had called for five location shoots. While the cracking glacier earlier had been a bonus, I was technically required to do three more. I glanced over at her, caught the shiver she tried to hide. 'Or are you ready to call it a day?'

Her gaze shifted to the covered equipment at the back of the sled. 'Did I spot a tent in there?'

I frowned, inexplicably tensing. 'Yes. Why do you ask?'

'Did you plan on spending the night on the snow?'

'Not tonight.' And certainly not with her in tow. The last thing I needed was her kind of distraction.

'When?' she pressed.

'At some point. When you're not here,' I added pointedly.

Again she surprised me by smiling where I'd expected her to be offended. She approached, not stopping until our bodies were six inches apart.

'Guess what my favourite game is, Mr Scott,' she murmured, her voice low, husky and sensually loaded enough to achieve its aim of curling tight around my cock.

'Winding people up?'

'Wrong,' she breathed. 'That's my *second* favourite. My first is Tug of War. Care to know my percentage on wins?'

'Sure. Enlighten me.'

She leaned up and in, until our condensed breaths mingled. And fuck if that didn't heat my blood. 'It's high, Mr Scott. *Very* high.'

'Very high doesn't mean one hundred per cent. Which means on occasion you lose.'

Her smile widened. 'Perhaps. But you're contractually obliged to give me what I want.'

'Or what? You're going to fire me? I'm the best,' I answered, with a tinge of well-earned arrogance. 'Your PM told you that or you wouldn't have hired me.'

'Nothing as melodramatic as firing you. More along the lines of thinking you wouldn't want to deny a client's reasonable request. Would you?'

'I've yet to hear what this reasonable request is.'

'You want me to spell it out?'

'Just so we're clear, yes.'

'You. Me. In the tent. Tonight. Doing whatever you were planning to do.'

Her words were deliberately phrased to get a rise out

of me. And fuck, did they just. My cock hardened at the imagery, my gaze unable to shift from the perfect curve of her lips. No wonder she had men in a lather all over the globe.

She already had me in a lather, all over the innocuous idea of spending the night in a tent under the Alaskan sky. Time to defuse this before it got out of hand.

'I always travel with a tent. You don't know when the weather will turn. Or when a night shoot will reap rewards.'

'What particular reward were you hoping for?'

I shrugged. 'The forecast is for a clear night. I was hoping to score a borealis on video as part of the project.'

I caught the faintest hitch of her breath. She didn't outwardly show her excitement, but the thought of witnessing an *aurora borealis* was a phenomenon most people rhapsodised over.

She slowly lowered her heels and slipped her shades back on, but even with the shield, I felt the power of her hypnotising stare. 'In that case I'm going to have to insist on staying,' she said after several seconds.

My pulse tripped, then raced at full speed. The thought of spending the long hours of the night with her in a tent, a woman even the most red-blooded alpha males feared, filled me with equal measures of dread and anticipation.

Overlay that with the persistent thought that she could be a Domme…

Again, where I should've refused, I found myself

shrugging, moving to the back of the sled to grab a thicker anorak. Returning to where she stood watching me, I held it out. 'It's a bit of a trek, sometimes over rough terrain. Bumps and bruises are unavoidable but wear this and you won't freeze to death.'

She took the anorak and shrugged it over her suit, then sent me another spine-tingling smile. 'Thanks. And when we arrive at our destination, you can tell me what her name is.'

I froze. 'Excuse me?'

'The name behind the baggage you're running away from. I'm sure she has one. I'd love to hear about her.'

CHAPTER THREE

I WATCHED HIM attend to the dogs, his movements efficient, capable, and yet sexily streamlined in a way that made me want to watch him on an endless loop. Which was absurd in itself, because I was used to beautiful men, wealthy, filthily pampered men who strutted about, cushioned by power and privilege.

Even hardened men like my brothers, Gideon and Bryce, who had been through their own versions of hell and back but had somehow managed to rise above, didn't hold as much interest for me as this man did.

You should've paid more attention, because they both seem to have found answers to love and acceptance that you haven't.

I pushed the thought away, my gaze lingering on Jensen as he petted his dogs, his back turned decidedly on me.

Why was I pursuing this? Why was the urge to needle and probe sliding like a narcotic through my blood? Something about the man had captivated me from the first, even *besides* the strong possibility that he was a sub. While I'd had my own versions of *no* in the past—

my parents delivering the most gut-wrenching one of all—I wasn't sure why this particular reluctance from him made me even more determined.

Determined to do what, precisely?

Exactly how did I expect this to go? I was emotionally bankrupt, according to myriad blood relatives, past lovers and strangers. I had nothing valuable to give, save my money, of course. After years of tossing those opinions away like so much chaff, I had finally been forced by my innate stubbornness to admit that perhaps they—and my mother—were right.

Every relationship was doomed to failure. Hell, even my brothers were avoiding me, my bitterness and emotional inadequacy making them run for the hills rather than spend time with me.

I couldn't even blame them any more. And it certainly didn't help that I was the spitting image of my mother. The mother who'd callously abandoned us decades ago and never looked back.

The urge to grab the satellite phone, summon my helicopter and get the hell off this barren landscape pulled at me.

I reached for the phone just as Jensen rose and pivoted towards me. Thoughts of leaving evaporated. Something about this man captivated me, made me want to dig deeper beneath the thick layer of concrete he wasn't shy about putting up.

I would've admired his resolve, if he hadn't ignored me for the better part of an hour and a half.

We'd arrived at his chosen site twenty minutes ago

and set up camp on a flat landscape with nothing but snow for miles around. Being born into wealth and spending most waking minutes in the lap of luxury where every whim was catered to had inevitably culti-vated healthy jadedness about most things well before I hit my twenties.

But looking around now, I couldn't help but be over-awed by the stunning beauty around me. And as much as I wanted to dismiss it, Jensen was a big part of that draw.

I'd perused his portfolio on the plane ride to Alaska. He was unapologetically talented at his job and had no modesty or pretensions about it. Sure, it grated that he was pretending I didn't exist at the moment. I would've been amused had it not been for the wicked little thrill that tunnelled inside me every time he glanced my way. It pleased me that he was fighting this connection be-tween us. And failing. The man couldn't help but look at me every few minutes.

He hadn't answered my question, though.

His gorgeous face had grown taut and forbidding, warning that my question about who had treated him badly wasn't going to be answered.

Yeah, I'd probably stepped over the line with that one. But, hell, wasn't that one of my many flaws, ac-cording to those who branded themselves experts on me?

I summoned one of my 'ice princess' smiles as he approached. 'Is this going to be an exercise on who blinks first? If so I'm happy to throw in the towel. You don't have to answer the question if you don't want to. I'm happy to let it be.'

He stopped at the entrance of the tent, his gaze pinning me where I sat in the folding chair he'd provided when he'd started setting up the tent. He'd firmly refused my offer of help, a move that'd stung a little more than I cared to admit. So what if I was out of my depth in this whole…snowy outdoors thing, and I'd probably have got in his way more than helped? I could follow instruction. On occasion.

'Are you?' he asked, his voice a little stiff and that edgy look still on his face.

'Not really,' I admitted. 'I still want to know.'

'Why?'

'I'm a hopelessly curious creature, Mr Scott. I can't help but wonder why a man like you would consign himself to this wilderness for weeks on end.'

'And you automatically assume it's because of a woman?'

'Isn't it?'

Something flickered in his eyes, something that sparked a kindred light inside me. One that burned brighter with every second he held my gaze.

'Maybe it was, maybe it wasn't,' he muttered eventually. 'But that's all you're going to get.'

I didn't tell him, of course, that his little addendum had only fuelled the need for satisfaction. That need for resolution born of stubbornness and desperation that had brought me more heartache than I cared to catalogue.

He ducked into the tent, emerging a minute later with a weatherproof bag he set down a dozen feet away. In silence, he lit a camp stove and started dinner. When he handed me a cup of coffee five minutes later, I answered with a smile. He stared down at me for a second longer than necessary before returning to his task.

I sipped the coffee, groaning as the warmth chased away the worst of the cold.

That drew his gaze again, as if he couldn't help himself. I hid a smile and finished my coffee, just as the aroma of pasta carbonara drifted towards me. Jensen dished out two bowls and held one out to me.

'Thank you.'

He nodded, went into the tent and brought out a thick rug, which he tossed onto the ground. Watching him fold his six-foot-plus frame before me, a cross-legged position that placed him at my feet, punched a deep longing that made my breath catch.

Perhaps he was aware of what he'd just done—that right up there on a Dominant's most cherished wish was a willing submissive at their feet—because he froze too, his eyes holding mine for a charged moment before returning to his bowl.

We ate in silence, eerie white darkness gathering around us as night fell and the moon rose.

'Her name is Stephanie,' he volunteered grudgingly.

I nodded, torn between satisfaction that he'd answered of his own free will and a peculiar dart of jealousy that I now had the name of the person who'd contributed to Jensen's wary reserve. I concentrated on eating, attempting to ignore the latter emotion.

'Not going to push for more?' he asked after a long stretch. 'Now you know, you're no longer interested?' he added with a trace of snark.

'You used the present tense just now. I may be many things, but I'm not a woman who encroaches on another woman's territory. Not even to satisfy simple curiosity.' I was lying, of course. I was way more interested than simple curiosity dictated.

'She's no longer in my life. Feel free to encroach away.'

Why did that invitation make my heart jump? Make temptation surge high? 'Are you sure?'

He shrugged.

'Maybe I won't encroach. Maybe I'll simply sit back and savour the mystery of you, like a fine wine.'

The lamps he'd set outside the tent illuminated enough for me to catch the slight flare of his nostrils at my words. The strong movement of his throat as he swallowed.

He wasn't unaffected by me. Far from it. And the longer we stayed out here under the star-dappled sky, for all the world the only two people left on this planet, the more I was tempted to discard the vow I'd made to myself.

The vow of no more relationships.

The vow to focus on the things I could control, like my charity work. So why the next words tripped from my lips, I would never fathom. 'Do you like the idea of being savoured, Jensen?'

He tensed at my use of his name, but it wasn't affront that bristled from him. It was something far more potent. Hot and wicked and carnal, it reached out in the space between us, wrapping itself around us the way only two people dangerously attracted to each other could be affected.

In the silent landscape disturbed only by intermittent faint cracking ice, he stared at me, want and need and lust building in his eyes until his chest rose and fell with rapid rhythms.

Beneath the thermal layers, my skin tightened, heat pooling as my body answered with equal fervour.

But slowly his face hardened again. 'I'm not one of the men you can toy with and discard when it suits you.'

Needles of hurt stung deep. I pushed the sensations away, telling myself it was better this way. Better that he thought he knew enough about me to believe the lies and make judgements for himself. That meant he was interested *despite* his better judgement. That meant neither of us would be seriously invested.

'The last thing I want to do with you is play, believe me.'

His fingers tightened around his bowl, the last bite forgotten. A second later, his jaw gritted. 'My bedpost-notching days are behind me. Sorry.'

'Are we talking about my bed or yours?'

'Yours is purportedly far more interesting than mine.'

This time the grating lingered longer, sharp disappointment lancing me as I stared at his averted profile. 'I'm surprised. I wouldn't have pegged you for a tabloid chaser.'

'I'm not,' he said tightly.

'Really? Because I could've sworn you just judged me by the contents spewed out on a regular basis in gossip rags.'

His gaze returned to mine, digging, attempting to see far more than I was willing to show him. 'I'm an experienced adventurist and can easily prove that there can be the smoke without fire. Is that what you're asking me to believe?'

I could've responded in a great many ways, batted him away with sarcasm and flippancy. But when I opened my mouth, only one raw, unguarded word emerged. 'Yes.'

His gaze was sceptical and probing, but it wavered for a moment to reveal another expression.

He wanted to believe me.

My heart leapt, a foolish action that I immediately condemned.

There was nothing to be excited about here. Bitter experience insisted that, regardless of how it started, inevitably every relationship ended with acrimony and pain. Trust wasn't a commodity I gave away freely; lately, I wasn't sure I possessed it any more.

That bracing reminder cooled some of the heat rampaging through my blood. It drove me to my feet, and I glanced around for somewhere to put the bowl.

Jensen rose too, once again towering over me as

he reached for it. With quick, efficient movements, he rinsed the bowls out and tucked them away.

Within a minute he was back, tall and mouth-watering, in front of me. But the past remained a hard reminder, a harsh voice that said I couldn't even explore, out here in the middle of nowhere, without further risking the last of my emotional reserves.

But does it have to be that heavy? You could just no-strings fuck him.

Temptation slithered inside, quickening as my gaze dropped to his sensual lips, slowly parted as he stared at me. The air thickened between us, his eyes darkening with every second that ticked away.

'Careful there, Jensen,' I murmured. 'Or I'll think you want me to truly savour you.'

One corner of his mouth tilted in a sexy little smile that jerked the strings attaching my brain to my pussy. 'Better that than being downed like a shot and forgotten about.'

'That's what you're worried about? That you'll be forgettable to someone?'

A shadow cast over his features, indicating I'd hit near enough to a bullseye. The urge to probe deeper surged through me. But then his gaze dropped, to rest somewhere near my throat, possibly at the frantic pulse beating there. Or, as I suspected, the submissive nature screaming out to me was rising, despite his attempt to ignore it. Need flared again, intensifying with each second.

'What if I am?' he murmured.

Unable to resist, I raised my hand, brought it close without touching his taut jaw. 'False modesty doesn't become you. You're as far from unforgettable as it's possible to get and I'm pretty sure you know that.'

He smiled, but the shadows remained in his eyes. And because I'd exhausted the willpower to remain this close to him without touching him, I ignored every last reservation, leaned up and pressed my lips against his.

He tensed for a frozen moment, and then his lips were clinging to mine, opening up beneath the pressure of my kiss, a grunt escaping his throat as he leaned down, granting me access to better explore him.

He was delicious. Heady, in a way that made my senses swim even before I'd taken my next breath. I swept my tongue over his slightly parted lips, and he groaned, pressed closer, wanting more. That fierce connection, that need to have my instincts satisfied, drove me to kiss him deeper, start an erotic dance with him.

Gloriously, he followed, met me stroke for stroke, intensifying the kiss. His teeth nipped, nibbling and tasting. My clit swelled, need building till the slickness dampened my panties.

Through it all, Jensen held his hands at his sides, adding another degree of certainty to my instincts that when it came to all things sensual and sexual, Jensen Scott would truly submit, wouldn't proceed without express permission.

My permission. My *domination*.

My heart and senses raced at the thought, saturating me with a sense of promise until I swayed under the strength of it. But it was short-lived, my spirits deflating. In less than twenty-four hours, the real world would beckon, and with it the knowledge that nothing this good ever withstood the pressures of a Mortimer life.

If we were really going to do this, all I had was this one night to savour him as I'd loftily offered.

I'd warned him about believing everything he read in the paper. Was I really about to embark on a one-night stand, my very first with a mysterious but intriguing man I'd only just met?

Why not? If that's what we both want?

But was it?

I trailed my hand over his jaw, neck and down a chest ridged with his rock-hard muscles. He jerked, reacting to me despite the layers of clothes between us. Insanely thrilled by his response, I took my time with him, fingers lingering as I headed south.

I disengaged from the kiss just before I reached his belt. I watched him, absorbed the almost haggard arousal etched into his face; took in the lowered gaze resting on my breasts. Pulling my lips between my teeth as anticipation blazed through me, I trailed my hand the last scant inches and gripped his hard length through the layers of clothes.

'Fuck,' he breathed.

I bit back a moan of my own, unwilling to admit how much his unguarded reaction pleased me. Despite the warnings shrieking in my head to slow down, think this through properly, I continued to stroke him, learning his length and girth and glorying in the heat and power of him. After a minute, I leaned closer, brushed my lips against his in a light kiss. 'Do you feel savoured yet?'

He gave an abrupt shake of his head, his tongue flicking out to taste my lower lip. 'More. Please.'

I curbed my smile, even as my heart jumped. This was so foolish. Disappointment surely lurked around the corner. But for the life of me I couldn't stop touching him.

A harsher wind swept over us, and, despite the insulation of clothes keeping the worst of the chill out, I shivered. Immediately, he unzipped the opening to the tent.

'Let's go inside. It's freezing out here.'

He held back the flap of the tent, and I went inside.

The large sleeping bag stretched out over a waterproof mattress was more than adequate for one person. Not two. I turned to comment on the feasibility of our situation.

The raw, ravenous look in his eyes stopped me.

That look became the deciding factor.

He was an adventurer. Used to taking risks and reaping stunning rewards.

Wouldn't it be a kick to take a leaf out of his book?

I reached for the zip fastening my suit. His gaze dropped to trail the movement, his harsh breathing so insanely sexy, my nipples beaded harder. Within the atmosphere of the closed tent, with double space heaters warming up the space, arousal bit harder.

'You want to help me with this?' I asked, my voice sultry with excitement.

With a firm nod, he stepped forward, taking over my unzipping. 'It'll be my pleasure.'

He was way taller than the tent and had bent his head when he stepped inside. Still, my heart lurched when he dropped to his knees. But his position in no way diminished him. Jensen was overwhelmingly large, his sheer size making my mouth water as I stared down at him. I dug my arms out of my outer suit, then held onto his shoulder as he manoeuvred the material down my legs.

I'd just stepped out of them, leaving my thermal all-in-one underneath, when he inhaled sharply. 'Shit. The aurora.'

I wanted to laugh, weirdly amused by the notion that the phenomenon was enough to distract him from what we were doing. 'Is it happening now?' We'd been in the tent only a handful of minutes.

He shook his head. 'No, but I don't want to miss it if it does.'

Even as he sprang into action, his gaze locked on my body, eyes heating up as it lingered on the twin diamond-hard points of my nipples, brazenly outlined in the thermal suit. After a thick swallow, he veered away, his movements graceful yet efficient as he dug through his equipment, took out three powerful-looking cameras and tripods and then swiftly exited the tent.

Minutes passed as he set up the cameras outside the tent. Then he was back, sealing the flap closed behind him. Need clamoured through me. Impatient to be naked, to feel his hard body and hands upon mine, I swivelled away from him, exposed my nape where the zip of my thermal suit rested.

Eagerly, he went back to work, his expert fingers lowering another zip, this one exposing my naked back to him. His sharp intake of breath made me smile, eroding a few more layers of doubt.

Jensen's reaction gratified, salved a wound I didn't want to admit needed soothing and I revelled in the warm hands that undressed me, pleasure gliding through me as I looked at him over my shoulder, watched his eyes linger on my behind, where my thong dissected the globes of my ass.

'You're beautiful,' he breathed, his hands shaking as they trailed up my legs, pressing into my calves on the way to wrapping around my hips. He leaned forward, pressed his face into the gap between my legs, shamelessly breathing me in before letting out a thick groan. 'And you smell amazing, *min elskerinde*.'

The foreign words were almost whispered against my skin, under his breath. I wanted to ask what they meant, but he was nipping at my flesh, using his teeth to wreak havoc.

Doing things I hadn't quite given him permission for.

I twisted in his hold, braced my hands on his shoulders. 'You've seen me. Now I get to see you. Undress.'

His hands reluctantly left my body, pulled at the fasteners securing the neck of his snow suit, but his movements were slow. Perhaps because his lust-dark eyes were fixed on my breasts, still encased in the burgundy bra that matched my panties. Lingerie was an expensive weakness of mine.

It was partly why I'd kept in touch with Bryce's childhood friend and now girlfriend Savannah Knight, and ordered a new selection from each of her Voluptuoso lingerie collections the moment it hit the stores.

Perhaps lace and silk that barely covered my intimate parts were impractical for sub-zero weather temperatures, but it was a decadence I didn't feel bad about indulging.

Judging from Jensen's reaction, it was well worth it.

'Hurry up, or I might change my mind about all of this.'

He attacked his zip without taking his eyes off me, hissing when it went over his engorged cock. He wore the same thermal under gear as I did, but in a blinding white two-piece trousers and long-sleeved T-shirt combo to my black one-piece. I was sure there were some Freudian connotations in our colour preferences but all I could absorb in that moment was the way the material moulded his sculpted shoulders and chest, the way it outlined his mouth-watering abs. With each movement as he shrugged out of the garment, I was exposed to even more of Jensen Scott's perfection.

I wanted to lick him all over. Then devour him in large, choking chunks.

The strength of that need alarmed me. But the sight of him on his knees, ready to surrender to me, overpowered the apprehension.

I was a grown woman, perfectly ripe for my first

one-night stand in a tent somewhere in the Arctic Circle if I wished it. Empowered by the thought, I cupped his strong jaw, leaned down and pressed an open-mouthed kiss to his lips. Before the flames could leap out of control, I eased away, walked past him to where the sleeping bag was laid out.

Like everything else around here, it held a chill as I lay back on it, but it warmed quickly. I let out a pleased sigh, watched as he swivelled to follow my movement, kicking away his suit as he did.

I beckoned him with a finger, and he rose.

He was gorgeous. Built like a true Viking with thick thighs, chiselled calves and lean hips, he was fantasy made flesh.

A fantasy I intended to make reality before the night was over.

'Come and show me what else those talented hands are capable of,' I invited sultrily, moving my arms to rest them above my head.

'Just my hands?' he asked, his voice a thick rasp.

'No, Mr Scott. Not just your hands. Every inch of that delicious body is definitely on my to-do list.'

My fingers brushed the side of the tent, and the brief contact with the cold sent a delicious shiver through me, making my nipples harder.

He groaned, then, erupting into movement, he dropped onto the sleeping bag, dark blue eyes devouring me as he started to reach for me.

'Wait.'

He stilled, his nose flaring in the silence I let drag out for several seconds.

'The beanie. Take it off. I want to see your hair.'

The white cap—he really had a thing for white, didn't he?—slid off easily, and I suppressed a groan. Hell, even his hair was magnificent. Burnt gold, threaded with hints of dark honey, it was enough to make a woman weep with envy. And a shampoo manufacturer scream with joy. But it was still tied at the back of his neck.

'All of it, Jensen.'

With an impatient tug, he freed the length from the simple elastic band. My breath caught as the heavy mass fell over one shoulder. With movements that were perfunctory rather than exhibitionist, he dragged his fingers through the thick strands, tossing them off his neck. They fell well below his shoulders. And while I wasn't into the whole man-bun craze, I couldn't deny there was something wildly sexy about a guy with the confidence to wear his hair this long.

Eyes darkened with arousal raked over my body again, unfettered lust parting his lips. 'What do you want, *min elskerinde*?'

'For you to finish undressing me,' I instructed.

He fell on me, callused fingers grazing my skin as he reached behind me to unclasp my bra. At the first sight of my breasts, he groaned. 'God, you're so fucking sexy.'

I arched my back, silently inviting him to touch.

He touched. Squeezed and caressed me until he dragged a moan from my throat. The thought of the frozen tundra right outside the tent and the sizzling effect of his hands on me was one of the headiest encounters I'd experienced.

I wanted more of it.

As if he'd read my mind, his hands tiptoed down my ribs, leaving a trail goosebumps, to catch and drag my panties down my legs.

In the dim light, I saw a flush stain his chiselled cheekbones. It was a unique enough reaction to elevate me from mere lust to…something else. Something that was exclusively mine.

Something that didn't remind me of my uncanny resemblance to my mother, a fact many chose to comment on, either with reverence or with cruelty. While these days I'd stopped reading the tabloids, I'd once spent a useless, soul-shrivelling month scouring newspapers and magazines for mentions of my name that didn't involve my mother. Not a single one had been entirely about me. Because of course I wasn't my own person. I was a churned-out product, a means to an end dictated by a few lines scrawled in a centuries-old trust, discarded at the very first opportunity.

If only I could look into the mirror and not see the exact replica of just who had done the discarding—

Callused hands tightened on my inner thighs, dragging me back to the present. To the man who crouched before me, his eyes fixed on me with complete, unwavering focus. 'I feel as if I'm losing you,' Jensen said, a displeased little light in his eyes that absurdly thrilled me. The idea that a man who barely knew me would fight for my attention, when my own mother had—

Dear God, enough already!

'Well, you've got my clothes off. Now what do you want to do?' I asked, momentarily content to let him make the decision. I was merely loosening the reins, not handing them over.

He swallowed, his gaze darting from my breasts to my pelvis, hunger etched deeper on his face. His grip grew even firmer, subtly nudging my thighs apart. I was shamelessly wet, could feel the hot dampness in the cool air.

'I want to taste you. Devour you. Make you come,' he said.

Breath hitching, I spread my thighs wider. 'Then we're in accord, Jensen, because I want the same thing.'

With a rough grunt, he lurched forward, wrapped both hands around my breasts and sucked a nipple between his lips. Expertly, he rolled the hard nub between his teeth, nipping and sucking until my back arched clear off the sleeping bag. He showered attention on the twin peak, then utilised his hot and skilful mouth on a trail south.

Jensen didn't tease and titillate his way into a slow build-up. He wanted to devour me, and that was exactly what he did.

With a full-on, dirty French kiss, he launched a spine-melting assault on my sex, tasting and licking with unashamed pleasure that made me gasp in shock.

'You taste so good,' he growled, his gaze rising to

clash with mine for a second before it dropped to my sex. Minutes ticked by, the only sound in the tent the decadent acoustics of wet, aroused flesh and pleasured moans.

Then his fingers parted me wider, exposing my engorged clit to the wicked assault of his tongue. Pleasure piled high, drawing wild tremors through me. Like a freight train, my climax bore down on me. Relishing the added friction of his stubble against my thighs, I gathered the long strands of his hair in one hand, the other cupping my breast to squeeze a nipple as I prepared to surrender to rabid lust.

It arrived in flashes of wild lightning, jerking my hips in hard spasms. Jensen's hand slipped beneath me, effortlessly holding me up as he continued to taste my climax. When it all grew too much, I tightened my grip in his hair.

With endearing reluctance, he diverted his attention from between my legs, dropped kisses down the length of my inner thighs before prowling his way up my body.

The decadent kiss tasted of my musky satisfaction. Eventually, he drew away, and I saw the building tension on his face.

I forced myself not to tense in response, despite the less than euphoric sensation moving through my stomach at the thought that he already regretted what had happened. 'If you're annoyed by the lack of accolades, I'd say give me a chance to catch my breath, then I'll—'

A sharp shake of his head halted my words. 'It's nothing like that.'

'Okay.' I waited.

His gaze rushed over me, as if he couldn't help himself. And call me vain, but it eased my tension a little.

'I'm not sure how far you want this to go…' he paused, jaw gritted, as if he didn't want to say the words '…but I don't have a condom.'

I froze, mildly stunned that the need for protection hadn't occurred to me. While I was on the Pill, and fairly certain pregnancy wouldn't be an issue, I'd never *not* used the extra layer of protection. The last thing I needed with my various issues was to add a baby to the mix. Or a different type of health issue.

In a way, this was the perfect get-out clause. A moment of reprieve to rethink this insanity before it got out of hand.

So why was I reaching for him, bunching my fist into the front of his thermal T-shirt to pull him closer? 'I'm sure we can find middle ground that works for both of us. Take this off, please. And kiss me again,' I said, reclaiming my true nature now the first hazy orgasm was out of the way.

He pulled the T-shirt over his head, and I barely managed to stop from gaping. He was glorious, a perfect synergy of sleek musculature and light golden skin.

I wanted to touch him, but he had other ideas. As per my instruction, the moment he tossed the clothing away, he fused his lips to mine. My hands went to his hair, gathered it in one hand. He gave a rough groan.

I used the pressure to draw him back, revelled in his wild shudder. 'You like your hair pulled?'

His rabid gaze remained on my mouth. 'Yes.'

I tightened my fist, applied pressure until his head bowed back, exposing his delicious throat to me. Unable to resist, I trailed a kiss down one side of his Adam's apple. 'What else do you like?'

'Everything.'

I laughed. 'That's too broad a spectrum. I deal in specifics. I'm a woman in a position of power and responsibility. I have a burden of literal billions in donations on my shoulders. I can't afford to waver or prevaricate over my decisions.'

His eyelids flickered, but he didn't lift his gaze. His submissiveness was so ingrained it was breathtaking. 'It's more than that, *min elskerinde*, and we both know it.'

My heart banged against my ribs. 'I should punish you for arguing with me.'

'But you won't because it's the truth. Being in control is who you are.'

It was my turn to shudder. But not with arousal. It was his recognition of my true self that threatened to move me. 'I'm still waiting, Jensen.'

'I'd very much like to fuck you. But since that's not on the table, I'd love to make you come again.'

As generous as the offer was, it reeked a little too much of pandering to the desires of the spoilt little rich girl, in the hope of banking brownie points. 'Why that, Jensen? Why not ask for a blow job?' My gaze dropped to the thick outline of his cock, straining about his thermals. 'I'm sure you could use a little relief?'

He shuddered against my lips, but still he shook his

head. 'The taste of you is…intoxicating. I want more,' he confessed thickly.

And what the hell…who was I to refuse such a request?

'Wake up, *elskerinde*.'

I snuggled deeper into the warm sleeping bag. 'What…why? Is it morning already?' It felt as if I'd fallen asleep minutes ago into what had surprisingly been restful sleep.

'No, it's not. But the borealis is happening. I don't think you want to miss it.'

My eyes popped open. 'Seriously?'

Jensen's eyes were amused as he nodded. 'Seriously.'

About to launch myself out of the bag, I remembered I didn't have a stitch on. The thought of piling on layers of clothes, while necessary, made me grimace.

Silently, he held out my thermal under suit, the jacket he'd given me on the last leg of the sled ride, and a blanket. 'This should be enough to keep you warm for a short time.'

I reached for the clothes with a grateful smile, something sharp and profound lurching in my chest. I was just his client. A client he didn't want to freeze to death on his watch. No big deal. Certainly no reason to read any more into this than a mere kindness.

I accepted the items, tugging the leggings of the all-in-one on without bothering with my panties or bra. As I punched my way into the jacket, I noticed that he was already dressed.

'How long have you been up?'

'About five minutes. I stepped out to check on the cameras and saw the lights.'

I hurriedly zipped up the jacket and searched for my shoes. Again, he produced them, the laces in my boots eased apart and ready to be tugged on. 'Am I going to miss it? How long does it usually last?'

The moment I stood he eased the blanket over my shoulders. 'Each one is different. If we're lucky, it'll last for a good while.'

He held open the tent flap for me. And I stepped out into the most spectacular sight.

Against a black velvet sky pierced with brilliant stars, breathtaking swathes of coloured light swirled and danced. Greens, blues, purples and yellows, they looked close enough to touch.

'Oh, my sweet Lord.' The cold Arctic slap of wind forgotten, I stared, my breath held at the wondrous sight. 'It's…indescribable.'

Ja,' he concurred, his tone a little gruff. 'No matter how many times I see one, it still takes my breath away. Each one is unique enough to make me feel like I'm seeing it for the first time.'

I could believe that. 'How many times have you experienced this?'

I sensed more than saw his shrug. 'Not as often as I'd like.' There was a wistfulness to his tone that almost distracted me from the sight.

Almost.

The beauty displayed above me was too powerful, too sacred to take my eyes off it.

So I watched, even as I sensed Jensen's subtle movements around me. Even as I heard the soft, shuttered clicks of his camera, circling. Stopping. Circling some more.

It was only as the spectacular display started to fade several minutes later that I paid attention to what Jensen was doing.

His camera was going off a mile a minute, his movements near balletic as he leaned in, then leaned back, dropped a few inches, then rotated the camera while adjusting the lens. There was something deeply hypnotic and breathtakingly beautiful about watching him at work, which was why it took several seconds before, alarmed, I realised that I was the focus of his attention, and not the spectacular display electrifying the sky around us.

Years of being photographed without my permission had engendered a hatred of having cameras trained on me, triggering a knee-jerk response. 'I hope you're not thinking of selling pictures of me to make a quick buck.'

He froze, then slowly lowered his camera as he rose from a deep crouch. In the pool of light from the lantern he'd brought with us, I watched shock and fury chase across his face.

'I get by well enough on my own hard work without the need to peddle images of celebrities, princess. I leave that kind of asshole move to pond scum who aren't familiar with concepts like respect, privacy and basic human decency.'

The bite in his voice rivalled the Arctic wind sweeping against my skin.

For a moment I was ashamed at my harsh rebuke, but even that emotion was swept away by the wild panic at the thought of having offended him. I stepped forward. He turned away, his back stiff as he went to check on his equipment.

I opened my mouth to say what I wasn't exactly sure just as the name he'd called me struck hard and deep.

Princess.

He called me *princess*. A predictable insult from someone who claimed not to read the filth and lies the media wrote about me. The world's favourite derogatory term for me, but searingly painful coming from Jensen. Anger mounted, and I stewed in my righteous fury, but beneath all that I was totally confounded by how much his slur had affected me.

Why?

Because we'd rolled around in a tent for a few hours?

It was supposed to mean nothing. And it *did*, I insisted to myself.

As passing time and work went, it hadn't been a bad day. I'd seen three spectacular sights, been the recipient of two mind-blowing orgasms, and could now tick a traipse to the Arctic Circle off my bucket list. Not bad for a twenty-four-hour jaunt.

First thing in the morning I'd order the chopper to come back and get me.

Jensen could complete his assignment on his own. If his work produced a less than satisfactory outcome, I'd hire the next best person. He might think himself the best, but surely there was someone out there equally qualified.

With that thought in mind I turned towards the tent, but at the last moment, unable to resist, I looked over my shoulder. In his white gear, he should've blended into the landscape, but there was an aura about him, the type that made him impossible to miss. Impossible to ignore. Even in these final moments of seeing Jensen Scott in this environment, I knew he'd be as unforgettable as he'd wanted to be.

The thought irritated as much as it disturbed.

Enough to trigger another unfettered response. 'This ice princess needs her beauty sleep. I'd appreciate not being disturbed when you come back in.' Yes, it was a cheap shot, but I didn't care.

Not when I zipped myself into the bag and immediately felt the lack of hard male body warmth that'd helped me sleep soundly only a few hours earlier.

Not when he didn't return for the better part of an hour, leaving my mind whirling, making me wonder where he was, whether I was that loathsome that he would stay out in the cold rather than share a tent with me.

Not when I felt another clench of my heart at the thought I'd screwed up something as simple as a one-night stand.

The same way I'd driven my brothers away.

The same way I'd screwed up and sent my mother away from me at the age of nine.

CHAPTER FOUR

THINGS WENT FROM bad to worse between Graciela and me while I was in the middle of kicking myself for over-reacting the night before.

Now I'd had time to cool down, I couldn't blame her for assuming the worst. The British media were notorious for privacy invasion, and with a family like the Mortimers, with their well-documented clashes with the tabloid press, it didn't surprise me that she'd be wary.

So what if we'd shared a few intimate moments the night before?

Everything about our encounter reeked of *temporary*.

Regardless of certainty, though, a hard bite caught me every time I thought of this project being over, that what happened in the tent last night would never be repeated.

Fuck, if I wanted the blood to relocate from what felt like its new permanent residence in my groin, I needed to stop thinking about last night and concentrate on the real threat of the snowstorm heading our way.

It'd caught me unawares, much like a lot of things had since meeting Graciela Mortimer.

Jaw clenched, I resisted yet another urge to glance behind me. To catch another glimpse of her face. She'd been asleep, thankfully, when I eventually returned to the tent last night. Knowing I couldn't join her inside the sleeping bag, despite being sorely tempted, had been another unpalatable lesson in self-control. Common sense had been little comfort as I'd shivered in the blankets on the other side of the tent.

Breakfast had been predictably chilly, and I wasn't surprised when she treated me to haughty silence as we packed up and reloaded the sled. Nor could I stem my disappointment when she informed me of her plans to cut short her involvement in the project.

There was no avoiding talking to her now, though.

I glanced over my shoulder. 'There's a storm headed our way. We're not going to make the rendezvous point to meet the chopper.'

Her eyes narrowed before leaving mine to scour the landscape and sky. 'The sky is clear. I don't see anything resembling a storm.'

I curbed a smile. 'This isn't a trick. We have about half an hour tops to find shelter before the storm hits. Your pick-up point is ninety minutes away.'

'Can't we hunker down somewhere, wait for it to pass?' she asked.

I shook my head, feeling almost sorry for her. Almost. Her hurry to get away from me rankled. 'No, we can't. It's better to find solid shelter rather than camp out.'

She reached for her satellite phone. 'I'll call my pilot, and you can redirect him here to pick me up,' she said.

'If the storm's as bad as I think it is, he won't be allowed to fly out at all. And if he does, you'll be risking everyone getting stranded—' The sound of her phone ringing interrupted us. 'I bet that's him now calling to tell you the same thing.'

With an icy glare at me, she answered. 'Hello?' She listened, her expression growing tighter by the second. Any moment now, I expected her to snap at her pilot to come, regardless of the procedures. But, surprising the hell out of me, she nodded. 'Fine. If you can't fly, you can't fly. Let me know as soon as you're given the all-clear.'

She hung up and, for a moment, I caught a lost expression in her eyes. And then she was back to glaring at me. 'So what now?'

A low hum of electricity vibrated through my bloodstream. 'My cabin is ten miles away. Provided the dogs cooperate we might beat the storm.'

Wariness crossed her face. 'And if we don't? What happens if we get caught in the storm?'

'We might catch a bit of it, but don't worry, if we need to stop, I'll keep you safe.'

Again, a raw expression crossed her face, but it was quickly stifled. 'If that's our only option...'

It wasn't exactly a ringing endorsement, but it was enough. I was prepared to risk getting us inside four solid walls rather than braving the elements, no matter how many sparks had flown in our tent. Before I'd ruined it.

I checked my watch's GPS tracker to make sure

we were headed in the right direction and whistled at the dogs.

They responded immediately, eager for brisker exercise, and turned east, towards the isolated cabin I'd been using for the last two weeks. The thought of Graciela in my personal space, alone with me under my roof, heated my blood, hardening my cock despite the possibility that she wouldn't move from her stance of clearly not wanting anything to do with me.

For a moment, I mourned refusing the blow job she'd offered last night. Bloody hell, how I wish I'd taken her up on it. Then I wouldn't be so fucking wound up tight, repeatedly dwelling on how incredible she had tasted, how snugly my tongue had fitted into her. How much I was dying to hear those control-wrecking little noises she made when she came.

I'd passed up the chance and I only had myself to blame for my state of raging blue balls.

The storm hit much quicker than I'd anticipated, catching us out a good ten minutes before we reached the copse of fir trees that signalled the beginning of the woods leading to the cabin. The dogs, sensing the turning weather, strained at the leash, barking excitedly at the thought of being given leave to go even faster. The moment I loosened the reins, they were off.

I checked over my shoulder. 'Hold tight.'

She nodded stiffly, although I caught a hint of excitement in her eyes as her hand tightened around the iron handlebar in front of the seat. She probably wouldn't admit it, but she was enjoying this, being at the mercy of the elements. I knew I was.

There was something raw and unfettered about pitting oneself against nature and coming out on top. It was mostly why I'd chosen my profession.

That and the freedom it gave me once upon a time to immerse myself in something else other than the turmoil going on at home. Turmoil that had ended up shaping my life.

I relished the icy wind lashing at my cheeks, making my eyes water as the wind picked up speed. The snow came, thick and furious, falling horizontal with the force of the wind. I checked on Graciela every few minutes, confirming that she was indeed enjoying this by the hint of a grin toying at her lips. Which stunned me a little.

The only time I took Stephanie on a shoot after her endless badgering for me to bring her with me, she'd complained the whole time, demanding to go back to *civilisation* at the earliest opportunity.

While I wanted to enjoy Graciela's pleasure for a few minutes, I was still relieved to spot the familiar treeline that signalled the boundary to the cabin, grateful to see an end to enduring what was quickly turning into a white-out.

Minutes later, I pulled to a stop in front of the compact log structure that comprised my cabin.

I hopped off the sled and helped Graciela off. 'Wait for me on the porch. I'll get the dogs squared away and bring in the equipment.'

She shook her head. 'It'll be quicker if I give you a hand.'

I nodded, located my camera bag. 'Okay. Take this up with you. I'll just be a minute.'

She grabbed the bag, lifting the heavy load without complaint onto one shoulder. Then she grabbed the blankets and sleeping bag and hurried onto the porch. I grabbed the rest of the equipment and followed.

The key was tucked into a nook specially created in one of the overhead beams on the porch. I unlocked the door and held it open for her. A full day with no heating meant the interior was icy-cold but, luckily, the electricity was still working. I turned on a couple of lamps and activated the portable space heaters we'd used in the tent. She set the stuff down next to the fireplace, and I disposed of my own load before waving her towards the wide, comfy sofa. 'Take a seat. I'll be back in five minutes.'

She nodded, but didn't sit down.

When I paused at the door and looked back, she was gazing around the cabin, inspecting the large open-plan space. It was rustic, far removed from the luxury she was no doubt used to. Nevertheless, as basic as it was, something about having her here in the space I'd made my own appealed to me.

I turned away, berating myself for getting carried away. She'd be gone as soon as the weather cleared. Besides the pictures on my camera, there'd be just my memory to evidence her brief presence in my life.

What the fuck is wrong with you?

I shut the door behind me, concentrated on relocating the dogs to their habitat in the heated shed where they slept. Ensuring they had food and water and that their blankets were dry, I returned to the cabin, grabbing Graciela's small weekender from the sled on the way.

She'd lowered the zip on the outer snowsuit, but hadn't taken it off. Which was a blessing, I supposed. The memory of her insanely beautiful body, smooth skin and the sweet flesh between her legs was vivid enough without a visual reminder.

I held up her case. 'I brought your stuff. I'll get the fire going if you want to change clothes?'

'I do, thanks,' she said, her voice a little stiff.

I sighed. Did I even have the right to be disappointed that she was giving me the icy princess treatment? What did it even matter? I'd come out here specifically to get away from women like her; taken this assignment because I'd believed I'd be alone, working while licking my wounds.

Trust-fund princesses with entitlement issues were supposed to be permanently off my menu.

What about trust-fund princesses with pussies that tasted like fucking honey?

Blood surged into my cock at the reminder, and my legs felt a little stiff as I went to the fire and tossed in a couple more logs onto the half-burnt ones I'd put out before leaving the cabin yesterday.

I lit the fire purely from muscle memory, what with my brain stuck back in that tent, reliving every second of how it'd felt to make her come, wring those insane sounds from her throat, to feel her fingers in my hair as she'd directed me on how to maximise her pleasure.

And that's what's right and so fucking wrong with this picture, isn't it? You got a taste of her and now you can't get her out of your head?

I ignored the voice, stayed right there on my knees until the fire was in full rage. The sound of a zip lowering made me turn. She was freeing her arms from the outer suit and tugging her hair loose.

I'd been so blinded by her body last night I hadn't quite clocked the long strands of her raven hair cascading halfway down her back. The urge to sink my fingers into the silky mass made me clench my fists. Realising I was staring at her like some hormonal fool, I busied myself by shrugging off my own suit.

Since I didn't want to risk her seeing her maddening effect on me, I unzipped to the waist and left the arms hanging down. Hell, she'd see the bulge below my waist soon enough if I spent any more time standing around staring at her breasts, thinking about how good she tasted.

Thinking about what else to do brought up a different dilemma, though. I eyed the sofa and hid a grimace.

She followed my gaze, but before she could speak, I grabbed her case. 'There's not much to the cabin but I'll show you around,' I offered. 'Let's start upstairs.'

I headed up the stairs and down the short hallway leading to the bedroom tucked in the eaves of the cabin. I heard her following and opened the bedroom door as she reached me.

The huge king-size bed took up most of the room because, what the hell, I liked my comfort when I slept. Besides that, though, I had very little else in the way of creature comforts. A dresser, bedside table, and closet that held a handful of clothes were all I needed when I used the cabin. I set her bag down beside the bed. 'You can have the bed. I'll sleep downstairs.'

'Why? Because I'm a spoilt ice princess?' she bit out, her face cold once again.

I gritted my teeth, regret and irritation warring inside me. 'You want me to apologise for what I said last night?'

'I wouldn't want you to waste your breath, since we both know it would be false.' She was back to using that snippy, upper-class voice.

As much as it came naturally to Graciela, it reminded me a little too much of the posh voice Stephanie had adopted to impress clients—and me—when we'd first met. It'd turned out to be as false as everything else about her.

With Graciela, I was beginning to recognise the snippiness as a facade. I'd caught enough glimpses of her vulnerability to guess the truth. Last night, for instance, even as she'd ordered me not to disturb her beauty sleep, I'd caught the hurt in her voice. Seen the way she'd held herself stiff and closed, as if she didn't want to show her vulnerability.

And, dammit, something about that made me want her more.

Perhaps even more than I yearned for the sultry creature who'd raised her arms above her head last night and invited me to use my hands on her.

'I see you're not bothering to deny it.'

I sighed, dragged my beanie off to run my fingers through my hair. She followed the movement and I did it again, a shockingly large part of me wanting to preen for her. Wanting to reawaken the Dominant I'd received an oh-so-brief taste of last night, just so I'd experience the unique pleasure of surrendering to her once again.

She seemed nowhere in sight now, though, and, for whatever reason, I wanted another glimpse of her. Wanted to test her authenticity. Wanted to—

What? See if she was real or a fake as Stephanie turned out to be?

Why?

I ignored the far too difficult question and focused on answering. 'Maybe I could've been a little less... spiky about it.'

One sleek eyebrow arched. 'Maybe?'

I hid a smile at the tight demand. She was one hell of a ball-breaker. 'Fine. I definitely could have been.'

The icy disdain didn't leave her face. I sighed again, then waved at the window, indicating the snowstorm raging outside. 'I've no idea how long this thing is going to last. I'd rather we didn't spend the whole time being at each other's throats.'

'Oh, you don't have to worry about me, Jensen. Ice princesses are experts at maintaining a dignified silence.'

My jaw gritted. 'I don't want that either.'

Her head tilted, her hazel eyes mocking as they met

mine. 'Let me guess, you want a cosy conversation by the roaring fire?'

No, I wanted to growl.

Conversation could come way later, after we stopped playing games and she showed me her true self. Long after we established a baseline of trust and she let me surrender to her from my rightful place at her feet. Long after I'd undressed her again and given her everything she wanted from me, which I hoped involved long hours spent between her thighs.

Then I wouldn't mind a conversation or two with her. A chance to discover what else lay beneath those dense layers besides the vulnerability I'd occasionally caught glimpses of yesterday.

Since even the thought of that was making me hard again, I forced a shrug. 'If that's what you want. But first you really should get out of those clothes. And you can have the bedroom. I insist.'

The barest hint of a smile ghosted her lips. 'Oh, you do, do you?'

I nodded. 'Call it my peace offering for offending you.'

A layer of iciness receded, and something tight eased inside me. 'Where are you going to sleep? Don't tell me you're going to take the sofa. It's barely long enough to accommodate me, never mind you.' She waved a hand at me.

I shrugged again. 'There's an air mattress around here somewhere. Or I can use the sleeping bag. I'll be fine.'

She didn't answer, but her gaze swung to the bed and she approached it. A smile playing over full, sensual lips, she sat down and dragged her fingers over the comforter. I bit back a groan, locked my knees as a punch of lust knocked the breath out of me. I wanted those fingers on my body, caressing me.

Before things got out of control, I waved at the door. 'You want to continue the tour?'

'It's more or less a two-room cabin, isn't it?'

'Yep. The bathroom's next door, and I have a dark-room downstairs next to the pantry, but yes, that's about it.'

Her eyes stayed on mine. 'That's all I need to know, thanks.'

'Okay.' I turned towards the door.

Her voice, firm, sexy, minus the icy disdain, stopped me. 'Jensen?'

I looked over my shoulder. 'Yes?'

'Apology accepted.'

Another knot unravelled inside me, disconcerting me as much as the smile that took me by surprise. I wasn't going to examine either right now. 'Great,' I said. 'Coffee will be ready in five minutes.'

Before I did something else insane, like beg her for another kiss, I hurried down the stairs and crossed the living room into the kitchen. I busied myself measuring coffee beans into the coffee-maker—another perk I'd allowed myself—while ignoring the noises from the bathroom and thoughts of a wet, naked Graciela. The coffee was brewing when I heard her footsteps behind me. I turned, unable to help myself.

My breath flattened in my lungs.

Dammit. She was fucking gorgeous.

Black leggings showcased long, shapely legs and feminine hips. Above that, a waist-skimming grey cashmere sweater, designed in a wide-necked sexy way to reveal one shoulder, left a creamy expanse of flesh I couldn't help but devour with my eyes as she moved towards me. 'Why the bedroom upstairs?'

'What?' I forced my brain to track.

'Why not attach a bedroom to the living room downstairs?' she elaborated.

'To conserve space. The initial plan was to make it one big room, get a big sofa that converts to a bed to use when I needed it, but I realised I'd need to make room for a bathroom down here too. I wanted to reduce the square footage so I went up rather than out and split the extra room downstairs into a pantry and darkroom. Rustic is one thing, but I draw the line at an outside bathroom.'

The barest hint of a smile curled her lips, and I was struck with the wild urge to see her truly smile. 'Surprisingly I do too.'

'Then we're in agreement.'

She looked around again. 'So, you own the cabin?'

I nodded. 'Built it with my own two hands three years ago.'

Her gaze dropped to my hands and for some reason I wanted to spread them out, offer them to her.

Get a grip, Jensen.

The coffee machine beeped, giving me the perfect excuse to use my hands on something other than supplication.

'How do you take your coffee?'

'Black. No sugar. Thanks.'

Damn. Girl after my own heart.

Woman.

Graciela Mortimer was all woman. A woman I wanted more with every passing minute. I poured two cups of coffee and handed one to her. She lifted the cup to her lips, gently blew on it before taking a sip.

Her gaze lifted, boldly spearing mine for one tight little second. I wondered if she'd seen my desire. If she had, what would she do with it?

Nothing, I told myself firmly.

I'd sworn off entanglements, remember? I took a large gulp of coffee, wincing when it scalded my mouth and throat. But it brought a modicum of common sense, enough for me to exhale somewhere near normally as her gaze swung from me to the window.

'Is there any way to find out how long this thing is going to last?'

My insides dipped, mocking the mental slap I'd just handed myself. 'In a hurry to get somewhere?'

Hazel eyes returned to clash with mine. 'Of course I am. Even charity magazines don't run themselves.'

'I don't want to start an argument, but don't you have people to ensure things run smoothly in your absence?'

'Doesn't mean I don't enjoy being in charge.'

My next breath strangled in my chest. I'd got a small taste of her being in charge and it'd sparked a red-hot fire in me. But there was something else, something she wasn't quite saying. I decided to leave it be. For now.

'You've got your satellite phone. That's enough to stay connected for the time being, right?'

Her gaze lingered on my face. 'I like to be fully present in every situation. Phones are one thing, face to face is quite another.'

Yep, we were definitely talking about something other than her business. Something that charged the blood in my veins triggered feral hunger inside me. My cock hardened. 'I get that.'

'Do you?'

My throat dried, words taking a little while to form in my brain before I replied. 'That you like being in control. Relish being in charge? Yes, I do. Am I wrong?' Fuck, I hoped I wasn't. Being taken for a fool by Stephanie was one thing. Getting it wrong *twice*…

'You really want to know the answer to that?'

I shifted as the ground beneath my feet lurched. We were straying into forbidden territory, slipping beneath the roped-off cordon and into space I'd designated off-limits since that last, soul-wrecking showdown with Stephanie. Where she'd admitted the depth of her duplicity. Admitted, *finally*, her interest in me had been mere facility, that I—and my celebrity—was a stepping stone to the bigger pool of clients she'd wished to cultivate. That she'd only *pandered to my proclivities* because she thought I'd grow out of it eventually.

I wanted to set my cup down, walk away from this subtexted conversation before it got any more dangerous. Before Graciela's sizzling gaze compelled me to disregard every reason why this was a bad idea.

'What if I said yes, Jensen? What if I told you that being in control is everything I live for? That I'm the Domme your senses are screaming at you that I am?' she stated, her voice deep, firm. Totally controlled.

My stomach went into free fall, my heart hammering a wild, feral beat as we stared at one another.

End this now. Don't risk another Stephanie episode when you know how it'll end.

What if I was leaving myself open to a new, untested form of hell?

But even as the warning shrieked inside my head, I knew this wouldn't be like that. For one thing, this would be temporary.

I was looking at hours, maybe a day with Graciela, rather than the months Stephanie had wormed her duplicitous way into my life.

Everything with Graciela Mortimer was already on a countdown clock controlled by the weather. It would end and we'd go our separate ways. So why not indulge in whatever open-ended proposition blazed in her eyes? Experience an epic adventure right here in my cabin?

And if it turned out not to be as epic… I mentally shrugged. I couldn't be more disappointed than I'd been in the last few years.

But if it was…

If she was offering me another chance to fulfil the deep craving, a chance to be rid of this hard-on threatening to cut me in half, no fucking way in hell was I to deny it. I swallowed another mouthful of coffee to buy myself some time; unable to deny the clamouring in my blood, I answered. 'Prove it.' The words fell from my lips before I could stop them. 'If you are who you say you are, prove it to me.'

She sucked in a sharp breath. 'You want me to…' She stopped.

And right before my eyes, her gaze sharpened, her features tightening with calculating purpose. Purpose that wouldn't be denied.

'For starters, you know I would never allow a sub to address me that way. Don't you?' Soft, menacing words that pounded the locked door to my soul ajar, demanding entry, demanding a glimpse of what lay beyond it.

I knew the moment she saw it. Her nostrils flared, her lips parting for just a second before she pulled the reins of the control tight.

'Yes.'

'And you are a sub,' she breathed. 'One who's yearning to find his freedom in surrender in a way he hasn't for…a while. Aren't you, Jensen?' It wasn't really a question. It was a searing acknowledgement.

Something shifted inside me. Something wild and elemental.

A key finding a lock.

Turning. Turning. Turning.

I couldn't halt my response.

'Yes, *min elskerinde*.'

CHAPTER FIVE

FIRE BLAZED IN her eyes at my answer, the flames raging as she continued to stare me down. 'How long?'

Flashes of shame and regret tore through me. 'Not as long as I've wanted to.'

'What does that mean? Explain yourself clearly to me.'

Shit, was I really doing this? Letting her open that door wider when I needed to be more circumspect? Graciela wouldn't be the first woman to profess she understood what I needed when she didn't have the first clue.

Case in point—Stephanie. First-class liar and con artist. She'd taken my trust and warped it without second thought to progress her career. Had been prepared to go even as far as *marriage*.

While I'd once upon a time made allowances because I was finding my own feet, I wasn't prepared to do so any more. Submitting to a worthy Domme for a night, or for however long we both wanted, wasn't something to frivolously toss around. I wanted a woman who knew what she was doing in the bedroom. Who understood my needs without flinching from fulfilling them. Part of that involved honesty. And openness.

I exhaled my apprehension. 'I didn't fully embrace my needs until a few years ago. Don't get me wrong, I'm not ashamed of who I am.'

'That's good to hear,' she murmured.

'I just choose not to be a raging advertisement for the lifestyle. But I know what I want in the bedroom and I'd rather not have to settle for a diluted version of it.'

She nodded. 'Again, good to hear.'

'Because?' I asked, my insides jumping, the need for confirmation running amok inside me.

She didn't answer immediately; her gaze drifted to the snow falling hard outside the window. 'Because I have a proposition for you, Jensen.'

'*Ja?*' I replied, slipping into Danish. My mother tongue was comforting, I'd found, in times of stress. Probably something to do with it irritating the bastard who I'd had the misfortune of calling my father. The bastard who'd made his wife and children's lives a living hell for a decade and a half before doing a disappearing act.

Sure, this was stress of a different kind, but it didn't make enduring it any easier as I waited for Graciela to respond.

Her gaze pinned mine, resolute. Commanding. My fingers tightened around my coffee mug, anticipation rushing through me.

'As long as that storm rages just outside, you will be mine.'

'Yes,' I responded immediately. Without reservation.

It was temporary. A start and end date. What could be better?

'You don't want to know what being mine entails?' she asked, a little amused.

'I do. Very much,' I said thickly, barely able to get my vocal cords to work.

'Put that coffee down and come here, Jensen.'

I set the cup down without taking my eyes off her.

But I didn't move from where I stood. I needed something from her first. 'Before we start...whatever this is, I want you to promise me one thing.'

A flash of a grimace twitched her nose, but I suspected it was a flippant gesture to hide a deeper reaction. 'People break promises all the time. What makes you think I'll keep mine?'

'I'll give you the benefit of the doubt and accept you at your word.'

She seemed momentarily startled. Then she shrugged. 'Fine. What do you want?'

'That whatever you're feeling, be truthful with it.' I'd had enough of lies and half-truths to last me a lifetime. Refusing to face up to reality was the reason my relationship with my mother was still strained, even now, years after the stain of my bastard father should've been erased from our lives, Stephanie's conniving ways and betrayal the reason I'd ended up here in Alaska. With my past and my present riddled with deception and duplicity, I was one hundred per cent sure I wouldn't take it well if Graciela Mortimer fucked with me that way.

Her head tilted in that way that said she was tunnelling furiously towards the truths and wounds that resided in my very core. And sure enough… 'Is that what she did to you? She lied?'

'Graciela…'

She didn't even bat an eyelid at my warning tone. Man, she was fearless. Not that she needed to fear me, but one day she was going to poke a wounded bear and get herself in a whole world of hurt.

'Gud hjælpe mig.'

'What was that?'

I inhaled slowly. 'Nothing.'

'Are you sure? Only it sounded like you said, "God help me".'

I stiffened. 'You speak Danish?'

She shook her head. 'Not one of my many talents, sadly.'

I exhaled. Sure, the words were similar enough to translate.

Note to self—watch yourself in future.

I snorted under my breath. What future? The sharp rip of something in my chest told me it wasn't as laughable as I was attempting.

'I gave you a command, Jensen.'

I took the vital step that brought me close to her.

'Take my cup,' she instructed.

I took it, turned and set it down next to mine.

With a soft snap of her fingers, she pointed to the floor.

I dropped to my knees, my heart threatening to

burst out of my chest as I lowered my gaze. She inhaled sharply and moved closer until only inches separated us.

She placed her fingers beneath my jaw, nudged my gaze up before leaning in even closer. 'I've seen you out there in your element, owning and bending nature to your will. That's great. Out there, you can be in charge all you like. But in here, you hand over control to me. I own your every move, your every breath. Do you understand?'

The knot I'd carried since Stephanie's lies unravelled, the raging need for the thick promise in Graciela's words shocking me to my soul. 'Yes, *min elskerinde*.'

She gave a brisk nod. 'Let's establish rules. You have my word that I'll be truthful. That I won't do anything to degrade you. We're both free to end this any time we want, storm or no storm. Agreed?'

Relief washed through me. Something else threatened to unravel, but I kept a tight hold on it. I wasn't ready to trust. Not just yet. 'Agreed.'

'Good. Safe words. Do you have one for me?'

I wanted to tell her I didn't need one. That I'd willingly follow her every instruction. But that was a slippery slope. Checks and balances were in place for a reason. I couldn't go into this ignoring rules right from the start. Besides, if she truly was a Domme, she would insist upon it.

I cast around for a suitable safe word as she stared down at me, eyes blazing.

And then it became laughably clear. The *only* thing it could be. 'Hazel,' I said, the word ringing inside me.

'Hazel,' she repeated, a smile curving her lips. 'I can work with that.'

Her gaze swept up and down my body, lingered on my hair. I couldn't quite read her expression but I could tell she wanted to touch me. More specifically, drag her fingers through my hair the way she did last night in the tent. And, boy, did I want her to.

I didn't vocalise my need, however. The words would remain locked in my throat until she gave me permission. She didn't give it.

Instead, she stepped back, casting a critical eye over the cabin. She paused at the fireplace and glanced back at me. 'I'd like you to set up the bedding you spoke about in front of the fireplace. Then undress and wait for me there.'

I rose to my feet, barely able to think through the wild roar in my ears at the thought of pleasing her. The blankets we'd brought in from the trek still lay in a heap next to the fireplace but I went to the supply cupboard to grab fresh, more comfortable ones.

Made of thick merino wool, three would do the job of providing adequate cushioning, I judged. If things went the way I hoped they would, we'd be there for hours. If we needed it, I'd blow up the air mattress later. Or, better still, Graciela might decide on the king-size bed going to waste upstairs.

Adding a handful of pillows, I silently thanked Mrs Percy, the old lady in the small town twenty miles away, who I paid to keep the cabin cleaned and fully stocked. When I'd told her I was coming, she'd filled the pantry and fridge with enough food and essentials to last for weeks.

Keeping Graciela warm and comfortable for as long as the storm raged wouldn't be a problem at all. Suddenly, I didn't want the snowstorm to end. Not for a long time, at least.

I crossed the living room to the fire, resisting the strong urge to glance over to where she stood next to the sofa, her arms crossed. I was head and shoulders taller than her, but her presence filled the room, filled my senses in ways that I was a little too scared to describe. Unfurling the blankets, I laid them down, tossed the pillows onto them.

A little too eagerly, I attacked the snow suit, stepped out of the thermal set and boxers, grimacing at the rock-hard erection that bobbed eagerly, excited at being freed.

I wrestled the insane need to wrap my fingers around my cock, ease the ache tearing through me, and slowly sank to my knees at the edge of the blanket.

I heard her approach but kept my gaze fixed on the fire. She stopped behind me and for the longest time didn't move, although I felt her gaze on me, hot and possessive, tracking every inch of exposed skin.

'You're beautiful, Jensen, do you know that?' she murmured.

'If you say so, *min elskerinde*.' I was used to women admiring the outer package, but knew that, when it came right down to it, it was what was on the inside that mattered. My father had been one handsome bastard with a heart as black as tar, proof that beauty was only skin-deep.

Fuck, I wasn't going to think about him. Definitely not right now.

'You don't like compliments?'

'I like whatever pleases you.'

'I'm not sure if that's a nice save or a cop-out I need to punish you for.'

'It can be whatever you want it to be.'

She circled me once and then stopped in front of me. 'This man bun thing you've got going on. What's that all about?'

I managed a smile despite the strain in my groin. 'A six-month assignment in the Amazon. Barber shops were a little thin on the ground there. I've grown rather attached to it. Plus it keeps me warm in the cold.'

'Hmm, I'm getting rather attached myself. You're not allowed to cut it while we're here. Is that understood?'

'Yes, *min elskerinde*.'

'Is that Danish? I don't know what it means but I'd prefer you call me mistress when you address me.'

My smile widened. 'I already do.' I hesitated for a moment and added, *'Min elskerinde.'*

She inhaled sharply and her eyes widened. 'That's what it means?' Mild shock echoed in her voice.

'Yes.'

Her eyes narrowed. 'You started calling me that last night.'

It wasn't a question, so I let my gaze speak for me.

'Jensen?' she pressed.

'I wanted you like this before our encounter in the tent. But you knew that already.'

'So you started calling me your mistress even before this thing was established between us? Do you know how dangerous that is? Some woman out there could take advantage of it.'

My heart lurched. She sounded almost protective so I didn't tell her I'd sworn off entanglements before I met her. That no other woman would be given the leeway I was giving her. 'Does that displease you?'

Several emotions flitted across the face, but eventually she shook her head. 'People are far too predictable, but you're not one of them.'

A layer of tension eased out of me. 'Is that a compliment, *min elskerinde*?'

'You can take it however you want to,' she answered with a wispy smile, then slowly her face grew tight, controlled arousal settling over her. 'Undress me, Jensen.'

I didn't even care a little bit that my hands shook as I caught the hem of her sweater and tugged it over her head.

She was lovely. She had on a new set of underwear, a deep night-blue that accentuated the smoothness of her skin and the luscious globes of her breasts. Reaching behind her, I unclasped her bra. Her breasts fell free, heavy and gorgeous, tantalisingly close to my hungry lips. I resisted the urge to pull one pink tip into my mouth, instead concentrating on removing her leggings. Unlike last night, she didn't touch me to steady herself, exercising control that only made me harder.

I'd always had a thing for delayed gratification, which was probably another reason my soul yearned to submit. She wouldn't reward me until she deemed it appropriate, and every minute she withheld it, the promise of release became that much headier.

This gloriously naked, insanely gorgeous creature before me already knew how best to satisfy me. And we'd barely got started.

She placed her hands on her hips and stared down at me, her gaze imperious. 'Tell me we have condoms in this cabin, Jensen.'

I flipped back one corner of the blanket near my feet to reveal the box of condoms I'd grabbed from the supply closet.

She smiled, and my breath caught at the lusty fire reflected in the hazel depths. My cock bobbed in excitement as she examined the box and dropped it between my knees.

'We'll get to that in a little while. Right now I want you to place your hands on your thighs. Don't move them until I say so. I've been dying to lick you all over and I'm going to do just that.'

Shuddering with anticipation, I did as instructed.

She stepped behind me, depriving me of the joy of seeing her beautiful body. Moments later her fingers delved into my hair. She caught it up in one fist and before I could take the next breath, her teeth sank into the skin at the top of my spine.

Pleasure rained through my body and I groaned.

'You like that?'

'Yes, *min elskerinde*.'

'Hmm, I think those two are becoming my favourite Danish words.'

I smiled, pleased. 'I'll teach you Danish if you like.'

Her small teeth grazed over my skin again. 'Yes, Jensen, I'd like that very much.'

My eyes squeezed shut of their own accord as she continued to taste me, tongue and teeth and hot breath wreaking havoc all over my skin, following my spine down my back as she explored me.

Fists bunched on my thighs, need pummelling me hard, I glanced down at the thick swell of my cock. Teeth gritted, I fought the urge to touch myself. To surrender to the need to blow my load. But I couldn't come. Not yet. Not until she commanded it.

The freedom in being shackled and under her control made my senses soar.

That need to step outside myself, hand the reins to someone else—a need absurdly born from having to be in control, to keep my family safe from the monster who called himself father—was like nothing else I'd ever experienced, not even the thrill of climbing the world's highest mountain.

I shuddered as her grip tightened in my hair, as she bent low behind me. One hand caressed my butt, squeezed and released at leisure then strutted back to my front. She leaned in, her breath feathering my face without her lips making contact with mine.

'Where was I?' she demanded sultrily.

My breathing grew frantic, erratic as her lips worked

her way down my throat, nipping and tasting my hard nipples, then my abs, until, with one long look at me, she crouched lower and licked the head of my cock.

A tight groan erupted from my throat, my fists bunching harder until my knuckles bled white. Fuck, I was one breath from erupting.

As if she knew the strain I was under, wanted to test my control, she sucked me deeper into her mouth while her fingers crept under my cock to take hold of my balls.

After a few swirls of her tongue, she straightened. 'Look at me, Jensen.'

I wasn't aware my gaze had dropped to the blanket until I lifted it at her bidding.

'Would you like to come?'

'Only if you want me to.'

She smiled. 'I'd love to see you lose that iron control for me.'

'Keep doing what you're doing to my balls and you'll find out soon enough,' I croaked.

Slowly, only one hand crept down her front, two fingers sliding between her legs. I wasn't aware of the strength of my opposition until the sound erupted from my throat.

She stilled. 'Problem?'

I breathed deep, the need to vocalise my need scrambling through me. We were in this thing, for better or worse. Why deny my true nature? Nodding at the fingers moving erotically between her legs, I rasped, 'I want to do that for you.'

Her smile was a pure strain of power and femininity. 'But you're not in charge here, are you?'

'No, *min elskerinde*.'

'So if I want to touch you, while touching myself, you won't have a problem with it, will you?'

'No, but it'll torture the fuck out of me,' I confessed raggedly.

She laughed, the sound wickedly sexy. But gradually, humour died, taken over by need and insistent lust. She released my balls, took hold of my cock, and, her gaze on my face, stroked me up and down.

'I want to suck your cock, and you're going to come when you're ready but you're still not allowed to touch me.'

I jerked out a nod, my lungs struggling for air as her strokes grew tighter. Faster.

She spread her thighs wide and leaned forward, bending over with her bottom in the air. The sight of her luscious cheeks sent me to a whole new stratum of frenzy.

'Fuck, fuck, *fuck*!'

Her sweet lips wrapped around my engorged head, drew me deeper into her hot mouth. Raw shouts left my throat and my hips pumped involuntarily. My head dropped back for one fast second until the need to avidly watch her suck me off redirected my gaze.

Control shredded to nothing within minutes. My vision hazed as she pumped my cock faster. I started to unravel. Undone with a raw shout, I let go, erupting into her mouth. She made pleased sounds of approval at the back of her throat as she sucked me deeper for endless minutes.

Eventually, she rose, sultry satisfaction on her face as she stared at me. 'Thank you, Jensen. That was beautiful.'

I didn't want the words to touch my soul, but they did. And it unsettled me a whole lot more than I cared to admit. Not enough for me to consider putting the brakes on this thing, though. Not enough to stop me from leaning closer, staring deep into her eyes. 'May I touch you now, *min elskerinde*?'

'I'd like that very much, Jensen.' She sank back against the bedding and, like last night, lifted her arms high above her head. 'Come here. And bring the condoms with you.'

CHAPTER SIX

My voice might have been calm and masterful, but inside I was anything but. I was shaken down to my core, terrified of the emotions sweeping through me.

I hadn't expected Jensen to readily admit to being a submissive, nor had I been prepared for the profound awe his admission would make me feel.

My mood had swung from being disgruntled about the snowstorm stranding me here to wanting it to last for a few hours. Maybe a whole day. Or two.

I wanted, no, *needed* the freedom to explore him. Explore myself in a way that I hadn't truly been able to in a very long time. But even as greed and lust and anticipation built inside me, so did a knot of tension. I couldn't afford to get carried away with this. Not when I had enough baggage to fill this cabin a dozen times over.

Not when he had his own baggage, in a Stephanie-shaped form specifically, that I couldn't help but resent even though I knew it was unfair. I had no claim on him, nor he on me.

But for as long as the storm raged outside, he was mine.

I watched him roll the condom between his fingers,

his eyes on me. At my nod, he tore it open and glided it down his long, delicious cock. Because it seemed as if I'd waited for ever, I didn't beat about the bush. And he either had amazing recovery skills or he was just as desperate as I was. He positioned himself between my thighs, and I looked into his eyes. 'Fuck me, Jensen. Fuck me hard.'

'It'll be my pleasure, *min elskerinde*.'

My mistress.

Power and gratitude surged through me, coated with the soul-deep yearning that threatened to break the leash I'd kept on it. I slackened the tight reins on my emotions, coaxed into almost feeling safe in this isolated cabin in the middle of nowhere. It was the least I could do considering Jensen had gifted me with his sublime submission. Wasn't it?

Rationale ceased to matter as his cock probed my entrance. Like the confidence with which he'd gone down on me in the tent last night, he slid in with one firm stroke, powerful, stretching me with enough friction and pressure to make me gasp. Pleasure rolled through me, intensifying as I saw it reflected in his blue eyes.

He muttered something in Danish.

'I like it when you speak in your mother tongue,' I said, my voice not quite steady.

He gave a strained smile, his nostrils flaring as he withdrew and thrust hard inside me.

'Talk dirty Danish to me,' I commanded.

Bracing himself on his elbows, he brushed his lips against mine. Then the sexy torrent began. Lyrical, alien words spilled from his lips, saturating my skin as he pleasured me with his cock and his tongue.

And, simply because I couldn't resist, I dragged his head down for a deep, tongue-tangling kiss. Our breathing turned harsh, the sizzling act of our coming together pushing us both to the edge far too soon. The urge to reward him ramped through me. That meant not giving in to climax too quickly. I needed to push him to the edge without making him go over, so I broke the kiss.

'Slow down,' I mouthed against his lips. 'Now.'

He gave a jagged little groan, but his movements slowed, his thrusts turning shallower, and his eyes squeezed shut in his effort to control his arousal. My fingers slid through his hair, caught the tresses at his nape and tugged.

He shuddered, a sheen of sweat breaking out over his sleek muscles. When he next pushed inside me, I tightened my muscles, gripping him as best I could despite the slickness of my sex. Fine tremors began unravelling over him and, heaven help me, but I loved seeing him on the edge, vulnerable and utterly lost in his pleasure.

Greedy need and the soul-deep yearning to unleash my true self prowled through me. Before I could withhold it, I pulled his earlobe between my teeth, bit lightly and relished his deep groan.

'I'd love to keep you like this for ever. Right here on the edge until you lose your mind for me. Or you beg me to end the unbearable pain. Maybe I will. Maybe I won't.'

Slowly, his eyes dragged open, intoxication drenching them as he stared down at me. 'Whatever pleases you, *min elskerinde*.'

My heart lurched wildly, the leash slipping another terrifying fraction.

This was too good to be true. *He* was too good to be true. Every single relationship I'd invested in since childhood had crashed and burned.

Whether initiated with childlike abandonment or after careful introspection and tending, each one had eventually turned sour, mocking my every effort to cultivate and maintain a sustainable connection. I couldn't need him this much, crave him this deeply.

The reminder threatened to dampen my spirits, caution seeping into my blood, cooling a layer of the frenzy triggering my yearnings. His fine tremor focused me, fine-tuned my pleasure so I could concentrate on him.

He really was perfect. Despite hard arousal etched on his face, he still moved inside me to the steady rhythm I'd instructed. I leaned up again, nipped at the skin beneath his jaw, revelling in the shudder that racked his frame.

'Beg me to make you come. Beg me to let you fuck me harder,' I whispered in his ear.

'Please, *min elskerinde*,' he said hoarsely.

'Please what?'

'May I fuck you harder? Make you come?'

'That wasn't quite what I ordered, was it?'

He shook his head. 'No, but I'll come harder for you if you go first.'

'Satisfying me gives you pleasure.' It wasn't a question. More like a shaken realisation that cracked another layer of the foundation I'd striven to safeguard myself with.

'Yes.' A simple, gruff admission that floored me. And intensified my hunger for him.

He registered the fresh wetness between my legs and his eyes lit with pleasure.

Jensen Scott might be a submissive, but he was a clever, powerful one who knew exactly which buttons to press. The thought of him doing this with another woman, somewhere in the hazy future away from this warm and toasty cocoon, drove my fingers into his flesh.

He gave another sexy growl, his hips jerking for an uncontrollable second. He righted himself immediately, his strokes measured as he awaited my command. Keeping my grip on his hair, I slid another hand between our bodies, beneath where we were joined, to grip his balls.

'Christ!'

Despite his harsh breathing, he kept up the steady pace. Impressive.

'How much longer can you hold out?' I taunted.

His jaw gritted before he replied, 'For as long as you need me to.'

I wanted his complete surrender, for the beautiful body poised above mine to drown in utter bliss along with me. The sweat drenching his skin said he was close. I wrapped my legs tighter around his hips, clenched him deep within me. 'Give it to me, Jensen. Give me everything you've got.'

Like a lion uncaged, he scooped a hand beneath me, angled my hips up, and then pounded me deep, hard thrusts that stole the breath from my lungs. Sounds of our decadent fucking filled the quiet cabin, adding another layer of erotic desire that drew me closer to the edge. Within minutes, I was mindless, a scream ripping from my throat as my orgasm hit with earth-shaking force. My internal muscles milking him, I heard him growl against my throat as he followed, coming with endless shudders until we were both spent.

Minutes passed with his arms wrapped tight around me. I floated in stunned euphoria, unable to form sensible words to fill the silence. The realisation that I didn't need to, that this wasn't another artificial encounter where I needed to deny my true self, filled me with an alien emotion that suspiciously resembled... contentment.

For however long this lasted, Jensen was my willing sub and I was his mistress. I could do with him as I pleased. If that included silence, it was my right.

Again, the thought shook me to my core. Enough to make me avert my gaze when he eventually eased up to look down at me. When there was enough space between us, he glanced down. 'May I?' he asked gruffly.

I nodded.

He eased out of me, rose and went into the kitchen. The supply closet door opened and a minute later he was back at my side, a towel in his hand. He cleaned me up, then himself, then tossed the towel away and resumed his position next to me.

It took a few minutes to wrestle my emotions under control. Striving to lighten the mood, I cast a deliberate gaze around the cabin. 'No TV. I'm assuming no Internet either?'

'In good weather my satellite phone's reliable enough to keep me connected but in this weather it's probably non-existent.'

It was a little disconcerting to be so cut off. Well, I still had my satellite phone for however long the battery lasted, but the thought that I wasn't in touching distance of a ringing phone felt…strange.

Admittedly, in a way that wasn't…awful. The lack of urgency to be in the centre of everything I'd built was freeing. Enough to trigger a smile. 'I'm assuming no board games either?'

He shook his head, his eyes twinkling. 'I wasn't exactly planning on entertaining when I came out here.'

I wanted to ask him why he'd come out here when, like mine, his professional life was booked solid for months. But the emotional wind tunnel I'd gone through a few minutes ago made me shy away from the personal. 'So what do you actually do here to occupy yourself?'

He smiled, an open, carefree smile that melted my insides as he caught a strand of my hair and toyed with it. 'We didn't get around to the full tour. My darkroom doubles up as office and studio. Most times I bring my work with me. When I'm not working, I hike the woods or take the dogs out for a run.'

Great, he was one of those healthily outdoorsy types.

He caught my expression and grinned. 'Yep, I'm one of those. I find it difficult to sit still for long.' His fingers left my hair, drifted over my shoulder and down my arm. 'Unless I have suitable distraction.'

I nodded, understanding him perfectly. After all, I was one of those. But, sadly, *my* restlessness had nothing to do with the need to be at one with nature and everything to do with running away from the demons haunting me.

'Why adventure photography?' I asked, despite my intention to steer clear of anything personal. But this wasn't personal. We were professionals exchanging professional courtesies. He was working on a project close to my heart and I had every right to know the man behind the camera.

Yeah, keep telling yourself that.

'My stepfather bought me a camera for my seventeenth birthday, a peace offering for sending me off to summer camp when I wanted to spend the holidays at home. I had every intention of hating it, along with everything and everyone at the camp,' he said with a grin.

'But you didn't?'

He shook his head. 'I fell in love with it. I photographed everything I could. When I returned and had the pictures developed, I realised I didn't suck at it, so I stuck with it.'

'And don't tell me, since you'd suddenly gone crazy about the outdoors you decided to throw a few risks in there?'

'It was easier to convince my mother that the purpose behind climbing mountains to get one unique picture out of thousands was worth it rather than climbing just for the hell of it. Although that was a seductive draw too.'

'And she was okay with that?'

His face tightened. 'She wasn't. Not for a long time.'

'Why not?'

His gaze shifted away from mine, reluctance in the fingers that absently caressed my wrist. Clearly his relationship with his mother wasn't smooth sailing. 'She found it difficult to let go, generally. At least she did before my stepfather.'

There was much more to that story and I probably should've changed the subject then. Hell, hadn't I earned a reputation for interfering where I shouldn't, pushing when I needed to step back? 'What about your father?'

He froze, his fingers sliding away from my skin. 'He's no longer in the picture,' he said tightly, his jaw clenching as his gaze swung to rest on the fire.

Was he dead? Had he abandoned Jensen as my parents had abandoned me? Questions teemed in my head, but I reluctantly accepted that he'd given me more than I intended to give him.

Minutes passed. When he looked back his expression was cordial enough to display no hard feelings but wary enough to warn me my probing questions were no longer welcome. The brief flare of disappointment and anxiety threw me. I throttled them down as he spoke.

'I'd very much like to feed you, *min elskerinde*.'

Hunger pangs immediately registered in my stomach, deciding our next activity. Summoning a smile, I nodded. 'I could eat.'

His smile returned. 'Do you have any preferences food wise?'

I shrugged. 'I don't mind, as long as it's hot and tasty.'

His gaze slid down my body and I could tell he was thinking about something entirely different from food. Nevertheless, he answered, 'I can rise to that challenge.'

He caught my hand in his, trailed kisses on my knuckles before rising. 'Stay here. I'll be about half an hour.'

I shook my head, reaching for my sweater. 'No, thanks, even princesses have to take a break from endlessly lounging about, waiting to be adored and pampered.'

He grimaced. 'I'm not going to live that down, am I?'

'Not for a long time, buster.'

He watched me pull on my sweater, disappointment in his eyes as I covered myself from chest to hip.

'Would you like some socks?' he asked, holding out a hand to help me up. 'There's underfloor heating but it's patchy in places.'

The cabin was warm enough. 'I'll be fine. I want to explore the pantry.'

Again, he smiled. My heart tripped foolishly.

'It's right through there.'

I left him to tug on his boxers and headed for the pantry. The room was about eight feet deep, with shelves that stretched from floor to ceiling, and packed with enough food and supplies to last a good few weeks. Even months.

How long had he been planning on staying here? What had Stephanie done to make him retreat from the world?

Questions lingered while I clocked the types of food Jensen liked. I was reaching out for a packet when he materialised in the doorway.

I couldn't help myself—I gaped at his delicious body. Watched him watch me as I adored him with my eyes, his cock thickening behind the stretchy fabric of his boxers. When my gaze returned to his face, his eyes were dark, gleaming in a way I'd learned signalled his arousal.

'I make a mean chicken fettuccine. Will that work for you?' he said, his voice a husky rasp.

'Good to know. The question is can you make a mean chicken fettuccine…naked?' I countered.

He delivered another one of those insanely sexy smiles, right before he yanked his boxers down his thick legs and kicked them away. I suppressed a gasp, my heart racing as he prowled towards me. 'Whatever my mistress wants, my mistress gets.'

He plucked the packet from my nerveless fingers, calmly collected the rest of the ingredients and left the pantry. I followed, worried that I was seriously in danger of becoming addicted to Jensen Scott.

It became clear very quickly that he was a maestro in the kitchen. He diced vegetables and smashed garlic with shameless aplomb. I wasn't even annoyed that I was reduced to simply fetching and carrying, the joy of watching him enough to dissipate my disgruntlement.

'Like a glass of wine?'

I hadn't spotted any wine when I fetched groceries from the fridge. He wasn't storing it outside the cabin, was he? 'Not if I have to venture out in that storm to get it, no.'

He laughed. 'There's a cooler in the pantry. I can't promise the vintage will meet your high expectations, but it's perfectly drinkable.'

My spirits plummeted, that stain of *spoilt little rich girl* cooling the atmosphere. I sensed his gaze on me as I went to the pantry. I'd missed it the first time round, probably distracted by a near-naked Jensen, but there it was in the back, a slimline cooler filled with a dozen bottles of white, and a wooden shelf next to it, holding bottles of red. I grabbed a white without reading the label, irritation warring with hurt as I returned to the kitchen.

He was leaning against the centre aisle, naked as the day he was born with his cock at half-mast. 'Look, I didn't mean—'

I stopped him with the dismissive wave of my hand. 'If you're going to throw another apology at me, don't bother. I know I come with a few unsavoury labels. It's not your fault if you can't help but go with the evidence bandied about.'

'You're upset, so I'm guessing they're not just meaningless labels?' he pressed.

'Is this just curiosity or do you actually want me to prove to you that I'm not what the media label me as?'

He shrugged. 'I want to know you. To see the woman behind the labels for myself.'

My fingers tightened around the bottle, a profound shaking starting inside me I was loath to outwardly display.

It stunned me how deftly he continued to pull the rug from under my feet. First with his unguarded admission of his sexuality and now with this. I dragged my gaze from his, but only strayed as far as the window, at the snowstorm raging harder with no signs of stopping.

The wind picked up then, and a loose branch smashed against the window, echoing the elemental force churning inside me. There was too much going on here, deep waters I was scared to wade through.

Ignoring him, I went to the drawer and searched for an opener.

Behind me, another drawer opened. A moment later, he appeared beside me, holding out the corkscrew. I took it, keeping my gaze on the bottle as I worked the screw into the cork. Tension vibrated through the cabin until a pop echoed in the silence. I'd spotted glasses in a cupboard earlier and I went towards it.

Jensen beat me to it, reaching up to the tall shelf to hand me a glass.

'Aren't you having one?'

Silently, he handed me another glass. 'I will if you want me to, *min elskerinde*,' he murmured, darkened eyes rapt on my face.

He was too much. Everything I was scared to desire.

I poured two glasses, handed him one and downed half the contents of mine.

An expression flitted across his face, too fast for me to decode as he raised his own glass and took a moderate sip. The sight of him, sipping wine while he stood there stark naked, comfortable in his own skin, yet with his eyes a little troubled as he stared at me, made me want to laugh. Or scream. Or hide.

From the first moment I'd laid eyes on him, he'd commanded extreme emotions from me. As if *he* were the Dominant.

Topping from the fucking bottom.

Well, if he wanted personal, he was about to get it.

I forced a shrug. 'No need to go on an extended expedition. I'm everything the media proclaims me to be. Spoilt. Rich. Some would even label me a ball-breaking bitch.'

A smile ghosted over his full lips. 'I can refute that last one. My balls were in your hands only a short while ago and I can attest they're still whole.' He cheekily glanced down at himself and I couldn't help but follow his gaze. Hell, he really was too perfect to ignore.

I wanted to end all of this by jumping him again, to dilute the heavy emotions with soul-drenching sex. I resisted the urge. 'Don't you need to look after the food?'

He shook his head. 'We're good for another ten minutes or so. Enough time for you to answer one question.'

I met his gaze with a deliberately sceptical one. 'Just the one question, is it?'

'Satisfy my curiosity. Just one innocent question.'

'I can order you to shut up. You know that, don't you?' I taunted softly.

His nostrils flared, but despite the mournful look in his eyes, he nodded. 'I'm aware of that. Do you want to?'

Emotion, thick and charged, arced between us, tugging tight and pulling me towards him. Several feet away from him, I stopped, bracing my hip against the centre aisle, wondering what the hell was wrong with me. Why my heart raced with alarm and anticipation of what his question would be. Why I was even considering answering in the first place. 'Ask.'

'Who's your favourite person in the world?'

I blinked in surprise. 'That's what you want to know?'

'I find the company one keeps says a lot about a person.'

'What if my person is not a person but a cat?'

His lips twisted and he shook his head. 'I'm willing to bet my favourite camera it's not. You don't strike me as a cat person.'

He was right. I actually preferred dogs, but I was a little miffed he could read me so easily. He continued to watch me in expectant silence, his hand casually twirling his glass.

We were straying into forbidden territory.

Heartache territory.

The branch slapped against the window once more, pushing me to answer.

'When I was younger it was my brother, Bryce, but

then…shit happened.' I shrugged, attempted to lighten the mood, alleviate the heaviness around my heart that reminded me of my inability to sustain relationships. My own brothers barely spoke to me, and when they did it was only to discuss Mortimer Group business. 'Right now, I'd say my aunt Flo is it for me. She doesn't take any shit, doesn't mince her words. She can be funny as hell with it, but she shoots from the hip and I…like that.'

Jensen nodded, his eyes locked on me as he took another sip. 'When was the last time you saw her?'

Technically, he'd used up his free pass. I wanted to tell him to stop. Opened my mouth to do exactly that. 'Why? What does it matter?' I asked instead.

'Humour me,' he replied.

I didn't see where he was headed with this, couldn't spot any real danger, so I responded. 'On her birthday, a few months ago.'

'So you're birthday, Christmas and anniversary friends?'

'How is this relevant to anything?'

'Is she a good person?'

A shaky sensation filled my chest. Aunt Flo was as close to love as I could manage, considering my issues. 'She's the best,' I said, my voice strangely tight.

Jensen smiled. 'She's your emotional compass. You go to her when you need centring. That means you hurt when someone causes you pain. You act spoilt when it suits you, but it's just that, an *act*. It means you may take life by the balls, but you'll never break them. Am I right?'

I set the glass down with a sharp click. 'What the hell is this?'

He shrugged, setting down his own glass to walk past me to the stove. 'Simply getting to know you, *min elskerinde*.'

He lifted the lid on the sauce, bent forward to stir it. As he did, thick strands of his hair parted at his nape. The glimpse of ink drew me to him.

'What is this?' I asked, parting his hair to reveal a dark blue tattoo etched into the skin between his shoulder blades.

Given our conversation just now, I gasped at the sight of an elaborate compass. It wasn't a common one. For starters, the lettering that should've clearly indicated correct points were different. Instead of N, S, E and W there was A where south should've been, D for east, M for west and the space for north left blank.

He stirred the pots for another few minutes before setting down the ladle. Then he faced me. 'We all have our ways for centring ourselves. This is mine.'

'What does the lettering stand for?'

'Family, for the most part,' he said a little tightly, reiterating my suspicion that things weren't warm and cosy on the family front for him either.

Nevertheless, his family seemed to be his guiding light. A compass guiding him when he needed it. I couldn't help the searing jealousy that lit through me before the curious burst of joy that immediately followed.

Even more confused by my jarring emotions, I let his hair fall back into place. 'Are we done with the interrogation? I'm hungry.' I was aware that my voice was several shades cooler, but couldn't seem to help myself.

The glance he sent me over his shoulder held empathy I didn't want.

'I don't want to risk being ordered to shut up so, yes, *min elskerinde*, we're done. And the food is ready.' His voice was even, bordering on gentle, which absurdly riled me up even further.

Feeling out of sorts, I busied myself gathering plates, cutlery, and setting the table. In silence, we dished out the food, took stools on opposite sides at the far end of the island that doubled up as a dining area.

I poured more wine while Jensen spooned mouth-watering fettuccine, sauce and lashings of grated cheese.

He stared, not touching his food, as I took the first mouthful. Grateful that we'd moved on from emotional subjects, I happily gave my verdict. 'This is good. Really good.'

He smiled, picking up his cutlery to dig into his own food. By mutual agreement, we stayed on safe subjects.

Why anyone would choose to risk life and limb the way he did as he described his most adventurous shoots was beyond me. I told him as much.

He laughed. 'Training reduces the risk of injury. Working with people you trust and will have your back also helps.'

Reminded of his question earlier, I asked, 'So you have your own group of friends you work with?'

His smile dimmed a little. 'I wouldn't call them

friends exactly. They're just a team I've worked with over the years. When we're done, we go our separate ways until the next assignment brings us together.'

'So who is your one true friend?' I pressed, tossing his question back at him. His gaze swept down, and he feigned interest in the contents of his plate. After a moment he shrugged. 'No one fits the label. Not any more.'

The finality of his statement tugged something inside me. 'Stephanie?'

His eyes narrowed, displeasure bristling from him as he stared at me across the island. He opened his mouth, but I pre-empted his reply.

'You can tell me to mind my own business if you want to. I'm just as curious as you were about me.'

His lips pursed, the last bite forgotten as he set down his fork. When he shrugged, his shoulders were stiff. 'We were lovers. But I thought we were friends too. I was wrong.'

'Was she a Domme?' I asked boldly.

He gave a bitter laugh. 'She went all out to fool me into thinking so, that's for sure.'

I gasped, unable to help my shock. 'Why…how?'

'Same way con artists fool people. She studied her craft, learned to imitate until she'd convinced herself she was an expert on the lifestyle. We met shortly before I went away on a three-month-long shoot. She made all the right moves, made me think she was what I wanted.' His eyes captured mine, boldly spearing me. 'But the truth always comes out, doesn't it?'

I wanted to snap back, punish him for daring to question me. But didn't his experience reflect mine? How many times had I fooled myself into thinking I was in a committed relationship only to discover differently? 'Yes, it does,' I found myself replying, my voice nowhere near sharp or scolding.

Understanding passed between us. Then memory etched harsh lines into his face. 'Unfortunately, Stephanie's little performance went beyond trying to fake her way into my bed.'

I looked around the cabin. 'So you came here to lick your wounds?'

I was poking the bear. Regardless of his submissiveness, he wouldn't appreciate his emotions being dissected, especially if the wounds were raw.

'Once I accepted your assignment, this was the logical base to work from.'

It was a half-truth. We both knew it. But when he stood and collected the plates, I let it go. In the space of twenty minutes we'd navigated landmine subjects with the power to blow us apart. I was all for taking a breather. Rising, I gathered the remaining dishes and joined him at the sink.

We cleaned up in companionable silence, and in ten minutes we were done.

I dried my hands as he headed for the freezer compartment of the fridge, pulled it open and peered inside. 'What would you like for dessert? We have…ice cream, ice cream and…ice cream. But in different flavours, I'm pleased to report.'

I grabbed the hem of my sweater and yanked it over

my head. 'I'm in the mood for something hot,' I said, adding sultry notes to my voice.

Slowly, he straightened. My gaze moved hungrily over his body, lingering longest at the cock rising to attention beneath my gaze.

He slammed the freezer door shut, prowled towards me with a mouth-wateringly virile swagger that made me suck in a breath. 'Your wish is my bidding, *min elskerinde*. You need only ask.'

'Return to the fireplace and lie back down. I'm in the mood to sit on your face.'

CHAPTER SEVEN

We sat on the sofa, Graciela's feet in my lap, my thumbs digging into the soft arch of her foot as she sipped a half-decent glass of Merlot.

Turned out she wasn't as snobbish about her wine as I'd insinuated.

Outside the snowstorm powered on, showing no signs of abating. We'd been snowed in for two full days. The only time I'd ventured out was to feed and water the dogs, make sure they were warm. They weren't exactly thrilled about being cooped up inside, but it couldn't be helped.

Despite it being well into the night, the wall-to-wall white-out cast a brightness over the landscape.

Winter had well and truly arrived in Alaska and I couldn't be happier.

I watched her watch the fire, enjoyed the dancing flames reflected in her hazel eyes. I'd almost fucked this up with that conversation in the kitchen on the first afternoon.

Since then we'd both avoided deep, personal issues, mutually choosing other forms of entertainment. Surprisingly, we'd found a few. Graciela loved hearing tales of my adventures. Her eyes lit up with almost childlike anticipation with each recounting. As much as I wanted to downplay it, having her hang on to my every word was a thrill I could get used to.

Turned out my mistress had a not-so-secret hankering for danger. As for the sex, it was beyond fucking sublime. Graciela was unapologetically demanding while generous in return. She was extremely sensual, breathtakingly intuitive, knowing exactly what I needed when I needed it. Her demands were equally challenging, a spine-melting edge to her dominance that led to the most intense climaxes I'd ever experienced in my life.

Besides the sex, touching her was my second favourite thing. In those moments between conversation, when the only sound between us was the quiet warmth of the cabin, the crackle of the fire, and the storm raging outside, my soul felt…right. My heart as close to contentment as I could manage.

I hid a smile as she moaned—I'd hit a particularly tight muscle.

'If I didn't hate the idea of robbing the world of your unique talents, I'd seriously consider hiring you as my full-time masseur.'

'I'm that good?' I smiled.

'You know you are,' she murmured, a small smile curving her beautiful lips.

My gaze dropped to the luscious curve of her lower lip reddened from wine and kisses, my blood heating up. She clocked the look and gave a wider, smug smile in return. Arching her beautiful body, currently clad in one of my white T-shirts, thong and nothing else, she leaned forward, ran her fingers down my jaw. 'I'd love to shave you,' she murmured, a definite savouring in her tone.

The stubble I'd kept when I arrived at the cabin had grown into a short beard and, just like my hair, she loved to play with it. Now she wanted to shave it off?

'I thought you liked the friction between your thighs?'

'I do. But I like the idea of shaving you even more. I'd use one of those old-fashioned blades, take my time with you.'

I stared at her, trying to work out which kink she had in store for me next. Much more than delayed gratification, she liked to keep me guessing. Not that I minded anything she'd done to me so far. Everything we did culminated in a wild and new experience. I was swiftly becoming addicted to it. *To her.*

I glanced out of the window, sending out a silent plea for the storm not to end just yet. I needed a few more days of this. Hopefully by then, this wild fever in my blood would've abated. Enough for me to let her go with no hard feelings?

My gut knotted, a hollow sensation taking up residence in the pit of my stomach.

'Tell me another story,' she softly commanded, relaxing against the cushions again and taking a sip of wine. 'Tell me about your very first assignment.'

I grimaced. 'I'd rather tell you a different story, *min elskerinde.*'

Her eyes sparkled, intelligence scheming in her eyes as she stared at me. 'You know evasion merely triggers my curiosity, right?'

Yes, I'd discovered that about her. But I didn't want to delve into this particular subject.

Her eyes narrowed. 'Why don't you want to tell me?'

'Because my first assignment was professional and also deeply personal.'

Her eyes widened. 'And you can't tell one without the other?'

I shrugged. 'I could, but it wouldn't be much of a story.'

She waited, one finger trailing along the rim of her glass.

And against my better judgment, the words tumbled from my lips anyway. 'I was hired by the owner of a sex club in Copenhagen to take shots for her revamped website.'

Her smile turned a little wicked. 'A different sort of adventure, then?'

I didn't return her smile. 'An enlightening one, yes.'

Slowly, her smile switched off, her face getting serious. 'How personal?'

'Helga, the owner of the club, became my first Dominant. She took one look at me and she knew.'

'How old were you?'

'Twenty-four.'

Something close to envy flashed in her eyes. 'How long did it last?'

'Six months.' I let out a wry smile. 'Then she moved on to somebody else.'

Sympathy shone in Graciela's eyes. 'She broke your heart?'

I shook my head. 'I thought so at the time, but in hindsight she was breaking down my barriers so I could accept myself.'

Graciela nodded, understanding brimming in her eyes. 'Why does that make you sad?'

'Because even after all of that I was still searching.'

'Searching or denying?'

I shrugged, the memory painful to vocalise. It'd been both. After the nightmare of my father, and the need to take control and keep my mother and sister safe from his abuse, surrendering that control had felt like a betrayal. One I'd struggled with for years before accepting the freedom of submission.

'So she was your first. Who was your second?' she asked after swallowing a mouthful of wine.

Shit, it looked as if we were doing this after all. 'No one memorable.'

One sleek eyebrow arched. 'Your third? Fourth or fifth?'

'All imitations of the real thing that have disappointed more than satisfied. Till…recently.'

She gave a soft gasp. 'Jensen…are you saying…?'

Fuck, I didn't want things to slip into hot and heavy territory, didn't want this perfect flow we'd found to hit the skids. But she was looking at me, expectant. And I was helpless to deny her any damn thing.

'You're the first to make a meaningful impression since Helga? The verdict is still out.'

She looked a little…relieved, and my stomach churned.

Damn, maybe I'd laid it on too thick?

Dial it back a notch, Jensen.

She held the glass against her lips, eyes spearing into me. 'Tell me about Stephanie.'

Fuck no.

'Graciela…'

She reached out, laid her hand over my arm. 'It's not an order. I just really want to know.'

I took a deep breath, wrapped one hand around her delicate foot. Then I lifted it, placing a kiss at the soft pad of flesh beneath her toes. She gave a soft gasp, her eyes darkening momentarily before she pulled herself out of my grasp. Great, that distracting technique wasn't going to work either.

I sighed, sifting through the torrent of memories I didn't really want to relive. 'We met at a party in London. She's an event planner, but her clients tend to be more on the risqué side of entertaining.'

'She throws sex parties?'

'Not always, but yeah, some of the time. She said all the right things, made all the right moves. We went out a few times and then things got…serious.'

'How serious?'

'I asked her to move in with me.'

She nodded, encouraged me to go on.

'Then the cracks began to appear. It started off by her telling me she didn't want to role play any more.'

Graciela frowned. 'Role play?'

'That's what she called it.'

'She thought it was a *game*?'

Bitterness drenched my mouth. 'Apparently. She'd been biding her time, hoping I'd snap out of it. When I pushed her on it, she confessed she'd read a few books, watched videos and used what she'd seen at her parties to expand her knowledge.'

'Bloody hell,' Graciela muttered under her breath. 'Where the hell did she do her research? The fucking children's library? Because the first real Dom or sub she met would've told her this isn't a damned game! That you don't simply play at it.'

'She was convinced she could make me happy. As long as we had regular sex like a *normal couple* and only did the Dom/sub thing on occasion.'

'My God. I kinda want to do…bodily harm,' she bit out, her breath hissing before she regained control. I was touched by that reaction. Ashamed to admit that I'd been looking for those signs of outrage, signs that she understood that this was as vital and necessary to me as breathing. Seeing her reaction only made me want her more.

'You trusted her?' she asked, her tone gentle with sympathy. 'Enough to surrender yourself to her? You must've or you wouldn't be…' She stopped and I was grudgingly grateful she didn't spell out what a fool I'd been taken for.

Still, bitterness flayed me, gouging deep at the soul-searing betrayal. 'Like I said, she walked the walk, convincingly enough to believe she had enough to achieve her ultimate goal.'

Graciela frowned. 'Which was what?'

I paused, unwilling to admit that last piece of Stephanie's deplorable intentions for the simple fact that I'd never seen it coming. But...what the hell? 'She ingratiated herself into the lifestyle merely to land herself a meal ticket either through a husband with a fat wallet or blackmail.'

Graciela jerked upright. 'She blackmailed you?'

My nod felt jerky, my emotions ragged and raw. 'Her next move after I threw her out was an email threatening to expose our sex life unless I paid her a million pounds.'

'I... Why would she—?'

My smile was crooked...off. 'She believed I would be too ashamed. Real men didn't submit. Her words.'

Graciela's jaw tightened. 'Now I definitely want to do harm. What did you do?'

'I called her bluff.'

Fire lit in my mistress's eyes. 'That's...ballsy.'

I basked in her quiet admiration, meeting her gaze, mine unwavering. 'I'm not ashamed of who I am. I may have taken a while to embrace that part of myself, but once I did, I was all in. *Am* all in.'

'I understand that, but there's a difference between moving on and having your business displayed all over the streets. Especially a man in your position. That's what she was counting on, right?'

'Yes. Her business was doing okay, but she had far loftier aspirations. She craved prestige, and she was willing to do anything to achieve it. Unfortunately for her, she thought threatening to expose me to my family would be the way to go. She was wrong.'

My mention of family drew a watchful look. 'So your family knows?'

I shrugged, unwilling to admit the undercurrent of tension between my mother and I meant that while I'd protect her to my last breath, inhabiting the same room for a long period of time was a strain. One I avoided until it became unavoidable. Like at Christmas. I pushed the looming visit from my mind and answered. 'We haven't had an open conversation about it, no.'

'You think they'll be okay with it?' she asked, a touch apprehensive as she awaited my answer.

'I am what I am and that's not changing. They'll have to be.'

'Even your father?'

'Stepfather,' I gritted out. 'My father is no longer in the picture. Hasn't been for years.'

Questions blazed in her eyes, but she didn't press me for answers.

Which was redundant because I confessed anyway. 'He was a deplorable human being.'

Her eyes softened in sympathy. 'I know a thing or two about deplorable human beings.'

'Yeah?' I encouraged.

She remained silent for several seconds and then she shrugged. 'My parents. They were probably as deplorable as your father.'

Despite the warmth in the cabin, icy fingers danced down my spine as memory pounded like a tide against rocks, battering my need to keep them on a tight leash.

'I really hope not.' Just the thought of Graciela being subjected to what my sister and I had gone through made my insides ice over with cold fury. 'Did your father batter your mother every damned chance he got for no fucking reason? Did your mother make excuses for his behaviour, lie about the true extent of the abuse, even though it was plain to see?' I didn't blame my mother for her inability to end the cycle of abuse before I took matters into my own hands, but it sure as fuck made trusting her an issue.

Her mouth dropped open, eyes filling with raw pain. 'No,' she whispered. 'Not to my knowledge, anyway.'

'Did he lay his hands on you or your brothers?'

She paled. 'He did that to you?'

I nodded, memory scraping over wounds still raw despite the passing years. 'Until I was tall and strong enough to stop him. But I didn't know why then and I sure as hell don't know why now. Some people are wired that way, I guess.'

'Jesus, Jensen, I'm so sorry.'

I laughed, the bitter sound grating my throat. 'How the hell do you do that?'

'Do what?'

'Slide so easily beneath my skin?'

She looked startled for the moment and then she shifted her gaze to the wine glass, examining its contents before she took a sip. 'It's a unique talent not everyone appreciates.'

'By everyone you mean…?'

She lifted her gaze. 'It's got me into more trouble than it's worth.'

'What kind?'

Her nostrils flared, more with pain than the discomfort of laying her secrets bare. 'I drove a wedge between myself and my brothers, for one.'

'How?'

She averted her gaze again, staring long and deep into the fire.

I recaptured her foot, massaging her instep as she tapped a finger restlessly against the glass. 'My parents didn't abuse us physically, but they didn't think twice about abandoning us when we were young. I was too stubborn to accept that. Hell, I believed I could single-handedly fix our dysfunctional family. So I pushed and I pushed until it broke us.'

I opened my mouth to ask, but she sent me a look that drove the words back down my throat. 'Tell me another story,' she commanded.

My mistress was fully back in residence and I wasn't allowed to deny her.

I didn't want to.

I raised her other foot, kissed her in exactly the same spot. This time she didn't pull away.

And it scared me shitless how pleased that made me.

* * *

My euphoric state lasted for another mind-melting twenty-four hours.

Another day filled with sex, conversation, good food cooked together and more sex. We barely slept for more than a couple of hours.

No surface within the cabin was left un-christened by Graciela's sizzling demands. More than her blinding, more frequent smiles and the intelligence that shone from her eyes when we discussed the diverse topics that captivated us both, it was the siren-like fire in her eyes just before she ordered me to fulfil a desire that stoked a craving in my soul I was beginning to suspect would never be equalled once this thing was over. It was the reason a knot of dread had taken up residence in my stomach at the thought of it ending.

The force of the storm had lessened, snow falling with less frequency in the last half-day. I'd taken the coward's way out and avoided checking the weather forecast.

We couldn't stay here for ever, but I could sure as hell enjoy whatever hours we had left. Her favourite setting for fucking was in front of the fire, but, for the sake of extra comfort, we'd relocated to the bed last night and promptly fallen asleep.

Our limbs were tangled together, her head on my shoulder as she breathed, deep and steady. I was turning into one of those corny idiots who even enjoyed the way his woman slept, unable to help my smile as I stared down at her.

Even in slumber, Graciela Mortimer remained a Dominant. One leg rested over both of mine, her arm firmly anchoring my middle. If I weren't miles stronger than her, I'd remain pinned in place until she decided to let me go.

And fucking hell, I liked her wanting to keep me close even in sleep. I glanced at the window, willing the snow to start falling again.

But after an hour of lazing about in bed, when my prayers weren't answered, I eased away from her. Restlessness that usually drove me outside for a walk in the woods or exercising the dogs, regardless of the time of year, sent me downstairs to my office.

Sitting at my desk with my camera, I scrolled through the pictures I'd taken for Graciela.

The perfectionist in me was pleased to see there were several exceptional ones she could use for her magazine, with more shots on autofocus that I could use to make an interactive video for the digital version of her magazine if she wanted. I was confident I had everything she needed.

But my reason for coming to my office had nothing to do with work right now. I scrolled until I reached the one I wanted. Connecting the camera to my laptop, I sent the image to print, my breath stalled as the machine spat out a single portrait, glossy photo. On a wild impulse I printed off another five in various exposures to make an even half-dozen.

I placed them up at vantage points in my office, playing with the lighting and scrutinising each one critically from a different angle.

As I experimented, an idea began to form in my head, excitement building in my chest.

Graciela Mortimer was without doubt the most beautiful woman I'd ever seen. Her unique beauty, the light she tried to hide needed to be stoked. Kept alive.

I sat down at my desk, fingers flying over the keyboard as I activated my emails. As suspected, there were over two dozen emails from my office and a handful from my agent. I ignored them all, typing up an email of my own. The Internet was patchy and probably wouldn't send for a good few hours, but I didn't care. It would take a few emails to get this project under way, but I set the ball rolling, smiled as I slammed the laptop shut. My agent would be thrilled. She'd been pushing me in the direction of holding another exclusive show, since my first and only show had become a runaway hit.

That show, purely based on a series of photos I'd taken, had snowballed into a wild, insane juggernaut, with awards, book deals and insane amounts of money thrown my way to add to the small fortune I already had in the bank, guaranteeing I wouldn't have to work another day in my life if I didn't want to. It'd been more than a little disconcerting, truth be told. The only reason the furore had eventually died down several months later was because I'd taken an assignment to Papua New Guinea, one I knew would last three months. My absence had done the trick of granting me a modicum of privacy and normality.

The memory sobered me.

Was that what Graciela went through on a daily basis? As a child born into a powerful and influential family, she'd been the cynosure of rabid, relentless interest probably before she could walk. My interaction with social media was selective, getting involved only where it pertained to my work, but technology made blaring headlines impossible to ignore. I knew the kind of hellish media attention she and her family garnered, the kind of invasion of privacy that dogged her every waking hour.

She'd lived with it all her life, so was it any wonder she was wary and instantly suspicious of anyone wielding a camera?

Would she think of my burgeoning idea in those terms?

No. This was different. It would be special. A celebration rather than an invasion. Hopefully a prelude to…something else.

I drew back from putting a label on it, though the curious churning in my gut wanted to delve headlong into dissecting just what it was I felt for her.

The last three days had been illuminating. I'd caught more frequent glimpses of the woman beneath the powerful surname. Discovered her previous relationships had been just as ultimately unsatisfying as mine. That she hadn't taken a submissive in a while. Selfishly, that'd pleased me. I wasn't magnanimous enough to be the kind of guy who made accommodation for other prospects when it came to the woman I was interested in.

She had no entanglements in London. Or New York. Or wherever it was she was heading back to once we left my cabin. As primitive as it sounded, I wanted to be the only man occupying her thoughts while she was with me.

And when she left? What then?

I clenched my fist at the hollow in my belly at the thought of it.

Yeah, I was dangerously straying into obsession. Had probably done so already. Yet the thought didn't terrify me as much as it would've a handful of days ago. My gaze fell back on her pictures. Maybe we could make this work outside this wilderness bubble.

Shit, I was licked if I was already factoring her into my future.

Would that be so bad?

The answer never formed, the door creaking open redirecting my thoughts to the present.

She stood in the doorway, a blanket drawn around her body, her hair sexily dishevelled. Lips I'd feasted on repeatedly last night were still swollen and the sight of her bare feet curling into the wooden floor was seriously arousing.

Fuck me, but she was breathtaking.

'I don't remember giving you permission to leave me alone in bed.'

The firm, hot dominating voice immediately triggered a fever inside me, fire licking through my blood. Before I took my next breath, my cock was hardening, my fingers tingling with the need to submit, to please, to hand over my surrender to her.

'I would be very happy to return there if that's what you wish, *min elskerinde*.'

She started to answer but then her gaze fell on the pictures. Eyes widening, she stepped into the room. 'What is this?'

The stiff note in her voice made me tense. 'I was going through the images on my camera and—'

'And you decided to print out pictures of me?' Her voice was hushed but stiffer with growing wariness.

I spread my hands to lighten the mood. 'Hey, it's no big deal. I just wanted to see the images in different lights.'

She turned from the one propped up on the shelf, her eyes suspicious. 'Why? Your project isn't about me, remember?'

I bit the inside of my cheek, reluctant to share my idea with her just yet. In this mood, I suspected she'd say no out of ingrained habit.

Once I presented the full picture, she'd know my intentions were honourable. I took the most direct cop-out. 'I'm aware of what my brief is. This is the way I work, Graciela.'

A trace of suspicion receded from her eyes, but she remained wary as she glanced at the pictures. It was part of the set I'd taken outside the tent as she'd stared up at the aurora borealis. The naked awe on her stunning face had needed memorialising. The instinct that few people, if any, were granted the privilege of seeing this powerful woman overcome with childlike wonder compelling me to take the photos.

I wasn't about to tell her any of that, of course.

While the past few days had revealed she'd push for the personal on occasion, she wasn't one for prolonged introspection or subjects that dwelled on her or her family for too long.

The snippets I'd gleaned formed their own story.

She wasn't exactly estranged from her brothers or the rest of the family, but her interactions with them were few and far between, instigated by both sides in equal measures. It was a situation that hurt her, regardless of how much she tried to deny it.

I started to gather the pictures, intending to put them away. But a wild urge stopped me.

Besides the wariness and suspicion, there'd been something else in her expression when she'd looked at her pictures just now.

An expression of...surprise.

As if she was seeing herself in this light for the first time. I wasn't letting the opportunity slip me by. I wanted her to rediscover whatever she'd had taken from her by her family or the world at large. And hell, I was playing with fire, risking whatever time we had left with this impromptu experiment that could blow up in my face.

But wasn't taking risks part of my life? My soul?

Her voice certainly called into question my sanity as she trailed me out of the office. 'What the hell are you doing, Jensen?'

She could stop me at any time, command me to destroy the pictures, and I would do it. I was still hers to command; had a feeling I would be far longer than the snowstorm lasted.

But even that disturbing admission didn't stop me from walking across the room to place one picture over the fireplace. The second one I attached to the fridge door, the next on the fourth step.

The fourth I pinned to the front door, the fifth on the coffee table next to the sofa, where she tended to place her wineglass. The last one I was saving for the bedroom.

'Jensen.' Her voice shook with warning as she watched me.

Hands empty, I faced her. 'I want you to see yourself the way I see you.'

She refused to look at the pictures. 'And how's that?' she sneered.

'Beautiful. Breathtaking. Full of wonder.'

Her hands bunched tightly over the blanket until her knuckles turned white. 'Instead of? Just how do you think I see myself?'

Crap, this had turned way heavier than I'd anticipated, but I didn't back away from it. 'The labels you call yourself are other people's opinion of you. And yet I think deep down you believe them, don't you?'

Her lips firmed, mutiny in her silence.

'You're not spoilt. If you were, you wouldn't have sent your team away and braved the elements with me with nothing but a phone and a change of clothes. You hate sitting back and being waited on hand and foot even though it's my privilege to serve you like that.'

Her hazel eyes darkened. 'I like control. That's all this is, nothing more.'

I shook my head. 'No, it's not. Control is one thing. *Consideration* is another. Beneath all that bristling you're a good person, Graciela. I just wish you would see that yourself.'

'I'm not. If I was, I wouldn't be alone,' she grated in a harsh whisper, her jaw tightening as she attempted to hold herself together.

More than anything I wanted to go to her, take her in my arms, but I suspected this would end very quickly if I moved from where I stood. 'You're not alone. You're here. With me.'

'For how long?' She glanced out of the window. 'In case you haven't noticed, the storm is over.'

'That doesn't mean we have to be.'

She inhaled sharply. 'That wasn't what we agreed.'

I shrugged. 'Agreements can change. Nothing is set in stone. The beauty of being adults is that we can change our minds. What's to stop us from making a new one?'

A light glinted in her eyes, but a moment later she shook her head. 'You're deluded. Or probably suffering from cabin fever or some such nonsense.'

My gut churned harder. 'Don't trivialise my emotions.'

Her face hardened. 'You're disappointing me, Jensen.'

'Am I? Why?' I dared.

I could tell I'd stumped her. That made me smile. 'I may be submissive, *min elskerinde*. But I'm not weak.'

She frowned. 'I never thought you were.'

'Are you sure? Were you not hoping to discover some flaw that would make it easier to end this?'

'Is that what we're doing right now? Ending this? Because I could've sworn you were pushing for more.'

'While you're simply trying to push me away.'

'Stop it, Jensen. Just…stop.'

'Is that an order, mistress?'

'Yes,' she snarled. 'It's an order.'

I moved then, reluctantly walked past her into the kitchen. 'The coffee is just about ready. Would you like some?'

I could tell my obedience was throwing her. Heck, this morning wasn't going quite how she had expected it to go.

Join the club.

I was feeling pretty damn raw and exposed myself. But what had I expected? In pushing her to accept a different version of herself, I'd bared my own needs. That I was way too invested in what was happening in this cabin.

Preparing coffee gave me something to do, and I gleefully ignored the yearnings rampaging through me as I grabbed the mugs and poured the beverage. Turning, I caught her gaze on the picture above the fireplace.

She presented me with her profile as I handed her the coffee, waves of displeasure emanating from her. But then, she surprised me by taking a seat on the sofa, right next to where her other picture lay face up on the coffee table.

Her gaze swept down to it for a moment before she sucked in a long breath and took a sip of coffee.

'Would you like some breakfast?' I asked.

She shook her head. 'No, thanks. I'm not hungry.'

My hands clenched around my mug.

The thought that I'd triggered an early end date for us slashed panic through me. I held it together, joining her on the sofa. I intended to sit next to her, but at the last-minute I sank lower to the floor.

My arm brushed her leg. Breath held, I waited for her move.

Seconds ticked into minutes. We drank our coffee. Then I felt her fingers, whisper-light against my temple. I stilled, barely breathing.

Her fingers slid deeper into my hair, brushing against my scalp in that firm, insistent way that sent shivers down my spine. As I predicted, she gathered the mass at the base of my skull, gripped it in her fist and used the pressure to tilt my head.

Our gazes met. Locked. She pushed. I parried.

She exhaled. 'Whatever it is you're doing, it's not going to work, you know.'

'I disagree.'

Her grip eased a fraction and I was absurdly terrified she was about to let me go.

'Tell me about the whales,' she said.

The whales. My life-changing underwater experience. The most profound moment of my life thus far.

I denied the deliberate distraction, nudged my head

at the picture. 'Tell me about the last time you felt like that before two nights ago.'

Searing pain clouded her eyes and she shook her head.

'Tell me,' I insisted. 'Lighten your burden by sharing it with me, Graciela.'

She stared at me for several seconds, her expression wavering. She released my hair. And a dark, thick hollow invaded my stomach. It lingered only for a moment because she touched me again, this time nudging my head onto her thigh.

I held myself stiff, instinctively sensing she needed the silence to delve beneath the surface of her pain.

CHAPTER EIGHT

HE WAS ASKING the impossible.

Demanding the forbidden. Asking me to rip my chest open, show him my shredded heart? When had that ever helped?

I had literal proof that it didn't. Every effort I'd made to connect, to *correct*, had turned to dust.

His hand wrapped around my calf. Warm. Solid. *Present.* Grounding me for the first time since I came downstairs.

I'd woken up in a wild panic and before I could put my finger on why, my heart was racing. It'd taken half a second to realise the primary reason for my anxiety. It was because Jensen wasn't beside me. The secondary because the snow had stopped. I was torn right down the middle between accepting that this wasn't just a casual fling and grasping the out that Mother Nature was handing me.

The latter had diminished within seconds, leaving a searing sense of loss.

The weight of it had compelled me out of bed, the need to see Jensen driving me.

Only to come downstairs to this stomach-hollowing situation.

He gently massaged my muscles, intent on grounding me in the present when I wanted to flee both it and the pain-ridden past.

And go where? Into a future filled with uncertainty? God, when had my future become so bleak?

When he knelt at your feet and gifted you with possibilities you knew you'd have to walk away from.

The raw, soul-shaking admission turned my insides out even more than the last few minutes had. My gaze lifted to the picture propped up above the fireplace. My breath caught; I barely recognised the woman in the photo.

He wanted to know when I'd last experienced that kind of…joy?

'It was the last time I saw my mother before she left me for good.'

I wasn't aware I'd spoken the words aloud until his fingers moved again, gliding up and down my leg in silent reassurance.

But with the words out, I couldn't hide any more. 'I didn't know it was the last time, of course. She was getting dressed to go to some function or other. I didn't ask because I was so surprised she'd let me into her bedroom at all, never mind her dressing room. Both were strictly off-limits to every one of us. But that day was different. She was…strangely indulgent, didn't berate me when I played dress up with the diamonds she'd expressly forbidden me from touching.'

'How old were you?'

'I'd turned nine a couple of days before.' The recollection brought a small smile, my mother's presence at my ninth birthday a wonderful phenomenon in itself that'd made my small heart burst with joy, the belief that my fractured family was on its way to becoming whole again, a sacred conviction I'd nurtured for days. A wish I'd refused to let Gideon's condescending sneers ruin. I'd later discovered that he'd somehow known it was a foolish dream. My clever brother, perhaps the cleverest one of us, had seen what was coming, used his trademark sarcasm and icy indifference to safeguard himself against hurt. He'd known what was coming but had kept it to himself.

I hadn't been so lucky…

Jensen's hand wrapped around my ankle, infusing warmth into me, as if it would lessen the pain of the recounting. Nothing could. But I appreciated the gesture.

'I was tall for my age and my mother and I were of a similar build.' We were more than that. My mother had given birth to a near replica of herself, the only differences between us the hazel eyes inherited from the Mortimer gene and my black hair to her chestnut waves.

'So she let you play with her stuff…' Jensen coaxed.

'Normally it took her hours to get ready. This time she took even longer. And I got to spend every minute with her.' My heart stuttered and my fist tightened at the recollection. 'I don't even remember what we talked about. I really wish I did. I wish I'd paid better attention…'

'The time spent was more important than the words said.'

'Was it, though? Because she left for her party and I never saw her again.'

His fingers tightened on my skin. 'What?'

'She was done being a mother. She wanted to live her life. Those hours in her dressing room may have been her way of saying goodbye. Or maybe it was just a meaningless indulgence for her. Thing is, I never got the chance to find out.'

Jensen exhaled slowly, then turned to drop a kiss on my knee.

I was glad he wasn't looking at me. I didn't think I could bear him witnessing my pain. Not that he didn't have a very good idea. He was far too clever for that.

'My brothers and I found out later that it'd been their intention all along. To leave that night and never return.'

Jensen frowned. 'Both your parents left?'

'Yes.' My throat was clogged with ravaging pain. 'It became sort of a recurring theme. My cousin Damien's parents did the same thing too.'

He cursed under his breath. 'Who told you?' he asked.

'My aunt Flo knew. Hell, she probably tried to stop them because...well, that's the kind of person she is. She didn't succeed, obviously. So a day after spending what I thought was the start of the mother-daughter bonding I'd dreamt about, I was effectively an orphan, despite my parents still being alive.'

'Min Gud,' he muttered under his breath.

My fingers weaved through his hair, anchoring myself. He made a thick, pleased sound at the back of his throat, leaned into my touch.

'Was that what drove you and your brothers apart?' he asked after a minute.

Fresh anguish washed over me. 'No. That was all me.'

'How?'

'I got it into my head that I could make things right, get my mother to come home. I begged and badgered my way into getting them to agree for us to write letters to my mother. It took a few months but I finally got them on board.'

'Did she reply?'

I laughed again, but the sound broke apart, catching the sharp edge of my grief. 'Oh, yes, she did.'

'Graciela...*kæreste*...'

I didn't know what the endearment meant, but I shook my head, eager to dispel the threat of tears and unlock the lump lodged in my throat. 'I'm fine. It's fine,' I insisted.

His fingers drifted up my calf. 'It's not. You know that as well as I do.'

'You're supposed to agree with me.'

'I do, for the most part. You did what you needed to try to make your family whole again.'

'No, I pushed and control-freaked my way into making things worse.'

'What did she say in her reply?'

That knot built in my throat again. 'In a nutshell? That I wasn't worth it.'

He inhaled sharply. 'Graciela…'

I didn't look down, didn't want to see sympathy or pity or embrace any form of gentleness. I was too scared my lacerated heart would fracture into a million pieces if I succumbed to the promise of empathy. Did I deserve it? When I'd dragged everyone down with me into the pits of despair?

'No one blames you for trying—'

I laughed again, my fingers tightening in his hair to stop his words. 'Oh, believe me, they do. Gideon most definitely did. He didn't hold back. Bryce was soft-hearted enough not to hurt my feelings with his words, but I could see in his eyes that he totally blamed me. I ruined us, Jensen. He went from being a loving and carefree younger brother to avoiding me every chance he got. I was a pariah in my own home. I'd enter a room and they'd leave. In the end I begged Aunt Flo to send me to boarding school. Then I charmed my way into mid-term breaks and school vacations with any friend who would have me because I couldn't face going home. And it worked. I didn't go home for two years, was terrified of returning home to the same hatred. It was why…' I pressed my lips together, holding in the last, heart-wrenching confession. But still he pressed.

'Why what?'

'Why I hated myself even more when I found out later that she came back.'

Blue eyes found mine. 'She returned?'

'For unannounced visits. She'd breeze in, drop off presents, then breeze out again. Or so I was told.'

'Maybe she wanted to reconnect?'

I shrugged. 'I wouldn't know. She never asked for me. She knew where I was but she never came to see me in school. She never reached out. It was almost like... I was dead to her. And that made me angry, Jensen. Angrier than I've ever been in my life.'

'That's understandable. She hurt you.'

'Yes, she did. But was it enough for me to wish her dead? Because that was exactly what I did. I wished her dead, and a few months later she died.'

The cold jagged pain of that admission froze me from the inside out.

I barely registered Jensen twisting around, his strong arms lifting me off the sofa and into his lap and wrapping around me. The tightness in my throat unravelled, dissolving into hot, gulping tears that shook the very foundations of my soul.

Through it all, he held me close, running his fingers through my hair and down my back without saying a word. When I was wrung dry, he brushed a kiss against my temple.

'You were heartbroken and lashed out. That makes you human. If wishing ill on someone actually guaranteed a desired result, my father would've been six feet under the first time I saw bruises on my mother and little sister. Life doesn't work that way, *kæreste*. Sometimes the assholes who cause pain get to live long, hopefully miserable lives.'

I raised my head, saw my pain reflected in his eyes. 'Your father?'

He nodded. 'I don't know where he is, but only because I've never bothered to find out. The third time I stood up to him, he went out drinking and never returned. So you see, I was responsible for driving my parent away too, but I don't regret it. I'd do it again in a heartbeat. I wanted him gone with every fibre of my being.'

I remained silent, unable to do anything but absorb his warmth, his sheer perfection. With his lips still trailing down my face, he reached for the box of tissues sitting on the coffee table.

I plucked out a few, blew my nose and scrubbed away the remainder of my tears. I didn't feel whole, would probably never be whole again, but I felt less... tormented, less burdened. The fact that it was Jensen who'd done this to me, for me, triggered a whole new layer of panic. The weight of what I felt for him terrified me. Everything I'd dreamed of had broken up beneath the pressure of my yearning.

Like a butterfly held too tight, I tended to crush the wings of things that were precious to me. And he was fast becoming precious, right up there with things I didn't want to lose.

Which brought its own bracing demand. What right did I have to him?

His lips drifted down my cheek, lingered at the corner of my mouth, and I conveniently sidestepped the questions teeming inside. 'I look a mess.'

He kissed me firmer, his lips more demanding. 'No, you look beautiful.'

Blind panic made me turn to him, seal my lips against his. I didn't want to hear the words. Didn't want to open my heart to a promise that would never be fulfilled. The contents of my mother's letter blazed through my mind, reminding me that I wasn't enough. I would never be enough.

His arms tightened around me, his eager lips surrendering to mine as I deepened the kiss. I wound my arms around his neck, repositioned myself so I was astride him on the floor. The blanket gaped open and his hands slid beneath, gliding down my side to grip my hips, hold me close as we leaned into the kiss.

Between my legs, he was rock-hard, a thrilling reality, a consuming storm I could drown in, forget about my emotional turmoil. I shrugged off the blanket completely, my fingers dancing down his muscled chest to stroke the bulge that promised oblivion.

'Fuck me, Jensen.'

He shuddered against me. Then he pulled back, just enough to meet my gaze. 'I'm dying to, *min elskede,* but we don't have a condom down here.'

I didn't want a reprieve from this madness; didn't want time and space to thrust me back into the emotional grinder I'd just been through. So I took a breath. 'It's fine. I...' *trust you.* I barely stopped myself, my heart lurching wildly at the dangerous words I'd almost uttered.

I'd only known him a matter of days. This was the proximity talking. We'd been cooped up in this cabin with no other outlet than to fuck and bare ourselves to each other. I was letting my emotions get carried away. Another mistake I'd regret if I didn't rein myself back in. 'I'm on the Pill. It's fine.'

His eyes lingered on mine, delving beneath the matter-of-fact words to find their true meaning. I rocked my hips over him, and the distraction worked like a charm. His fingers tightened on my hips and his gaze fell to my breasts. With a deep groan, he dipped his head and sucked one nipple into his mouth. I clutched him to me, throwing my head back in wild abandon as I drowned in the unique passion he invoked.

This was…should be…just sex. Good sex I was in danger of sullying with emotion.

Again my heart shook at the half-lie, another fastening tearing itself from my control. It was almost as if it wanted to free itself, soar where I couldn't allow it. I couldn't risk the responsibility of him, couldn't risk turning another person against me.

Thankfully thoughts ceased to matter as ecstasy took over.

He bent me backwards until my hair brushed the floor. Then he rained kisses down my front to the top of my mound. I revelled in the heat of his hands and mouth, in the thick Danish words he whispered over my skin.

His thumb strummed my clit and I cried out. He toyed mercilessly with the swollen bud, didn't stop until I was mindless. Until sating this insane need was all I could think of.

Repositioning myself back on top of him, I speared

my fingers through his hair and dragged his gaze to mine. His face, powerfully lust ravaged, was the most perfect image I'd ever seen. 'I want you inside me. Now.'

He raised his hips off the floor just enough to yank down his jogging bottoms. The moment his erection was freed, I braced myself on my knees, spread my thighs wide. Jensen gripped his cock, his other hand clutching my hip, and with his eyes rapt on my face, absorbing my every action, I lowered myself onto him.

'*Min elskede.* You feel so good,' he groaned.

The gruffness in his voice made me wonder if I'd misheard the word, but I didn't care. He was inside me. I was mindless with bliss, free from memories and pain. The lack of a condom's barrier was equally thrilling, adding a layer of intimacy I'd never imagined. It was probably that, and not the lightened weight in my heart. Or the hushed voice at the back of my head suggesting I wasn't quite as hopeless, quite as deplorable, that I might be worth something if this formidable creature possessing me believed so…which brought tears to the act. Which made me want to burrow inside this bubble and never emerge.

Whatever it was, it culminated in soul-searing pleasure that made me scream with the sacredness of it. My orgasm went on for ever, my whole body shaking, my heart hammering as fresh tears formed behind my eyelids.

I wrapped myself around him, rejoiced in his shout of release and the power of him pulsing inside me. We shuddered uncontrollably in the aftermath, clinging to each other, our breaths ragged as we slowly came down from the highest high. His hands trailed down my back, over my hips and thighs until our breaths returned to normal.

'I'd like to shower with you. And then I'd very much like to feed you. May I?' Jensen asked, his breath brushing my ear.

Normality. Or a semblance of it.

I wanted to kiss him for not making a big thing out of this. Instead, I nodded. 'Your mistress would like that very much.'

I felt his smile against my jaw as he adjusted me in his arms, then lithely rose from the floor without dislodging me.

God, that was sexy.

I managed a smile as he raced us up the stairs.

We were both wrung out, didn't speak as we entered the large shower stall. Jensen washed me from head to toe, his hands firm, adoring. When he was done, he sank down to his knees, silently offered the shower gel to me.

I returned the favour, lingering longest in his glorious hair before washing his sculpted, mouth-watering body. After dressing, we returned downstairs, where I was confronted with my images. For a panicked moment I wanted to order him to take down the pictures. I could tell he was bracing himself for it. The words never came. I'd revealed the worst of my secrets to him. What was a picture or six?

When he realised I was going to leave them be, a smile broke out on his face. A smile that made my heart bang hard again. Dear God, I was in danger of expiring from heart failure if this continued.

And it couldn't really continue...

As we ate breakfast mostly in silence, that thought solidified. After what he'd been through, Jensen needed someone unbroken. Someone not quite so...flawed. Twisted and riddled with dysfunction. Someone who didn't live in torment or trail bitterness and disappointment behind her.

So in a way, I accepted fate's decision when the unfamiliar sound disturbed the silence. We both started, Jensen's gaze narrowing as it swung upward to where the sound emitted from the bedroom. 'It's your phone,' he said, his voice dark and subdued.

My satellite phone. My route out of here.

I hadn't used it for days, not even to check in with my staff because I'd been wholly enraptured and encapsulated in this delusional bubble we'd created for ourselves. But now, my life was stridently calling. I ignored the ashen taste in my mouth at the thought of leaving, stood and went up the stairs to retrieve it.

'Hello?'

'Miss Mortimer? It's your pilot. I've been given the all-clear to fly. The forecast predicts another storm later today, so this is our only window.'

I heard a noise behind me and turned around.

Jensen stood in the doorway, his piercing gaze

pinned on me. For a long stretch, we both remained frozen.

'Miss Mortimer? Would you like me to pick you up?'

My gaze darted wildly around the bedroom, the place I'd experienced fulfilment such as I'd never known. When I glanced back at him, Jensen was striding forwards, his jaw set, but appeal in his eyes. It wasn't a request I could grant. Not without disappointing him eventually, hurting us both.

'Yes. Please come and get me. Hold on a second.' I held the phone out to Jensen. 'Can you tell my pilot how to find me, please?'

He took the phone from me, but didn't raise it to his ear. 'I thought we were going to talk about this?' he hissed. 'Make other plans—'

I shook my head. 'No, we weren't. The storm was going to let up eventually. And I was going to leave. You know that.'

'Graciela,' he gritted out, stormy shadows moving over his face. 'This isn't done. Stay.'

Every cell in my body screamed with the need to say yes. I shook my head harder. 'What's that going to achieve? You've wrung me dry. Be content with that.'

'Content? You think downstairs was about me being content?'

I stopped him before he could carry on, my gaze shifting to stare pointedly at the phone. 'I'd rather not do this with someone eavesdropping.'

A muscle ticced in his jaw, but slowly, he lifted the phone to his ear and coolly recited his coordinates to my pilot. Then he disconnected the line, tossed the phone onto the bed and fixed determined eyes on me.

I pre-empted him before he opened his mouth. 'I'm not going to change my mind, Jensen.'

'We have at least an hour before the chopper gets here. Are you planning on not talking to me in that time?' he taunted.

'Don't be ridiculous.'

I hurried to the closet where he'd placed my week-ender. Snatching whatever personal items I could locate within easy reach, I mentally dismissed taking things like my toothbrush and the toiletries scattered around his bathroom. They were easily replaceable.

Plus, moving around meant I didn't have to acknowledge the hard, painful knot in my belly that grew tighter with every second.

'Why the sudden hurry, Graciela?' Jensen asked, his voice deep, throbbing with challenge.

I didn't want to look his way, but, God, I couldn't help myself. His arms were folded as he lounged against his bedroom wall, his stance deceptively calm. But his eyes gleamed with purpose that stated he wasn't about to let me leave with a dismissive wave and a hollow promise.

'What are you talking about?'

'I'm talking about you, attempting to shut the door after the horse has bolted. What happened downstairs was unsettling, I know, but—'

I forced a laugh, one so false it grated my throat. And made his face tighten with irritation. '*Unsettling?*

Why, because I shed a few tears? Don't make it a bigger deal than it was, Jensen. Sure, I was due a little... catharsis, but it was hardly life-altering...'

My words trickled away when his face grew tighter, the warmth leaving his eyes. 'That's the second time you've attempted to dismiss something significant as nothing—'

'Because it was nothing!'

His arms dropped, his jaw rippling as he took a slow breath. 'It wasn't nothing. What happened with your mother was shitty and traumatic. You shame yourself by trivialising it now because you let your guard down. Did you forget what you promised me?'

My thundering heartbeat threatened to drown out everything. 'I warned you people break their promises all the time.'

An emotion that closely resembled bleakness filmed his eyes for a moment before he blinked it away. 'Yes, you did. But I chose to believe you when you said you'd be truthful about whatever you were feeling. About what happened between us.'

'And you think I'm not?'

His pointed look spoke volumes. 'I know a little bit about denial and the people who practise it, Graciela. My mother was an expert at it. And *you* are so fully immersed in it, it's any wonder you can fucking breathe,' he scythed at me, cold fury drenching his features.

The searing accusation, and the caustic acknowledgement of its truth, made me turn away from him before he saw his effect. I silently willed my pilot to hurry before I did something foolish, like beg Jensen not to be disappointed in me, to help me see myself the way he wanted to see me. But that was a road fraught with even more disappointment. After all, wasn't what I'd predicted already unfolding before my eyes?

Zipping the bag, I lifted it and blindly headed for the door.

'Aren't you going to say anything?'

I forced a shrug. 'What's the point? You seem to have me psychoanalysed inside and out.'

Without asking my permission, he stepped forward and took the bag from me. But he made no move to leave the room. His presence surrounded me, his beautiful masculine scent invading my every pore. 'And you're just going to take it?' he jeered.

Fear and frustration shook through me. 'Jensen...'

He exhaled, long and loud. Then he jerked towards me.

'*Min elskerinde...*'

The fury and mockery were gone, his voice low. Gentle. Coaxing.

'Stay. Take a day, let's sort through this.'

With every fibre of my being I wanted to scream *yes*.

My heart dropped to my stomach, acceptance that our agreement was officially over, that I was no longer his mistress, or he my sub, blinding me with pain so acute, I nearly gasped.

It if hurts this much, then why are you leaving?

Because what I wanted didn't matter. Because...

You're not enough. You'll never be enough.

My mother's words echoed and re-echoed in my head. And the heart I thought had shrivelled to uselessness after being steeped in years of pain and bitterness started to bleed.

'I'd stay if there was something worth staying for,' I forced out. 'It's been fun, but we both know that was all this was ever going to be.'

Gentleness evaporated and the cold scorn returned. 'Bullshit. Cut the lies and say it like it is. You're going to board your chopper and run away because you're scared.'

He waited, eyes fixed on me as a minute ticked by. Two.

I remained silent, holding my tattered emotions inside because I was terrified of opening my mouth. Petrified I would scream that, yes, everything he said was true.

With a tight curse, he left the room and jogged downstairs with my bag. I followed, mourning the sight of my bag propped beside the door. Avoiding the taunting images of a Graciela who apparently lived inside me but wasn't strong enough to reach for what she wanted, I perched on the farthest end of the sofa, staring into the fire and fighting the tears that threatened.

Stealthily, I watched Jensen prowl around the room, tugging on his thick coat and boots. When the ominous sound of a helicopter approaching shattered the silence, he strode to my bag, picked it up and opened the door.

A chill wind blew in, but it was nothing compared

to the cold seizing my insides at the thought of leaving this rustic cabin. Leaving Jensen.

'You'll hear from me shortly,' he said, his voice stony.

My heart leapt, then the true meaning sank in. He was talking about the project. The work I'd given just fleeting thought to over the past three days. 'My assistant will put you in touch with the editorial team.'

His jaw clenched and he shook his head. 'You're not fobbing me off on your assistant. You hired me. You're going to deal with me. I won't have my time wasted going back and forth with subordinates who'll feed me second-hand information. I'll be in London next week with the finished project. We'll meet, then hopefully we can be rid of each other.'

His words were firm, forceful, any hint of the earlier pleading and deep craving gone. I wanted to step back in time, accept the extra day, see where it led. But I already knew the outcome. Two more broken souls. More anguish that would keep me up at night. I couldn't take that. Not any more.

And yet, I couldn't make my feet move. Couldn't step off his frozen porch and climb the chopper patiently waiting thirty feet away.

'That's what you want, isn't it?' he pressed, his voice harsh.

I swallowed, forced my head to nod. 'Yes. Elsa will check my schedule and let you know.'

His lips tightened, assailing me with an urge to see him smile one last time that was so unbearable, I turned and hurried out onto the frozen tundra, my feet sinking into snow, towards the pilot who alighted and came to escort me.

Jensen handed him my bag, then stood, feet braced, cold eyes boring into my back as I climbed aboard.

He didn't back away or go inside as the rotor blades churned up snow.

Even when his white jacket was pelted with snow, he didn't leave. He stood there, his glorious hair whipping around his face, jaw set as he stared up at the helicopter.

Unable to help myself, I stared back, my eyes watering as he blended into the blinding white landscape.

Only when the chopper banked steeply did I look away, my heart already thudding with deep dread at the enormity of the misery that awaited me.

CHAPTER NINE

'OH, MISS MORTIMER, you're back! I wasn't expecting you till later this morning…'

Elsa's surprise registered hollowly in my head as she entered my office. I heard her stop a few feet from my desk, but didn't turn from my position at the window.

'Can I get you anything? Your usual coffee?' Her voice trailed hesitantly when I continued to stare at the window, glaring miserably at the view I didn't want to see.

It was the wrong view. For starters, London was wet and dreary and had been since my return two days ago, the rain unable to make up its mind whether to turn to sleet or mizzle.

I wanted a white-out, thick snow covering everything in sight and cutting off the world.

But more than anything, I wanted the man who I'd been snowed in with. As much as I appreciated her, Elsa's presence was just another reminder that I was half a world removed from where I wanted to be.

I forced myself to turn around, to paste a half-decent smile on my face as I sat at my desk. 'I came in a little early.' Understatement of the year. I'd abandoned sleep at two a.m., my queen-sized bed suddenly feeling like a wide, endless ocean of misery, determined to swallow me up.

The longer I'd lain there, staring at the ceiling, the deeper my despair and panic had taken hold. With the business day beginning, I'd decided to call it quits where sleep was concerned, and get a head start on my work.

In hindsight, I realised leaving the perfectly adequate loneliness of my Mayfair mews house to place myself in the operating hub of the Mortimer Group empire wasn't my finest decision.

Because the more the hive of activity moved around me, the deeper my loneliness had steeped.

The inter-family group email that someone industrious had set up a while ago was the first of many joy-shrivelling emails waiting to pounce on my vulnerable state when I fired up my laptop. Every single one of them involved some family member crowing about their personal success.

Apparently Gideon and his wife, Leonie, Damien and his new wife, and Bryce and Savannah were planning on spending the holiday season cruising the Mediterranean on the family's yacht. The invitation had been extended for anyone who wanted to join, of course, but last thing I wanted was to be a fifth, sixth or seventh wheel.

There was another email from Bryce, mildly berating me for my unavailability, and informing me of his engagement to Savannah. Apparently he'd tried to call several times in the last few days but had been unable to reach me to give me the good news.

Even while my heart had soared with happiness for him and Savvie, the depth of my despairing loneliness intensified. When we'd met up in Singapore a few months ago at the opening of Savannah's flagship lingerie store, he'd looked just as miserable as I felt. But evidently, he'd worked through his differences with Savvie.

Christmas was less than two weeks away. The thought of spending it with my dysfunctional collection of back-stabbing, acid-tongued family members filled me with dread.

...run away because you're scared...

My fingers shook over the mouse as Jensen's words struck hard and deep.

I'd been burned more than a few times, but...had some of that been of my own doing? Had I deliberately held myself up to the flame, just to see if I'd burn? For once, would it hurt to see what happened if I stepped back? Perhaps feel warmth instead of flames?

Before my courage deserted me, I pushed away thoughts of Christmas in a cabin in the wilds of Alaska and fired off emails to Gideon and Bryce, tentatively accepting their invitation to join them for New Year. I could always change my mind later.

'Give me five minutes, I'll grab your coffee,' Elsa said.

I shook my head. 'I don't want coffee, thanks.'

Her eyes widened at the uncharacteristic refusal. 'Are you all right?'

'Yes, I'm fine, thank you.' She didn't need to know that I only wanted coffee from one person. I didn't even care that Jensen hadn't given a shit about achieving the optimal temperature for his coffee. He'd served it with a blinding smile, a mouth-watering, naked torso and eyes filled with the desire to please his mistress that touched my soul.

Elsa frowned. 'Are you sure I can't get you anything? Maybe tea?' she said hesitantly, anxiety filming her eyes, as if she was afraid I'd say yes and confound her further.

'No, thanks. Do you have any messages for me?' I said, striving to keep my voice calm.

She looked down at the leather binder she always carried and back up at me. 'Nothing that can't wait—'

I held out my hand. 'I'll be the judge of that.'

She passed it over. I flipped it open, my heart racing as I perused the three neatly typed sheets containing my packed daily schedule. There was nothing about a meeting or call with Jensen Scott.

Bleak disappointment thudding through me, I handed back the binder, aware Elsa was staring at me.

'Is there something specific I should be looking at?' she asked.

'No.'

'Okay,' she said. 'Well…your first meeting is at nine. I'll give you the usual ten-minute heads-up.' She started to walk away.

'Is Larry in? Do you know if he's heard from Jensen Scott?' I blurted before I could stop myself.

Elsa turned around, her eyes flaring with interest at the mention of Jensen's name. I tightened my fist in my lap, attempting to breathe calmly so as not to give myself away.

'Larry left for Jo'burg last Thursday. He's taking his annual leave before he starts the next project. I emailed you about it last week.'

'Can you liaise with his assistant and let me know the minute Mr Scott gets in touch?' I said briskly, partly because I didn't want Elsa to linger, and slip into one of her girly chats about Jensen.

It worked, my solemn mood filtering through to her. With a nod, she left my office. My hands shook as I laid them back on the desk.

Jensen had said he'd be in touch next week. It'd only been two days, for heaven's sake. And yet it felt like a lifetime. I turned back to the window, irritated the rain was still falling, that it hadn't turned into snow while my back was turned.

I was still standing there, fighting a losing battle with dejection, when Elsa returned with the promised ten-minute warning.

Get your head back in the game.

But my performance was perfunctory at best, only years of experience seeing me through the busy day. The magazine I was so passionate about, nurtured from an often disregarded five-page newsletter into an award-winning mechanism for charity, had lost its lustre. And

I wasn't sure whether to be terrified or shocked at my apathy.

In between meetings, I rabidly refreshed my inbox, hoping for an email from Jensen.

It didn't arrive.

I held my breath each time Elsa entered my office with a message, each time a new email hit my inbox and I experienced a bolt of excitement, only to deflate when it wasn't the one I yearned for. By Friday afternoon, I wanted to hate him for sticking to his word. For cutting me off so clinically.

But how could I when nothing had changed for me, except the searing sense of loss every time I thought about him? How selfish did it make me to long this desperately for a moment of joy on what should be a conclusion to a business transaction for the sole purpose of alleviating my loneliness?

An email pinged and my heart leapt. It wasn't from Jensen, but Bryce's name caused a different sort of excitement.

I know you're thinking about joining us on the yacht for New Year's, but do you fancy Christmas Day with us as well?

My fiancée insists you join us if you don't have plans.

I would love to see you too.

Bryce

I read and re-read it, unable to stem the expanding hope in my chest.

In a moment of weakness a year ago while in New

York, I'd had lunch with Savannah, and blurted out my desire to reconnect with Bryce. Her store opening had been the perfect opportunity to fly to Singapore to attempt to salvage things with Bryce. I'd come away with a suitcase full of exquisite lingerie and a growing hope that my relationship with my brother would be rekindled.

I fought back tears that sprung out of nowhere, daring to accept that things weren't so hopeless with my brothers after all. I was dashing away tears when Elsa knocked and entered. She looked flustered, her eyes a little too bright. 'Umm, sorry to disturb you, but Mr Scott's just turned up. He says he has a meeting with you, but—'

I jumped up to my feet, despite the sudden nerves and the memories of our parting. 'Where is he?'

'I'm setting him up in the conference room, but you have an appointment in fifteen minutes.'

'Cancel it,' I blurted.

Her eyes widened as I rounded the desk and headed for the door. 'Which of the conference rooms is he in?' I asked, my heart slamming against my ribs.

'Conference Room Three.'

I nodded, pleased. It was the most secluded one, the one with the best soundproofing. Which we wouldn't need, of course, because this was purely a perfectly civil business meeting. A last meeting before we parted ways.

If you are so unaffected, then why is your heart racing? Why are you shaking?

I ignored the taunting voice, walked with measured strides to the door.

'Umm… Miss Mortimer?'

'Yes?' I answered, impatience and anxiety ramping high. 'Was there something else?'

Elsa nodded at my face. 'You might want to fix your make-up.'

I grimaced and reversed direction, tossing my thanks over my shoulder as I headed to the private bathroom adjoining my office. When I saw my reflection, my jaw dropped in shock. I looked a mess. No wonder Elsa had been casting me concerned looks all day.

My mascara was smudged to clown-like proportions, my lipstick non-existent from stress nibbling. My hair looked as if I hadn't brushed it in days.

Who cares? He's seen you without make-up for three straight days.

That didn't mean I wanted to present myself looking like a scarecrow.

I repaired my make-up, tugged a brush repeatedly through my hair until it fell in acceptable waves over my shoulders. My suit was professional but stylish, uniquely edged with purple stripes against black adding an unapologetic touch of femininity to the outfit. After gliding nude gloss over my lips, I left the bathroom.

My heart banged harder against my ribs, my palms growing sweaty as I approached the conference room and opened the door.

Jensen looked up from where he lounged in the seat

at the head of the table, eyes just as chilled as the last time I'd looked into them.

Despite the cold reception, I froze, my senses needing a moment to absorb him.

He wore a dark navy suit, clearly bespoke, gloriously highlighting every superb physical attribute.

His hair was combed, but it still achieved that sexily dishevelled look. The stubble he'd cultivated during our time in the cabin had now grown into a short, sexy beard, making his face even more wickedly handsome.

'Good afternoon, Miss Mortimer. I hope I'm not disturbing you too much?' His deep, gravel-smooth, desperately missed voice slid over me like silk.

Ice-cold silk.

My fingers tightened on the door handle as I shifted my gaze to where Elsa stood frozen next to him, her eyes wide with interest as they flicked from Jensen to me and back again.

'You can leave now, Elsa.'

Her lips drooped with disappointment, but she nodded. 'Oh…er… Okay. Sure thing. The projector for your presentation is all set up for you, Mr Scott.'

His smiled warmed for her but turned frigid a moment later. 'Thanks, Elsa.'

I shut the door behind her and approached, only then taking in the leather case that contained his trays of photos before my gaze swung back to him.

In time to catch a flash of hunger before he checked his expression.

I wanted to pepper him with questions, demand that

he tell me everything he'd done since we last saw each other. But wouldn't that be prolonging the agony?

I took a deep breath, forced my gaze away from his face to the photos laid out on the conference table. 'Shall we begin?' I said briskly.

'Yes. Let's,' he rasped, his voice brisker, perfectly emulating the Arctic wind I yearned to feel against my skin. Because, absurdly, it suddenly symbolised bliss and freedom I was terrified I'd never experience again.

A different sort of shudder moved through me, a forlorn little forecast of what my future held. Desperately, I pushed it away. 'Is this everything?' I waved my hand at the tray.

He laughed, harsh and bitter. 'Are we really going to do it like this?'

'Do it like what, Mr Scott?'

Without answering me, he rose, strolled down the length of the conference room to the door and turned the key in the lock.

A million butterflies fluttered in my belly. 'What the hell do you think you're doing?'

He ambled back to me, looking sleek and delicious in his suit. 'I thought giving you a week to think things through would work,' he repeated.

I deliberately raised an eyebrow, despite my heart leaping at that fixated look in his eyes. 'Then you obviously don't know me well.'

He stopped a few feet away, his gaze not leaving my face. 'And whose fault is that? One of us ran away the moment things got a little too personal, and that person wasn't me.'

Shame engulfed me but years of staring opponents down weren't easy to dismiss. 'Is that why you've locked the door? To physically restrain me?'

Distaste washed over his face. 'That's so we're not disturbed, not so you can't leave whenever you want to. I'll never keep you prisoner, Graciela. Not unless you specifically ordered me to.'

A fever started in my belly, heating me up from within. I fought to deny it. 'Not going to happen.'

Briefly, his nostrils flared, his expression dimming before he turned to the table. He shrugged off his jacket and tossed it over a chair before curtly nudging his head at the tray. 'Fine. Looks like you want to keep hiding from reality, so let's get on with this, shall we?'

He started the projector. I grabbed the remote and dimmed the lights and took a seat, forcing myself not to glance his way. Not to breathe him in.

He negated all of that by dragging his chair closer, until he was a tempting arm's length away. For the next long while hundreds of pictures scrolled across the screen, each one stunning enough to make paring it down to the essential twenty-five I needed for the magazine near impossible.

When we reached the images he'd taken on the night of the borealis, fine tremors shook through me, memory attempting to shake free everything I needed to hold inside. Every frame he'd captured was overwhelmingly breathtaking, unique enough to draw a gasp.

I felt him lean in close but couldn't move away. Didn't want to.

'I'll never be able to experience another borealis without thinking of you,' he breathed in my ear. 'You know that, don't you?'

I didn't answer. I couldn't. A lump had lodged in my throat; with selfish pleasure I took from his words. Yes, I didn't want him thinking of anyone else but me.

Abruptly, he moved away, hit the button again, and we scrolled through the last of the images. When Jensen activated the lights, I blinked, still awestruck by the power and beauty of the pictures.

'How the hell am I going to choose?' I blurted.

His smile was stiff and cold. 'I'll take that as a compliment.'

I stared at the display on the table, at a loss as to where to start.

Impatient fingers drummed on the table, then, 'Do you want my help?' Jensen offered.

I hesitated, the idea of handing over such an important decision to him stopping me for a moment.

The drumming stopped. He lounged back and folded his arms as he watched me back. 'Don't worry, Graciela. You're still in charge. I'm merely lending you support.'

My heart fell at the mild sneer in his voice. And again, I wanted to throw caution to the wind, rewind to the blissful moments on his cabin sofa. To the intense, transcendental hours spent before his fireplace. But I needed to stay in reality. *My* reality, not the one Jensen believed I needed to face. Anything besides strict professionalism would only be adding to the heartache I'd experienced in the last week.

If that meant letting this animosity ride out for the duration of our meeting, then so be it.

I nodded my consent. He didn't move immediately. His arms remained folded, his piercing gaze narrowed at me for a stomach-tingling stretch.

Then, lips firmed in a line of displeasure, he went to work, sorting out forty pictures with jaw-dropping efficiency. 'I think these will work for what you have in mind. They have an element of each topic you're discussing, and, together with the interactive video in the digital version, I think your message will be heard.'

I stared down at the pictures he'd chosen, added another ten of my own, and, refining down again, halved the photos and rearranged them in the order I envisaged them laid out in the magazine.

We both stepped back and admired the mock-up, and he nodded. 'That's even better.'

I wanted to preen at his compliment, but I couldn't even give myself that little leeway. 'I'll leave them there for now, and come back to it in a while. See it with fresh eyes.'

He nodded. 'Good idea. You don't want to saturate your senses before you make a decision.'

I turned to the rest of the images, totalling over eight hundred. 'It seems a shame for all of these to go to waste.'

'They're yours. Do with them as you will.'

Again there was a distinct timbre in his voice that

caught me on the raw. I looked over and he was staring straight at me.

Hunger tore through me. I licked my lips and his eyes darkened, his gaze rapt on my gliding tongue. Face tight, he took a half-step closer. I averted my gaze from him, back to the photos, terrified of the wild leap of my heart. 'I can make a coffee-table book, donate the proceeds to charities in Alaska?'

I felt his gaze linger on me for a few seconds more before he answered. 'You have enough here for two books, easily. Even make it an annual thing.'

The idea thrilled me, but even more was the thought of a possible future collaboration with Jensen.

Terrified of the frenzied leap of my senses, I focused on the pictures, killing the idea of an extended connection with Jensen. There wouldn't be a different outcome in the future. I would always disappoint and fall short.

He joined me, handing me images on one subject, then the other. Within a short time, I had over three hundred photos for the first coffee-table book. He reached for the last set of photos at the same time I did. I jumped back, the electrifying effect of his touch lighting through me.

His face froze over and he reached for his jacket. 'It's getting late. I need to be somewhere else.'

'Where?' I asked before I could stop myself.

He shrugged. 'I have a prior engagement.'

A vice clamped around my heart. Was it business or pleasure? Was he seeing someone else? So soon?

What right did I have to be distressed by it? I'd

pushed him away. Still, the thought of him leaving strangled my insides. 'We're not done here.'

He paused, raised a mocking eyebrow at me. 'Aren't we?'

'We have an executive chef in the building. I can order something for us to eat while we finish up here.'

If anything, his expression grew more remote. 'You sure you want to risk indigestion by spending more time with me? Aren't you afraid I'll want to get *personal* again?'

'It's a professional courtesy, Jensen. That's all.'

His smile lacked any trace of warmth as he leaned forward, right into my personal space. And, God, he smelled so good, looked so mouth-watering, I wanted to leap across the gap between us, press myself against him and never let go.

'What makes you think I'll play by your rules of professional courtesy?' he rasped.

Because he brimmed with integrity. Because not a single time during our cabin seclusion had I had reason to call his character into question, the way I did so many people in my life. 'Because I know I can take you at your word.'

He hissed in a breath. 'What the fuck do you think you're doing, Graciela? I won't let you toy with me.'

My heart kicked hard. 'I'm not—'

'Did you decide some time in the past week that you weren't quite done with me as you purported to be? That perhaps I'm good for one last fuck, maybe two?'

Until I witnessed it for myself, I would've deemed

it impossible but Jensen's gaze was both sizzling and frigid as it swept over me, lingered on my face, my breasts, my hips and legs before returning. He wasn't bothering to hide his hunger and each look triggered, until I couldn't stand it any longer.

When I stepped back, he followed. I didn't order him away, couldn't even get my tongue to work, the electricity zapping through me freezing my vocal cords.

My hip bumped the table, halting my momentum.

Slowly, he raised his hand, brushed the pulse leaping at my throat with his knuckles. My nipples immediately puckered and I bit back a moan.

He tossed his jacket away, and captured my wrist. Holding my hand within his, he turned my wrist, his gaze on the fingers he was running over my racing pulse. 'So tell me, did you miss me, *min elskerinde*?'

I gasped, my senses cartwheeling at hearing those two words fall from his lips even while I was searingly aware I was foolish to open my heart up to it. 'Don't call me that,' I forced out. I wasn't worthy, not if I couldn't be what he wanted me to be. Open. Wearing my pain on my sleeve. Vulnerable to seismic emotions that would eventually consume me whole.

He exhaled long and deep. 'Why not? You're my mistress, whether you want to acknowledge it or not.' His gaze still downcast, he raised my hand and placed an open-mouthed kiss on my wrist.

I sucked in a sharp breath, arousal lighting through me as he slowly tasted my skin.

'Staying in the cabin without you was fucking hell,'

he confessed roughly. 'For the first time since I built it, I couldn't wait to leave. Return to London.'

Something deep, profound, moved through me. 'Jensen,' I attempted again, my heart hammering hard.

'I'll stop calling you *min elskerinde* if that's what you truly want. After today, you don't need to hear it again, anyway, right?'

I didn't pull away. I loved what he was doing so much more than the bleakness that awaited me once I ended this.

He trailed erotic kisses down my arm, drawing closer with every caress.

Something cracked open inside me, letting a flood of hope and desperate craving rush in.

'Not going to answer?' he mocked as he bit the sensitive skin. 'I'm afraid I'll need an answer to my next question, though.'

I cleared my throat, forced my voice to work. 'What question?'

Glacier-coloured eyes met mine, blazing lust and censure fighting for supremacy. 'Despite the bullshit we're rolling in, I want you. Fucking badly. So may I have you one last time, *min elskerinde*?'

I should've said no, of course. Should have snatched my arm away, shown him the door, tossed whatever temptation he was dangling out with him. But of course, I didn't. Because this was Jensen. Gorgeous. Wickedly talented. Pure sex on two legs. As close to a perfect sub as my jaded heart and broken spirit could appreciate.

So I cupped his jaw, caressed my fingers over his nape before sliding them into his hair.

My fist tightened around a handful of glorious hair.

He sucked in a sharp breath, his eyes squeezing shut as a hot shudder shook his towering frame. His hands stayed at his sides, his breath panting as he waited for my next move.

'Maybe I won't let you have me. Maybe I'm just going to make you watch me come.'

Harsh, razor-sharp need twisted his features. 'If—'

'You're not allowed to say *if that's what you wish*. You're so big on being real, then tell me what you truly feel. Not what you think I want to hear.'

His Adam's apple bobbed. 'Fine. I want to be the one to make you come, *min elskerinde*.'

'Why?'

Stark need darkened his eyes, transformed his beautiful face into a mask of pure masculine arousal. 'Because you can't hide from me then.'

Another rivet yanked free, a slither of hope flaring high before despair doused the flame. 'Did you stop to think that maybe I'm protecting you, Jensen?'

His nostrils flared. 'What from?'

'From me!' I released him, started to step back.

He yanked me close. 'Why the hell would I need protection from you?'

'Because I'm not enough! You think you want the whole, sordid truth? I haven't sustained a single relationship in my life. Not a single one. Everything I touch turns to fucking dust. I may be successful in business but I'm a mess in private.' The unfettered confession snagged several emotions inside me, twisting up into a knot of need so acute I feared the power of it. 'You think I'm hiding? Maybe I am. But I'm hiding for a reason. You judged your mother for living in denial. Did you stop to think she may have been protecting you? That she didn't want you to witness every single sorry detail of her trying to hold it together?'

His face tightened into a taut, angry mask, his skin losing a trace of colour. 'We're not talking about me. Or my mother—'

'Why not? Because you feel *exposed* when we do? Maybe even a little unsure about that high horse you're perched on?'

Anger slowly dissipated, leaving behind a poleaxed look I'd never seen before. He dragged a hand over his mouth and jaw, and his gaze shifted from mine as he processed. Frowned as he turned his back on me and strode a few paces away. A different sort of tension rode him as the minutes ticked by in silence.

'Could you have got her wrong, Jensen?' I pressed softly.

He whirled back, traces of alarm and uncertainty in his eyes. 'Whether I have or not, that's for me to deal with,' he gritted out. 'Right now, we're talking about you, Graciela—'

'No. I don't want to reason this out. I've lived with this for years, Jensen. The promise of my mother's love and her abandonment wrecked me for any relationship.

I've tried. Believe me, I've tried everything. Nothing works.'

And the end result had turned me inside out, raw with anguish and guilt because not only had I brought pain on myself, I'd dragged my brothers into that dark hellhole. I'd ended up ruining not just my childhood, but theirs.

Silence stretched, tight and fraught. 'Fine. So what now?' Jensen demanded, eyes narrowed.

I shrugged, surprised my shoulders could move beneath the heaviness weighing me down. 'I'm more than done with this crazy emotional roller coaster you seem determined to make me ride. So we can end this right now. Or we can end this an hour from now on condition the hour is spent the way we intended ten minutes ago.'

I held my breath, praying he wouldn't take the first option. Praying for a precious sixty minutes more with him before I had to let him go.

He stepped forward, paused for an infinitesimal second, then lifted his hand to my cheek with a wry smile. 'I'm not idiotic enough to walk away given those options. But know this. We might be fucking instead of talking, but we'll still be having a conversation, *min elskerinde*,' he said with quiet confidence that angered me, even as my heart wept at the gift of those two words.

A gift I didn't deserve, but was too selfish, too greedy to turn away. 'I hope you're not awfully disappointed if that conversation is one-sided,' I sniped, distressed by the dominion he seemed to have over my emotions. 'Undress,' I ordered, kicking my shoes off before stepping out of my own clothes.

Naked, I pulled out one of the conference room chairs, sat down and then slowly cupped my breasts and toyed with the peaks as I watched him tear off his clothes.

His cock jerked, a drop of moisture already beading the tip of the broad head. Tugging, twisting, tormenting the hard tips, I opened my senses to self-pleasure, intensified by the rapt look on his face as I arched my back.

My pussy throbbed and clenched around the promise of his cock. When I moaned, his lips parted on a harsh pant.

Abandoning one tight peak, I trailed my hand down my midriff, my fingernails drawing shivers over my skin and trailing goosebumps down my navel to my hairless mound. There I rested for a moment, revelling in the agitated rise and fall of his chest and my own dark pleasure.

Slowly, I parted my thighs. His gaze zeroed in on my wetness, and I spread my legs wider. He groaned and licked his lower lip.

Stark, anguished need intensified on his face and his thighs shook beneath the force of his desire.

I slid two fingers on either side of my wetness, pinching my labia tight. The zap of lust was nearly my undoing. Jensen growled beneath his breath, and I knew he was on the verge of begging.

Except he wouldn't. He had his instructions, and,

sublime sub that he was, he would obey to his dying breath.

Enjoy this while you can.

I refocused on him. His gaze was still riveted to the fingers gliding up and down my folds. 'Do you want to taste me, Jensen?'

He groaned. 'Yes, *min elskerinde.*'

I slid one finger inside. Then two. Deep. Deeper to my second knuckle. Rolled my hips to get them deeper, then drew them out. Held them up in front of his face.

He inhaled long and deep, licked his lips again. But he didn't move. Didn't even beseech me with his eyes. He simply…waited.

Flooring me with his control. Making me want to reward him. 'Taste.'

The words were barely out of my mouth before he grasped my wrist, wrapped his mouth around my fingers, drawing deep. The strength of his suction made me flinch. He felt it and immediately eased, his eyes flashing an apology as he glided his tongue over my digits, eagerly lapping up my essence. His deep grunt of satisfaction trebled my need. Hunger flaring wider, I dropped my other hand between my legs and slowly fucked myself.

He followed every movement, cock bobbing up and down. A thicker bead welled, then trailed down the underside of his cock. Veins stood out in hungry relief. I knew he was suffering.

'Would you like to come with me, Jensen?'

Again, he hesitated a fraction. 'I would like to fuck

you, *min elskerinde*. It would be a privilege to come inside you. But…'

'But what?'

Pure torment darkened his eyes. 'I don't have a condom.'

'I feel like we've been here before.'

He jerked out a nod.

'Has anything changed since then?'

His eyes narrowed, a gleam I couldn't decode lighting the depths. 'Not sexually for me, no.'

'Nothing has changed for me, either.'

His gaze swept down, and I got the feeling my answer had pleased him. More than anything I wanted to know what he was thinking…feeling.

I didn't ask. I didn't have the right. Never would.

Best keep this to just sex. Pure, unadulterated sex.

'If we're agreed, then what are you waiting for?'

He insisted on taking me home afterwards, dismissing my driver with a few words when we exited the building. Words that seemed to be the last he was going to utter as we rode through London in charged silence. Maybe it was the after-sex endorphins zipping through my blood I didn't want to deplete by acknowledging the dark, bleak finality racing towards us. Or worse, that Jensen had finally accepted it too.

At my door, he stared down at me for tense seconds, his eyes inscrutable.

I opened my mouth, but words refused to form, thoughts fraying to nothing because there was nothing to reach for. Hell, even uttering *goodbye* felt insurmountable.

'Goodbye, Graciela,' Jensen murmured heavily, apparently having no trouble with the word.

I didn't respond. Couldn't.

Could only watch as he sauntered back to his car.

I thought I knew what pain was.

The days that followed Jensen's departure introduced me to a whole new level of desolation.

So when Elsa slid the envelope addressed to me on my desk, I barely glanced at it. Barely had the strength to lift it.

When I summoned the energy to open it, the power of my need floored me.

Hands shaking, I read and re-read the words.

Don't fire her, but Elsa tells me you have no firm plans for Christmas.

Join me for a private event in Copenhagen next week.

I guarantee a misery-free and unforgettable adventure.

Spend a day or a week. Your choice.

Come and I'll tell you about the whales.

Jensen

CHAPTER TEN

I SHIFTED AGAINST the soft leather of the town car, my booted foot bouncing on the foot well carpet.

Nerves threatened to turn me inside out. But my gaze remained fixed on the entrance to the airport's arrival hall. Jaw clenched, I tried to regulate my breathing.

Adrenaline was good in any situation. It kept you sharp, focused. Nerves, on the other hand, were…bad. And since I couldn't remember the last time I'd been *this* nervous, I was lost as to how to deal with it.

I laughed under my breath. That seemed to be the recurring theme when it came to dealing with Graciela.

She'd kept me in suspense for six long days, refused to give me an answer to my invitation, drawing out my nerves until I'd thought I would snap. When she'd eventually answered, she'd done so through Elsa, giving just a date and time of her flight and nothing more.

I'd wanted to meet her inside the airport but decided against it.

The last thing I wanted was to set the tabloid press after her. And while I could fly under the radar in most countries, I was as recognisable here in Denmark as the Mortimers were around the globe.

I'd fucked things up, not once, but twice with my righteous bullheadedness. I wanted, no, *needed* to get this right this time.

But what if I didn't even get the opportunity? What if she didn't turn up?

I'd replayed our conversation in her conference room countless times, each recount a little more eye-opening. Each one shaming me a little.

Did you stop to think she may have been protecting you? That she didn't want you to witness every single sorry detail of her trying to hold it together?

A handful of words that had rocked me, more than she knew. She'd changed something fundamental inside me during those three days at the cabin, then completely shifted the axis of my world in her conference room.

A saner man would flee from such a seismic shift. But what the hell kind of adventurer would I be if I didn't explore to see where it led?

A surge of travellers heading for their holidays ebbed and flowed out of the entrance, but there was no sign of Graciela. At this time of night only two flights were supposed to land. As the last of the passengers trickled out, my insides plummeted.

She wouldn't leave me hanging like this. Would she?

My fingers gripped my thighs, then immediately unclenched to tap a wild beat, in direct contradiction to the dull thudding within my chest. I was so intent on debating whether to call her mobile or not I didn't see

the figure walking up until a knuckle rapped sharply
against the window.

I jumped, then waved the driver away as he made
to alight, yanking on the door handle and stepping out.
She was dressed in the sort of classy chic I'd come to
associate with her. Dark glasses despite the time of
night, dark designer denims, black cashmere sweater
and thick parka, and a stylish scarf with slashes of colour wrapped around her neck.

Thigh-high boots that were totally impractical for
winter in Denmark adorned her feet but, of course, she
carried it off effortlessly, looked seriously sexy.

'You're here,' I said uselessly.

Her smile was wary, her eyes apprehensive. Unlike
the confident Dominant I knew. 'I hate mysteries. I had
to come and see what that second line was all about.'

I reached for her suitcase, a little disconcerted by
how small it was.

She either intended to stay for a short visit or she
didn't intend to wear many clothes while she was here.
I fervently hoped it was the latter. I tossed the case
into the boot and joined her in the back seat. She un-
wrapped the scarf from around her neck and ran her
hands through her hair, and I searched her features as
the car joined traffic. I was willing to admit my approach hadn't been the most risk-free. I'd titivated and
cajoled without knowing what the outcome would be.

'So when do I get to see my surprise?' she asked.

'The day after tomorrow.' I held my breath, waiting
for her to tell me she only intended to stay one night.

She didn't, but a curious look crossed her face. 'Tomorrow is Christmas Day.'

'I know. The idea was for you to spend Christmas with me.'

She shook her head. 'We never agreed on where I spent Christmas. I'm supposed to be in the south of France.'

Chains tightened around my chest. 'The south of France?'

She nodded, naked emotions shifting over her face before she expertly masked it. 'Gideon and Bryce invited me to join them.'

I wanted to be pleased for her. But I wanted her here with me more. 'Are you going?'

She shrugged. 'I haven't decided yet. The idea was for me to come here and for you to show me whatever it is you want to show me.'

'I would've elaborated if you'd bothered to answer me directly. You spoke to me through your assistant.'

'Is that an accusation?'

I sighed. 'Are you going to allow me to be a charming host or are you going to turn this adversarial?'

Her eyes widened, surprised at my daring. 'Your insinuation that I was a charity case was not appreciated,' she snapped.

I frowned. 'I never said that.'

A sad little smile curved her full lips. 'That's what you meant, though, wasn't it?'

'If I recall, my exact words were, *I guarantee a misery-free and unforgettable adventure.*'

She waved her hand out of the window at the twinkling lights strung up in festive cheer. 'So what is this? An experiment to see whether you can cheer up the poor little rich girl at Christmas time?'

'If your brothers are reaching out, then things aren't as hopeless as you think, surely? Self-pity is not a good look on you.'

She gasped, hurt reflected in her eyes. After several tense seconds, she looked way. 'I don't think this is going to work.'

'Giving up already?' I pushed.

'How dare you?'

'No, how dare *you*, Graciela? How dare you waste your beautiful life?'

'I'm not—'

'You are and you know it or you wouldn't be here. You're curious. If you want a different experience, let me give that to you. You can start by letting me give you a proper welcome to Copenhagen.'

She arched a brow. 'What, with a visit to a sex club?'

'A kiss. I was simply offering a hello kiss.'

Nostrils flaring, her gaze dropped to my lips.

Silently, I held out my hand. After a beat, she put hers in mine.

I pulled off her gloves, warmed her chilled fingers between mine before brushing a kiss over her knuckles. Then, leaning close, I pressed my lips to hers.

It was all I permitted myself. All I could control against the need clamouring to rip free. It was gratifying to see her disappointment when I pulled away.

But then a determined little light glinted in her eyes as she glanced at the window. 'Where exactly are we?'

Despite the nerves eating me up again, I played the tour guide for her, answering questions until we drew up in front of my apartment building. I ushered her into the lift, my hand on her waist as we soared up to the penthouse suite I bought five years ago.

I watched her look around my apartment. Watched her take in the countless pictures documenting every project I'd worked on. She ignored the million-dollar view, her interest sparking as she went from frame to frame. 'These are amazing.'

A layer of nerves settled inside me. This could work. Either way I was going to give it my best shot.

'Thank you.' I set her case down, and went towards her.

Another wary little look crossed her face.

'There's no need to fear what's coming, Graciela. I promise you it's all good.'

Defiance replaced wariness, her eyes snapping with irritation that did a shoddy job of covering the alarm beneath. 'I'm not afraid. I just don't like surprises.' Her head tilted, fire sparking in her eyes. 'Give me something at least, Jensen, or all we'll be doing is making meaningless conversation while I wonder what you have in store for me.'

I smiled. I couldn't help it. She challenged and terrified me. Brought me alive in ways that I could never have imagined a short while ago. Ways I didn't want to have to do without. 'How about instead of telling you, I show you?' I offered.

Her gaze started past me, down the wide hallway that led to my bedroom. It was the only hallway in the apartment. So I'd correctly guessed her thoughts. I laughed.

'Hopefully the sex will come later. I need your clothes on for this one. Or we'll risk shocking a few people.'

'People,' she echoed, tensing.

I reached for her hand. 'I know we only just arrived but we need to leave again. We're expected.'

She opened her mouth, most likely to demand I tell her. But a different light shone in her eyes. One that thrilled me far too much. It was a light of trust. It said she was willing to take this small step.

She nodded, and my hand tightened around hers. We took the lift to the underground garage. She looked around, curious as I led her to the late-model sports car. She remained silent for the twenty-minute journey to our destination, but every now and then she'd glance at me, bite her lip, the first sign of nerves I'd ever seen on Graciela. It was endearing. But also a little sad that she'd be so afraid of the unknown. Sad that she didn't know her strength or underestimated her worth.

I was equally nervous when I pulled up in front of the large, familiar suburban house. The past few days had been enlightening, and Graciela was about to find out how instrumental she'd been.

I took her hand and kissed the back of it.

'I'm beginning to associate you kissing my hand with something that'll freak me out.'

I smiled. 'You liked something about my invitation or you wouldn't be here.'

She shrugged. 'It beats spending the night listening to my cousin Jasper drone on about our family feud with the Binghams, that's for sure.'

'The fondness in your voice tells me he's not all bad.'

She shrugged. 'I tolerate him, probably because I hardly see him.'

It was more than that and we both knew it, but I let it slide. We stepped out and I walked her to the red-painted front door decorated with garlands and Christmas lights. As we approached, sounds of festive music filtered through the air.

'You brought me to a party?' There was no disappointment, but neither was there anticipation. She was guarding her feelings and I couldn't blame her.

The door opened before I could knock, a woman of slim, tall build throwing her arms wide.

'Jensen! You made it.' Her wide smile didn't cover the wariness I glimpsed in her eyes but the tight band that usually gripped my chest when I was in my mother's company had loosened. Enough that I could return her smile.

Beside me, Graciela tensed. I tightened my fingers around hers, infusing reassurance. 'Mor, meet Graciela Mortimer. Graciela, my mother, Agnetha.'

Graciela held out her hand, but her face remained politely neutral as she greeted my mother. 'It's lovely to meet you.'

My mother's smile widened. 'You too. I was thrilled when Jensen said he was coming home and bringing a guest with him. Usually I have to beg and plead.' She threw the door wide open. 'Come in, meet the rest of the family!'

As we entered, I slanted a glance at Graciela, gauging her reaction.

Her face gave nothing away, not even when the rest of my family descended en masse. Not when Dag, my gregarious stepfather, enfolded her in an embrace. She remained coolly polite, upper-class and boarding-school-honed manners fully in place.

Dread slithered down my spine; the notion that my plan had backfired, that I'd probably killed any chance I had with her, became a reality when she cornered me in a quiet alcove while pre-dinner drinks were being served.

'I was right, wasn't I? I'm just some guinea-pig experiment to you!' she hissed with quiet fury.

Frustration boiled inside me. 'Only you would see it like this.'

Her face tightened. 'What's that supposed to mean?'

'Look around you, Graciela. We're not perfect. Hell, some of us have been through a lot of shit. But we don't wallow in it.'

I knew the words coming out of my mouth were wrong the moment I said them. 'Dammit, I didn't mean it like that.'

Pain dulled the fire in her eyes. 'No, I think you meant it exactly like that. You either meant to show me what a fuck-up I am or to rub my face in your idea of happy families,' she said.

'Or maybe there's a third option? How about gratitude? Wanting you to feel affection? Warmth? Conversations that didn't start and end with who could hurt whom worse or whatever version of hell you were too scared to face this Christmas?'

Her eyes grew bright with unshed tears. Furiously, she blinked them away. 'I don't need you to deliver whatever message you feel you need to deliver. I've survived holidays with my family for the better part of two decades.'

'And you still choose to accept things the way they are? What are you, Graciela? Deluded or coward?'

The blood drained from her face, her eyes turning into twin pools of torment.

I dragged my fingers through my hair as my words replayed in the shocked silence.

What the hell was wrong with me?

Showing her that her powerful words had changed my relationship with my mother was one thing. But this…?

Hell, I hadn't even got around to telling her why we celebrated Christmas on the twenty-fourth instead of on the traditional Christmas Day we used to celebrate in England.

She started to walk away. I held on. 'Wait. There's something I need to tell you…'

'You want to give me more of the same, you mean?' Her voice was ragged, her face still tight.

'I'm sorry. Dammit, that came out wrong. So fucking wrong.'

She held my gaze for a blazing moment. 'I can't leave without appearing rude. I can't order you to take me away from here because that would make me a bitch who's stealing the precious son away at Christmas. So I guess I'm fully immersed in your little experiment, aren't I?'

Without waiting for my response, she darted into the living room, the centre of revelry. For the rest of the evening, she placed at least half a room width between us, finding an excuse to distance herself whenever I got close.

If my mother and stepfather noticed, they decided on diplomatic silence. Merete, my sister, however, repeatedly shot me questioning glances, which I silently warned her not to vocalise.

Merete tended to shoot her mouth off before she engaged her brain. As much as I loved her, I wasn't in the mood to accommodate her adorable foibles tonight.

Not when I could feel the woman who'd gained monumental importance in my existence slipping through my fingers. The loud, obnoxious gong sounded for dinner. I rushed to my feet, crossed the room towards Graciela.

She ignored me, turning instead to Mikkel, Merete's five-year-old son, who'd spent most of the evening gazing at her in wide-eyed adoration. 'Would you like to show me where I'm sitting, Mikkel?'

He nodded eagerly, and I couldn't help the bite of

jealousy I felt towards my nephew. I followed, my spirits sinking lower when I clocked the place-settings.

I was seated as far away from Graciela as possible, next to Merete. I gritted my teeth, suspecting my sister had been instrumental in the arrangements.

Short of making a scene, I had to let it go.

Dinner was a loud, boisterous affair. But Graciela picked at her meal, offering a shallow smile as my sister peppered her with questions. I wasn't surprised when she excused herself the moment the second course was cleared away, to go to the bathroom. I stared at her back as she disappeared down the hallway, refocusing on my family when the throat cleared loudly. My mother was staring at me, her gaze a mixture of curiosity and sympathy.

'Whatever's going on, son, you need to fix it. Fast.'

I nodded, a curious little lump in my throat as I contemplated hunting her down again. Going down on my knees to beg forgiveness. I didn't give a fuck who saw me. But perhaps it was best to give her a little time to cool down?

Five minutes later she hadn't returned, and my foot was bouncing again.

Bloody hell.

Was it supposed to be this complicated? Was reaching for the most perfect thing I'd ever experienced supposed to be this hard?

I snorted under my breath. Of course it was. I'd nearly lost a couple of fingers climbing mountains all over the world. But regardless of how treacherous and agonising the climb, it was worth it every single time once I reached the summit. That kind of euphoria was indescribable.

It might have backfired spectacularly today, but there was always tonight. And tomorrow.

Cold, misery-filled shivers rippled down my body as I sat through the rest of dinner. They continued to surge, drowning out the sound of merrymaking until only my mother's voice remained in my head.

He's trying to prove his point. You're a charity case. The poor little rich girl he's taken pity on because he's got nothing better to do. You read his invitation and allowed yourself to dream. Deep down you know you're not enough. You'll never be enough.

I barely heard Jensen making his excuses to his family. Barely registered that we were leaving when he approached, my jacket in his hand. I held myself stiffly as he helped me into it. Desperately holding onto the last reserves of composure as I said my good-byes.

In silence, we walked out to the car in the freezing cold.

I felt his penetrating gaze on my face as I slid into my seat, through the tense drive back to his apartment. My heart thudded dully as I walked through his front door.

A few hours ago, I'd been elated that he was sharing his private space with me. Just as he'd shared his cabin in Alaska. This was a bigger deal, of course. And, contrary to the guard I'd wanted to place around this whole visit, I'd fallen in love with his apartment the moment I walked in.

It wasn't so much the stunning view outside the glass windows, but the testaments to his brilliance scattered everywhere. He loved what he did and wasn't afraid to show it. He didn't need to brag about his talent. The evidence was everywhere. His apartment felt like home in a way that I hadn't felt at home anywhere else for a very long time.

But…it turned out I was deluded. I glanced at my case, sitting there on the floor, waiting to be scooped up again sooner rather than later.

Stomach in miserable knots, I went towards it. 'I'm going to stay in a hotel tonight.'

He grunted an angry sound, one of the first I'd heard him make. 'No, you're not. This is insane. You don't need to leave, Graciela. Let's talk about this.'

I turned on him, anguish and fury boiling inside me. 'Again with the talking? Fine. Admit what you hoped to achieve by taking me to your parents' tonight.'

He stalled for a moment and then his lips firmed. 'For most of my childhood we celebrated Christmas the English way, until my mother decided to revert to the Danish way of celebrating the day before. Do you want to know why?'

I shook my head, impatient with his deviation.

'It's because my father ruined every Christmas for us, without fail, for as long as I could remember. He'd pick a fight over the smallest thing, use it as an excuse to ruin the whole fucking day. One time, my mother stood up to him, and he destroyed all the presents. Smashed everything to pieces with a fucking baseball bat.'

I flinched, my heart going out to him despite my own despair.

'When she met Dag, they decided to revert to Danish tradition, head off the day before bad memories ruined it.'

'Well, I guess it was a good way to counter what your father did, but by not celebrating both days, wasn't he winning?'

'Don't get me wrong, we still celebrate Christmas Day, but over the years, the Danish celebration has become a bigger deal.'

'A bigger deal you wanted to throw me in at the deep end of, to see whether I sank or swam?'

His face hardened. 'You really think I would do that to you? Deliberately sabotage your happiness?' His voice was rough. Ashen.

'I don't know. Tell me why you did it.'

'Because I wanted you to be happy!' he all but bellowed.

'Why? Why does this mean so much to you?'

He exhaled harshly. 'Do you remember what my mother said when she opened the door?'

I frowned. Shrugged. 'Something about bringing a guest?'

'No, the bit about having to beg and plead for me to visit.'

'Yeah. So?'

'So I avoid going home as much as I can. Excuses were easy to find and I wasn't ashamed to use them.'

'Sorry, you've lost me.'

'I walked you to your door last week, then drove straight to the airport. Because something you said pulled the rug from under me. Made me see what a selfish bastard I'd been to my mother.'

My heart kicked. 'Something… I… What did I say?'

'That she was trying to protect me by keeping the painful details of what my father was doing to her from me. I'd secretly blamed her for years for staying, failed to see her choices were limited. It's easy to stand back and judge. And I'd judged her harshly until you forced me to face the truth. Taking you home with me tonight… I wanted you to see what you'd done for me. Show my gratitude. Instead, I fucked it up.'

The different, enlightening slant to the whole evening shook my world. He'd invited me here to witness something beautiful. Something wonderful *I'd* helped create.

The haggard sob caught me by surprise. Jensen too, from his stunned expression. Then he cursed. 'What the fuck did your mother do to you?'

Instantly, a vice tightened around my heart. 'Jensen…no,' I warned.

'No, I really want to know. What did her letter say?'

'It's none of your business,' I bit out through lips gone numb with pain.

'Oh, but I think it is. Because here you are, on the

verge of throwing away something precious because you can't or won't move from the past.'

More icy shivers drenched me. 'God, you're really in full flow tonight, aren't you?'

He dragged desperate fingers through his hair, his eyes spearing into me. 'I have to. Because I want you, Graciela, *min elskerinde*.'

My heart shook, as it did every time he called me that. 'You will not call me that again,' I said, my voice firm enough to make him freeze.

For a moment, stark bleakness darkened his eyes. 'You have my word. I won't address you like that again until you ask me to. But I meant it when I said I want to know what she said to you.'

With compulsion I couldn't stop, my gaze darted to the handbag I'd dropped on the sofa when we arrived.

His gaze followed mine, enlightenment and shock sharpening his eyes. 'Jesus, you carry it with you?'

I glared at him. 'So what if I do? What's it to you?'

His lips flattened as he strode across the room.

'Don't you dare—!'

He grabbed the bag and held it out to me. 'Show me,' he growled.

'No.'

Tense seconds ticked by, then he dropped the bag on the coffee table. 'Fine, if you won't show me, then get rid of it.'

Anguished ravaged my insides. 'I beg your pardon?'

'You heard me. I'm not sure how long you've been

carrying that toxic thing around with you, but you need to get rid of it, Graciela.'

'I don't know where the hell you get off—'

'I get off where I fucking love you so much it kills me that you won't give yourself a chance to be happy!'

My heart dropped to my toes, my brain ceasing to function. 'You...*what*?'

He reached out, seizing my wrists and dragging me close until we shared the same air. 'I love you. I've loved you since the second day at the cabin when you ordered me to tell you a story.'

I shook my head wildly. 'I... You can't.'

'Is that an order? Because if it is, I'm afraid I'm going to have to disappoint you by declining.'

My mouth dried so hard I feared I'd never form words again. So instead, my soul unfurled, eager to absorb the promise of his words.

'I can't, I'm no good for you.'

His fingers caressed my jaw. 'Oh, but you are, *min elskede*,' he insisted thickly. 'You're everything I will ever want in this lifetime and the next. And before you give me some excuse about not knowing you, or you not being right for me, remember that I'm a risk taker who's been diving headlong into dangerous situations since I could get away with doing it. Whatever you think you're hiding underneath this strong, beautiful heart that will scare me away, don't bother. I feel like I've been preparing all my life for this chance to win you.'

A rough, shocked laugh took me by surprise. 'So I'm just a challenge to you? While you tell me you love me?'

He grimaced, then shrugged. 'Shock therapy was part of my game plan in bringing you here.'

His admission should've angered me but, dear God, he wasn't taking any of it back. He wasn't grabbing my suitcase and tossing me out of the door with it.

Because he loved me...

Slowly, he released my hand and sank onto his knees.

I gasped, the act shockingly blunt, cutting through the noise in a way his words hadn't been able to convey. His hands curled around my calves, glided up slowly until he was gripping my hips. He leaned forward, laid his cheek against my stomach.

'With everything that I am, everything that I will ever be, I am yours, Graciela Mortimer. *Min elskede.*'

'I thought you weren't going to call me that until I gave you permission?'

I felt his smile against my stomach. 'You're *min elskede*—my love. I intend to do whatever is necessary to earn the right to call you *min elskerinde* again.'

The tremor started from the depths of my soul, rolling out like a tsunami until I was shaking and he was clutching me harder. The tickling on my chin I absently registered as tears pouring down my face. My hands sank into his hair, my grip loose as I nudged his face upward to meet my gaze.

'I don't know that I can love you, don't know if I'm capable.'

He nodded, pure understanding in his eyes. 'For now,

I'll be confident for the both of us. But you will. I believe in you.'

Dirty, soul-racking sobs seized me then, as they had at the cabin. He caught me when I broke, held me until I was wrung dry, then he rose, swung me into his arms. The bedroom was on the minimalist side, from the little I spotted before he crossed over to lay me down on the bed. He went to the bathroom and returned a minute later with a towel. After drying my tears, he tossed it aside. Then he climbed on, fully clothed, and folded me in his arms. Silence reigned for a few minutes and then he nudged my chin up.

'Why do you carry the letter around with you?'

Shame and pain twisted my insides to knots. 'Because it's the only thing of hers that I've got.'

He frowned. 'What do you mean?'

'Remember when I told you I was very angry with her for a very long time?'

He nodded.

'After she died, the lawyer told me I'd inherited all her clothes and any jewellery that didn't belong to the Mortimer family trust. I told the lawyer I didn't want any of it. Aunt Flo talked me into getting them. I don't think she believed me when I said I *really* didn't want it. Anyway, her things arrived a few days later. Boxes and boxes of pretty things I'd only been allowed to touch the day she left me. I set everything on fire that night, staying to make sure everything was turned to ash. But the letter, I kept. It's the only thing I have that's truly...hers.'

He gave a grim nod. 'I understand why you want to hang on to it, *min elskede*. But I still want you to destroy it.'

I tensed, ready to launch myself out of his arms, but he held me tight. 'You won't truly move on and heal until you do.'

I kept mutinously silent, my heart shaking at the enormity of what he was asking.

But…what if he was right? What if I was chaining myself down by dragging that letter through life? I'd kept it partly as a reminder not to make the same mistakes I'd done with her. Not to hope or love or reach for happiness in case I proved the failure she'd predicted I'd be. But that had happened anyway, hadn't it?

Until Jensen had battered through that toxic fortress, taken the chance on me I was too afraid to take for myself.

What if… *I was enough*?

My breath shuddered out of me.

His piercing eyes were fixed on me; he knew the moment I reached for courage and made the decision. He vaulted out of bed and held out his hand to me.

Together we walked into the living room and crossed over to the coffee table. Wildly shaking, I dug through my purse until my fingers brushed the corners of the worn, folded paper.

The words were seared in my memory, trickled through as I held it…

You'll never be enough for any man, woman or child.

You cling too hard, love too deep.

We Mortimers have an addiction problem.

Yours is emotional addiction.

Wean yourself off it or you'll be nothing but a disappointment.

You already are to me, and I suspect to your brothers.

I'm not coming back, Graciela.

One day you'll see it's for the best. You might even thank me for it.

I held it out to him. 'Do you want to read it?'

He shook his head. 'I don't need to. Whatever it says in there, it's not true. Very soon, you'll believe it too.'

With quick strides, he went into the kitchen and returned with a large ceramic bowl and a box of matches. Heart in my throat, I dropped the paper into the bowl. He handed me the matches, and when my fingers shook too badly, he cupped my hand, steadied me.

When I struck it, he released me.

I held the flame to one corner of the paper, my heart in my throat as it immediately caught fire. In less than a minute it was gone.

He gently cupped my face, dropped a reverent kiss on my lips before catching me in his arms once more. I refused to look into the bowl.

Couldn't mourn a mother I'd never really had.

With each step away from the blackened remains of words that had weighed me down all my life, the tightness in my chest eased, smothered hope breaking through the fog of doubt.

A clock chimed somewhere within the apartment as he walked us back into his bedroom. This time he set me down next to the bed, his face lighting up in a smile.

'It's Christmas Day and I would very much love to unwrap you.'

My heart hammered hard enough to power up a small city, yet I still managed to raise my chin, to stare him down despite our height difference.

'I may just allow you to, but only if you address me the way you crave to.'

I'd bared myself to him, admitted that I wasn't sure how capable I was of returning the feelings he craved from me. But *this* I could give him. He dropped to his knees, and I was awed all over again by how magnificently comfortable he was in that position. How magnificent he was, full stop.

With reverent hands, he took my clothes off and then, at my nod, he undressed himself, pulled back the coverlet and helped me into bed.

Sliding between my thighs, he wrapped his arms around me. '*Jeg elsker dig.* I love you.' He dropped a long kiss on my lips. 'Merry Christmas, my heart. *Min elskerinde.*'

'Merry Christmas, Jensen.'

We spent Christmas in bed making the most sublime love I'd ever known.

Jensen was searingly sweet, attentive and generous

with his love. With every second that passed, my soul healed.

When Bryce called out of the blue, I bit back tears as I wished him and Savvie a merry Christmas. A text from Gideon an hour later *daring* me to spend New Year with him and Leonie brought on another emotion bout.

I'd never discovered what my mother had written to them in their letters, and I didn't need to. Not any more. Somehow we'd all found happiness despite the abysmal odds, and that was enough for me.

I was a little apprehensive when Jensen strode into the room the next night, breathtaking in his tuxedo. I was also formally dressed in a strapless gown, with shoes and a matching clutch. Diamonds sparkled at my throat and in my ears, and my hair was slicked back and down my back, a simple enough style that'd surprisingly taken more time than I'd anticipated, making me a little late and a lot flustered when Jensen halted in his tracks.

'Holy fuck, you look incredible,' he breathed, his voice rough.

'All this wasn't achieved without huge effort, I'll tell you that.'

He shook his head, his hands sliding over my waist to grip my hips. He loved gripping me there, and I loved his big, calloused hands on me.

'The outer package is merely the support act to the real diamond beneath that shines through your eyes, your smile. I taste it when I kiss you. Feel it when I'm inside you.'

I fanned my face, swallowing more than once before I could speak. 'You're going to make me cry again and ruin my make-up and make us late to wherever we're going.'

He gave a wicked smile, kind enough not to point out how many times I'd dissolved into tears in the last twenty-four hours. It was as if all the grief, anger and bitterness I'd bottled up inside had needed an outlet immediately. He'd never once complained.

He'd simply gathered me in his arms and held me until the storm passed. That simple act of kindness had helped me heal faster, enough to tentatively embrace the phenomenon of his love.

He held out his hand and I slipped mine into it, my heart flooding with joy as he walked us out of the door and downstairs to his car.

The bright lights of Copenhagen flashed by as we headed into the inner city. When he stopped in front of a futuristic-looking glass building, I stepped out, looking for clues as to where we were.

'If you're trying to guess where we are, don't bother. Unless you've become fluent in Danish in the last day and a half?'

I shook my head, laughing. 'I'm good, but not that good.'

Jensen tossed his keys to a valet and held out his arm to me. I slipped mine through and we walked together into the building that turned out to be an art gallery.

My eyes widened. 'It's your exhibit?' I guessed, thrilled.

He nodded with a smile. 'My agent thinks it's about time for another one.'

'I wholeheartedly agree.'

He mock-winced. 'I hope the two of you never meet. My life would become unbearable.'

'It's because we both believe in you. Your work is magic.'

He leaned down, his lips brushing my earlobe and making me shiver. 'That's what you keep insisting in the bedroom. And I might just start to believe you, *min elskerinde*.'

I was laughing when we walked into the first, largest room.

My laughter died, my senses overtaken by a different sort of pleasure.

The space was filled with Jensen's work, starting from the first time he'd picked up a camera to his latest project, which happened to be mine. The whole place was hushed, the guests admiring his work in reverent silence.

We walked slowly through the gallery, stopping every now and then when a guest stopped him to congratulate him or express their wonder at his talents. He accepted accolades with a simple nod and smile, but as we drew closer to the end of the exhibit, he grew apprehensive.

'Something wrong?'

He flashed a smile. 'I hope not.'

About to ask what he meant, I held my tongue as his mother, stepfather and sister approached. His mother was smiling, her smile a little tearful as she addressed her son. Dag simply beamed, the proud father.

After a quick exchange in Danish, Agnetha turned to me. 'Your lovely presents arrived this morning, Graciela. Thank you so much, but you really shouldn't have. You've given me the best Christmas present.' Her gaze veered to her son, fresh tears filming her eyes.

Tears clogging my own throat, I waved her away. I'd woken a slightly disgruntled Elsa and had her raid the emergency presents stash I kept in the office. Agnetha's scarf, Dag's vintage bottle of red, and Merete's crystal bracelet had been hand-delivered this morning, along with Christmas cards and a present for Mikkel.

'Excuse us, please,' Jensen said to his family, then smoothly led me down a short, darkened hallway.

'Where are we going?' I asked, excitement mixing with a touch of anxiety.

'You'll see,' was all he said.

I was learning that in some things Jensen was immovable. He was mine to command and cherish in the bedroom. But it was equally fulfilling for both of us for the reins to slacken a touch. It was all the more rewarding and thrilling when I pulled them back and took control.

I watched him grow more tense as we approached a set of double doors. With one last, furtive look at me, he threw them open.

Every surface, from floor to ceiling, was covered

with images of me. All taken on the night of the bore-alis. There were easily over two hundred, but I could swear each frame had captured a different expression.

I turned to him, my heart in my throat as I stared at him, my soul bursting with feeling I couldn't quite de-scribe but wanted to embrace.

'This, *min elskerinde*, this is how I see you. This is how you should look every day for the rest of your life,' he said, his voice thick with emotion.

'Thunderstruck?' I croaked.

He smiled. 'Starstruck. Awestruck. Filled with won-der and joy. Beautiful. Hopeful. Breathtaking. Fulfilled. Beautiful.'

'Your already said *beautiful*.'

'I know. It deserves repeating.'

His fingers interlocked with mine, I slowly spun around, my gaze lighting on each picture, tears brim-ming in my eyes as his words nurtured my soul, watered it and helped it sprout wings of belief. And as I came full circle, he was waiting, arms wide open.

I flew into them, my heart full. 'I love you,' I con-fessed, the words a vow I knew I'd never doubt or break.

His body shook, his breath expelling long and deep as he held me tight. 'I know, my darling. I got there a little faster than you, but I knew you'd catch up.'

I laughed. I cried, uncaring that I was becoming emotionally wrecked again as I basked in his love.

'We can enjoy this just between us, or you can show it to the world. You direct the narrative of your life from now on. I'll merely provide the support. But I'd like the world to see the real Graciela Mortimer.'

Eventually, I dragged my head from his chest and looked up into his eyes. Watched him slowly sink down, uncaring who saw him on his knees in front of me, waiting patiently for my reply.

'I want what you want, Jensen. Today, tomorrow, for always. If you see me like this, then I would be proud to show myself like this to the world.'

I leaned down and kissed him, my fingers gliding through his hair, catching the knot at the back of it and gripping it tight. He groaned into my mouth, then drew back for a spell. 'I love you.'

'Jeg elsker også dig,' I repeated back to him, watched his eyes light up and knew that within that light my soul had been reborn.

EPILOGUE

'TELL ME ABOUT the whales, Jensen.'

He gave a thick groan and I hid a smile. 'You want me to tell that story right now?' he asked, his voice strained.

It might have had something to do with the fact that I was completely naked and astride him, and he was deep inside me, doing everything in his power to hold absolutely still at my command. Or perhaps it was the old-fashioned folding razor I was using to shave off his stubble that made him a little nervous. I had a feeling it was the combination of edgy danger and surrendering himself to me that gave us both the ultimate thrill.

I carefully scraped the sharp edge beneath his firm jaw, the sandpapery rasp curiously making me wetter. 'It's been a crazy couple of months. But I think we have a little time now?'

He snorted. 'By a little time, you mean you plan on being fashionably late to your launch party?'

I couldn't hold back my grin. Hell, I'd been smiling so much lately, I was surprised my face hadn't fallen off from the well of happiness growing inside me.

My life had changed in the space of a few weeks.

First, Jensen and I accepted Gideon's invitation and joined him and Leonie on the family yacht in the south of France a few days into the new year. My apprehension melted away within minutes when my hitherto fearsome and formidable brother greeted me with a wide smile and swept me off my feet into a bear hug. The second surprise, in the form of Bryce and Savvie stepping onto the deck, was equally heart-warming, starting what had become the best family time I could remember. That they were coming to the party tonight filled me with warmth I wouldn't have believed possible a short time ago. My heart swelled as I acknowledged that it all had to do with the man beneath me.

'Don't change the subject,' I said, projecting sternness into my voice.

'I wouldn't dare. Not when you've literally got me by the throat and cock,' he joked, but he swallowed hard nonetheless, a fine tremor shivering through his body as I slowly rolled my hips. 'Christ,' he swore thickly under his breath.

'The whales, Jensen.'

'What do you want to know, *mit hjerte*?'

My heart. I loved the Danish endearments that fell so effortlessly from Jensen's lips because I knew the wealth of emotion behind them.

'Everything. Start from the beginning. Did you know they were going to be there?' I finished with his left side and angled my body to his right.

The movement dragged my inner heat over his

length and he gave a deep groan. Then took a shuddering breath. 'I wasn't going to shoot any underwater stuff that day. We were in Tonga to film the active volcano. I spotted a couple of whales on my morning swim, grabbed a few of my guys and headed out on the boat for a closer look.' He stopped. I paused, overawed by the transcendent look on his face. 'There were dozens of them, just…frolicking. Mothers with newborns. Older ones. I couldn't get into my scuba gear fast enough.'

I smiled. 'Tell me about that picture.' The one that had made him famous. The iconic one everyone raved about when they spoke about Jensen Scott.

His throat moved as he swallowed again. 'Until very recently, it was the most profound thing to happen to me.'

'Tell me how it felt. In that moment. Were you terrified?'

'The smallest was easily the size of a bus so, yes, I was plenty terrified going into the water. But…all I know was that one moment my chest was pounding, then the next all I felt was…incredible, soul-quietening peace.' The last word was gruff. 'I don't know why they stopped playing or why they came close the way they did.'

The picture of seven sperm whales surrounding him in a perfect circle with Jensen suspended in the middle had rocked the world. The perfect synchronicity of giant tail fins moving as one while the whales all stared at Jensen had moved millions. Thousands had believed the picture was fake. When it'd been authenticated, Jensen Scott had shot to fame, winning a clutch of awards both for the stills and for the ninety-second video he'd shot with the camera pointing up.

'What made you leave the camera where you did?'

He exhaled. 'That was nothing new. I always dive with multiple cameras. You never know where the perfect shot will come from. Everyone thinks there was just that one camera but there were three, set up on the ocean floor on tripods. The one I released captured the best angle.'

I gasped. 'There are others? Can I see them?'

'They're in the Denmark apartment. You'll have to come back with me next week if you want to see them.'

I leaned close and brushed my lips over his. 'I was planning on coming with you anyway.' We hadn't quite worked out where or when we'd move in together. All we knew was that we were rabid about spending every spare moment together.

I leaned back again, watched his eyes fall to my breasts before darting back up to meet mine. His cock jerked inside me, and he sucked in a desperate breath.

'How many times has your video been watched?'

'According to my agent...two and a half billion times.'

'God, that's incredible.'

He made a pained sound and squeezed his eyes shut for a moment. He was almost at breaking point, just where I loved him to be.

'Last question,' I murmured as I passed the razor along his taut cheek, shaving the last bristled spot.

'*Ja, min elskerinde.*'

'You said it was your most profound moment until recently?'

Ice-blue eyes met mine, blazed with steel-forged love, before dropping in submissive surrender. 'It was. At the time I thought nothing would ever equal it. Then I met you.' His voice was hushed and solemn, reflecting everything he felt. An expression I was still finding hard to fathom belonged to me and only me. 'Now I simply accept that it was a moment that was destined to happen just so it would bring me to you.'

I heard the razor clatter to the floor without fully taking it in. I gripped his nape, nudging his head up until I captured his gaze with mine. 'You can't say things like that to me.' God, was that mess my voice?

His nostrils flared. 'Why the hell not?'

'Because there's only so much room in my chest for how big my heart gets when you say things like that.'

The most dazzling smile stretched across his face, making my heart swell even bigger. 'Will you punish me if I say I'm not sorry?'

I slowly circled my hips, biting back a moan at the scalp-tingling sensation. 'I most definitely intend to punish you. Later. Right now I'll reward you for sharing your beautiful story with me.' I pressed a kiss to his lips. 'And for loving me,' I added in an even thicker voice.

His smile altered, weighted by emotion as he bared himself even further. 'I intend for us to have many beautiful stories to share, *min elskede*,' he vowed.

'Then share one with me right now, Jensen. Touch your mistress. Show her how much you love her.'

The words were barely out of my mouth before he was switching his death grip from the chair to my hips, slamming me back down on his steely length.

I held on tight for a moment, then simply let go as I was swept under a torrent of love. One I was beginning to believe would stand the test of time.

An hour later, after a quick but carnally eventful shower, we stepped hand in hand out of the lift ten floors below, in the tallest building in London, which just happened to have the Mortimer name stamped on it, and into the glitzy affair that was the ice-themed party to celebrate the latest release of *Mortimer Quarterly*. The climate-conscious theme had resonated powerfully, with many media outlets running features off what Jensen and I had put together.

We circulated, holding on tight to one another.

A loud wolf whistle cut through the music and chatter and I turned to see Bryce, grinning, with one arm slung around Savvie, the other waving me over. Next to him, Gideon also kept his wife close, as if they were both afraid of letting the women they loved stray too far.

My fingers tightened around Jensen's, my own possessiveness engulfing me.

'Everything okay?' Jensen murmured, sensing my emotions.

I swallowed the lump in my throat. 'Yes, Jensen. Everything's great.'

He smiled, kissed my hand again.

'This is some shindig, Gracie,' Gideon said when I reached him.

'The whole thing's amazing,' Leonie, his wife, added, looking stunning in a green sequinned dress.

More accolades flooded in from Savvie and Bryce. Inexplicable tears prickled my eyes. Perhaps the women sensed my surfacing emotions. They excused themselves to go to the ladies'. Jensen kissed my cheek, then headed to the bar to get us drinks.

An easy silence settled between my brothers and me. Bryce broke it. 'What the fuck is wrong with Jasper? He looks like he's about to deck someone.' He nodded his head towards the opposite corner of the room, where our cousin was staring daggers at his drink while ignoring the tall, stunning woman next to him.

Wren Bingham.

Daughter of the late Sheldon Bingham, brother of Perry Bingham, the man currently fuelling the flames of the decades-old family feud between the Binghams and Mortimers.

I was surprised when Jasper listed Wren as his plus one to my party. Reading the fiery undercurrents between them now, my thoughts echoed Bryce's.

'Maybe he's in the mood for a little self-flagellation,' Bryce answered his own question with a smirk, then his face grew serious. 'Fuck me. Would you have ever believed we'd get here?' he said gruffly.

Gideon lifted a snarky eyebrow. 'Here?'

Bryce slugged him on the arm. 'Yes, *here*, and with

other halves who tolerate us for more than five minutes rather than, I dunno, in the bloody nuthouse.'

'And why the hell wouldn't they?' Gideon demanded. 'Beneath all the bullshit, we're fucking awesome.'

I laughed.

Bryce joined in.

Gideon chuckled.

In that flawless moment, I realised I did indeed have more room.

For infinite love.

* * * * *

DOUBLE DARE YOU

CARA LOCKWOOD

For PJ, the stars and moon in my sky.

PROLOGUE

HIS LIPS CLAIMED hers and, in that moment, her entire body came alive. The rumors about this sex god were true, beyond true, she realized as he pulled her into his arms, flat against his muscled chest, and the world outside faded away. Nothing existed but their bodies before the woodstove in this small lodge on the top of a remote peak in the Rocky Mountains. He tasted like pure animal magnetism, pure white-hot desire, everything she'd ever wanted and more she hadn't dreamed of. Her clothes came off. Before she knew it, she was naked, and then it was electric skin against skin. She could almost feel the pulse of his need against her belly. She didn't know where her heat began and his ended, and she didn't care to draw boundaries. She wanted them all gone. God, how she'd fantasized about this moment, with this man, and how she'd never believed it could ever happen, not in a million years. He had his pick of women in Aspen, but now, finally—and at long last—it would be her turn.

The blizzard howled outside the wood lodge, a

mournful call she felt in her chest, mirroring her own desperate need. She'd wanted him since she first laid eyes on him but had been so long denied. She'd pined in silence for months, even years. She'd yearned for this since she first fell in love with him, only she'd been in hell ever since. She'd been slowly chipping away at that friendship line, and now, finally, she'd gotten him to cross. She knew she was risking everything, his very friendship, and yet she didn't care. Her need for him was just too great, her want burned in her hotter than the crackling wood in the stove. She couldn't have stopped herself any more than she could stop the snow battering the windows outside. This might be her only chance, and she'd take it, her head buzzing with wine. She understood the dangers here, knew she was playing with fire. He didn't do relationships, didn't do love. He'd break her heart if she let him. This man wouldn't settle down with anyone, wouldn't be tamed, but that was why she wanted him so badly, she realized. She wanted to stand in the wind and howl, she wanted to consume some of his wildness and feel it run riot inside her. She wanted to be obliterated, completely, and then put back together again. She wanted him, the chaos he brought, and she wanted to ride it until she couldn't ride anymore.

He laid her down on the bearskin rug, its fur surprisingly soft against her bare back. She soaked in all the details, because she'd want to remember this, now and always. She didn't care about tomorrow. She only cared about right now, this man she'd stupidly fallen in love with. The man who might never love her back, but she didn't care. She'd have his body even if she couldn't have his heart.

CHAPTER ONE

Two months later

WHAT WAS *HE* doing here?

Allie Connor froze at the bar, her ruby-red cranberry vodka in the martini glass stopped halfway to her mouth. Liam Beck, looking too damn fine for words, eased through the crowd at the Aspen lodge, seeming like he already owned it in his ruffled-blond, leather-jacket glory, with more than a hint of stubble that said he only marginally cared what anyone thought about his shaving habits. He looked just as cocky as ever, and ridiculously fit, chiseled from free rock climbing, river rafting, snowboarding or whatever *extreme* thing he could think of to do to his body lately. What crazy-ass thing was he doing now? Bungee jumping without a bungee cord? Free-climbing up cliffs? Jumping into ponds of alligators?

When it came to Liam Beck, anything was possible. And whatever crazy risk he was taking suited him. He looked good enough to eat.

Not that Allie was falling for it. Not this time.

Stay in your lane, she told herself. *This all happened because you didn't stay in your lane.* She needed a straitlaced nice guy who regularly contributed to his 401(k). Not somebody who liked to hurl his body off snow-covered cliffs with nothing but a snowboard and his wits to save him.

"Trouble, two o'clock," Allie murmured, pushing up her round, nearly clear-framed glasses, careful not to gaze directly in Liam's direction again, lest he see her. She half turned, keeping him in her peripheral sights. Some upbeat, too-bright Christmas song floated through the crowd. Behind her sat a roaring fire in a stone fireplace, circled with small pub tables, and to her left a giant bar made of reclaimed wood, old antique iron fixtures hanging from the ceiling giving the pub a modern take on the gold rush times. Allie tried not to think that two months ago she'd had the misfortune of tumbling into Beck's bed. Or, actually, the tremendous fortune. He'd been—bar none—the best sex she'd ever had in her life.

And then he'd not called her after that weekend. Or texted. Or acknowledged her at all. She might have thought he'd had a horrible skiing accident, except for the pictures of him plastered across social media smiling with a parade of pretty tourists. She'd expected more from the man who'd claimed to be her friend before they'd taken their clothes off. But deep down, she knew she had only herself to blame. She tangled with something wild. Was it a wonder it came back to bite her?

"What the hell?" Allie's best friend, Mira, frowned as she first saw Beck clap a friend on the back. Beck was six-three and impossible to miss in a crowd, his tawny blond hair and perpetual tan from practically living outside in summer *and* winter standing out like a beacon. Somehow, he was moving *closer*. She felt that familiar pull in her chest, as if he'd buried a beacon for himself there, one that lit up only in his presence. Why couldn't she even stay mad at him? It hardly seemed fair.

"I definitely did *not* invite him. You know I didn't."

"Someone did." Allie suspected that someone might be Channing, Mira's roommate, who happened to be secretly hoping for a hookup with one of Aspen's most famous bachelors. *Good luck with that*, she thought, as she saw the sleek blonde light up from across the room and squeal Beck's name. Then again, since when did Beck ever need an invitation anywhere? He was used to showing up to adoration wherever he went. Allie did not have time for this. She sucked another deep drink of her nearly full cocktail and thought about bolting. Was sticking around for a round of free holiday drinks at the resort worth it?

"Maybe I should go." The minute the words were out of her mouth, she felt like a coward. She should be able to be in the same room with him, after all. She'd known what she was getting into that weekend, but she hadn't cared. That was her mistake.

"Do *not* let that X Games junkie scare you away from *my* party." Mira's dark eyes flashed with fire.

Technically, it was Mira's boss's party, the man who owned the upscale Aspen resort, Enclave, where Mira worked as an events coordinator. But Mira had planned and organized the party for Enclave's various employees. She was running the show tonight. Mira had made sure to add Allie as her plus-one, to take advantage of the holiday party and the free drinks. Allie self-consciously patted her loose bun, finding an errant strand of auburn hair had fallen loose at her temple. She tucked it behind her ear and wondered if Beck would notice the new bright red highlights in her auburn hair, and then hated herself for wondering. *I don't care what he thinks.* "You are *not* moving to Denver because of him, okay?"

Allie was considering a job offer in Denver, one that would take her three hours away by car. An old college friend had reached out on LinkedIn, and the accounting firm had a new position opening in the New Year. She would've turned the job down flat two months ago, but since then, she'd started to think maybe a change of scenery would do her good. Maybe getting away from Beck's gravitational pull would help her heal.

"I haven't decided about that job yet. I've got time. They don't need the position filled until after the New Year."

"Don't let him scare you off," Mira added.

"I'm not scared," she hedged. She wasn't frightened of Beck, exactly. It was more the case that she was scared of herself around him. Of what she might do. Of how she might feel. She hated that, even now, her body responded to the fact that he was in the same room, breathing the same air. As she watched his big shoulders part the crowd, her stomach instantly wound itself into a Gordian knot. Despite the fact that a throng of people blocked him from her, she could still track almost every movement he made, no matter how small. She hated that her whole body seemed tuned to his frequency, a channel she couldn't seem to change no matter how hard she tried.

Remember what it was like, she told herself, waiting for him to call the morning after. And then the week after, and then the month after. Remember the stupid messages she left, the rambling ones, trying to be cool, but failing miserably. Remember how she spent hours combing over every delicious position she'd shared with him in bed, and then worried that, somehow, she'd come up lacking. And then pretending none of it mattered at all, when, truly, she was horribly heartbroken. Knowing it was all her fault. She knew what Beck was. Local ski and sex god. Gods didn't wind up with mere mortals like her.

"I just don't want the hassle." Allie wished she could be one of those immensely mature adults, the ones who could stay friends with hookups or exes, but Liam wasn't the kind of man any woman could just be friends with. He exuded pure sexual energy. There literally *was* no friend zone with him and that was his whole problem. Even when they were "just" friends, she'd harbored a secret crush on the man.

She saw, from the corner of her eye, that he'd been cornered by Channing. Good. Let Channing realize she was playing a dangerous game with a man who lived his life with no rules at all. Despite Allie's better instincts, curiosity got the better of her and she found herself turning toward the couple, and staring directly into Liam's ice-blue eyes.

Dammit.

Now he'd seen her.

A slow smile crossed his face, amused and almost a little...dangerous. The man knew his own power, and he wasn't afraid to use it.

Look away, Allie, for God's sake. But then she glanced away too quickly, like a rabbit who'd locked eyes with a wolf. Now he'd know he rattled her. She fiddled with the frames of her new glasses, self-conscious.

"Brace yourself. He's coming over here," Mira warned as she sipped at her glass of white wine.

"God, no." The last person on earth she wanted to talk to was Liam Beck. Yet her body vibrated with the excitement of doing just that. Her body, ever her mind's betrayer. They had never been on the same page as far as Beck was concerned, and might never be.

"Al?" he said, and she felt his baritone in the pit of her stomach, a vibration that tingled all the way down to the crease between her legs. She almost flinched a bit at the sound of her nickname. He'd called her that warmly when they'd been friends, but it took on a new meaning when he'd whispered it in her ear that weekend they'd spent together, naked on the floor of his wood lodge, tangled up on the bearskin rug, the thick wool throw on top of them. The memory of his taut skin against hers, his strong hands on her body, made heat flush her cheeks.

"Get lost, Beck." Mira narrowed her eyes at him, flicking her black hair over her shoulder. "She doesn't want to talk to you."

Allie cringed. Mira's full-throated defense made her sound like she *cared*. She didn't. Not in the least. Her body might, but she told herself that was just pure animal instinct. Lust, really. What straight woman didn't lust after Liam Beck? But human beings were made of higher stuff than just base instinct, thankfully. Allie shot her friend a glance, but Mira was focused on Beck, her head tilted up, her shoulders squared. Not that the five-foot-three, part-Asian former marathon runner could do much against him, but the warning look in her eyes told Allie she'd try if she needed to.

"Is that so?" A grin split Beck's face, as if he was mulling over a joke at her expense. He probably was. Could he see the blush? Would he know he caused it? Of course he would. He thought everything was about him. She glanced upward at his perfectly chiseled features, reminded again that he was one of the few men so much taller than her. At five-ten, she never felt tiny. Except around Beck.

"I don't really care, actually." Allie congratulated herself on sounding pretty even-keeled. Bored, even.

She sipped her drink and deliberately looked away from Beck, using all of her willpower to drag her attention away from those powerful blue eyes. She could still feel him studying her, the attention feeling like the heat of the summer sun on her face. What did he think of her hair? Worn up in a loose, messy bun? Or her new glasses? Did he notice that she'd lost ten pounds since that ominous weekend? She knew it was silly to be so affected by two days at a lodge, but there it was. After Beck cut her from his life, Allie had trouble choking down food. She had trouble sleeping. She had trouble doing everything. But day by day, week by week, she'd gotten better.

"New glasses?" he asked her. He'd noticed. That was something.

"Yeah," she said and nodded.

"I like them." She beamed in the compliment and then mentally berated herself. Why did she care if he liked her glasses? His gaze flicked downward, slowly, taking in her tight cashmere sweater and skinny jeans, paired with a sky-high pair of stiletto boots. Impractical for the Aspen weather, but necessary for navigating the single scene. "You look…thin, Al."

She heard the note of concern in his voice. As if he had a right to be concerned. Aspen was a small place, and so avoiding her for the last two months took some doing. He'd been almost surgical in his precision. So it was clear that he'd done it on purpose. So why did he care how she was now? She glanced up at him and wished she hadn't. A little worry line etched his forehead, marring his otherwise perfect skin. He almost looked as if he truly cared. That, she knew, would be her undoing. "You doing okay?"

The air felt suddenly thin then, and she knew it had nothing to do with the altitude, even though they were perched probably somewhere around 8,000 feet high in the Rocky Mountains. She'd lived in Aspen for years, and the altitude never got to her. Her sudden light-headedness had everything to do with Beck.

"Al?" he prodded, and Allie realized she'd not answered his question. She was busy just staring at him like a fool. Her baser instincts had taken over, clearly, her body in control. But her brain wasn't going to tolerate it for long. It hummed the truth: it was none of his damn business how she was doing. He hadn't cared two months ago, so why should he now? He was the one who'd run away. She wanted to ask why, but she wasn't sure she wanted to know the answer.

"I'm fine." There was an edge to her voice, one she hadn't intended. Unable to handle the weight of his gaze any longer, she looked away. She tried to find something—someone—more interesting at the bar but failed. Even the moderately cute-ish bartender with the floppy brown hair and the lopsided grin who kept sending looks her way suddenly paled in comparison to Beck. His massive shoulders, the easy way he held the beer he was drinking, the bottle looking small in his huge hands, like a doll's plaything. She looked at the bartender, even though all of her other senses were completely focused on Beck, standing less than two feet from her. She could almost feel his body heat through the T-shirt he wore beneath his worn leather bomber jacket. His defined pecs begging to be stroked beneath the thin cotton fabric. Why did he have to look so damn…delectable? She suddenly hated Beck and his stupid muscles and the caring look on his face. His just-rolled-out-of-some-model's-bed sex appeal. *Remember, he probably did.* That musky, manly scent coming from him was probably just stale sex.

The thought jolted her to the present. He was a walking rabbit hole. One step too close and she'd fall in again.

"Beck!" squealed Channing, as the tiny blonde bounced up to the three of them and locked her arm inside his. She was wearing a ridiculous Santa hat and a red corset top that she was practically spilling out of and too-thick false eyelashes that made it look like spiders were crawling across her eyelids. Trying too hard, Allie thought. She knew Beck well enough to know he hated that. One of his biggest turnoffs. Channing didn't even acknowledge Allie or Mira, choosing instead to tug her prize away from them. "You *have* to meet my boss. She's right over there. She's the one I told you about. The one who books tours."

At the sound of possible new business, Beck's interest diverted from Allie to Channing. Not that he needed new business. His extreme mountain tours and heli-skiing excursions were the best in Aspen. Everyone knew that. At the height of tourist season, he had to turn away customers. Everybody wanted to go on a ski expedition with the two-time silver medal Olympic champion. Few people seemed to care if he had a death wish, always pushing things a bit harder, a bit farther than he should. Channing glanced at Allie. "Don't waste time here. Come on." Before she left, she turned and murmured "Greenie" beneath her breath. Allie wasn't even sure she'd heard right. *Greenie?* What the hell did that mean?

Channing pulled Beck through the crowd, and he went, casting one more look over his shoulder. Concern once more on his face. *Don't fall for it*, she told herself. *He's not really worried. It's all just part of the game.*

"Good riddance," Mira almost spit, glaring at his retreating figure.

"What does 'Greenie' mean?" Allie asked Mira, who glanced at her, suddenly looking guilty.

"Nothing," Mira said, but she bit her lip, a telltale sign she was lying. Allie had known Mira for years, and she was one of the first people she'd met in Aspen.

"You *know* what it means."

Mira hesitated. "Well…"

"Spit it out." Now Allie was beginning to be frustrated. It had to be bad, because Mira was stalling. The strand of hair popped loose from Allie's ear, and she twirled it around her finger. Suddenly, she felt anxious.

"Well…look, I saw somebody's Snap about you. It

was one of Beck's...*friends*." She said it with disdain, so Allie knew she meant one of the many women rotating through his bedroom. "I guess...well, I guess someone—I don't even know who, actually—gave you a nickname." Mira took a deep breath. "Greenie, as in a green run."

"What does a bunny hill have to do with me? I'm a decent skier." She wasn't an Olympic champion, but she was a black-diamond skier. She'd been skiing for years and thought she was pretty good.

"It doesn't have anything to do with skiing," Mira said. "They mean that you play it safe."

She was an accountant born in a family of non-risk-taking accountants. Of course she played it safe. The only risky thing her parents ever did was occasionally go about two miles over the speed limit. Her parents had raised her to be afraid of almost everything: strangers, trampolines, drugs, driving too fast in the rain, and the list went on and on.

"And what's wrong with that?" Allie challenged.

"Well, nothing—except when you're in bed."

"Wait... You mean..."

Mira gave her a knowing look and the full realization hit Allie. Beck thought she was boring in life *and* in bed. Plain Jane. Greenie? The unfairness of it felt like a slap. She was *not* boring in bed, at least she didn't think she was with Beck. In that damn lodge, she'd done things with him that she'd never done with anyone else. But maybe Beck's pulse had barely ticked up a notch. Oh, God. Maybe that was why she'd never heard from him again. Maybe...she'd bored him so much he ran away.

She felt a deep, stinging embarrassment, and heat rushed through her from her nose to the roots of her hair. Had he measured her against the dozens and dozens of other women he'd taken to his bed and found her wanting? Had the best sex in her life... turned out to be the worst for him? She felt a hard, slick pit at the bottom of her stomach, an oily nause-ating mess. She suddenly badly wanted the floor of the bar to open up and swallow her whole.

"But you're not. You know that, right? You are *not* boring." Mira was babbling now, trying to comfort Allie in a rush. "You're badass awesome, and if he can't see that, then screw him. Who cares what he thinks or anybody else thinks? I know you're amaz-ing and fun, and if he doesn't, that's his loss. You are one of the most exciting and dynamic people I know. If he can't see that, then he's blind."

"I can't believe he thinks I'm boring." She felt... crushed. Completely and utterly crushed. She wanted to run home—immediately. Or she needed to drink. Literally everything in this bar. She grabbed her cock-tail and took a huge gulp.

"On the bright side, do you know how many women in Aspen would *kill* to get a nickname from Liam Beck? Even a bad one?" Mira was just grasp-ing at desperate jokes, trying to make her feel better, but Allie felt like she'd had the wind knocked out of her. At the very least, she'd thought Beck had been...

her friend. Friends didn't treat friends like this. It felt like one more betrayal. "Oh, geez. I'm making this worse." Mira shook her head. "Look, do *not* let him into your head like this. This is why I didn't want to tell you. Who cares what he or any of his loser groupies say?"

Allie did. She wished she didn't, but she did. It was that simple. The worst part was that, deep down, she didn't believe it was true. She'd seen Beck's face when he'd come; she'd looked right into the man's eyes. He didn't look bored. He looked...electric, enthralled, completely and utterly focused on her. And would a bored man have gone back for seconds...thirds...*and* fourths? It seemed like his frantic want had matched hers, that he'd needed it as much as she had.

But maybe she'd read him all wrong.

After all, he hadn't called her. On the contrary, he'd deliberately avoided her. And now...that damn nickname. Greenie. She wasn't timid or boring or any of those things. She might be an accountant raised by helicopter parents, but she wasn't a mouse. She glanced over at Beck and saw him throw back his head and laugh, his teeth almost too white against his tanned face. Maybe he and Channing were laughing at her right now.

"I think I should go." Allie didn't want to run scared, but she also didn't want to be in a room anymore with Liam Beck.

"Stop that right now," Mira commanded and snapped her fingers near Allie's face. Once more, her attention was on her best friend. "Don't let him ruin your night. You hear me?"

"He can't ruin my night," Allie said. "Not if I don't let him."

"That's my girl," Mira said, her dark eyes fierce. She glanced over at the bartender, and her face lit up. "Why not get your mind off Liam Beck. I know!"

"What?"

"Go kiss that bartender." Mira nodded over at the floppy-haired server who had a silver martini shaker high above his head. He was no Beck, but he was cute. Kind of. In a slightly-out-of-shape, cuddly way. But, on the bright side, he probably wasn't the type to go free-climbing up one of the highest peaks in the Rockies, without even the thought of a harness. The bartender was one hundred percent nonthreatening. Not like Beck, whose flick of a single eyebrow offered a whole menu of dangerous options. The bartender did have kind eyes, and Allie liked the flannel shirt he wore. He seemed nice. Maybe after Beck, *nice* was what she needed. Though, her body rebelled at the thought. Her body didn't want nice.

"I couldn't," she said, laughing self-consciously.

"Why not? I bet *he* won't think you're boring. Because you're not. You will knock his socks off."

"No, I won't!" Allie laughed.

"I *dare* you." Mira's red lips slipped into a devious grin. "I *double* dare you."

"Mira. Come on. We're not in third grade." She didn't need to prove anything. She knew who she was.

But she also knew that the one weekend she'd spent with Beck had kept her head spinning for two months straight. Nothing quite seemed normal.

"No, and hold that thought—my boss wants something." Mira nodded over to a dark-haired man in his forties who was signaling her. "Probably wants to make sure we have extra bottles of his favorite champagne. I'll be right back. Meantime… Get *on* that bartender, would you?"

Allie was tempted. She glanced over at Channing, who was practically rubbing herself on Beck like a cat.

Why the hell not? How did she even know if she didn't like "nice" until she tried it? Maybe the cure for Beck was to hop into bed with his exact opposite. And she was no coward. She wasn't going to let Beck run her out of the bar. That would mean he won.

"Well, then." Allie took a deep breath and slipped off her new glasses, putting them in her pocket. "Looks like I'm going to do this."

"Atta girl," Mira called over her shoulder.

CHAPTER TWO

BECK SAW ALLIE move from the corner of his eye. He was only half listening to Channing. She loved talking about herself, and while she found the subject endlessly fascinating, Beck most certainly did not. He wanted to head right back to Allie. She looked tired. Worn down. Had he done this? Guilt pricked the back of his neck, feeling like the scratchy edge of a clothing tag he'd forgotten to cut out. If he didn't know better, Allie looked heartsick and he hated himself. He *knew* she couldn't handle casual, but he'd gone in anyway. It was just that…he couldn't resist her. That was the problem.

If he were truly honest with himself, those two days with Allie in that snowbound lodge had blown his mind. He couldn't even say that if he had to do it all over again, that he'd do anything differently. Afterward, he'd spent weeks dreaming about her petal-soft skin, and the fact that he'd never in his whole life had a woman so attuned to him, so willing, so completely focused on the moment. Plus, he practically sneezed and she came. Once, twice…and again, and again and again. And none of them faked. That was the amazing part. They were one hundred percent real, just like Allie herself. Most of the women he took to his bed seemed to be only there to star in their own personal porn, acutely aware of which angle looked best for them, as if performing the whole thing for some imaginary audience, but Allie wasn't like that. Allie was carefree, completely authentic. Because of that, she was the sexiest woman he'd ever met.

But he'd crossed a line he'd promised he'd never cross with her. She'd been one of the few women he'd managed to be friends with and he'd gone and let a little wine and a blizzard get in the way of his good judgment. All he'd been trying to do was minimize the damage afterward. He thought if he made himself scarce it would somehow be easier. Sure, for him, but also for her. She could recover and they could both pretend those two days never happened. Maybe, even, after a little time, they could be friends again. Because what was he going to do? Settle down? Ask her to marry him? Have two kids?

Marriage, kids, a picket fence—those were never going to be in his future. He had too much Beck blood in him. Becks didn't do families. Or when they did, they did them all wrong.

He'd disappeared for her own good, but it looked like she'd done a lousy job of recovering. And it was all his fault. It didn't look like she was thriving. Sure, she was as gorgeous as ever, especially with the new hair—yellow and red like a single flame—and those sexy AF librarian glasses. God, they made her look razor sharp and…so delectable. But the faint circles under her eyes told him she wasn't sleeping, and her too-slim hips told him she wasn't eating enough. Beck knew that when she was stressed, she didn't eat. Like during her busy time at work last year when he'd have to practically force-feed her dinner, because she fretted so much about her deadlines that she forgot she needed food to fuel her. Who was making sure she ate now? Her cheekbones were sharper, her waist thinner than usual. She needed to eat, that much he knew. He wanted to scoop her into his arms and take her to the nearest burger joint and watch her gobble down a large order of fries. The instinct to take care of her burned in him.

That was why they'd made such good friends. He wanted to take care of her. But now they'd slipped into bed together and everything had changed. He'd known it would, but he'd crossed the line anyway. He was a fool.

She moved like the model she should've been: tall, elegant, lean. Just watching the bar light catch those fire-engine red highlights of hers made him want to put his hands in that messy bun and tug it down, unraveling the silky strands with his fingers. He remembered the feel of her waves in his fingers, soft but strong, and the feel of her thick lips on his. He recalled, too, her sheer lace underwear—and garter belts. She might be a buttoned-up accountant on the outside, but peel off that first layer, and any man was in for a surprise. Her lingerie had matched perfectly— a shock since the blizzard had taken them both by surprise, and they'd ended up stuck at the same lodge by sheer accident. He had wanted to study it and rip it off at the same time. He wondered what she might be wearing beneath that tight cashmere sweater. Red lace? God, he hoped it was red.

His groin tightened at the mere thought.

Stop it, he told himself. He wasn't crossing that line again. It was best for her. He knew that even if she didn't yet. He'd plowed through a couple of rebound trysts since then, but he'd had to choke them down, force himself. Liam Beck had never been the kind of guy who had to force himself to oblige a willing woman, and yet, lately, sex had become a chore. In fact, he hadn't even touched another woman in a full month. Because the more women he took to his bed, the more he realized they were nothing like Allie. He'd been through enough plain cotton thongs and mismatched sports bras and fumbling awkwardness to last a lifetime. They all seemed immature some-how, even though none was more than a couple of years younger than him. Even Channing, with her corset and plunging cleavage, seemed just like a girl playing dress-up.

Allie, on the other hand, was a woman. Complex, grown-up, sexier and infinitely more dangerous. He watched her glide through the crowd, the men and women parting to let her to the bar. She was tall, lithe and graceful as she leaned in to get the bartender's attention. Not that he needed a signal. He dropped everything and scurried over to get her order, his eyes lighting up at the sight of her. Of course. She was gorgeous, that auburn hair and delicate pale neck. She was a knockout, not that she knew it. Her power over men always came as a surprise to her. Not to Beck.

He frowned as he watched the bartender's eyes light up as he bathed in her attention. He remembered the feel of being the focus of those clear green eyes, and the feeling, too, of truly being *seen*. He noticed their conversation dragged on longer than should be right for a quick order of drinks. The man laughed, too, at one of her jokes, he assumed, and then Beck wondered with a shock if she were *flirting* with him. The dad-bod bartender? The one with the patchy beard? Looked like he couldn't grow any in on the middle part of his chin. Was she serious? He was maybe a three, and she was most definitely a nine. Was she doing this to get his attention?

If so, goal achieved.

A muscle in his jaw twitched. Why was she leaning so far over the bar? The bartender's eyes drifted down to the V-neck of her sweater, which barely contained her. And he suddenly wanted to fly across the bar and remind the man about good old-fashioned manners. The jingly, upbeat Christmas music drifting out through the speakers suddenly grated, as his mood turned dark. This wasn't the happiest season of all. He hated Christmas. It reminded him of the day he watched his dad being led out of their house in handcuffs. He hadn't come from the kind of family who baked cookies and sang carols.

The whole season got him into a defensive mood, and it didn't help watching the bartender fall all over himself to serve Allie right now. He had a goofy grin plastered on his face as if he couldn't believe his luck. Well, of course. He'd just won the lottery with the sexiest woman in the bar whispering something directly into his ear. Whatever she said, she seemed to make his night. And then he realized with a shock that maybe she *knew* him. Was she dating this guy? Were they a…thing?

Then, in a flash, she was kissing the guy, *on the mouth*, in front of everyone in this damn bar. That answered his question then. What the holy hell? If he hadn't seen it with his own eyes, he wouldn't have believed it. What was Al doing sticking her tongue down that guy's throat? Then he had to remind himself that he'd set her free *for this very reason*. He clutched his beer harder. Didn't make the reality of her using that freedom any easier to take. Whoops and hollers of approval went up from the bar, as the nearest revelers seemed to enjoy the show. The attention didn't bother Allie at all, which confounded Beck. How could this be? She hated the idea of people watching her. Then the bartender reached up and *put his hands in her auburn hair*, threatening to bring the whole messy bun down.

He couldn't watch anymore. He turned away then, chugging a big swig of beer.

None of your fucking business, Beck.

He set her free, and it was for her own damn good. If this was how she used her freedom, then that was her choice. He'd had this stupid notion that he'd nobly let her go and she'd find the man of her dreams, a boring lawyer type who'd deliver all the things she wanted: an engagement ring, a white picket fence and kids—the life he'd sworn he'd never have. He wasn't the kind of man to be domesticated. He had serious issues with his father, but the one thing he'd learned from the drug addict was that it was best not to put someone in a cage who didn't want to be there. Otherwise, he'd hurt everyone around him trying to escape.

He took another drink of his beer. Then a cry went up from the bar—Allie's cry. He whirled in time to see some other patron at the bar deciding to get in on the action. He had an arm around her and was dragging her to him against her will, asking for a kiss as well, though the look on Allie's face told him she was in no mood to oblige him. The bartender was gesturing and yelling at the man, but whatever the threat from her new boyfriend, it wasn't enough. Before he could stop himself, he'd stashed his beer on a ledge near Channing and was on the move, every muscle in his body telling him that he had to intervene. He felt a sense of possessiveness he had no business feeling rising up in him, a ridiculous primal instinct he knew was wrong but couldn't fight. Nobody touched Allie without her permission. Ever. Period.

He made it to the bar just in time to see Allie give

the patron a good stomp with her stiletto ankle boot on the inside of his foot, and he leaped back, cursing. Allie's frown and the wagging finger in the man's face told Beck she had the situation handled. But then, she always did. He felt a fierce swell of pride in his chest. That was his Al, all right. Lord help the man who underestimated her. God, he missed her. She swiped past him, glancing up for a split second, her green eyes ablaze. He watched her head to the ladies' room, and without thinking, he followed her into the small corridor. He found her outside the locked door, leaning against the corner and fiddling with her heel. He watched as the heel fell off the sole of her shoe. She'd broken it against the man's foot! He couldn't help himself—a sly grin wiggled across his face.

"Well, that's one way to make sure he understands the value of consent," he managed, folding his forearms across his chest. "You okay?"

Her head snapped up then, her green eyes fixed on him, fury still flickering there. She'd stashed her librarian glasses somewhere, and now he could see her green eyes clearly, large and burning. The fire in them didn't cool when she saw him, either.

"I'm fine," she said as she tried unsuccessfully to reattach the heel. Whatever had held it there was useless now.

"I might have superglue in my truck," he offered. The idea of her wobbling about on lopsided shoes for the evening wouldn't do.

"I don't need your help." She ground out the words

as she glared at him. There was a series of novels in that one little sentence, added meaning behind every word. Frustrated with her heel, she let out a sigh and stopped trying to affix it to her boot, as she sagged against the wall one legged, like a depressed flamingo. He almost laughed but thought better of it. Laughing would make her only more furious and he didn't want to chance her breaking her good heel on *his* foot. She wobbled a little, biting her lip in frustration. She ducked down and tried to unzip the broken-heeled boot, but balancing on one stiletto in a small corridor with no good handholds made her less like a flamingo and more like an amateur athlete stuck on the end of a pole midvault.

"Al..." He leaned in now, close enough to get a whiff of her amazing perfume, the signature floral scent that always used to drive him mad. She smelled like the Rockies in springtime, all in bloom beneath the Colorado sunshine. "Please," he said with deliberate deference. He reached out and touched her elbow. Instantly, her wobble steadied. "Let me help."

She glanced up at him, an unanswered question in her emerald green eyes. He knew he wouldn't be able to strong-arm her any more than he could tell daffodils where to grow.

"Please, Al."

She softened a bit. Fairly confident she wouldn't try to stick her good stiletto in his eye, he knelt before her and helped her unzip the broken boot, her delicate foot slipping out, revealing sheer lace socks. His eyebrows rose in appreciation. Only Al could make socks sexy. He saw the bright green polish on her toes and thought of her eyes. Still kneeling, he held her tiny foot on his knee, giving her a steady base, and tried not to think about the warmth of her toes against his jeans. He studied the shoe, and the heel that she wordlessly handed to him. He wasn't sure if glue would work after all. Beck studied the slope of the boot's sole, surprised to find it more like suede than leather, more pliable.

"Can I see the other one?" He reached for the good boot. She hesitated, but then let him, slipping her socked foot on the mat near the bathroom doors and raising her other foot. He slowly worked the zipper down the side, trying not to think about how he'd taken off her boots just this way…that night at the lodge. Boots…then jeans…then the delicate lace beneath. She stood very still, eyes watching his every move. He freed her from the second boot, and now she was standing in her lacy socks, her freshly painted green toes a beacon. He wanted to kiss them and stroke her calf all the way up to her knee. He watched as she shifted uncomfortably from one foot to the other.

"Floor cold?" he asked her, and she gave him a swift nod. He glanced around, seeing a stack of kitchen towels stashed in the shelves near the bathrooms. He grabbed a thick one and dropped it down near her feet. She tiptoed on the terry cloth delicately and stood there on the balls of her feet. He managed to divert his attention back to her boot in his hand. The good one. He'd put the broken one down on the floor. He straightened, as he studied the black suede boot, an idea coming to him. An idea she wouldn't like, but that would help prevent her feet from freezing for the rest of the night.

He took the boot, which seemed so delicate and small in his hands, and quickly snapped the other heel off.

"What the hell!" cried Allie, her face beet red with anger. "Beck!"

"You can walk in these now and your feet won't get cold," he said, even as she gave his chest a shove. He tried to defend himself against her blows. "And calm down. I'll buy you a new pair."

She angrily swiped the boot out of his hand and jammed her foot in it. "I don't need you to buy me anything."

"I know," he said. Allie could take care of herself, but that didn't mean that he wouldn't want to if she'd ever let him. Her head bounced up, a tendril of auburn hair falling across her forehead.

"I just want to make sure you're okay, that's all."

"So you break my shoe?"

"I *evened* the pair," he managed. Now her ire was fully focused on him, the jerk at the bar long forgotten. Suddenly, the heel fiasco was all his fault, instead of the handsy SOB who'd started all this—or the wimpy bartender who couldn't defend her even in his own place. "I didn't want your feet freezing, or for you to fall and break your knee hobbling around like a pirate."

She stuffed her other foot in the other boot and zipped it. They both glanced down at the flattened boots and saw her toes pointing oddly in the air. The once sexy ankle boots looked a bit like something that one of Santa's elves might wear. Now Beck really did want to laugh. Hard. But he had to swallow his chuckle as she glared at her feet, exasperated.

"I look ridiculous now."

Beck said nothing. She did, kind of, look ridiculous in her elf shoes. Not that any of the guys at this bar, or any other bar, would care. No man would be looking at her feet. She could wear a pair of stuffed bear paw slippers and still get hit on by every straight guy in the place.

Allie frowned, more tendrils of loose hair falling forward in her face, her bun all but coming undone. He wanted to put his hands in her hair and finish the job. He longed to see her face framed by the silken auburn streaked with red, wanted to feel that silky hair once more on his bare chest. He mentally shook himself. More thoughts like these and he'd have a hard-on in the bar, right there. And he'd promised himself: hands off Allie. Period.

"I don't think your new boyfriend will care about the shoes, if that's what you're worried about," Beck offered.

"Boyfriend?" Confusion crossed Allie's face.

"The bartender?" Beck reluctantly nodded toward

the bar, still not quite believing that the solidly below-average man was Allie's choice to replace him.

"Him?" Allie laughed, confusing Beck. "He's not my boyfriend. Any more than you are."

The sting of the comment was surprisingly sharp. Beck blinked fast. "Sure seemed like you guys were friendly."

Allie's gaze focused on him with the intensity of a lion looking for the weak member of a pack.

"Were you watching me?" she asked, a note of accusation in her voice.

"Of course I was." If she were in the room, then that was where his attention would be. Plain and simple. That hadn't changed, might never change. "So you're not dating him?"

Allie laughed. "The bartender? No."

Relief flooded Beck. "Good." That bartender couldn't handle a woman like Allie. She was way out of his league.

"I don't even know his name," she added.

This felt like a punch in the gut. "You *kissed* a guy and you didn't even know his name?" Beck felt like an alien had come down and taken over his friend's body. She was not the make-out-with-strangers-in-a-bar type. Allie picked her lingerie with care, and her men with more deliberation. It was one of the things that made Allie…Allie. They'd spent enough time at enough happy hours to know how the other operated, enough time together lamenting the Aspen dating scene to know what made the other tick. It had been why they'd been such great friends. Until the blizzard that had snowed them in on top of the mountain and everything changed.

"Why?"

Allie shrugged. "Because Mira dared me to."

"Dared you?" None of this made sense. "What the hell is that?"

Allie laughed. "I'm playing a game of double dare you. So why do you care? Don't you have some mark to make tonight? Is it Channing?"

Beck flinched. They were back in Allie and Beck mode, friends mode, where she'd be his wingman at the bar and he'd reveal the real truth about what it was like being Aspen's most-talked-about bachelor. It was comfortable. Dangerously comfortable.

"No, I can't stand Channing."

"She sure likes you." The words seemed to have some weight to them. Beck tried not to think about what that meant. Despite the fact they were acting like good old friends, something was off. Beck knew exactly what. It was because he'd tasted every inch of her body and he'd liked it. Liked it so much, he craved another round. And another. "Well, I'm sure you'll have your pick of the bar. Anyway, I've got to go. The bartender told me he's off in fifteen minutes."

Now Beck felt like he'd been hit with a ton of bricks. She was going to take that lame guy *home* after that pathetic show at the bar when he let that patron slobber all over her? She was going to show him her red lace? His brain felt short-circuited. The world he lived in no longer made sense.

"You're going to fuck him?" He stared at Allie as if seeing her for the first time. "You don't even know his name."

"That never stopped you before."

"Yeah, but, Al. You're not me." He thought this was obvious. Al didn't do casual. She'd never done anything casual in her whole life. She was all in or nothing. There wasn't an in-between with her.

"I'm not?" The challenge in her voice was unmistakable. "Maybe I've been going about my life all wrong. Maybe I've been *boring*."

What was she even talking about? "You're not boring." She was anything but. And taking after him was the last thing she ought to do. If only she knew how little he'd enjoyed anything or anyone since the weekend they'd spent together, how he drifted aimlessly through nights with strangers like a robot. He could go through the motions, but he felt numb inside, as if he was stuck in a performance trying to convince himself that sex could be half as good with anyone else. He already knew it would never be as good with anyone as with Allie.

"Al…" He sighed. He knew all he had to do was pull out his phone right now, and in seconds he'd probably have a Tinder hookup waiting in the parking lot. There was no way she'd believe that was the last thing he wanted with her standing in front of him. "If you take that guy home, it'll be a mistake." Then she'd feel the emptiness he felt, the uselessness of it all. "You'll regret it."

He was speaking only the truth, but she immediately took offense.

"I'll be the judge of that," she said. He recognized Allie's stubbornness, but not this newfound determination to sleep around. She didn't avoid her problems by having sex with strangers. That was Beck's coping mechanism, as ill-advised as it was.

She cared too much, that was Allie's problem, and she wasn't built for casual sex. It was why it had been a colossal mistake for him to go there. He wasn't a relationship guy. Allie deserved the guy who bought her flowers and wrote his own sappy poems in Valentine's Day cards. Not the guy who didn't plan his life more than a week in advance. "Please don't take him home." Beck realized he had no sway anymore. As much as he wanted to protect her and keep her safe from scruffy-bearded bartenders, he actually didn't have a say in her life.

"Why do you care?"

"Because..." He never stopped caring—that was the whole problem. Because he was jealous, even though he had no right to be. "Because I don't want you to get hurt."

"I think it's a little late for that." She blinked, and he worried for a second she might cry. If she cried, he'd be undone; he wouldn't be able to keep his resolve. He'd pull her into his arms and beg her for forgiveness. And that wouldn't help either of them.

How could he tell her that he'd just find a way to disappoint her? Later, five or even ten years down the line, the Beck genes would come roaring to the surface. They always did.

"I'm..." He almost said "sorry" but stopped himself. Sorry wasn't enough. "Just...please don't do this."

She took a step closer to him and he felt his own heart tick up, the thought of pain and heartbreak slipping away. Her perfume was in his nose, and all he wanted to do was inhale. She was so close he could dip down and kiss her now, show her what it meant to be properly kissed, not slathered on. He could kiss her in the way he knew she liked. Every bit of him wanted to. Wanted to feel her lips once more against his. Make her sigh into his mouth.

"You can't tell me what to do anymore," Allie said, voice low.

Beck couldn't help it. He chuckled and shook his head slowly. "Al, I never could tell you what to do." And he wasn't dumb enough to start now. "I just don't think the bartender is the answer to your problems," he said. "Trust me, I know." He couldn't even remember the names of the women he'd been with but he knew that they'd only made him feel lonelier.

"Maybe the bartender is just what I need." Her green eyes were ablaze with defiance. "Maybe I'll just accept any crazy dare that Mira or anyone else throws my way. Not because I'm scared of what Mira or anyone else thinks, but maybe I'll do it *just because I can.*"

Allie stabbed a finger in his chest, and Beck felt laughter bubble up in his throat, which he promptly squashed. There was no way he'd tell her that her anger coupled with her elf shoes made her off-the-charts adorable.

"Look, you don't have anything to prove to me, okay?" he managed. If this was about trying to make him jealous, he needed to stop this right here and now. She needed to get past him if she was ever going to truly be happy with someone else.

"Why do you think it's about you? None of this is about you." Allie's right eyebrow twitched, her tell. She was lying.

"This isn't about me?" Beck knew he shouldn't poke the bear. Knew he should just let her leave the little alcove feeling like she'd won this fight. But Beck couldn't let it go. She needed to face her feelings, or they'd always have control over her. She'd never get over him, if she was always trying to prove she was over him. The ultimate irony.

Not that he'd done much better. He'd faced his feelings for Allie every day since that weekend, and it hadn't helped him one bit. He had no idea how forty-eight hours had upended his life, but they had.

"You think it's about that weekend? It's not." Again, her eyebrow twitched. "I don't even *think* about that weekend."

Now he knew for sure she was lying.

"You don't?"

"No. I don't." She glared at him. He'd made her come more times than she could count, and she'd shouted his name in a hoarse ecstasy that he'd never heard before. She absolutely remembered. He would bet money on it. Hell, he'd bet all his money on it. "You think I won't take that bartender home? Just dare me. I will." He almost wanted to catch her up in his arms right then, show her who she should be taking home tonight.

"If you need me to dare you, then maybe you're not all that into the idea," he said dryly.

She flipped her hair from her eyes and looked as if she might breathe fire, burn him to ash if she could. *That's it*, he thought. *Get angry.* Angry was much better than sad. Anger could help her get stronger. Sadness would eat her alive, but anger would help her fight. Help her recover. "You're impossible. I'll take him home anyway."

"You'll take him home and you'll think of me."

Shock bloomed on her face as her mouth fell open. He'd rendered her speechless—for once. He grinned. He knew she needed to get angry, for her sake, but he was also enjoying pushing her buttons. He'd forgotten how easy she was to bait and how much he loved her temper. He was drawn to that heat, that fire, in her.

"I *will* not," she managed, once she found her voice again. "How dare you even think that I'm somehow hung up on you…"

"Because you are."

"I'm not." Now the teasing was going too far. Annoyance bubbled in Beck. Why wouldn't she just admit it? He knew it was about pride, but if she just admitted it, she could move on.

"Okay," Beck said, his mind feeling like it was crawling with ants. Allie was getting under his skin. He took a step closer and almost felt like he wanted to drown in those green eyes. So defiant, so full of ire and so stubbornly unwilling to admit that she still had feelings for him, which she clearly did. He was going to do something rash, something that broke his own rules, but he had such a hard time toeing the line. Hell, he didn't even see the line with her right in front of him. "If you are over me, and I don't mean anything to you, then prove it." She blinked fast. He grinned, slowly, letting the tension build. He was going to enjoy this. "I dare you to kiss me."

CHAPTER THREE

ALLIE FELT THE entire world on the other side of their little nook fade away into nothing. For a second, she forgot to breathe and there was just her and Beck, the only two people on earth. Because it all seemed more than absurd, she laughed. A brittle, bitter laugh.

The man must be joking. That was the only way she could think to explain it. How else was it that Beck, who'd been happily sleeping with the tourists of Aspen for the last two months, wanted to kiss her? He was the one who'd made it clear to her that they had no future, and yet now he wanted to come back for more?

"Why are you laughing?" His steady, serious gaze told her she'd miscalculated. He was deadly serious.

"Because you have to be joking."

"I'm not." He was so close now, she could see the darker flecks in his blond stubble. The man seemed as if he belonged in the middle of a snowboarding commercial beneath the bright mountain sun. She wanted to put her hands in his hair. Touch it, see if it was as soft as she remembered. She had to shake herself. That was not an option. Not now. Not ever. "If you don't care for me at all, then kiss me. I'll be able to tell, and then I won't bother you anymore, and you can take that scruffy bartender home."

"This is ridiculous." She shifted her feet in her broken boots, the soles feeling oddly angled against the bar floor. She felt exposed.

What was the man's game? He could have anyone in the bar, and in fact, Channing was already in a pout across the room because she'd lost her prize.

There was only one reason why she could think that he'd be interested in her again.

Was the adventuring ski god of Aspen…jealous? He didn't want her for himself, but didn't want anyone else to have her?

"So? What about that dare?" His blue eyes never left hers. They were steady, serious.

She laughed again, but this time it came out sounding thin and a little nervous. "No," she said and folded her arms across her chest.

"Why not?" Now he moved a beat closer. She could almost feel his body heat, and she'd forgotten how broad he was, and the nook they were in barely contained them. He was all muscle, and if he wanted that kiss, he could get it whether she wanted it or not. But that wasn't Beck's way. She knew it as well as he did. Besides, women in Aspen would line up for a chance to kiss Liam Beck, for a chance to do much more than that.

The worst part was that even though he'd discarded

her just two months ago, her body didn't seem to care. Right in that moment, all she wanted to do was reach on her tippy toes and kiss that man right here. After all, he was a phenomenal kisser. A man with that much practice couldn't help but be.

"You know why," she said, voice low. *Because we had amazing sex and then you dropped off the face of the earth. Then I hear you think I'm boring.* But Allie couldn't get herself to say those things out loud.

"If you take that bartender home, but you're still hung up on me, it's not going to be good for you."

White-hot anger rushed through her, warming her right through her toes. "It's my mistake to make, then." She could not believe this man. He ghosted her, then spread rumors she was a dud in bed, and now he was micromanaging her dating life?

"You don't get to pick who I sleep with, Beck."

"I know." Beck glanced away, almost looking guilty. "I know that."

The vulnerability he showed in that moment sliced through her. He seemed so lost...so untethered. For a second, she wondered if the breakup had hit him hard. Harder than she'd imagined. Here she thought he'd just resumed his life, no worse for wear, but the look of pain across his face told her a different story. Could it be that he had suffered, like she suffered?

It almost made her want to kiss him, just to make him feel better. She nearly laughed. She wanted to make *him* feel better? What was she thinking? She wasn't. She never did when it came to Beck.

"Go ahead, then," Beck said, sounding resigned. "Go back to him."

She hated that in that moment of him dismissing her, it made her only want to stay. Why, she didn't know. The more Beck pushed her away, the more she wanted to be with him. She hated that weakness in herself. She glanced over Beck's shoulder and saw the bartender eyeing them from the bar. He'd come to her rescue if she signaled him, she thought. But part of her didn't want to be rescued. She wanted to stay just where she was and that was what worried her.

"Maybe I will."

Beck stared at her for a beat. "You're not moving."

No, she wasn't. It felt like she was caught in Beck's gravitational field, fixed like a moon in orbit.

"I don't think you want to go," Beck said at last. Damn him for reading her mind. She scooted a bit against the wall, but her elf boot hit the edge of a nearby mat, and she stumbled. He caught her, steadying her. His strong hands on her elbows made her remember how talented they were in exploring other parts of her body. How she felt so delicate, so little, in his arms. Allie froze then, the moment turning serious suddenly. He ran a finger down the outside of her upper arm. His touch felt hot. She watched his finger trail the seam of her sleeve, remembering how well his hands already knew her body. Despite all her logical misgivings, some part of her still burned for him. "I think you want to kiss me. I think you haven't gotten enough of me."

There was no boast in the words. It was true, after all. How could he read her so well?

She blinked fast. Her heart ticked up a notch. She wanted to kiss him, but she was scared. One kiss and she might be a slave to him again, a slave to her own passions, all logic and will gone. Beck moved forward, and she was in the dark corner of the alcove now, away from the bar, out of the line of vision of anyone there. The bartender wouldn't be able to help her now, but she didn't want anyone's help.

She decided then and there, she wasn't going to be afraid of Liam Beck. She could kiss him and not feel anything. She could do this and prove to him and herself that she was beyond him.

"I'll kiss you, just to prove that weekend meant nothing," she said. "I don't feel anything for you, Liam Beck."

Beck nodded, once. "Good. If that's true, then I'll leave you alone."

She needed Liam Beck out of her life. And if kissing him one last time was the way to do it, then she'd do it. *It's just a kiss*, she told herself. It would mean nothing. And then she'd be free of him.

"Fine." She tilted her head up, lips ready. Beck wasted no time. His big palm sneaked behind her back, and he pulled her to him. In seconds, she was pressed flat against the massive muscles in his chest. He was so big, she felt tiny. She held a breath, her heart fighting like a rabbit trying to get out of its cage. Beck took his time. His eyes studying hers and then moving ever so slowly down her face to her lips. They parted on their own accord, already tingling in anticipation. *It won't mean anything. I won't feel anything*, she told herself.

He pressed his full lips against hers, tentatively at first. Gently. She kept her lips still. *If I don't move, then everything will be fine.* But she knew already this wasn't going to be a quick peck on the lips. Beck had something else in mind. The second his lips moved on hers, the entire last two months disappeared. It was as if they'd never spent a second apart and they were right back in that lodge.

His mouth, warm and determined, found hers in just the way she liked. Instantly, all her senses lit up, like blinking lights on a massive Christmas tree, and she felt the surge of electricity down to her fingertips. She didn't know whose tongue sought the other's first, only that soon the kiss turned deeper, more dangerous. He anticipated every move she made and countered it, in a way that made her feel like they were partners in the world's oldest dance. There was something about the way the man tasted, something so irresistible that she didn't want to stop. In seconds, her hands, with a will of their own, had crawled up the back of his neck and into his hair. Yes, that thick, soft shock of blond, and his neck thick with muscle. His hands kept firm on the small of her back and she was reminded how big his hands were, how they seemed to span most of her waist.

And then Beck's hands snaked up the back of her

sweater, and she felt his palms on her skin. The heat from his hands traveled all the way through her. Want, powerful and raw, came to life in her belly, and she realized how she'd stuffed down her own desires for weeks, how she'd denied herself, how she'd tried so hard to forget how Beck felt. Now here he was, mouth on hers, and all she could think was *more. I want more. I want his lips. I want his hands. I want everything.* She felt as if she'd only just woken up to the fact that she had been starving for this.

His hands roamed downward, outside the fabric of her jeans, and he cupped her possessively, pushing her flat against him, and then she felt the hardness bulging in the front of his jeans. He wanted her, too. Badly. The discovery made her kiss him even harder; she wanted to devour him. Stand in that chaos once more that was loving Beck, cling to him in the ferocious whirlwind that was him. Kissing the bartender was now a distant, faint memory. Here, right here, this was what passion was meant to be. His hands roamed freely now, as did hers, neither seeming to be able to stop groping. She realized the stark truth: it wasn't that she *couldn't* stop kissing Beck. She didn't want to stop.

Distantly, she heard someone come out of the locked bathroom behind them, and in a second, Beck was steering her inside. She went willingly, unable to believe how fast things were moving, but then, that was what Beck did. He tackled everything fast: slopes, cars, women. Beck himself was like a thrilling roller coaster ride, one without a safety harness. She pushed him against the bathroom wall, running her hands up his thick, fit chest. And then she realized that she could have him, right there in the bathroom of this bar. No one would have to know.

She pressed her hand to the front of his jeans and found him hard and ready. All she'd have to do was free him, a single zipper standing between her and him. That was all she wanted. One more time. One more and she'd be done with him.

Or would she? She wondered if she'd ever, truly, be over Liam Beck, or if he'd stay in her blood forever, like a dormant virus, ready to come to life at the first touch. She pulled away from Beck first, breaking the spell. She saw surprise on his face, as he panted, out of breath. The extreme snowboarding athlete that never met a mountain he couldn't climb or ski seemed winded and disoriented. God, she wondered what she looked like. Hell, probably, her lipstick smudged, her hair a mess. She felt as surprised as Beck looked. Well, guess he wasn't expecting that, either. He'd forgotten, just as she had, how electric they'd been. How much like gasoline on flames. It was why he was so addictive, so hard to quit. That kind of fire didn't come along every day. Or, hell, every lifetime.

"Al…" Beck's voice was a guttural growl. His blue eyes nearly black, his pupils were so big with desire. His hair was ruffled, too, she noticed. That was where her hands had been two seconds ago. "Al, oh, but I missed you."

The words sliced through her. She wanted to tell him she'd missed him, too. She wanted to take him home to her bed and show him just how much she'd missed him. But she couldn't. Things were different now. They'd never be the same.

She slid her hands down the front of his pants and he groaned. A flicker of mischief ran through her. She glanced downward, at her hand covering his fly, and then she slowly worked his zipper down, a centimeter at a time. She expected him to…what? Stop her? Tell her they weren't right together? That this was all some kind of mistake. Would he warn her about tomorrow or the next day when he wouldn't call?

But the want in his eyes was like flame, and she knew he wasn't going to stop her. She reached into his pants and wrapped her hands around his thick shaft, and he sucked in a breath. Smooth, hard and thick, just as she remembered. Absolutely, blindingly perfect. Then, just as quickly, she released him.

She smiled, slowly.

"Looks like *you're* the one who's not over me, Beck."

And then she turned, leaving him leaning against the wall, face frozen in shock. She left him there, and he let her go, the look in his eyes telling her that whatever it was between them was far, far from done. Why did she have a sudden and definite feeling that she'd kicked a hornet's nest?

CHAPTER FOUR

"You did *not* seriously do that! Left him, dick literally in his hands!" squealed Mira the next day, as she jabbed a piece of spinach salad and forked it into her mouth. They sat in the retro-styled café near the slopes, which seemed both quaint and modern at the same time, with sleek stainless-steel tables and leather-bound booths. More Christmas music blared happily from the speakers and the restaurant was decorated floor to ceiling in freshly harvested garlands and wreaths. The whole restaurant smelled like pine trees. Allie was busy explaining why she'd made a hasty exit the night before, leaving well before the party was over. Mira had to stay until the end—it was the party she'd helped organize, after all. "Serves him right. That'll teach him to ghost you. And here I thought you were in hot water with Beck. I knew he'd gone after you, but I didn't think... Well, damn, girl. I didn't think you had it in you."

"Why? Think he'd kiss me and I'd beg for more?"

Mira glanced at her friend, wary. "Well, yes. The man is a sex god. *Look* at him." Her friend sent her a sympathetic look. "And you did say he was amazing."

"Whose side are you on?"

"Yours—obviously." Mira leaned closer. "You sure you didn't feel anything when he kissed you?"

"Nope." Technically, she didn't feel anything. She felt everything. Every possible nerve ending in her body lighting up, like a power grid that only Beck could ignite. But she couldn't let that derail her. She knew Beck, knew that he could never truly be serious about anyone.

"Good. I thought you might be sucked into his web again. He's not the kind of man who's ever going to settle down. Or if he does, he'll be sixty and opt for a twenty-year-old."

"I know. I should never have thought about him as relationship material. That was my mistake. He was a good time, nothing more." The more she said it, the more she hoped it would be true. The problem was she'd had feelings for Beck for a long time before they rolled into bed together. Again, her fault. She'd always prided herself on being the girl who wasn't sucked in by the guy every girl wanted. Then again, she'd always been bookish, so it wasn't like the hottest guy in school was after the honors society president, either. Still, she told herself it was mutual as she'd steered well clear of the popular and gorgeous egomaniacs who devoured her friends' self-esteem and left them used and mangled. But then came Beck. She thought being friends with him was a safe bet, but it turned out to be anything but. She'd fallen for him hard. Just like most of the women in Aspen. She was almost disappointed in herself for stumbling into the same trap, for being so ordinary. She thought she'd had better sense than every other woman in town.

"Not to mention, who wants to be his girlfriend anyway? Waiting for him to come home after one of his skiing trips in avalanche country?"

Mira nodded. "He's an adrenaline junkie. It's like he's addicted to it."

There was something in Beck that seemed hell-bent on self-destruction. Some people did it with drugs or alcohol. Beck did it with crazy stunts on the mountains. Allie always wanted to show him things could be different, but he didn't seem willing to see that. And now she wouldn't really get the chance.

"He'll probably be dead by forty."

"Don't say that." Allie's voice was sharper than she intended. They might not be a couple, or hell, even friends anymore, but Allie couldn't bear the thought of an accident taking Beck's life. She realized she'd just shown Mira that she still cared, and she hated that. She wondered when there would ever be a time she truly could care less about Liam Beck.

"Sorry." Mira backed away quickly, her dark eyes full of apology. "I didn't mean it."

"I know you didn't." She sighed. Allie fiddled with her spoon. Suddenly, the steaming hot bowl of cheesy onion soup in front of her didn't seem so appetizing anymore. The upbeat jangly holiday music grated, and all she wanted to do was skip over the cheery holiday mood and land in bleak late January. Allie pushed around some of the melted cheese in the bowl in front of her.

"It's just that if he really cared about you, he would've called."

"I know."

"And not just that." Mira searched for the right words. "If he cared, he would've made room for you in his life. He seems like a man who puts everyone in a box. As long as you were in the friend box, that was okay. But then, when you hopped on out of there and wanted a bigger box, a girlfriend box, he freaked out."

Allie nodded. "Well, that's the nice way of looking at it. He freaked out because he cared too much about me, instead of the fact that sex with me bored him to tears."

"Look, you're no *Greenie*. I may never have slept with you…" Mira raised her eyebrows. "And as your *straight* best friend, never will, but I am willing to bet you are great in bed. You are like the hardest worker *I know*, so I can't imagine you're lazy in bed."

Allie laughed a little. "Thanks, Mira." Allie felt a little bit better. "I do think I have some skills."

"Of course you do!" Mira chirped. "I do have a question for you, though. So, all that time you were friends with Beck before *the weekend*…did he ever invite you on one of those crazy tours of his? The heli-skiing?"

Allie shook her head. "Me?"

"You're a kick-ass skier," Mira said. "You eat black diamonds for breakfast."

"Yeah." Allie glanced downward. She was a pretty good skier. It was the one thing she'd split with her conservative parents on—she'd learned to ski and kept skiing, despite the risks. Of course, she wore one of the best helmets money could buy—at her parents' insistence. "But even if he'd invited me on one of those tours, I would've probably said no, anyway."

"Bullshit. If Beck had invited you, you would've bought a new skintight ski suit, gotten a full-body wax and *then* you would've gone. Girl, please." Mira spoke the truth. Even Allie had to admit it. "But he never asked you. Even though you guys were friends who hung out almost every week."

"Yeah."

Mira jammed another bite of salad in her mouth, chewing fiercely. "It's all because you didn't fit into that extreme sport box. It's that he likes to keep his life arranged in neat little boxes: his one-night stands in one, his friends in another, adrenaline junkie stuff in yet another. He reminds me exactly of a guy I used to date in college." Mira waved her now-empty fork in the air. "Even *if* you dated him, or hell, even if you could get him to marry you, he'd probably just put that in another box. Along with each kid you had. Never the two or three or four or five boxes shall meet."

"I don't think he'd do that." Why was she defending Beck? Mira was probably more on target about Beck than even Allie wanted to admit.

"Really? Is that why when you tried to climb out of that friend box and get into that sex box he decided he was better off without your friend box than having someone who wouldn't stay in it?"

Allie felt the punch of truth. She wasn't going to finish her lunch for sure now.

"Ugh. I'm sorry." Mira reached across the table and clutched at Allie's hand. "Your face looks like I kicked your puppy. God, I need to shut my mouth and mind my own business."

"No." Allie gave her friend a weak smile. "I know you want what's best for me."

"And I'm proud of you for not trailing after him like some stray cat, like half of Aspen." She squeezed Allie's hand one last time and let it go. "I want you to see that you can do better than Liam Beck. He's never going to rearrange those boxes for you in his mind. He'll always be trying to put you in one."

Allie let out a frustrated breath. She knew logically that might be true, but in her heart, she simply wanted to believe he could change. And part of her wasn't so sure she could do better than Beck. She could feel his lips on hers, how he'd made her whole body come alive with a single touch. What other man could do that? He'd been as good as she imagined—no, even better.

"It's probably just Christmas. Between Thanksgiving and Christmas, more ghosting and breakups happen than any other time. Too much pressure with the holidays."

"Is that true?"

"I saw it in a meme somewhere, so probably not." Mira laughed to herself as she dabbed her mouth with a napkin.

"Probably is true with Beck. He hates the holidays."

"Did he ever tell you why?"

"Not exactly, but it has to do with his family." It was one of the many secrets Beck kept. She knew the broad outlines of his childhood: addict dad, absent mom, and the fact that Beck spent his childhood in and out of foster care before he turned eighteen and set about taking care of himself. It was the same story that had made him such a favorite in the Olympic Games. Kid from a broken home makes good with two silver medals. But none of that explained exactly why he hated Christmas so much. Allie had just assumed Christmases had been hard for him, growing up. But he refused to talk about them, or pretty much any of his childhood.

"You're sure he didn't rattle you?" Mira asked, looking suddenly concerned.

Allie let out a false laugh, which sounded a little too forced. "No, of course not. I'm the one who left him in the bathroom."

"But you also kissed him."

"Right, to prove that there was nothing between us," she said. "Which there's not." Now, that was definitely a lie. But Allie told herself she'd keep on telling it until it was true. *Fake it till you make it*, she told herself.

Mira stared at her friend a beat. "Okay," she said after a while. Allie was glad her friend didn't push it. Suddenly, she didn't want to talk about Beck anymore. Allie took a gulp of ice water from her glass.

Mira's face softened, and she reached out and clutched Allie's hand on the table.

"I didn't mean to doubt you," she said. "I just care about you, and Beck is trouble."

"I don't want to be hurt again, either." Allie sighed, dunking her spoon once more in her soup. She pushed it away from her, frustrated. "Look, don't worry. I can handle myself. It's not like he's…" She glanced at the waiter who strode by carrying a tray filled with two decadent chocolate desserts. "He's not double-fudge brownies with extra chocolate sauce and whipped cream."

"Don't even talk to me about chocolate right now." Mira munched another bite of her salad and glared at the desserts. "I couldn't even zip up my jeans yesterday. I've already gained the holiday ten pounds and *it's not even the holidays yet*."

Allie laughed at her friend's exaggerated expression of disgust. "You look your adorable little self as always."

"No, I don't. And if this keeps up, Dockett will fire me just because I don't look the 'hospitality part' anymore." Allie frowned at the mention of her boss, Bill Dockett, who owned Enclave. Dockett subtly pressured his employees to stay trim, put together and trendy. Allie thought it absurd and likely illegal, but Mira was paid well, and she was doing what she loved, and the only downside was working for a dinosaur of a boss who'd never heard of #MeToo. Mira looked at her friend. "You're lucky you're tall. You've got more places to stash the weight." Mira cocked an eyebrow. "Not that you need to worry about that. *You're* the one who needs another brownie. You're literally wasting away."

"I am not," Allie protested.

"The heartbreak diet has done its job, but now you need to eat, my friend." Mira pushed the bowl of onion soup toward Allie. "You need to at least have three more bites." She dipped the spoon in and lifted up a bite, as if she planned to feed Allie herself.

"What am I? A toddler?"

"I'll make the airplane noises for you if you want," Mira joked. Allie made a face at Mira, the woman who'd answered her post for a roommate back when she first moved to Aspen. The two had hit it off immediately since they'd both been from Nevada. What were the odds she'd find someone else who learned to ski in the Sierra Nevadas and then moved to Aspen to get more snow? Allie dutifully took the spoon and had a bite of now-lukewarm soup. "Seriously, though. Come out with me tonight. You need a do-over from yesterday. No Beck this time."

"I don't know." It wasn't that work had been busy at

her small accounting office, but Allie wasn't usually a hit-the-bars-two-nights-in-a-row kind of woman.

"Don't flake out on me!" Mira scolded. "I double dog dare you," Mira teased.

"Don't start that again!" Allie cradled her head in her hands in defeat. "Pretty soon, I'll be jumping off a cliff because someone asked me to. You know I can think for myself, right?"

"I know," Mira said. "But maybe you're too much in control. Maybe you need to give it up a little bit. Shake things up. Come on, admit it. Last night was fun. The bartender?" Mira banged the table with her open palm, making the silverware jump.

It wasn't the bartender Allie was thinking about, as she remembered Beck's strong hands at the small of her back, the feel of his hands in her hair.

"It was fun," she admitted. Not the fun she planned to repeat, if Beck was involved.

"But seriously. It's fun to shut your brain off now and again. Let someone else do the steering."

Allie couldn't help but feel that her friend spoke the truth. She'd always held on to things in her life so tightly: her job, her friends and even Beck. But look at where that had gotten her. She thought the tighter she held on to Beck, the more he'd be hers, and yet the opposite had happened. He'd walked out of her life anyway. Maybe the way to happiness wasn't keeping a tight rein on everything in her life. Maybe it was all about letting go. Letting chance take the wheel.

"Come on," Mira said. "Let's play this game to-night. See if we can't get more people involved."

"More people?"

"Let's ask *our* friends to give you a few decent dares just for fun. See where it leads. Come on. You need some fun. *This* will be fun."

Beck spent the night and following day thinking about Allie. Her soft lips, her delicate voice, how that vixen had grabbed him literally by the balls and then left him wanting. She was the only woman who could do that, wrap him around her finger, make him do what she wished and then leave him panting for more. He should be mad, but instead, all he could do was admit to himself that he deserved it. He never should've kissed her like that. He'd crossed a line *again*. He was always doing that with Allie and it was getting to be a problem. Not that he'd planned it. The woman lit a passion in him that burned white-hot, woke desires in him he didn't know he had, his basest primal instincts.

He knew there was a kind of darkness in him, one that invited in the chaos, but when Allie was around it boiled in him, almost impossible to control. Even now, thinking of her delicate cool fingers around his cock made his heart pound. The fact that she'd left him with a nasty case of blue balls just had made her hotter. No woman toyed with him like she did, no woman left him wanting more. That bombshell au-burn hair with the highlights of fire. That electrifying kiss that had all but made him come right there. And part of him wanted to have her ride him until she was spent, but another part also wanted to just curl up with her naked and cuddling in bed, her snug in his arms. That was what made Allie so dangerous. It wasn't just the sex; it was how he wanted to take care of her after.

"Uh, hello? Anybody in there?" Willis waved his hand in front of Beck's face, and he realized his business partner had been talking for quite a while and Beck hadn't been listening. He straightened, taking his feet off his messy desk in the small office of Aspen Adventure Tours, the business the two old friends owned together.

"Sorry, man. I zoned out." Beck gave Willis a sheepish grin. He'd known Willis since the Olympic Village in 2006. Willis invented some of the tricks that were now staples on the half-pipe.

"Mmm-hmm." Willis studied him. "Doesn't have anything to do with Allie Connor, does it?"

"Why would you say that?" Beck's voice was sharp, defensive, even to his own ears.

"Because I know she was at the party last night, and rumor has it…well, that you two had a reunion of sorts."

"It's not like that." He didn't like the idea of anybody spreading rumors about Allie. The muscles in his neck tensed. There it was, that rise of protectiveness in him.

Willis leaned back in his seat, dark eyes focused

on Beck. Judging him. Willis had never much liked Allie, though Beck was not certain why. Part of him thought Willis was jealous of the attention she sucked away from the business, and the way she was always trying to get him to scale back on some of the more dangerous tours.

Willis, however, thought people paid more for danger, and that was what they were in business to deliver. The two friends couldn't be more different. Beck was blond and blue-eyed. Willis, dark haired and wiry, was almost all beard, which went all the way down to the third button on his shirt.

"Look, it's none of my business, man, but she's your polar opposite. Yet that girl has you *wrapped*."

Beck knew this was true, remembered how he'd stood frozen in that bathroom while she'd walked away from him. Still, he could think of worse things than to be in love with a woman as amazing as Allie Connor.

"So?"

"So, didn't she try to change you? Try to get you to sit home and knit or something? All those accountant types are the same."

"That's not exactly it."

"You're going to retire, then? Give the business over to me? I wouldn't mind." Willis grinned.

"I'm not retiring." Beck glanced at Willis, feeling heat at the back of his neck.

"Okay, then, maybe you should do some work instead of stalking your ex on Instagram." Willis nodded at the smartphone lying faceup on his desk, Allie's profile up on it. He quickly swiped the screen away on his phone.

"I just wanted to see if she's okay."

Willis shook his head slowly and absently smoothed his beard. "Right. Sure. Hey, it's your life, man. I'm just glad you didn't give all the accounting over to her."

Beck had been tempted. Allie had offered numerous times to do their accounting work. As of now, she just calculated their taxes at the end of the year. Beck was not a numbers guy, but Willis seemed to be happy to pay their bills and do the payroll and Willis didn't see why they should pay an outsider to do it.

"Have you thought more about my suggestion of expanding to Vail and Breckenridge? Maybe Keystone?" Willis's eyes lit up at the prospect.

Beck might take risks on the mountain, but when it came to finances, he made only deliberate, safe decisions.

"They already have adventure tours. The competition is thick there."

"With your name? We could blow them all away." Beck hated playing off his fame. He hadn't gone to the Olympics for fame. He'd done it to prove he could.

"But I live here. I'd hardly ever be on those tours."

"So what? Your name is what sells, man. Go for the opening, stay a week, then come back here. You'll have people lining up in droves just to say they skied the same backcountry trails Liam Beck did." Willis was pushing this hard. Beck didn't know why. They both had enough to get by. More than get by: thrive.

"Aren't we already making enough?" Beck asked.

"Is it ever enough?" Willis countered.

Beck didn't think much about money. He had enough in his bank account and his bills were paid. He didn't worry about much more beyond that. They were doing well and he didn't see the point in risking overextending for a few extra bucks.

"What if the new venture failed?"

"I'd run it for the first year. It won't," Willis promised.

"How could you run both Vail and Breckenridge?"

"I'd figure it out," Willis said.

"I don't know." Beck shook his head. "Why do we need to expand so fast? We've got a good thing going here. And if we save up for another year or two, then maybe."

"By the time we do that, it'll be even more competitive. And somebody else will have a name they can use, too. You know there are a ton of other punks out there, fresh off the last Olympics, probably planning their own gigs right now. We've got to get out there, make our mark, first. We could *own* Colorado."

Beck still didn't like the idea of spreading himself so thin.

"You're asking me to take on all the risk," he said.

Willis paused a moment, seeming to contemplate what he planned to say next.

"I'm asking you to open your eyes to the possibilities, that's all. I'd like my paycheck to be as fat as yours one of these days." This was Willis's way of reminding Beck that he didn't think their deal was fair. Beck knew Willis hated the sixty-forty partnership split, but what could Beck do? He'd already laid down most of the capital—all the money he'd made from snowboarding endorsement deals after the first Olympics—and had taken on all of the risk of losing it all. Willis had come later, bought in after Beck had laid the groundwork. Sure, Willis worked more hours on the mountain than Beck did these days, but that had been the deal from the start. "Listen, just read this, okay?"

Willis held out the folder stuffed with paperwork he'd put together, numbers for what it would cost to open two new locations. Reluctantly, Beck took the folder. He owed it to Willis to at least read the stuff.

"It would be a nice Christmas present if you said yes," Willis said as he nodded toward the folder, his eyes full of expectation.

"You don't watch it, you're just going to get coal," Beck joked, and his old friend's face broke into a smile, not that he could see most of it, covered as it was by his mountain beard. He glanced at the folder, which was brimming with numbers and spreadsheets. God, how he hated spreadsheets. "I guess I can take a look."

"That's all I'm asking you to do." Willis's mood

seemed lighter, happier. "Want to grab a few beers tonight?"

It had been a while since Willis had asked him out for a beer. The two kept monstrously busy schedules, but also, Beck had felt his friend grow a bit more distant lately. He knew he should say yes, but, frankly, he didn't quite feel like it. He wanted to sit and brood about Allie. Maybe scroll through her social media accounts once more. Willis would definitely not approve.

"I think I'm gonna call it an early night," Beck said. Willis shrugged one shoulder.

"Sure, man," he said and stood. "See you tomorrow, then." Willis grabbed his big silver puffer jacket from the coatrack and headed out the door. He shot one parting glance over his shoulder at Beck, but Beck couldn't read his partner's expression. He wondered if he'd made a mistake not taking his friend up on that drink. What was he doing sitting at his desk and cyber-stalking Allie? But he knew why. He couldn't get the woman out of his head. Or his heart. Or his life. The harder he tried, the more she dug in, somehow.

Beck's phone dinged then, an alert that Allie had posted something new to her account. He turned his phone over and checked, seeing a new photo of Allie at the bar, holding up her own phone and a list of new contacts she'd entered into her phone—all men's names. Beneath it read the caption *Dared to get five men's numbers in fifteen minutes. Dare complete.*

Beck sat up. What the hell was this? Five numbers in fifteen minutes?

He read backward and quickly surmised the game: Mira had sent out a post asking all their friends for suggestions on dares to help Allie "get out of her shell."

Beck's back teeth ground together. He liked Allie just fine in her shell. There was no need for her to come out of it. He also took note of the several shots she'd already downed that night and it wasn't even six yet. What was the woman doing? She had the tolerance of a mouse—and that was before she'd dropped ten pounds. Now she was out there getting men's numbers and probably kissing more bartenders and doing who knew what else. He looked at the last picture and recognized the miner's big telltale copper bell at the end of the bar. That was the North Star.

North Star was one of the oldest bars in Aspen. It was where silver miners used to go to celebrate their finds or drown their sorrows, and the big bronze bell still stood at the end of the bar—the bell miners rang when they had found a big lode of silver and planned to buy their fellow miners a drink. Beck loved the feel of the place. It was what Colorado was all about: adventuring souls who shared their good fortune. And now the bar catered to locals looking for cheap pitchers of beer and several big screens of whatever game might be on. If Allie was going to North Star, that meant she might be hitting on people he knew. Why didn't she just go to one of the nice resorts that he knew she preferred? Sleep with tourists he wouldn't know and would never see again?

Just leave it alone, Beck. She probably doesn't want you crashing her big get over Beck *night.* It was a mistake, though. Aspen might be a major ski resort, but in the end it was really just a small town. About ten thousand residents lived in the area all year round, but tourists doubled that population on average every day. So the locals ran in tight circles and mostly kept to themselves. And they gossiped. So much. It was why Beck tended to keep to the tourists. He could have his fun and then not worry about the consequences. If Allie took a local home, there'd be rumors swirling around them for weeks. Even months. Locals got bored, especially around the holidays, and they loved nothing more than to talk about each other.

Another photo came up, a new one, and this time Allie was standing next to a rough, tattooed dude with a beanie cap on and a loop through his nose. He looked like one of the many pipe rats that littered the slopes these days—kids thinking they'd invent the next big trick that would land them on the podium at the Games. Beck took a closer look. Wait a second. He wasn't just any pipe rat. That was Taylor Johnson and he was nothing but trouble. First off, the man was married. He'd gotten hitched two weekends before in a hasty ceremony since his girlfriend was eight months pregnant. So Beck had no idea what he was doing out at the bar, posing for pictures with Allie and *not* wearing his wedding ring. Beck wondered if Allie knew any of that.

There was one way to find out. Looked like he was headed to the North Star.

CHAPTER FIVE

ALLIE WAS HAVING the time of her life. At least, that was what she told herself, and the more she drank, the more she believed it. In the last hour, she'd gotten five strangers' numbers, bought another man a drink and had exchanged her scarf with Taylor's checkered scarf, which she now wore draped around her neck like a trophy. Beside her, her new friend Taylor was showing more than a little interest, and his frame was enough like Beck's that she kind of liked it. He was tall and blond, though he had streaks of bright green in his hair, a look that normally she'd say was trying too hard to broadcast that he liked to risk life and limb trying a double backflip, or double cork, in the half-pipe. She hadn't met him before tonight, but he was actually quite nice, and eager to buy her drinks and feed her compliments, and for once she wasn't thinking of Beck.

"Have I told you that you're the sexiest woman in this room?" Taylor leaned in, his brown eyes earnest as he slid another beer her way on the ornate but old-fashioned bar. Beneath her feet lay the sticky floor and mismatched tiles. This was a far cry from the trendy, upscale places she usually preferred—the tourist hangouts with the trendy drinks, where she and Beck would so often run into each other. But that was the whole point. She was hoping *not* to run into Liam Beck.

The bar was small and standing room only since they were running a locals' happy hour, with beer on tap half-price. Mira and Allie claimed a small corner of the bar by the wall, and Taylor maneuvered himself between Allie and Mira, and now almost had Allie pinned against the wall. Normally, Allie hated guys who were so instantly territorial, but given how much kissing Beck had rattled her the day before, she was eager to put that in her rearview. That meant Taylor would get a pass.

"You're so sweet," she said and took another drag of her beer.

"You've got another dare!" Mira chimed in, beside her, as she sipped at her vodka soda and glanced at her phone. "Ooh, this one is good. Kiss the first bearded man you see."

Mira glanced up and looked around the crowded bar, and Allie did, too. Usually, beards were a dime a dozen in Aspen, the longer the better, but tonight the place seemed all stubble and no beard.

"Seriously?" Mira asked no one in particular. "*No* beards?"

"How about I go grow a beard and you kiss me?" Taylor suggested, and he moved closer to Allie, and now her back lay flat against the wall. Allie felt a little uncomfortable with his hemming her in, so she laughed a little and wiggled to the side.

"I don't think that would count."

Taylor leaned in and whispered low in her ear, "Why don't we get out of here and go to your place?"

Allie couldn't believe his boldness. It was barely nine, she'd known him all of fifteen minutes and Mira was standing right there. Not that she'd heard.

"That's not part of the game," Allie said, deflecting him.

"Ooh! Here's another dare," Mira said, pulling up her phone. She read it, squinted and read it again. "Uh…"

"What is it?"

"It's Beck," she said, frowning at the screen. "He's asking if he can play, too."

Beck? What the…? Allie turned then and locked eyes with Beck, who was already moving through the crowd, parting the patrons easily as they shifted to make room for him. His eyes were focused on her and she hated how she felt a little flame of excitement tickle the back of her neck, how her body reacted instantly, how she was already leaning into him, even though he was still across the room.

"Well, this is going to be interesting," Mira said in the understatement of the year.

Allie looked amazing, even if she was wearing that ridiculous scarf around her neck. That was Beck's first thought. His second was that he wondered why every time he saw her his breath caught a little as if, somehow, all the way across the room, she was managing to squeeze him from the inside. She wore dark shadow around her eyes that made them pop and told him tonight she planned to take no prisoners. Good. Neither did he. Allie was silently sending him about a dozen messages across the bar, most of which he could tell started and ended with *WTF*. Well, he'd explain himself later. And she probably wouldn't be grateful, but he wasn't going to let her hang with a man who was clearly deceiving her. All he wanted to do was get to Allie. He was there in a few long strides and clapped the man—hard—on the shoulder. Taylor whirled, a frown on his face, and then it lit with recognition.

"Liam Beck." He said the name as if it left a foul taste in his mouth.

"Taylor. You don't sound happy to see me." Beck kept his hand on the man's shoulder a beat too long. He could smell the beer wafting up from him. He'd had a lot to drink already, which could make what came next messy.

"I thought you'd be too busy losing gold medals to come out drinking." Taylor sneered at Beck, as he usually did. The punk thought that silver was a loss, that he could do better in the next Olympics. Beck welcomed him to try. The sport only got more competitive every year, harder and more dangerous.

"At least I have Olympic medals," he muttered

beneath his breath. "So, Taylor. Where's your wife? Melanie?"

Taylor turned as white as the beer coaster on the bar. "Home," he said.

"Wait. You're married?" Allie clearly had no idea.

"Has she had the baby yet?" Beck had to admit he was enjoying this just a little bit. Taylor and Allie both looked like a light wind would blow them over.

"Baby?" Allie echoed, horrified.

But Taylor didn't even bother to answer. He had defeat written all over his face as he finished his beer, set it on the counter with a thump and then put his back to them all and left without so much as a word.

"Did he just leave?" Mira cried, staring after him.

"He's married, though?" Allie said. "But he was trying to kiss me."

"That's what you get for playing with amateurs." Beck leaned into the spot Taylor had left.

"I cannot believe the nerve of that man. I'm going to out him," Mira said, and she began furiously typing on her phone, probably posting something not so nice about Taylor.

Beck kept his attention solely focused on Allie. "So I'm here. I'm ready to play double dare."

"Beck, you can't play," Mira said, not looking up from her phone.

"Why not?"

"Fine. I *dare* you to leave, then," Mira suggested.

Beck shook his finger slowly back and forth. "I'll only take dares from Allie. This is the game we started last night, and I just wanted to finish it." He stared at her long and hard, and almost thought she was imagining the same things he was: her lips pressed against his, his hands running up the tender skin of her back. She was the most beautiful woman in this bar—hell, in this state. Could she feel that current running between them? The invisible tether that connected them? He wondered if the whole bar could feel it.

Mira glanced back and forth between Beck and Allie. Clearly, she'd noticed the connection.

"Can you give us a second?" Allie asked Mira at last.

"You sure about this?" Mira eyed Beck like he might be a poisonous snake. He couldn't blame Mira for looking after her friend. He would've done the same in her position.

"Mira, it's okay," Allie said. "We have some things to settle."

"You sure that's a good idea?" Mira asked, but Allie gave her a long look, and she swallowed her protest. "I was going to go get another drink anyway. And I think I see some people from work I know over there." Mira nodded to the corner. "If you need me, that's where I'll be."

Allie stared at Beck the entire time Mira moved away. Mira sent worried glances back at her friend, but Allie never looked in her direction.

"What are you doing here?"

"I'm here to finish our game," Beck said and grinned. "You didn't let me finish last night."

"That was on purpose." She tapped her foot angrily against the floor. "That was for…breaking my boots."

He laughed and shook his head. "I was only trying to help."

"Right. Like you're only trying to *help* me now."

"I am," Beck said. He leaned in and got a whiff of Colorado wildflowers. God, he loved her smell. "Or was one of your dares sleeping with a married man?" He cocked an eyebrow.

Allie let out a frustrated sigh. "No, that was *not* one of the dares. I can't believe he was pretending to be single. He wanted to go to my place!" Allie smacked her forehead. "What would've happened if we'd gone? I feel like an idiot."

"You're not the idiot." Beck blamed Taylor. "He's the idiot. For thinking you'd fall for it. Even if I hadn't come along, you would've figured it out. I was just trying to spare you the trouble."

"You think?"

"I know." Beck nodded once, swiftly. "Come on. You see through all my bullshit."

"True," she said and gave him a playful nudge with her elbow, her eyes suddenly grateful. He saw how hard she was trying to be on her own, how much she wanted this all to work. He knew she wanted to believe there was nothing between them, when even Beck could feel it there, like a living thing between them, this bond, this connection. The lodge mattered, no matter how either of them tried to deny it to themselves. He hadn't been the same since, and he knew she'd felt the aftershocks in her life, too. Why else would she be acting out like this?

He just wanted to pull her into his arms, tell her to stop trying to fight against it so hard. But then again, wasn't that what he was doing?

"Al," he began. And he was going to tell her… what? They were going to live happily ever after? He was never going to break her heart, when that was all he seemed to know how to do with the women in his life? That was all Becks were ever taught.

"Yes?" She seemed so hopeful in that moment, that part of him broke.

"How about tonight, just take a break," he said.

Confusion flickered in her eyes. "From what?"

"From trying to be me." The best way to get out of this emotional quagmire was a good distraction. And Beck was the king of distractions. Divert, tease, make light of any situation. Whenever any conversation got a little too close to the heart, he'd pivot. He'd been doing it his whole life.

"I'm not *trying* to be you."

"You are," he teased. "Double dare you is like my favorite game."

"Not true. Strip poker is," she deadpanned, and Beck barked a laugh.

"Okay, *second* favorite game. Come on, Al. Let me play. Please?" Beck could see Allie weigh her options. He could also see her physically trying to fight his charm. But he should tell her it was a losing battle. She'd give in eventually. "I promise not to get in the way of anything. And, upside, I make an excellent wingman."

"You? You want to be *my* wingman?" Allie coughed in disbelief. "You want to sabotage me."

"I do not. Look, you set the rules of the game. Anytime you want me to leave, I'm gone."

"How about now?" she joked.

"Not yet." He grinned. "We have to play first."

A playful spark lit in her, and Beck could tell she was warming to the idea. "Okay, so we dare each other to do things."

"Fine."

"And if you don't complete a dare, then…" Allie thought for a moment. "Then *you* have to personally apologize to every woman you've slept with this last year."

"What?" Beck was taken aback.

"You have to personally apologize for loving and leaving them."

Beck shook his head. "The women I sleep with know what they're getting into. I don't pretend otherwise."

Hurt flickered for a second across Allie's face before her brave mask came back up, and Beck mentally gave himself a swift kick in the ass. What was he doing? He knew Allie was the exception to this rule. He knew it. Yet there was something about Allie that was like walking truth serum. He couldn't *not* tell her the truth. It was unnerving, especially for a man who'd spent his whole life carefully boxing away all the things he didn't like to unpack.

"I mean, yes. Fine. I will."

"You'll apologize publicly. Social media, wherever, and promise to do one thing to make it up to them." Beck knew Allie was talking about herself. Okay, then.

"Fine. I'm not worried about losing." Beck had never faced a dare in his life that he hadn't easily taken on. There was very, very little that scared him in this world.

"And if *you* renege, then you stop this game. Once and for all," he said.

"Deal," Allie said and held her hand out for a shake. He took it, and the second her small palm pressed against his, he felt a small bolt of electricity that went straight to his brain. There it was again, the feeling of connection, that there was a bond between them, something both delicate and strong at the same time.

"Okay, I'll go first. I dare you to..." Allie considered this. "Order a frozen piña colada, with extra umbrellas."

Beck groaned. He was a strict beer or whiskey guy. But he had promised to play the game, so play the game he would. "So that's how it's going to be, huh? Fine." He signaled the bartender. "But I dare you to drink a single shot of jalapeño tequila."

"Ew." Allie made a face and stuck out her tongue in disgust.

"You started this," Beck said. "Ready to quit yet?"

"Hell, no," she said and slapped the bar next to them with enthusiasm.

Beck ordered their drinks and in seconds was staring at the frilliest drink he'd ever seen: four umbrellas, two cherries, complete with a tourist's take-home pink-rimmed glass, and somehow, against all odds, the drink was bright blue. He hoped nobody in this bar took a picture of him drinking the monstrosity. Allie, for her part, stared at her shot glass with disdain. She hated tequila. It was the one alcohol that always got her into trouble. Beck knew this all too well from last year's Cinco de Mayo.

"You're seriously going to make me drink this?" Allie said, sniffing the cup and making a gagging noise.

"I could ask you the same thing," he said, nodding at his umbrella monster drink. She laughed.

"Oh, you're going to drink that. And I'm going to take a picture." She whipped out her phone and snapped a quick shot. "And I am going to post it everywhere."

"Of course you are." Beck shook his head.

The two of them drank: Allie a tiny sip of the fiery tequila and Beck a big gulp of much-too-sugary blech. It was more like a slushie than an actual drink. In the standing-room-only bar, a high table opened, and Beck nodded to it. "Shall we?"

On their way, a college-aged kid brushed past Beck. "Hey…aren't you…?" Recognition dawned on the college boy's face. Recognition and reverence. "Aren't you Liam Beck?"

Beck glanced at the kid who looked suddenly star-struck.

"Two-time silver medalist at men's snowboarding cross? *That* Liam Beck?" The boy glanced at the fruity drink in Beck's hand and looked momentarily baffled.

"Nah, that's not me," he lied.

Allie flashed him a brief look of pity. Beck shrugged. The Olympics were a long, long time ago. He'd long since had his fifteen minutes of fame.

"No, you're definitely Beck, man. I'd know your face anywhere."

This time, Beck didn't argue. But he wished the kid would stop gushing. It always made him uncomfortable.

"You're my hero, dude. The way you shredded that course! Like…amaze-ing. I—I mean I *learned* to snowboard *because* of you!"

Nothing like a young punk to make him feel ancient.

Beck and Allie settled into the high top. "We'd like to finish our drinks, okay?"

"Oh, yeah, man. Sorry… Just… I mean, you're my hero!" He held up his hand for a high five and Beck reluctantly slapped it. As the boy slid away, Beck shook his head.

"Still don't like fans?"

"It's not that." Beck shrugged. How could he tell

her it all felt undeserved? "I didn't do it for the fame. I did it to prove something to myself. The fame is just kind of an annoying side effect."

"The same fame that helped you launch your business, though," Allie pointed out.

"Yeah," Beck said. "And Willis wants to use my name to open a few more adventure tours in other cities."

"Can you afford it?" Allie asked, concern wrinkling her brow.

"Not sure." Beck needed to look over those papers.

Allie studied him a minute. "Okay, next dare, then. I dare you to…tell me something you've never told me about the Olympics."

"What?" Now Beck felt on high alert. This game was supposed to be about putting Allie on the spot, not him. "I thought this was a game of double dare you, not truth or dare."

"A dare's a dare." Allie took another sip of her tiny shot of tequila and then coughed, patting her chest.

"You're supposed to slug that."

"You didn't say that in the dare," Allie pointed out. "So I'm going to sip this one. It tastes awful." She wrinkled her nose. "So? Go on. The Olympics. Tell me about it."

What was there to tell? His father had promised to go, and Beck had even sent him a ticket, but he'd gotten too high and missed his flight. By the time he arrived in Turin, Beck's event was over. His mother had just had another baby with the new family she'd created far from him in Florida and didn't feel like she could make the trip. By the time Vancouver rolled around, he hadn't bothered to invite anyone. It had been better that way.

"Not much to tell," he said. "I didn't do it for the fame. I did it to prove I could because everyone told me I couldn't. Just went there and skied hard. And wished I'd gotten gold both times." That was the short answer, the textbook answer, and she knew it. She knew all that already.

"Was your family there?" she asked him.

"No."

"Why not?"

Beck stared at her. "Why all the questions all of a sudden? And how many questions do you get to ask with one dare?"

"As many as I want," she countered. "This is my game. And you haven't told me anything I don't already know about the Olympics. Tell me one thing I don't know."

Beck sighed. "I don't like talking about it because I wanted to win gold and didn't, and now I won't have another chance." Beck shrugged. "I don't want to think that my best accomplishment is in the past, but it might be."

Allie studied him a beat. "Being a medalist doesn't define you."

"Doesn't it, though?" Wasn't that why people flocked to his adventure tours. Or looked at him twice when he went into a bar?

"Only if you let it." God, he missed her so much. Missed how she managed to cut through all the noise and make him feel seen. Few people had that skill and even fewer people could snap him out of a pity party. "And, by the way, thank you. For warning me about Taylor."

The gratitude took him by surprise. "You're welcome."

A woman walked past their table then on the way to the bathroom. She eyed Allie with some disdain and then sent a long, knowing look to Beck, who realized he knew her, vaguely. They'd had a night together maybe two or three years ago. Her name started with a *K*. Kayla. Kaylee. Something like that. "Hey, you," she murmured in a much-too-familiar way as she passed him. Then she leaned over as if to whisper something in his ear. "Why don't you drop by my place later?"

The petite blonde in the too-tight leggings and too-low-cut sweater glanced over her shoulder as she passed, seeming not to care that he was sitting across from Allie.

"What did she say?" Allie's voice sounded hard. Jealous.

"She wants me to come over."

"Will you?" Allie bit her lip.

"No." Beck shook his head. What he remembered was that she'd taken a selfie of herself *in his bed*. He didn't want to know what she'd done with it.

"She was one of your marks, though."

"More like, I was *her* mark." Beck shuddered a

bit. No way was he remotely interested in taking her home again. He felt like she'd probably steal things from his condo for souvenirs, or take selfies in his closet next to his medals and his Olympic jackets.

"Mmm-hmm." Allie looked at him, that old disapproval on her face. Before the weekend at the lodge, she'd teased him relentlessly about the women who rotated through his bedroom. Only she could make him feel moderately ashamed and more than a little bit shallow for simply doing what came naturally.

"Look, as much as you love talking about what a dick I am, can we just focus here? I dare you to…" He looked at Allie's big green eyes, attentive and watchful, and suddenly just wanted her to come back to his condo, so that it could just be the two of them, where he could hold her. She broke his gaze and he realized she was staring at Kayla/Kaylee's back. The girl had on a too-short tight sweater and her lower back was completely bare. There was a tattoo there, Olympic rings. Of course there would be.

Allie held up a finger. "Wait a second," she said, and then she downed the entire shot of tequila. He hadn't expected that. Then she grabbed a passing waiter and ordered another.

"You sure that's wise? Tequila doesn't agree with you."

"I'm sure I'm going to need it to get through this next dare."

"I dare you to…"

Meanwhile, from the corner of Beck's eye, he saw

the starstruck kid come back, carrying shots of tequila and slices of lime.

"Hey, man, just wanted to buy you these," he said, beaming like a little boy who'd managed to tie his shoelaces for the first time. "It's an honor to share a drink with you, *Liam Beck*, and you, uh…" He glanced at Allie, unsure.

"Allie Connor," she said and happily grabbed the shot glass. She took it a bit too quickly and it sloshed on the table.

"Allie, careful," Beck cautioned, but it was too late—she was already glugging it down. Since when did Allie shotgun tequila? She had the tolerance of a fly. Two drinks and she was buzzed. Three and she was on her way to hammered. And tequila took her there twice as fast.

The boy held up his shot glass, and she took that, too.

"Allie, give that back," Beck said, but she was in no mood to oblige him. She held on to it.

"Here, take mine," Beck offered the kid. He took it and drank.

"You're just the coolest ever, man. I'll go buy you another," he offered. Before Beck could argue, he was hurrying back to the bar. Beck refocused his attention on Allie.

"What the hell are you doing? Tequila makes you sick. Remember Cinco de Mayo? I only dared you to drink *one* shot."

"Well, this is the *new* Allie." Her eyes had already

taken on a glassy sheen. Not a good sign. She pushed back her chair. "I'm going to the bathroom."

Her mood had soured, and it had everything to do with Kayla/Kaylee and tequila. Beck knew it. This was why he was no good for her. He just brought a bundle of drama to her life that she simply didn't need. He couldn't help it if women approached him, but she seemed to take every single woman he'd ever slept with as a personal affront. How could they ever really have a go at a relationship if she let every woman who glanced at him twice get into her head? This was why Allie was better off without him.

She stumbled a bit getting off her chair. The tequila was working its black magic and fast. He steadied her, but she was determined to get away. What had caused this? Was it Kayla/Kaylee?

"So, I'm taking you home now."

"I don't need your shelp," she slurred. The shots took hold fast.

"You do need me. Or you'd fall down."

"Is that a dare? You daring me to fall down?" Allie asked, unsteady on her feet as she reached for the women's restroom door. Her eyes were having the slightest bit of trouble focusing on him. She'd had way too much to drink in a short amount of time.

"That would hardly be a dare. You're going to do that all by yourself," he said.

"Well, then, what are you going to dare me to do?" Allie asked, blinking fast.

"I…" But before he could get another word out, she'd grabbed him by the shirt.

"Too slow. My turn." Before he knew what happened, she'd arched on her tiptoes and planted her lips against his.

CHAPTER SIX

ALLIE HAD NO idea what she was doing. Her body was on autopilot, and she had her tongue in Beck's mouth before it even registered that she was kissing him. *Again. For the second night in a row.* Her brain was awash in tequila, and the room had already begun to spin a little. Was that the tequila buzz or Beck's mouth? She wasn't sure, but what she did know was that her body, even dulled with alcohol, felt the pulse of heat between them and the promise of more pleasure to come. It took her a moment to notice that Beck remained entirely still. For a heartrending second, she thought Beck might not kiss her back, but then his lips were on hers once more, his hands at the small of her back. *Yes, kiss me. I want you. I've missed you.*

The thoughts ran unheeded through her brain, and she suddenly forgot why she'd decided to kiss him in the first place. She was proving what exactly? That she was better than that blonde with the tattoo? That she could somehow compete? That she even *wanted* to compete? Why did she even care who Beck slept with? He wasn't hers, would never be hers.

Her head spun, literally spun, as their lips met. She felt they were both twirling in a fast circle.

Then, as abruptly as the kiss began, it ended. Beck pulled away first, chest heaving, his big strong hands on her arms.

"You're drunk," he said, his eyes telling her it took more than a little willpower for him to keep her at arm's length.

"Yes, I am," she conceded and hiccuped. Not that it mattered. She'd feel the same about Beck if she were sober. She felt wild, impulsive, and realized that being with Beck made her feel out of control, reckless. And she liked it. That was the problem.

"I'm going to take you home," Beck said. She wondered if he planned to stay the night in her bed. In her current state, she wouldn't tell him no.

"I don't need your help," she said, defiant. The room took another spin then, and she knew it had nothing to do with Beck's hands on her and everything to do with the tequila she'd hastily downed. Her stomach roiled, suddenly in revolt. She realized she was about to lose the last tequila shot she'd drunk and more, as she spun and ran into the bathroom, barely making it to the first stall before she lost the contents of her stomach. Beck must've heard the commotion outside because he rushed in, steadying her by the toilet as another wave of nausea hit her.

"What was that about not needing my help?" he asked her, holding her hair back, as she retched again.

* * *

Allie woke the next morning feeling like her head was a delicate soft-boiled egg, its shell cracked in a dozen places. Her hands flew to her temples as she groaned, the bright light on the other side of her closed eyelids like daggers to her brain. She didn't even want to open her eyes, afraid the sunlight would send more shards of pain pulsing through her head. What on earth had happened last night? She groaned as bits of the night came back to her…too many shots, the dares…that blonde at the bar and the way she was eyeing Beck, and then…how Allie had reacted like a scorned girlfriend and drowned her sorrows in tequila. What was wrong with her?

Then she remembered that she'd been sick. She remembered throwing up at the bar and…the game of dare. With Beck. What had happened? She couldn't remember. She moaned and pulled the covers up over her head, shielding herself from the memories of the night before and the morning's sunlight. Her head throbbed and all she wanted to do was stay in this warm, snuggly goodness forever. It was only then that she realized the blankets over her were heavier than her own. They had the feel of weighty down instead of the loftier, lighter cotton fill of her own comforter beneath her white eyelet duvet cover. The realization slowly came: these weren't her sheets. If they weren't hers, then whose were they?

She pushed her head out of the covers and opened one eye. The first thing she saw was the blue-and-white-checkered scarf she'd traded with Taylor the night before. One of her first dares. Oh, no. Did she go home with…Taylor? No. She didn't like him. He was married, the jerk. She remembered. And then Beck had arrived and… She sat up then and glanced around, realizing quickly this was not a stranger's room. It was far worse than that. She knew this bedroom.

Allie was in the middle of Beck's king-sized bed, the thick goose-down comforter with the navy blue cover tucked around her soundly. She knew the room from the dozens of times he'd invited her to parties at his place, big sprawling affairs with dozens of locals. In a panic, she glanced down and saw she wasn't wearing her clothes from the night before. They'd been replaced with one of Beck's long-sleeved T-shirts with his adventure tour logo emblazoned on the front. She reached down and was mortified to discover she had no pants on.

What had happened? She racked her brain trying to remember, but no more memories came. She was at the bar, she got sick, Beck was there and…what? Well, clearly he brought her home. Had they…? Good Lord, did they…? Allie pressed her hands against her body and was glad to find that she still had her bra and low-cut bikini on, her pink-laced ones. Okay, if they'd…gone there, then she probably would be completely naked beneath Beck's shirt. The worst part was that she couldn't figure out if she was relieved… or disappointed. What the hell was wrong with her?

Falling into bed with Beck would be the worst thing she could do.

She scanned the room. More important, where *was* Beck? That was when she heard rattling in the kitchen. She heard the sound of a pan coming out of the cabinet, and the high-pitched squeal of hot water through coffee grounds in his single-serve coffee maker. The aroma of freshly brewed dark roast drifted into the bedroom and she suddenly badly wanted some. Her uneasy stomach cried for coffee. The sizzle of freshly cracked eggs on a buttered pan hit her ears as she swung her bare legs over the side of Beck's massive bed. Her head revolted, almost sending her back to the sheets, but she knew coffee and food were her best ways out of this hangover. Her stomach felt dangerously empty, and she needed to fill it with grease and fast.

She glanced at the bedside table and saw her phone and her glasses there. Beck had left them in reach, which seemed sweet. She put on her glasses and headed to the door. The fact that she'd have to face Beck didn't occur to her until she'd cracked open his bedroom door and saw the man—shirtless—frying up eggs at his stovetop. He turned and saw her, grinning from ear to ear.

"Well, she's alive," he said and shook his head slowly, the crook of his lopsided grin telling her he was going to enjoy having fun at her expense. "It was touch and go for a while."

Embarrassment burned her face and she wished

she'd checked her reflection in his bedroom mirror before coming out. Too late now. "Was it that bad?"

Beck cocked a blond eyebrow. She tried very hard not to look at his smooth bare chest, the ripples of his muscles beneath his rib cage. The man was the only one she knew who actually carried a real six-pack. She remembered running her finger along those ridges that weekend at the lodge. How he would laugh and tell her he was ticklish. "You don't remember?"

Allie glanced at her bare toes, the green nail polish beginning to flake off. "Uh, no. Last thing I remember was being at the bar with you. Even that is spotty, but I think I..." She swallowed, recalling the humiliating trip to the bathroom. "Uh, I think I got sick in the bathroom."

She glanced up once more but found all that bare skin of his distracting. The man ought to put on a shirt, but she didn't want him to think his half nakedness was bothering her at all. He wore only a pair of mesh gym shorts, the ridges of a V pointing down beneath his waistband. She looked away, to his stark apartment, noticing that there weren't any Christmas decorations. He never decorated for Christmas. Not even a tree, for as long as she'd known him. Not even when he'd had a Christmas party here for half of Aspen two years ago.

He laughed and then flipped the fried egg in the small pan, and it sizzled in the butter.

"You did indeed. Is that all you remember? Nothing else?" He sent her a sly glance. Oh, no. Did she sleep with him? She woke up in his bed, after all.

She glanced at his pronounced chest muscles. Did she run her hands along that bare skin last night? She wasn't sure what bothered her more: the idea that she'd done it, or the fact that she couldn't remember it if she had.

"N-no." Now she was getting worried. He was enjoying this far too much. She was almost afraid to ask anything about the night before, but she had a feeling he would tell her anyway.

Her head still pounded from her hangover headache. She reluctantly moved to the breakfast bar, which at least obscured some of Beck's bare skin. He handed her a cup of coffee.

"With nonfat milk, just like you like it."

"You remembered," she murmured, surprised, wrapping her hand around the mug's handle and taking a long sip of the warm liquid. She didn't think a little detail like that merited a place in Beck's memory.

"I remember everything about you, Allison Connor."

He sent her a long, deliberate look. How did he manage to do that? Make her feel like she was the only woman in the world who mattered? She glanced away from him, not sure if prolonged eye contact with him shirtless, and her without pants, was all that good of an idea. Her headache might be going strong, but even it might fall to Beck's humming charisma.

She hugged the mug of coffee with her hands as

she watched Beck dole out a fried egg onto a piece of toast. He slipped the plate over to her with a grin.

"Thanks," she said, suddenly so grateful for the food she wanted to cry. Her stomach growled, and despite having clearly not fared so well last night, it was ready to consume. He cracked another egg into the pan and waited, studying her.

"Go on and eat," he said. "You need your strength." He grinned. "Don't wait for me."

She took a bite of breakfast goodness. It was just what she needed, and she moaned in gratitude. When she opened her eyes, she saw Beck watching her. The expression on his face had grown serious. He seemed intent on watching her eat. She felt suddenly self-conscious. She glanced at the counter and saw a folder stuffed with spreadsheets.

"What's this?" she asked, quickly, hoping for a distraction.

"Willis's spreadsheets. I'm trying to figure out if I have enough capital to expand the business."

"I could take a look at them, if you want. Just as a favor. I can let you know what I think."

Beck glanced at her. "That would be great, actually."

They stared at each other a beat. Allie didn't want to break the moment. She liked silence with Beck. It never really felt like silence, as she could almost hear the hum of their connectivity, the way being in a room with him alone just felt like all that she needed.

"So how much of a fool was I last night?" She

didn't want to hear the answer, but knew she'd have to face it eventually.

"Well, you kissed me at the bar."

"I…what?" Now Allie felt hot and cold all over. Allie furrowed her brow. She had no memory of kissing Liam Beck. "Was that all I did?" she asked, tentative. She sneaked a glance at his bare chest, feeling flaming heat in her cheeks.

Beck chuckled, a warm, low sound that traveled to her own middle. "No, that was definitely not all." He flipped the egg and crossed his fit arms across his chest. "You threw up in the bar bathroom, yes, and in the parking lot, and out the door of my truck, and then twice when we got back here."

Allie groaned. No wonder her stomach felt so empty and her head hurt so much.

"Beck, I'm sorry. Do I need to clean up? I…" She stood, a bit too fast, and a sharp pain stabbed her brain behind her eyes. The hangover wasn't going to tolerate any quick moves this morning.

"Sit. Eat. I'm just glad to see you human again." He slid the fried egg onto his own plate and then moved to sit next to her at the breakfast bar. She was reminded of the morning after their first night at the lodge, when he'd made her breakfast. He was good at it. She took another bite of her egg, the warm gooeyness melting on her tongue. The more she ate, the more she felt…closer to normal. She felt stupidly grateful he wasn't making too much of a big deal about it. He could've been lording it over her, teasing her relentlessly. She didn't have the energy to defend herself at the moment, but that was Beck. Beneath all his bluster and ego, he was amazingly kind. It always took her by surprise. When she expected him to be a jerk, he did something surprisingly nice. Thoughtful, even. It was almost as if he used the egomaniac, player persona to hide his real self, as if it were just a hard shell to protect the big softie beneath.

He took a bite of his breakfast.

"But… I mean, did you…? Did we…?" She trailed off. She couldn't get the words out of her mouth. *Did we have sex?* God, she couldn't believe she even had to ask him this. How had she let herself get into this position in the first place? But then she glanced at his amused crystal-blue eyes and knew the answer to that. Because this was Beck, and he was pretty much irresistible.

"You want to know if we had a reunion of the carnal kind?" he asked between bites. Her eyes drifted down to his bare chest and she ordered them back up again.

She could only just nod her head but failed to look him in the eye. What would she do if the answer was yes? She had no idea.

"And if we did… What do you think of that?" He patted his mouth with a paper napkin.

"Beck, just tell me, already. Did we or didn't we?" Now the suspense was really killing her.

"You hoping we did? Or…didn't?" He was enjoying this so much. She actually wanted to give him a good shove and tell him to cut it out.

"Didn't," she said, but then she glanced up and saw his pec flex as he moved the piece of toast on his plate to sop up the runny egg yolk and had a sudden change of mind. She wished they did have sex. Somehow, it would be a relief of a sort. Since they'd kissed at the holiday party she'd been worried that sex might just be inevitable, that she'd slip up, like an addict sneaking in a binge. If she had slipped up, then she could start walking the straight and narrow again… Maybe.

Beck sent her a rueful smile. "You're in luck. We didn't."

Surprise tickled the back of her neck, and something more… Disappointment? "What about my… clothes, then?" She nodded down to his shirt. "Did you…? I mean…"

"You were in no place to consent, Al. I don't take advantage of anyone that way." He shrugged. "Your clothes are in the wash. During one of your trips to the bathroom, your sweater and jeans got hit. Well… splattered. That's all. I got you out of them, and into bed—on your stomach—and then I slept on the couch. You were in rough shape." He glanced at her, clear worry on his face. It was the concern that rattled her, even more than his bare skin. Did he still care about her?

"So we didn't…" Allie frowned. She wished she

could remember the night, but no matter how hard she tried, no memories came to mind.

"No, but…" Beck grinned, as he laughed a little. "But not for want of trying on your part."

"Oh, no." Allie covered her face with her hands. She was worried about that. She had a hard enough time fighting her attraction when she was a hundred percent sober and in control. She didn't want to hear what uninhibited Allie might be like.

"I mean, you were definitely…absolutely…trying to get me into bed with you." He threw down his napkin and leaned back on the kitchen stool, enjoying himself.

"No, no, no." Allie shook her head and then regretted it, as the headache thrummed in her temples.

"You might have been sick, but you were tenacious. I had to peel you off me. You tried to take off my pants…three times."

Mortification stung her. And she realized arguing was futile. She felt the truth of his words in her bones. She could imagine herself doing it. That was the worst part. Maybe it was all this Greenie nonsense. Was she trying to prove something to Beck? To herself? Or was she just hot and heavy for the man, and no amount of time or distance would ever cool her desire for him?

Beck flashed her a grin and then gave her shoulder a playful nudge. "Don't worry, Al. You weren't that bad."

That just made her think she was that bad…and worse.

"Well…" She swallowed, almost glad she didn't remember the scene she'd made. "Thanks for taking care of me."

"Of course." Beck acted as if he'd always be ready to be called up to protect her. Not as if he was the man who'd walked out of her life. Everything about him confused her.

"I'm surprised Mira let you take me home."

"She didn't…exactly." Beck shrugged. "I'd gotten you into my truck already, and she was there, asking you if you were sure, and…" Beck took a deep breath. "And you said you were never surer of anything in your life, and then, I think, you called me a sex god."

Allie was going to die of mortification. Right there. She was going to die on the spot. At least, she hoped she did.

"God!" she wailed and buried her face in her hands again. "Oh…no. Oh, no, no, no."

"Mira said she knew it, and then she let you go with me. Is this what you call me to your friends? A sex god?" Even Beck couldn't quite keep a straight face. His ego was already out of control, and with this new feather in his cap, he'd be intolerable.

"I'm going to crawl under the bed and die," Allie murmured, more to herself.

"Do you think I'm a sex god? Is that right?" Beck flexed his arm muscles in a show of strength. "You never told me that."

"I'm literally going to die. Right now. I'm dead. Dying." Allie pushed away her plate and laid her face on Beck's breakfast nook. "Just leave me here to die of mortification."

"I'll just use my sex-god powers to revive you."

"You're never going to let me live this down, are you?"

"Of course not." Beck laughed. "This is too good."

Allie groaned and rubbed her face, as if trying to scrub this nightmare of the last twenty-four hours out of her head. Why had she had so much tequila? Why had she admitted so much? Now Beck held all the cards, and she had none. Again. Why did it feel like a game of poker she could never win?

"Al," Beck said, and he put both his big hands on her shoulders and gave her a gentle shake. "If it's any consolation, I think you're pretty much a sex goddess, too."

She lifted her head and squinted at him. "You're just trying to make me feel better."

"Nope. I'm not. You're sexy as hell, Miss Goddess." He grinned, mischief in his eyes. "And sex gods don't lie."

"Oh, is that in the Sex Gods' bible?" Allie teased. She was only vaguely starting to be okay with living.

"Sure it is. It's right in our holy book, the Kama Sutra."

Allie gave Beck a playful shove. "Okay, so if I'm so great, then why didn't you call…after? Why'd you ghost me?"

Beck sighed. Allie didn't even know why she'd asked. She didn't really want to know the answer.

"I didn't call because you need a steady guy. Not someone like me. I'm reckless. I run away. I'm not the solid relationship type. You deserve all that and more." He blinked twice and ran a hand through his thick shock of blond hair. He pushed his now-empty breakfast plate away and leaned back on the stool. "But now that you're flirting with other guys, I'm stupidly jealous. I can't stop myself, either. I know it's wrong. But there it is."

Allie's heart ticked up a beat. "You're jealous?"

"Yes. Any time a man lays a hand on you, I want to break it."

Allie laughed a little bit. "That might be the most honest thing you've ever said."

"Are you okay? Have you been eating?" he asked, blue eyes tinged with concern. "You look like you've lost weight."

"Why do you care so much?" She couldn't figure this out. Was it just guilt? Did he not like seeing his decisions had consequences?

"I never stopped caring about you." His eyes were so serious now that Allie couldn't look away from them. How could he truly care about her when he'd let her go?

"No, I haven't been eating all that well," she admitted, though she couldn't look him in the eye. "Or sleeping, actually." In fact, the night she'd spent passed out in Beck's bed was probably the first full night in many weeks. "It's stupid. It was only a weekend, and believe me, I know you. I never expected you to change. I knew what I was getting into. I just didn't expect..." She trailed off. She was about to say *didn't expect to fall in love with you.* And that would've been the dumbest thing she could've said.

Beck sucked in a breath. "This is all my fault."

"What's your fault?"

"That you're doing all this crazy stuff. These... dares?"

"No." *Yes, of course it is,* she wanted to shout. But that felt like giving him too much information. Too much power. And she'd already given him far too much of that.

"You're not trying to get my attention?" A look passed through Beck's eyes then. Something like hope? Though she told herself it was just smugness. On another man it would be ego, but with Beck, it was just fact. She and every straight woman in Aspen was interested.

"No, I'm not trying to get your attention," she said. "You're stalking *me.* I'm just trying to live my life. Without you."

He flinched slightly at the last two words.

"Look, I'm worried about you. That's all. Last night... You were a little out of control."

"And?" She raised her chin a little. She was her own woman who could do as she pleased. She didn't need a babysitter.

"What if I hadn't been there to take you home?"

"Mira would have." And Mira now knew the truth, if she hadn't already, that Allie was still hung up on Beck. So much for the brave face she'd put on for her friend.

"But what about Taylor? Or what if some other man had taken advantage?"

"You mean like you?" She took a swig of her cooled coffee, but wrapped both hands around the mug anyway, as if looking for a way to keep her hands busy. She felt fidgety suddenly, and vulnerable, all too aware that she was sitting on Beck's breakfast stool wearing just his shirt, her bare feet swinging above the ground.

"You know what I mean." Beck grasped her elbow and she turned to look at him. She saw genuine worry on his face. She slowly put the coffee mug down.

"I'm a big girl. You don't have to look after me, okay? I'm fine." She was glad her voice came out strong and convincing, at least to her ears. Besides, where was all this concern when she was curled up on her couch eating ice cream from the container and watching slasher films because that was the only way to get away from true love and big-screen kisses and everything else that might remind her of Beck?

"I think this is all about you regretting your decision to sleep with me."

She glanced up at him sharply, suddenly worried that her heart was written across her face in bold ink.

"I don't regret that decision." How could she? It

was the best sex of her life. It was like an out-of-body experience, only one that occurred deep within her body. An inner-body experience. The problem was the sex had been all she'd imagined and more. He *had* been a sex god, and she'd finally worshipped him like she wanted to, and it all made her feel stupid. She was a self-made woman. She made her own money, and took care of herself and didn't need a man to make her feel whole, and yet…and yet…with Beck, she worried that she did need him. Too much.

She studied her coffee mug, not quite able to look him in the eye. She didn't want him to see how much that weekend meant to her. "It was fun. We just took it too far."

She had a flash of his mouth on her breast, enveloping her nipple. She almost could feel the hungry heat on her skin.

"You're not acting like yourself, is all. Stop these silly dares. And wild partying at the bar and downing tequila shots and…"

"Wild? Maybe I like wild."

"Wild like almost going home with a married man?" Beck's attention was now fully on her, his blue eyes sharp.

"Okay, not my best moment, agreed. But I was never going home with him."

Beck slowly shook his head. He was now playing the part of the sage father type, but she thought he didn't do that. Hadn't he always railed against all things paternal? Yet he was lecturing her like a tired dad of a wayward teen. "You're going too far. You need to stop this. It isn't you."

"Maybe you don't know me." And now she was acting like a petulant teenager. She wasn't even sure why.

"I know you better than anyone." The way he said it made her feel a chill down the back of her legs. They stared at each other for a second and she remembered all the ways he had gotten to know her better than anyone, in his bed. She had to stop thinking about how his hands felt on her, but it was next to impossible with him sitting shirtless and barefoot next to her. Being the object of his full attention felt like being warmed, as if she were sitting by a roaring fire. She'd missed holding his attention, but also hated that she liked it so much. She'd never cared about the attention of other men. And now she'd gone and fallen for the one man everyone wanted. She was living a cliché and she didn't like it.

"I know that you like to play it safe, but you also like to flirt with danger *sometimes*. That underneath that good-girl, always-by-the-book, drive-the-speed-limit exterior, there beats the heart of someone who likes to take a risk now and again. You don't need to prove that to me. I *know* you."

"What makes you say that?"

"Because that's what made you fall into my bed in the first place. You *liked* the danger."

"No, I didn't." But the minute she denied it, she knew it was true. Hadn't she gone into Beck's bed knowing full well he'd do exactly what he did: make her come so often she almost forgot her own name and then disappear afterward? It was what he did to everyone else, so she couldn't expect anything different. She'd been beating herself up for being foolish, but maybe he was right. Maybe it was the danger that drew her to him in the first place. Maybe this had been what she wanted all along.

"Look, maybe I'm turning over a new leaf. Maybe this doesn't have anything to do with you." She wanted to say anything to keep him watching her, attentive. Why did she care about making herself sound interesting to the man who'd shown her how little he cared? She shouldn't, and yet keeping his focus felt like a perverse accomplishment. "I'm a *new* Allie, one you don't know so well."

Beck's lips quirked up in a patient, though patronizing, smile. "So, this new Allie Connor. Tell me about her."

"She takes risks. She's spontaneous," Allie began. "She doesn't need Liam Beck." She didn't need to know *everything about him*. She no longer felt the need to pry open all those secret boxes inside his heart and see what was inside.

He chuckled, a sound she felt low in her belly. God, she loved making this man laugh. She wanted to do it again, make him throw back his head and belly laugh.

"Or any man. And she's not boring."

"I never thought you were boring."

"Is that why you spread those rumors about me, then? Called me Greenie?" She looked at him sharply.

"What are you talking about?" Now Beck looked thoroughly confused.

"I heard that you'd been spreading rumors about me, about how dull I was. Like a green ski run."

"I have no idea what the hell you're talking about." Beck shook his head. "I never spread rumors about you. I swear to you, I've never said anything bad about you. Because there's nothing bad to say. You're damn near perfect, Allie Connor."

This shut her up completely. She felt stunned, down to her toes. The connection she felt between them thrummed, and she vibrated, like he'd pulled a guitar string that ran straight to the center of her.

"But you ran. You didn't even want to be friends afterward. I just thought… I was dumb, I guess, but I thought we'd at least be friends." Tears glistened on her lashes. She batted them away, frustrated. Why did she care so much? She knew she shouldn't care.

"I'm sorry, Al. I really am." She could almost feel him pulling away from her. She needed to stop all this heaviness. Beck didn't do heavy emotions. He liked to play in the shallow end of the pool. The more she lingered here, the more he'd want to run away again. "What were we supposed to do? We'd had some wine, and we were snowed in for thirty hours alone in a lodge."

Beck had offered to show her his ski lodge that he was thinking about selling. He wanted to ask her opinion about updating the bathrooms in the place, which slept twelve, and as his friend, she was happy to oblige. Hell, to be honest, anywhere Beck asked her to go, she would've gone. She knew that. She'd been secretly thrilled when she learned the lodge was accessible only by snowcat or helicopter. How she'd *wished* the snowstorm would move in earlier, and then it had. As if she'd willed it there.

He had plenty of provisions, and tons of wood to keep his stove and fireplace stoked and the lodge warm. They'd also dipped into his serious wine collection. It was a recipe for sex. It was what the place was made for. The sauna for two, the shower with the many, many hot jets of water pouring from the ceiling and the tiled walls, and, of course, Beck. She remembered how she'd wondered how many other women he'd taken there, how many other women had lain on his bearskin rug by the fireplace, how many others he'd taken into his massive bed made of pine and shown them what it was like to melt their bones. She hated that she'd so badly jumped into that queue, eager to take her turn.

"The weather forecasters were wrong. We were supposed to be long gone before that snow hit. And…" He sighed. "I knew I shouldn't cross that line with you, Al."

Line? What line? He hadn't crossed it at all. She'd pulled him over it with both hands. The thought that he seduced her was absolutely ridiculous. Beck glanced at her.

"You think you seduced me?" Allie couldn't believe her ears. "You thought you lured me into bed with you? That I didn't want to go?"

Beck glanced at her, momentarily puzzled. "Well, yeah. That's what happened."

"I was *hoping* for that snowstorm," Allie said. "I was hoping we'd get trapped there. Why do you think I asked to go later in the day? Why do you think I wore red lace lingerie?"

Beck blinked twice. "You were planning to sleep with me."

"Yes." She stared at him.

"You took advantage of *me*, then."

"Absolutely, yes." Allie stared at Beck, daring him to contradict her.

"You were going to risk our friendship?" Beck still seemed in disbelief.

Allie nodded.

"Even if I wasn't going to be your boyfriend or whatever normal people do when they date."

"I didn't care. I just wanted you."

"But you can't do casual, Allie. You're not built that way."

"I just want you, Beck. Any way I can have you."

Beck stared, and for a split second, Allie thought he might lean over and kiss her. Or maybe she just wished it, hoped for it. She'd laid herself bare, because she couldn't help it. Not around Beck.

"But I know you want something more."

That was the truth. She *knew* he refused to be serious in his relationships, yet part of her had hoped she was wrong. Believed that he might care for her more than he let on. But then, she chastised herself for believing that. Why did she think she'd be any different than any of the other women he took to his bed? Why did she think she could change him? It was the worst cliché of all time.

"I can handle it."

"You're not handling it." How could he do that? Beck just had a way of making her feel *seen*. She could never have any real secrets from him. It wasn't fair. She had no choice now but to lie.

"I'm the new and improved Allie. I am not who you think I am." And why did she care so much about what he thought of her anyway? Why did she care to prove to him that he hadn't hurt her?

"So, the new Allie will do what? Climb mountains?"

"Maybe. Ski more at least."

"Even backcountry trails?"

"Maybe."

Beck raised a blond eyebrow in surprise. Of course, he would be surprised. How often had she cautioned him about the dangers of skiing unmarked trails high in avalanche country? Every time there'd been an accident with a skier she'd pointed it out to him. Tried to convince him how dangerous his hobbies were.

"What else? Bungee jump?"

"Yes." She didn't flinch.

"And…?"

"And take anyone to bed I want." There, she'd said it.

"Anyone?" He quirked an eyebrow and Allie realized her mistake at once. She'd meant to tell him she planned to sleep with someone else, but the fact was, there wasn't anyone else she wanted to sleep with, and she felt like they both knew it.

"Dare me," she murmured, voice low. *Dare me to do anything.* To strip naked. To get on her knees and take all of him in her mouth. The worst part was that she wanted him to. Even after he'd run away, she still wanted him. She pressed her thighs together and felt a tingle there, the spark of want. She could almost imagine his hands on her, how they'd feel running up the softest skin of her thigh, his fingers exploring her. She realized that if he asked any of those things, she might just do it. She wanted to do it. Even after all that Beck had done, and all this time trying to recover, she still felt that magnetic pull to him, a force that seemed far out of her control.

"Okay." Beck was going to take his time asking for what he wanted. Allie's heart thudded in her chest and her breathing grew shallow. She could tell him she'd made a mistake, that she'd never take a dare from him. But deep in the pit of her stomach she knew she hadn't made any mistake at all. This was what she wanted. Ball in his court, see what he'd do with it. His face was so close to hers that she could almost feel him breathing. She was all too aware of her bare knees and his bare chest, and how little clothing they both wore, how quickly it could be shed.

"Yes?" She tried to keep her voice neutral, but it came out more as a hoarse whisper, something like a prayer.

"I dare you to tell me what you want."

CHAPTER SEVEN

SHE FELT SUDDENLY on the spot, as if he could sense the changes in her body, the white-hot heat that flooded her. Beck was asking her what she wanted. And it felt like the doorway to so much more.

"What do you mean?" But the mood in the kitchen had already shifted, grown more serious, more sensual.

"Tell me what you *want*." His blue eyes fixed her to the spot, dazzling her with a menu of daring options. But the fact was she wanted them all. Wanted him to kiss her. Wanted him to explore her with his fingers, wanted him inside her, the deepest parts of her. She wanted to lose herself in him, now and always.

"I—I…"

"I'm right here, Allie. You have my full attention now. I'll give you whatever you want." He glanced at her lips. "Just tell me."

Now, at last, there it was. The single shift of power. He'd given her the reins now, and she clutched at them. The heady, delirious power. What would she ask of him? There were so many options, and she wanted them all.

"I want you to touch me."

"Where?"

"Here." She spread her legs a little. He touched her inner thigh and she shivered. He took his time working upward, and then he met the soft lace of her underwear. He stroked the fabric.

"There?"

She nodded, and his fingers slipped beyond the fabric, finding her warm, wet center.

"Do you want anyone else to touch you here, Allie?" he asked, moving ever so slowly, building the heat within her. For the first time, she could see the real jealousy, the real hurt in him. He didn't want to share her, and that thrilled her.

She shook her head.

"No one else," she said. That was the truth.

"Good," he murmured and pressed his mouth against hers, as he slipped his fingers inside, finding the delicate ridges of her G-spot. She gasped in his mouth. Allie couldn't think with his hands in her, on her, his mouth devouring her. She wanted…everything. She wanted Beck to love her; she wanted Beck never to leave her; she wanted him…forever.

"Tell me, Al. Tell me," he pleaded, as if he, too, were swept up in the game, unable to stop himself. There was no dousing the flame she'd lit in her own belly. He was staring at her, blue eyes intent, and she was very much aware that they were both half-naked—her without pants, and him without a shirt.

"I want you to kiss me."

And then he reached up and gently took her glasses off. She blinked as he set them deliberately on the counter. Then his lips were on hers. And he tasted so damn good. She kissed him back, fervently, desperately, the last two months disappearing entirely. She might as well be back at the lodge, lying on that bearskin rug, Beck's delicious tongue in her mouth. Her brain switched off and her body took over. She wanted him, wanted him as much as she had then, as she had for the last seven years. She burned with need for him.

And yet was she ready for him to walk out of her life again? Was she ready for that to happen?

She broke the kiss, panting, and she saw the want in his eyes, a need that mirrored her own. He craved her, too.

"I thought you…didn't want…me." Her voice came out so low she herself barely heard it.

"I'll always want you, Allison Connor." He was so sincere, so serious, that something in her broke then. She'd thought she'd built up a wall of defense against Liam Beck, but now, with him so close, the wall she'd built crumbled, and she realized that it had only been made of paper this whole time. She almost laughed to herself to think that she'd thought she could keep him out of her heart.

They both knew it was wrong. They both knew they shouldn't go here. Not again. But she couldn't help it. And she had a growing feeling that neither could he. She kissed him then, softly at first. He didn't push her away. He wanted the kiss as much as she did. Her lips had a mind of their own as they returned his kiss, deepening it, as the hunger inside her for him grew. Her want was like a pilot light flicking on, igniting a flame that burned hot. Before she knew it, her hands slipped up his bare, muscled back, crawling up his amazingly smooth skin. She knew she should break away from him. She should stop this before it went further, before she wouldn't be able to stop herself from what came next. But her body screamed for this, for his hands on her, for every pleasure he could give her. She wanted him more than she'd ever wanted anyone in her life. No matter what she told herself, she'd always wanted Liam Beck.

He lifted her easily up off the stool and placed her gently on the breakfast bar. For once she was taller as he arched up to reach her lips. She wrapped her legs around his waist, pressing her hot center against his belly, nothing separating them but the thin, sheer fabric of her underwear. She needed to wake up from this dream. This would not change a thing between her and Beck—neither one of them had changed and hasty sex wasn't going to take away the last two months—but her body craved him, like an addict that needed a fix. And their bodies spoke a language that flowed so much better than words. Their bodies had an understanding their minds didn't. His hands were all over her, under her shirt, and the tee came off and she was there in nothing more than her sheer pink lace, bright against her pale skin. She didn't care as he cupped her breast gingerly over her bra.

Need exploded in her chest, white-hot and demanding, and her legs tightened their grip around his waist, her thighs burning with effort.

"God, Al," he murmured into her mouth. Their tongues lashed together in the most primal of dances, tasting each other, devouring each other. He pushed into her, and she knocked over his salt and pepper shakers, not that either of them took notice. All she could think about was the man's mouth and his expert hands and the way his muscled bare back felt against her calves. She wanted to squeeze him and never let him go. She wanted this forever.

She wasn't drunk now, had no excuse for the fever burning for him in her brain. This was just…Beck. All Beck. The way he was so strong, so built, yet touched her so gently, almost with reverence. He trailed a line of kisses down the delicate skin of her neck and she gasped, the heat building in her, pooling in slickness between her legs. She wanted him. She was ready for him. She needed him more than she'd needed anyone in her life. He pushed against her and an empty coffee cup rattled dangerously next to them.

Beck picked her up then as if she weighed nothing and carried her away from the crowded breakfast bar and over to the bare wall. He held her against it, her back pressed to the cool, flat surface. He held her there, pinned, his muscles working as he pushed against her warm center, his mouth on hers. She felt his need, hard and ready, straining against the thin mesh of his gym shorts. That was all that separated them now, bits of tiny fabric, all that stopped them from the reunion Allie had dreamed of so often, late at night in her bed, or in the hot stream of her shower. She'd be embarrassed by how often she'd thought of Beck, of him having her, just like this, again.

Her legs tightened around his waist as she held to his neck, and he moaned a little as he pressed himself, bulging and stiff, against her. Then he'd whirled her again, away from the wall and to the plush couch nearby. He laid her down easily, his blue eyes searching hers. He took one hand and pulled at the edge of her lacy underwear, tugging it down to her knees and then past her ankles.

Now was the time she should find the resolve to resist him. She should tell him no; she should tell him this was a mistake. What would sex do for them now? Show her all she'd been missing and break her heart all over again? But the distant thoughts felt far away, drowned out by the humming want in her body, all the nerve endings in her eagerly responding to Beck's touch. The cool air of his condo hit her bareness and she shivered, even as she watched Beck tug down his shorts. He was freed then, heavy and hard, and she remembered how often she'd enjoyed him in that lodge, how often she'd wrapped her hands around him and made him moan. She did that now, an instinct, her hands flying to him, finding him heavy and thick and ready. He bit his lower lip as she worked him just the way he liked, from the base of his shaft to the tip. She loved that feeling of power. *Yes,* she thought, *I know you. I know what you like. I know how to make you moan.*

She thought of how he must've had other women since her, perhaps just this way, on this couch. She knew that he'd have other women after her, too. She couldn't fool herself now. Beck was Beck. He wasn't going to change for her. But she didn't care. Not in this moment. Still, she hesitated.

"What's wrong?" Beck asked, and she wanted to say "everything" and "nothing" all at the same time. Everything was wrong because everything felt right. It didn't make sense, but then, nothing about them ever did.

"Do you want to stop?" he asked her, concerned.

"No," she murmured. She didn't want to stop and that was the problem. She wanted Beck deep inside her, possessing her in all ways, to hell with the consequences, with what any of it meant. For one small moment, she just wanted to be Beck's once more. When he was inside her, everything was perfect. And she desperately wanted to feel that perfection again.

"You sure?" he asked, but he had himself in his hands now, and he moved so that his bulging tip rubbed softly against her. She moaned at the contact, soft, delicate. Her hips moved to meet him, as he continued to tease her, rolling himself across her in a way that drove her wild with want. He kept working her even as he dipped down to kiss her, now the full length of him between the folds of her most delicate skin. His tongue found hers as he began to move against her. The torture was delicious. She wanted him inside her, yet he seemed happy to keep her wanting. It drove her mad as the pleasure began to build. She realized even this little bit of him against her was enough. This bare contact would take her over the edge.

She clutched at his bare back, the power of what was coming too big to control. She spread her thighs wider beneath him, a prayer for him to take her, to plunge deeper, but he refrained, as he skimmed her in a steady rhythm, stroking her clit, and before she knew it her body went rigid, and she was coming as she couldn't remember coming before. Pure pleasure exploded in her veins, running from the roots of her hair to the tips of her toes. She squeezed her eyes shut and cried out, unable to keep quiet as the tsunami of her climax washed over her. She opened her eyes to see Beck studying her, a look of admiration and awe on his face.

"You're so beautiful when you come," he said, voice low. "No one comes like you."

And that was when the words bubbled up in her throat. *I love you.* They almost tumbled out of her mouth, almost jumped straight out in the air, but she caught them in time, swallowing them back, realizing in horror that she'd almost done the unthinkable: admitted the hold he had on her. Then, suddenly, logic switched on again. What the hell was she doing? Letting Beck make her come, make her forget the last two months? Beck had been close to negating all of what she'd worked so hard to heal. He'd broken her heart, and if she let him inside her, let him come, part of her knew her heart would break all over again. What would happen after? When he'd had his fill, scratched his itch and realized he still needed the comfort of other women? She might not be able to recover this time. The thought of tumbling to rock bottom, climbing her way out of heartbreak once more, sickened her. Yet, looking at his intense blue eyes, she was willing to risk all of that and more. What she wanted was to give him the best climax of his life. She wanted to show him what he'd given up.

"Al…" he breathed, and she felt his hardness against her thigh, his want. "God, Al, I want to be inside you."

"How bad do you want me?"

"Bad."

She reached down and felt the thickness of his shaft, understanding all too well he was telling the truth.

"What did you do the other night? When I left you like this." She felt him heavy in her hands as she worked him, clutching him so tight he moaned for more.

"I finished it myself later," he admitted. "I…thought of you. I…always think of you."

She felt giddy with power then. Good. *Want me. Need me. Like I need you.* She shifted herself, and he moved, so that he was half sitting, half lying on the couch. She slipped off the side and found herself kneeling beside him, hands still working him.

All she wanted to do was put her mouth on his big, throbbing self, make him groan with every lash of her tongue, make him remember just how very good she was at driving him wild. She had never felt like this with any other man, felt the need to worship him with her tongue.

"Do you like this?" she asked, as she licked him, from base to tip. He shuddered at the contact.

"Yes," he groaned, as he lay back farther in the couch. She put her mouth around the head of his cock, flicking it with her tongue. He moaned again, closing his eyes. She released him once more.

"Want more?" she asked him, and he nodded, once. "Good," she said, feeling the vixen as she took him once more in her mouth. She worked him, with her tongue and her hands, the long, fast strokes that she knew he liked. His whole body stiffened and she relished the power she had over him. Now he would know what she felt like, when she was at his mercy, at the mercy to her own clawing want.

"Don't stop," he pleaded with her, his hands in her hair. "Please, don't stop."

But then she did stop. She pulled away, teasing him, relishing in bringing him to the brink of the ultimate pleasure, before backing away.

"You're torturing me," Beck moaned.

"You deserve it," she said and grinned, wickedly. She laughed, feeling heady with power. She straddled him then, grinding slowly against him, making him grow even more.

"You regret not calling me now?"

"I've always regretted it," he admitted, voice solemn.

She paused then, a whirl of emotions floating inside her. "So, what is this we're doing?" She rubbed against him, slowly, and he sucked in a breath. She could feel him grow stiff between her legs, this desire growing with his cock.

"I don't know," he admitted.

"Do you want me?" she asked, grinding against him, but not letting him in. Not yet.

"Yes," he said.

"Are you going to let me in? For real this time?" She needed to know. What this was. She needed a label put on it. She needed to know. She was tired of him running hot and cold.

Beck glanced away. "I don't know, Al. I want to, but…"

"But…?" She dug in, moving her hips, making him groan.

Beck said nothing, but his eyes met hers, full of want. "Is this all we are, then?" She slid her hand between their stomachs and grabbed his cock. "Is it just sex?" She rubbed him harder. "I told you, I've changed. Maybe Allie 2.0 just wants this. Wants sex and nothing else."

CHAPTER EIGHT

BECK REALIZED THAT the gorgeous woman on top of him, wrapping her hand around his throbbing cock, was giving him an offer no sane man would ever refuse. Sex with her? No commitment, nothing but the beauty of their bodies pressed together in the way nature intended, finding ways to please each other that had nothing to do with emotion, and everything to do with pure sexual chemistry. They'd always had chemistry, he and Al, and that didn't stop no matter how much reality got in the way. Any man would be crazy to turn down her offer, except that Beck wasn't just any man. He didn't want just her body; he also wanted her mind and soul.

"No, this isn't all we are." He managed to say the words out loud. He almost wished it was. Just sex would be infinitely easier. Infinitely less terrifying.

"Are you sure?" She laid a trail of delicate kisses down the side of his throat and he could feel the pulse there, thudding. There was no such thing as casual sex with Allie Connor. He already loved her. He'd forever love her. She was asking him to ignore every single beat of his heart.

"Yes," he murmured. "I'm sure. I've slept with other women. But I've never wanted to care for them like I care for you."

She dipped down and kissed him, long and hard. Then she pulled away.

"Condom?" she asked, and he involuntarily glanced over at the small drawer in the unvarnished end table beyond her. She slipped open the drawer and pulled out a thin package.

"I know how to help myself," she said, and then she ripped the package open. He should've stopped her, told her that he couldn't do what she asked: sex without emotion, and he doubted she could, either. He knew she was already as invested as he was, already in too deep. She slipped the latex sleeve on him, rolling it down slowly, so slowly that he thought he'd die from anticipation. He wanted her so badly. He'd been without her for so long. She moved him with her hand, guiding him between her legs, and then, before he could react, she'd moved him inside her. He felt the walls of muscle inside her constrict around him and he nearly came right there. They were the perfect fit, he and Al, made for each other.

She gasped, too, her beautiful green eyes widening with surprise, as she took him inch by delicious inch. He wanted to move faster, but he waited, letting her ease him inside, little by little. She bit her lip, and suddenly, he wanted to do the same, feel the delicate skin of her bottom lip held gently between his teeth. He wanted to feel all of her, all at once.

She began moving, ever so slowly on top of him, rocking forward, taking him ever deeper. He held on to her hips as she whipped off her T-shirt, revealing her delicate lace bra. She was spilling out of it, her shell-pink nipples straining against the sheer fabric. She looked like a sex goddess, that was all he could think, a woman who knew exactly what she wanted and how to get it. That was what made Allie a woman and not a girl, he thought. She was a force to be reckoned with. She never broke eye contact as she reached behind her and unhooked her bra. It fell forward and she tossed it gently aside, but his eyes were focused on her heavy breasts, now free, her pale pink nipples erect against her creamy skin.

He reached up for them, finding them too big for his hands, and he loved that, feeling as if there were just more of Allie than he could possibly handle. Defying logic, he grew even bigger, even harder inside her, his body pushed to its limits by his want for her. He felt like a man starved of sex, and it was because he'd been without Allie for far, far too long. She watched him, green eyes never leaving his, as she rode him slowly at first, and steadily faster. She dipped down and he reached up, taking one delicious nipple in his mouth. He gently grazed the tip with his teeth and she moaned. God, he loved all the little sounds she made. They were guideposts for him, signal lights as clear as any he'd ever seen on the street. He read the language of her body as if he'd been born knowing it.

He licked the other nipple now and she shuddered, squeezing him even tighter. She pulled away from him then, eyes on his, and then she moved faster, her need growing. He met her thrust for thrust. When she came, she cried out, but never closed her eyes. She kept her eyes intently on his, and he saw an amazing explosion of pleasure in them, of awe, and he thought he'd never seen a woman more beautiful in all his life, more raw or more authentic, than Allie.

And then, seeing the pure joy on her face, he came, too, feeling the deepest, most secret part of him come a little loose then, and threaten to bob to the surface. He cried out, but he worried that it was all too late, that he'd never fully recover.

She was looking down at him now, as she ran a finger down the side of his cheek.

"Why don't we spend Christmas Eve together," she said.

The offer came out of the blue. Christmas? His stomach tightened at the thought. The perfection of the climax fading quickly. He had a ritual at Christmas.

"Christmas Eve, I ski," he said. It was his tradition. He always hit the mountain, no matter how bad the weather, trying to outrun his memories.

"And Christmas Day?" Something in her voice felt like a warning. He knew he should heed it, but he didn't. Christmas Day, he'd wake sore in his bed, and treat it steadfastly just like every other day. That was how he coped with the holiday.

"Al…"

Allie rolled off him. He felt the loss of her warmth like a blow. She was unnervingly quiet. He didn't like it. What was going on in that head of hers?

"Why do you hate Christmas?" she asked him, voice low.

"Come back to here." He didn't want to talk about Christmas. Or his family. He wanted to hold Allie in his arms and forget all about everything else.

"If we're going to do this, then you have to let me in. A little." He knew by the rigid set of her back she was serious. "Maybe you should see a counselor. Maybe that would help."

"A counselor? No." Beck shook his head. The idea was preposterous. He'd seen what counseling had done with his father, when he'd gone to sessions for addiction, and it hadn't helped him, so why would it help Beck?

Allie blinked. "Counselors help a lot. My parents went to marriage counseling when they were having trouble a few years ago. It helped them."

Beck shook his head. "No," he said, determined. Going to a counselor felt like admitting defeat, admitting he was broken. He thought, with a little time, he could simply fix himself.

"Well, if you don't go see someone, then at least *talk* to me."

He sighed, feeling like he had no choice. "When I was eight, my dad was arrested Christmas morning. He'd been dealing and doing drugs. Opioids." Beck glanced at her, blue eyes steely. "It was the first of many Christmases I spent at Child Services."

"Beck, God, I'm sorry." She turned back to him, rubbing his chest with her hand.

"This is why I don't tell this story," Beck said. "I don't want pity."

"You're not going to get it from me. I'm Allie 2.0."

He laughed at that.

"How did he get addicted?" Allie asked, but Beck just wanted to close off this memory, wall it off and never think about it again, even as Allie seemed determined to drag it into the light and inspect all its ugly imperfections.

"I don't want to talk about it anymore," Beck said. "Come on, let's do something else." He ran a finger up the side of her leg. He knew it was meant to distract her, to divert. But she wiggled away.

"Did he get treatment?"

He stayed mute. Allie let out a frustrated sigh.

"I think I should go." She stood.

Beck realized she was serious. She was going to walk if he didn't share something. "It doesn't matter about the treatment. He quit that like he quit everything."

She sat on the bed then, near him. But he wanted her closer, wanted her in his arms where she was meant to be. "You know you're not him, right?" she said.

"Most people who think they aren't going to turn into their parents are just naive. It happens to all of us, eventually." Beck grabbed her hand and squeezed it. "We either turn into them, or we spend our lives fighting to be the opposite. Either way, they drive us. Whether we want them to or not."

"And you think you're going to be your dad or..."

"Whatever the opposite of him is."

"Well, that would be a good thing, wouldn't it? That would mean a sober family man."

Beck threw back his head and laughed. "No way that's where I'm headed. I've got too much of Dad's wildness in me."

Allie studied Beck. "I like the wild in you. That's my problem." She stroked his cheek. She looked suddenly sad, and Beck wasn't sure why.

"Come here." He spread open his arms, hoping she'd walk into them. He'd never wanted anything more in his life than for Allie to stop being so serious and to just get onto this couch with him. Once their skin was touching, he was sure he could convince her all was right. Their bodies shared a better language than their brains, anyway.

Allie sighed, though, and stood. "I think I'm going to go." She grabbed her clothes from the floor.

"Why? You could sleep here," he offered.

She smiled, faintly. "I think we'd better take it slow."

Beck didn't understand. He'd given her what he thought she wanted, but she was leaving anyway. "Why?"

"Because if I sleep here with you, then I'll think it's this whole thing that it might not be."

"Maybe it *is* this thing. Maybe it will be if you let it." Beck reached out for her.

"Or maybe I'll just grill you incessantly about your childhood and you'll flip out, and not talk to me again."

"I won't flip out," Beck promised.

She studied him, eyes growing cloudy. He didn't like that look on her face, that studious one. She was overthinking things again. "I think you only want me when I'm leaving," she said.

"What? That's not true. Al, you know it's not."

"When I'm all in, you run for the door." She considered this, nibbling on her bottom lip. "But when I leave, then you're all after me. It's all about the chase for you."

"That doesn't mean you need to leave." The thought of her leaving disturbed him greatly. He wanted to sleep with her in his arms, wanted to re-create that magical night in the lodge when they stayed together, bundled up, naked, for hours. Why didn't she want that, too?

She grabbed her bra and wiggled back into it, and then found her underwear on the floor and stepped into those. She walked to the already-open door of his utility closet and pulled her now-dry and clean clothes from the dryer. She dragged on her jeans and sweater from the night before.

He badly wanted to peel those clothes right off her. He wanted to hold her in his arms, whisper promises in her ear, but most of all, he just wanted her here. With her in his arms. Her leaving felt like an icicle in his abdomen.

"You don't have to go." This much was true.

"I know," she said. She tugged on one sock and then the other and twirled around until she found her boots near his front door. "But I'm going anyway. The old Allie, she would have stayed. I told you I was the new and improved Allie. This is Allie 2.0," she said.

She grabbed her phone and small cross-body bag off his console table, grabbed the folder of Excel spread-sheets she'd promised to audit and flipped her auburn hair back and gave him a vixen's grin.

He got up, but she held up a hand to stop him even as she reached out for the knob of his front door.

"I'll call you when I've looked at these," she said. "I'll see you around, Beck."

See him around? That sounded like something he'd say.

And then she'd swung open the door and disappeared into the cold December air. Well, hell.

Beck sat literally with his now-spent cock in his hands, feeling like he'd been hit by a tornado. What the hell had happened? But then again, he knew. Allie 2.0 had happened. He could feel himself slick with Allie's juices, the smell of her on his stomach, in his hair, seemingly everywhere. The ache for her burned in his belly. Would he ever stop wanting her? Ever tire of her?

The sex they'd just had didn't even scratch the

surface of his craving for her. He'd thought that two months away from her might break the spell she'd woven through his life, but two months without her had made him want her more. He should run after her, call her back, but… For what? Was she right? Did he care about her only when she was running away from him? Was he just a simple predator? Was she the gazelle to his lion? But, no, he didn't think that was true. It wasn't just a game of big cat and his prey. Not to him.

He wanted more than just sex. He wanted all of Allie Connor. He wanted to breathe her in every morning and pull her into his arms every night. He needed her. Sure, he'd take as much as he could get it, but he wanted her sharp mind, her quick wit, the way she always kept him accountable and on his toes.

She'd blown apart every last thing he thought he knew about his life, every assumption he'd ever made about how he wanted to live it. And then she'd just sauntered out.

Now what?

Allie kept his mind spinning. Just when he thought he had her figured out, she pivoted, changed tack and slipped from his grasp. The woman dazzled him, confounded him. All he wanted now was that fiery redhead in his bed all night. Hell, he wanted her in his bed for the rest of his life.

Could he break free from his father's ghost long enough to make this work? He didn't even know how to start. How did he even start thinking about his future now? How could he settle down? He ran extreme adventure tours. Taking on one big risk after another. That was not what family men did: put their lives at risk every day to make a buck. That was what he did, though, to remind himself he still was alive. What would he do if he couldn't do that anymore? He couldn't let go of the idea he'd had for his life to live fast and not worry about tomorrow. Yet he couldn't shake the feeling that Allie was meant to be his next chapter or, truly, his every chapter after this one.

Beck shut his eyes, remembering how quickly Allie had come for him, how she'd held nothing back. She never did, which was one of the reasons she was so damn hard to quit. Beck never quite shared everything. He always kept something in reserve. Living with an addict had taught him to be careful and hide his feelings. He'd never gotten out of the habit. Allie wore her heart on her sleeve, and he could see in her eyes how much she missed him even if she'd rather die than admit it.

But the real problem was that he missed her, too. She had gotten under his skin and made a home there, and no matter what he did, he couldn't shake her loose. Worse, he didn't want to. And he had no idea what to do about it.

Maybe he did need to think about seeing a counselor. Maybe he'd do it, too, if it meant winning Allie back. Convincing her he was worth her time. But maybe, it was really himself he needed to convince.

His mind was spinning. He needed to see her again. He also knew he was playing with fire, because the more Allie insisted she could handle a casual relationship, the more he knew she simply couldn't. But was casual even what he wanted anymore? His head felt like it was going to explode. And this was all Allie's fault.

What he did know was that a woman hadn't ever tried harder to get his attention all while insisting that wasn't what she was doing. And he'd never met a woman so insistent that she'd changed, when he knew she was exactly the same Allie she'd always been, and that Allie was pretty damn wonderful.

He pulled out his phone and scrolled through it, deliberately ignoring the many messages he'd received over the last day. Channing had texted. Willis, too. Everyone wanted a piece of him. He scrolled through his social media accounts, and there, in his feed, was a picture of the perfect necklace for Allie. Rose gold, two initials, which he could envision already—*Al*. It would make a perfect Christmas present.

And then he stopped himself. He was buying *Christmas* presents now? He didn't do Christmas. He hated Christmas.

Yet he could imagine that delicate rose gold necklace, the color of the blush in her cheeks when she came, hanging around her neck, the charm nestled in the hollow at her throat. He thought how surprised she'd be to get it. He wanted to see her face when she opened it. He wanted to be with her Christmas morning—and every morning. God, he was in love with her. It was so obvious that he didn't want to admit it even to himself. But it was the truth.

Liam Beck had fallen deeply, irrevocably, in love.

CHAPTER NINE

ALLIE HAD SPENT the next week battling wild mood swings as she fluctuated from relishing Beck's astonished look when she'd left his apartment to feeling hopeless that she could ever, truly, get through the emotional barriers he'd set like barbed wire across his heart. Beck had called and texted a few times over the next few days, but Allie was the one who went radio silent this time. She was still dealing with the realization that Beck seemed to be interested in her only when *she* was doing the leaving, when she left him wanting, and how was a decent relationship supposed to flourish like that?

Beck wanted her only when he had to chase after her, when she was grabbing his attention by kissing strangers at a bar, but what happened when it was just the two of them, when there was no chase? Beck was right. He wasn't the settling-down type, so why was Allie desperately trying to squeeze him into that mold? It was almost as if she were trying to trick him, trying to get him to chase her straight into monogamy. It seemed a foolhardy plan.

Her heart ached at the realization that Beck would always be Beck. What had she expected? *She* couldn't change Beck. Only Beck could change Beck, and he seemed not to want to or not to know how. Either way, she was silly to think they could really make it work. Besides, when she imagined them together, what did she think? That she'd be enough to satisfy his deep restlessness?

And if he truly wasn't interested in something long-term, was she really willing to sacrifice her wants, her needs, just to sleep with him sometimes? The fact was, she was actually considering it. She shook herself. When did this happen? When had the confident, take-charge Allie been replaced by a love-sick girl willing to betray her own heart just to keep Beck around?

But they weren't compatible if she really sat down and thought about it. He was a risk taker and she was an accountant. He flew by the seat of his pants and never planned anything and she had every bit of her financial future mapped out down to the monthly contribution to her 401(k). He was wild, and it was the very wildness that she loved that also repelled her. How could she love the core of a man and then ask him to change it at the same time? She couldn't.

So, she was ignoring his calls. She was tired of pushing so hard, trying to make him something he wasn't. But at least this time she knew she hadn't been imagining the incredible chemistry between them. Now she knew he felt it, too. It wasn't all in her head. *And that's all it is, or ever will be*, she told herself.

Allie stood in her office, staring out the window of her small tax accounting firm that she'd proudly started herself. She had a shop just off the main streets of downtown Aspen, in an old office that used to be a telegraph office, back when this was an old mining town. Silver had brought people here back in the late 1800s, but now it was the white-capped mountains that lured in tourists looking to spend cash on ski lessons and fine dining. The short wooden buildings were brightly painted, but she could still imagine them as they were back in the Old West, when the streets would've been made of frozen mud and snow. At the end of her street, she could see the Rocky Mountains jutting up, covered in snow and evergreens, a view that never ceased to take her breath away.

She lived in a small condo she rented above the office, so didn't even have to step outside for her commute. She took another sip of her quickly cooling tea and watched as a flutter of snowflakes taken by the wind swirled along the street. The view couldn't be more Christmassy if it tried: a dusting of fresh white snow on the cars, small shops and restaurants outlined in white lights, almost everything wreathed in evergreen and red ribbon. The afternoon sun shone on the snow, making it sparkle.

"Allie? Did you hear me?" came the familiar voice of her assistant, Maggie. Maggie was about her mother's age, midsixties, and helped Allie answer phones, pay bills and do simple accounting for her less complicated clients.

"Sorry, Maggie," she said, dragging her attention away from the window. "What did you say?"

"Well, you just agreed to give me a hundred-percent raise, so woo-hoo for me!" Maggie grinned, her silver hair catching the light.

"You'd deserve it," Allie said. "Wish I could afford it."

Maggie shook her head. "It's all that tax software's fault." Maggie made a disapproving noise in the back of her throat. She hated the tax software that seemed to be everywhere and was cutting into their business. Some people still preferred the old-fashioned way of doing taxes, but Allie wondered how long that would last. "Have you thought more about that job offer?"

Allie glanced at her assistant. A college friend had offered a job in Denver not long ago, to be an accountant at a big firm there. It would give her a twenty-percent raise, and cover the cost of her relocation.

"I don't know."

"Well, don't worry about me. I'm retiring in January, no matter what." She grinned. She had two grandkids living with her son and daughter-in-law in Florida, and she planned to move there to help them.

"I know and I'm going to miss you." This was the truth.

"You got a place to go this Christmas?" Maggie sent her a sympathetic look. Maggie had adopted her as her own, since her family lived so far away.

"Not sure yet," Allie said. The mention of Christmas sent a bolt of sadness through her heart. All she wanted to do was spend it with Beck, but he'd shut her out—again. He'd tried to stuff her down into her Allie box once more. But she wasn't going to stay there.

"Well, you know you always have a seat at my table." Maggie was the sweetest. "Maybe I'll invite Beck, too."

Maggie had been trying to get Beck and Allie together for years. She didn't know about the weekend in the lodge or the reunion the Saturday before, and Allie would like to keep it that way.

"He won't come if I'm there." It was the sad truth.

Maggie glanced at her a bit. "He will. He likes you."

Allie shook her head. Maggie was working from a point of what-ifs and what-would-bes, but Allie knew the truth. Allie saw a flash of memory from last Saturday, his magnificently naked body above hers. She pushed the memory away. Now was not the time for that. She needed to put Beck behind her, for her own sanity. She was tired of crashing herself against the wall he'd built around his heart.

"He called today."

Allie turned, surprised. "Did he leave a message?"

"He wanted to know if you'd looked over some papers."

Allie glanced down at Beck's open file on her desk, frowning a little. She'd gone through the paperwork and everything seemed all right, except some-

thing was bothering her. The payroll was off. It was
too high for the number of employees she thought
they had, but then maybe Beck had hired more help,
or contracted out some of the tours. She'd have to
check with Beck about it. She calculated that, based
on last year's numbers, the payroll had gone up thirty
percent, even though she didn't find any new recipi-
ents of the pay. Maybe Beck had been overly generous that year and given out bonuses. She'd have to go
over the numbers again, sometime when she wasn't
distracted by thoughts of Beck himself.

Maggie wasn't finished. "And…" Maggie paused,
dramatically. "And he mentioned something about bungee jumping? He said you guys had a date?" Maggie's
eyes lit up with excitement.

"Oh, no. No, no, no. We don't have a date." Allie
shook her head fiercely.

"You might want to tell him that." Maggie nodded
toward the glass door and Allie glanced up and saw
Beck there, wearing a fleece-lined bomber jacket, a
familiar knit skull cap covering his blond hair. His
breath came out in foggy puffs against her glass door.
He raised a hand in a wave and a question.

Her heart thumped in her chest, and her brain ping-
ponged from sheer shock to immense relief. But what
did the appearance mean? She tried to calm the fluttering hope in her chest that this meant something,
that he was here to tell her something important like
he'd decided she was the only woman in the world for
him, and that her life was about to turn into a climac-

tic scene from one of her favorite rom-coms. Except that this wasn't a rom-com, this was her life, and that was Beck, and she needed to calm the heck down.

Allie strode forward and pulled the door open.

"Hi?" she offered tentatively.

"Hi," he said, his blue eyes lighting up when they saw her. Or was that just her imagination? She'd imagined so much when it came to Beck, she needed to remind herself this was about her dignity. About not letting him see he'd hurt her. And that she was still, on some level, supposed to be peeved with him. Even though she'd forgotten why as he stood before her in all his Beck glory.

"Gonna invite me in?" He flashed a white grin that made her stomach twist. Feeling like she was over Beck was much easier when he wasn't standing right in front of her, when she wasn't imagining his big strong hands on her hips. Allie watched as he took in her outfit; her skinny jeans, hiking boots and thin wool sweater. She thought she saw the glint of approval in his eyes, the heat of desire. She felt heat rush to her inner thighs, and she knew if he peeled her jeans off her, he'd find her wet and ready. She hated that her body responded instantly to him—there was that frequency again, the one tuned straight to him.

"Oh, Allie, don't let the poor boy freeze to death out there," Maggie chided as she welcomed him in. Allie doubted Beck could freeze. He spent his days outdoors heli-skiing on some of the highest and coldest peaks around. Cold never bothered the man. Beck sauntered in and hugged Maggie, who had to stretch up on her tiptoes to fold her arms around the back of his neck.

"Beck! So good to see you," she said, grinning, and seeming to work hard to make up for Allie's lack of enthusiasm. Allie couldn't help but feel the two were in league against her.

"What do you want?" Allie asked, and then instantly wanted to slap her forehead. Why did she say that? She was trying to sound professional and cool, but she saw by the look on his face that he took it as an invitation to a menu of sex acts.

"You'd know if you ever answered my calls," Beck said dryly. "If I didn't know better, I'd say you were ignoring me on purpose. To get me here. Didn't you say I only loved the chase?"

"Beck." Allie let out a frustrated sound and rolled her eyes. "Seriously. I have work to do. So…?"

Beck's face broke into a devious grin. "Well, I had some clients cancel on me and I thought you might want to bungee."

"Oh, let me look at my calendar…" Allie pretended to thumb through an imaginary calendar in the air. "Uh, nope. I'm busy."

"Come on."

"I've got to work."

"I can watch the office," Maggie chimed in, grinning. "You go. Have fun. While you're young."

"Uh…" Why did Maggie do that? She sent her a glance to show she didn't appreciate it, but Maggie stubbornly refused to make eye contact. The woman was determined to get them together. She'd have to have a word with her assistant later.

"Well, sounds like your afternoon just freed up." Beck swiped Allie's coat off the rack and held it up. "So, let's go."

"No." Allie crossed her arms across her chest. Beck put her coat over her shoulders like a cape. "You can make plans, like a normal person. I need some notice."

"Well, I *would've* made plans, if you'd returned my calls or texts. But you didn't. So, now, here we are."

Allie shook her head. "Still not going," she said, firmly.

"Okay, then. So you admit Allie 2.0 isn't real."

"Oh, she's real." Allie 2.0 was about to smack Beck, that was what Allie 2.0 was going to do.

"Okay, then. What's the problem?" Beck leaned in and Allie was acutely aware of the man's massive size. She craned her neck to meet his blue gaze, something she never had to do with anyone else. She was used to being among the tallest in a room. Allie tried not to feel off balance, but Beck always seemed to mess with her equilibrium.

"You're the problem." Allie glared. Beck just stared back, as if he already knew he'd won.

"Well, I've got a whole afternoon and evening planned for you. Allie 2.0 will love it."

This made Allie hesitate. Beck never planned anything. "A plan? You? I don't believe it. You don't even believe in dinner reservations."

Beck laughed a little. "Well, maybe this is Beck 2.0."

"You can't copy me and my 2.0."

"As long as you're pretending to be me, I can pretend to be you. Fair's fair."

"Go on, you two, argue on the way. You're wasting sunlight," Maggie chimed in. Allie glanced at Maggie, who shooed her with both hands. Maggie would like nothing better than for her to spend the afternoon with Beck. The worst part was that Allie would like nothing better, either.

"Fine," she ground out between clenched teeth. She was too tired to argue with both of them, and if she was honest with herself, she wanted to see what Beck had planned. He grinned, and somewhere, deep inside, Allie knew she was going to be in trouble.

CHAPTER TEN

ALLIE WALKED BY Beck's side in the freshly fallen snow, the late afternoon sun glinting on the crystals. She was a little tongue-tied. What was she doing letting him convince her a date was a good idea? The main street with the wreaths and red ribbons all felt so very festive…and romantic. Ahead of them, the Rocky Mountains jutted up, a tall, snowcapped peak in the distance against the bright blue sky. She sucked in a breath, feeling lucky to be living in such a beautiful place.

She glanced up at Beck's profile, wondering if he felt the beauty of the place, too. Normally, he hated the town. He preferred the pristine peaks far above the reach of ski lifts and amateur skiers. She wondered if he was thinking of those right now.

"Do you want to tell me why you've been ignoring me all week?" Beck asked. "I've been calling."

"I know."

"And texting."

"I just… Maybe you're right about us."

Beck shook his head. "Allie, I know you're trying to *be* me, but this is ridiculous. I'm the only one that gets to ghost people." The way he said it made Allie laugh.

"I'm not ghosting you."

"You're not?"

"I'm just *taking things slow*."

"By ignoring me."

"Mmm-hmm."

Beck stopped near a light pole decorated with a green laurel and glanced at the motorcycle parked in the snowy space. "Here we are," he declared.

"What's this?"

"My new ride," he said. "Truck's in the shop getting new tires, so…"

She glanced at the motorcycle, which already had a dusting of snow on its black seat. It was all chrome and black leather, a mean machine that looked like it spit out danger from its impressive tailpipe. The motorcycle suited Beck. It was a little bit wild, just like he was. She almost felt drawn to it, wanting to touch the black leather seat. But she held her gloved hands back. Was she really considering riding a motorcycle in snow?

"Oh, no." Allie held up her hands and backed away from Beck and the two-wheeled death machine. "No way am I getting on that. It's *winter*. In Aspen. You'd have to be crazy to ride one of those now. We'll slip on ice and die."

"Well, maybe the snow will break our fall." Beck shrugged.

"No. *No.* I'm not getting on that thing." Allie had always been taught to fear motorcycles a little. Her uncle had been an orthopedic surgeon and had often said that motorcycle accidents and trampolines made up the bulk of his business.

"I thought you were Allie 2.0," Beck challenged, as he straddled the motorcycle. The cycle was big, but Beck was bigger and made it look small. "I thought you took risks and did things the old Allie wouldn't do."

"Yeah, but…"

"Yeah, but what?" He patted the seat behind him.

"You did this on purpose," she said, suspicious. "Is your truck really in the shop?"

"It is. But, yes, I did this on purpose." He laughed. "So? Come on, Allie 2.0. Part of you is curious."

To ride a motorcycle, no, she thought, but to sit behind Beck? Wrap her arms around his waist and snuggle against his broad back? Maybe. Feel the wild wind whipping over their bodies? Possibly. But to go hurtling down the ice-slick highway on one? Uh, no.

"I've got a helmet for you," he said, offering her one. "Even this date has some *safety* requirements."

Her fingers tingled a little at the word *date*. What was his game?

"I'll freeze to death." She realized she was just coming up with excuses now. Part of her wanted to jump right behind him, and she squished that part down, feeling at war with herself.

Beck laughed a little. "I'll keep you warm. And

it's a short ride, anyway." He patted the seat again. "What? Are you scared?"

"No." Maybe. A little. She sucked in a breath. Not that she'd ever let him know that. "Oh, hell. Why not?" Her reckless half won, as she grabbed the helmet and stuffed it on, and then took her place behind Beck. His shoulders were so broad she could barely see over or around them. It was a wall of Beck in front of her.

"You might want to hold on," he cautioned her. She reached around and wrapped her arms around his middle. Then the motorcycle roared to life, pure power between her legs as Beck backed up into the street and then hit the gas. The jolt startled her and she pressed her face into the back of his bomber jacket. The hum of the wheels against the newly plowed street made her worry that they would somehow slip, but Beck, as usual, controlled the machine with rigid precision. He was a man who could bend machines and snowboards to his will, so it shouldn't surprise her that he could maneuver a motorcycle with ease. The roads had been thoroughly plowed and salted by trucks after the last snowfall, so they were mostly clear. She found herself actually enjoying the ride, as he wound through the narrow streets of Aspen, past the adorable shops decorated for the holidays. Soon, she loosened her grip a tad, feeling every small shift of weight Beck made, and then she copied it, their bodies melded together in perfect harmony.

The smell of wood-burning fireplaces hung in the

night air and she inhaled the scent and tightened her grip on Beck's waist, thankful for the gloves on her hands as the cold December wind whipped across them. The sun, however, warmed her dark coat as they sped down the small two-lane highway, winding around the mountain. Up above, the snow clung to ridges, and the mountains stretched up into the sky. Allie was amazed by how much she could feel every last vibration, that she felt as much a part of Beck as she did a part of the bike beneath her. He kicked up the speed another notch and Allie sucked in her breath, nerves humming in her temples. But then she found herself loving the speed, the wind against the mask of her helmet as they passed a slow-moving truck and sped down the highway. There was freedom in the open road, behind Beck. She wanted to drink it in, savor it. She loved how his body talked to hers, telling it when to shift weight, when to hold on tighter.

The ride was over way too soon as he pulled off the road near a long metal walking bridge across a huge ravine. Far below, at least twenty stories down, the rush of the not-quite-frozen river flooded over boulders that were coated in snow. She recognized the spot. It was where Beck took clients who wanted to bungee jump.

"Oh, no," she murmured, but her helmet echoed the sound back to her own ears. "You were serious about this?"

"Well, that's what we've been talking about all this time. You said you'd bungee jump." Well, in theory she had, but now that she was here, she didn't much like the idea of leaping off a bridge tied to a rubber band. She hopped off the bike, her legs still vibrating from the engine. She tugged off the helmet and immediately felt the static electricity run through her hair as she shook it loose.

"I thought you were kidding."

"When do I ever kid about *bungee*?" He set the kickstand to the ground and left the bike and helmet near the steps leading up to the bridge. In minutes, he'd unlocked the storage unit attached to the foot-bridge and dragged out a harness and the gear she'd need to free-fall.

Allie felt a little weakness at the back of her knees.

"Am I?" she asked, peeking over the edge of the metal bridge and feeling her stomach shrink as she calculated the sheer drop down. She didn't do well with heights.

"Having second thoughts? If so, you can just admit that we're great together and stop running away from me."

"Says the man who ran away from me first." Allie crossed her arms across her chest and frowned. "You cannot take the high road on this."

"Well, I've grown. Matured. Seen the errors of my ways." Beck flashed a grin and she felt her insides melt a little. Felt the pull to him, the powerful tug. All he had to do was crook his finger in her direction and she'd do just about anything he said. The depth of that power made her dizzy.

"I don't believe you've matured." She shook her head.

"Well, then, seen the errors of my ways." He cocked his head to one side. "So...are you going to jump? Or admit you want me? That what you'd rather be doing right now is be naked in bed with me."

Maybe now would be a good time to call this whole thing off, and let Beck know she'd only been kidding about Allie 2.0, that he was one hundred percent right. It was just a ploy to try to prove that, what? She wasn't boring? That she wasn't a Greenie. Or that, above all else, she wanted Beck to notice her. And keep on noticing her.

"No," she lied. She glanced at the harness. It had a lot of buckles and loops, and while it seemed to be made of seat belts, she wondered if it would truly hold her weight. Oh, Lord. What happened if she ended up losing all control of her bladder? If her accountant parents ever found out about this, they'd have a fit.

"Come here." Beck motioned her over and her stomach clenched. She didn't know if it was because she was moving closer to Beck, or because he planned to hurl her off the edge of a bridge. She swallowed, hard.

"Do I have to?"

He nodded, and his blue eyes focused on her with an intensity she would've liked under different circumstances.

"Okay, Allie 2.0." He busied his hands slipping the harness over her legs, and she was achingly aware of how close he was. For a second, she completely

love with Beck was the scariest thing she could think of. Even if she knew it was true. Admitting she loved Beck would be the same as losing him forever. She knew him well enough to know that much. If she could keep it light, remind them of their friendship, then maybe she could keep him. As a friend. As a casual lover. As something. And as pathetic and silly as that sounded, she'd rather have something than nothing. And she'd rather have it and her dignity all at the same time.

"Yes," Beck said and dropped his length of bungee cord. She was inches from the edge. All she had to do was fall forward, and she'd be doing it: jumping into the ravine. "You look a little pale. You sure you want to do this? Or do you want to talk about your feelings about me some more?"

"I don't have feelings for you." Her voice shook a little, but she told herself it was the icy wind and the fact that she was at the edge of a thin metal platform about to free-fall. Her legs shaking had nothing to do with her feelings for Beck.

"You sure?" His gaze told her he knew she was lying. But she had to cling to the thin lie anyway. It was the only protection she truly had against him. She needed her dignity.

"Stop playing around, Beck." It was almost a plea. If he kept at her, she just might admit what she'd sworn never to tell him, ever. "Am I going to jump or are we going to gossip about our feelings some more like girls at a tea party?"

Beck threw his head back and laughed then. "Suit yourself." He tugged on her ropes, checking the safety harness once more. "You know, you really don't have to do this. But I also know, if you do it, you're going to love it."

He grinned. And in that smile, she trusted him, even though she *was* terrified. Every cell in her body, every survival instinct she had, told her that jumping would be suicide, no matter how secure the ropes might be around her feet. Still, she needed to do this. She glanced up at Beck.

"I am, but I want to do it."

"Or you could just skip this part and get into bed with me?"

She wanted to do that, too.

"So you can brag about being right? No way. I'm jumping."

"Okay, if you're really going to do this, then make sure to just dive off, like you're jumping in a pool. Try not to pinwheel your arms. It's best to keep them straight out by your sides. The bungee will catch you, but it shouldn't be too rough. And when you stop bouncing, then I'll reel you back in." Beck tapped the winch next to her head. "Are you ready?"

Allie nodded. She scooted to the edge of the platform and glanced down. Good grief, that was a long way down. A cold sweat broke out on her lower back as she stood near the edge. What was she doing? Her conservative accountant parents would literally have a heart attack if they knew. Yet part of her felt the urge to just take the leap. Feel the wind on her face. Feel the free fall and, for a delicious second, all that chaos that could clear her mind entirely of everything but that single moment.

"You sure you don't want to change your mind?"

Allie wasn't sure at all. But then she spread her arms and jumped.

Beck had never found a woman sexier in all his life. She dived off that platform like a pro, arms out, legs pressed together, a beautiful, lithe bird, diving straight into the ravine below. For a woman who claimed to like to play it safe, she sure took to danger. The bungee caught her and she let out a delighted squeal, a sound that Beck felt in his entire body. Her auburn hair had come loose from its tie. Beautiful waves of gold and red caught the sunlight as she bounced once and then twice, before she came to a stop at the end of the bungee. She stretched her arms out and shouted with joy, her voice ricocheting off the rocks below and bouncing up around them. He had to laugh at the purity of her celebration and felt himself a little envious. He remembered the rush of his first jump, and how it had made him feel invincible. There was truly nothing like staring down death to make you feel truly alive. Not that there was any real danger here, but try telling the body that. It doesn't know or care about safety harnesses. All it feels is the free fall and the pure lick of adrenaline.

"That was amazing!" she screamed, her face absolute joy, as he activated the winch and pulled her up. In seconds, she was in his arms and on the platform. He set her down, and she threw her arms around his neck and kissed him. Surprised, he stumbled back a bit, but then caught himself, the fierceness of her lips demanding his full attention. Her hands were in his hair and her tongue in his mouth before he knew what was happening. Not that he was complaining. He kissed her back, right there on that platform, feeling his body come to life, summoned up to do whatever she commanded. She pulled away, her green eyes bright.

"You never told me that would be so amazing. Is this what skiing unmarked trails is like? Or any of the other crazy things you do?"

"Even better," he said. It was true. That was what cheating death felt like. Addictive and wonderful.

"So this is why you do it. Pure thrill. God, my heart is beating so fast." Beck knelt to take off her harness, freeing her feet. She ran her hands through her hair. "It's just amazing. I've never felt so…"

"Alive?"

She nodded.

"Now, isn't this better than taking married men home for a one-night stand?"

Allie laughed. "Marginally better." She grinned. Allie glanced at the harness in his hand. "Wait. Can I put that back on? Can I do it again?"

Right there, with Allie standing in the sunlight, beaming from head to toe, her green eyes shining like emeralds, Beck knew he loved this woman. He didn't know how he'd do it, but he'd find a way to convince her they belonged together.

Something shifted after the bungee jump, Allie could feel it, though she couldn't say what. She rode with her arms around his back as he took her to dinner. It was the day before Christmas Eve and all the restaurants were packed with out-of-towners, tourists who'd flown in for the holidays. Allie never thought most people would opt to go away from home for Christmas, but Aspen was always full to bursting with those who did. After searching and failing to find a restaurant that didn't have an hour's wait, they ended up back at Allie's condo with pizza and a bottle of red wine.

Sitting in front of her blazing wood fireplace, with Beck lounging casually on her leather armchair, and Allie's stomach full of thin-crust spinach-and-sausage pizza, she felt strangely content. Maybe she could just be fine with this, whatever *this* was. Beck glanced at her small Christmas tree, the one she'd set near her window overlooking the street. It was lit with white lights and she'd filled it with all-silver ornaments. Allie knew how Beck felt about Christmas, and suddenly wished the tree wasn't there.

"It's pretty," Beck said, nodding at the tree. "Where did you find that star?"

"My father made it," Allie said. "He likes to repurpose odd pieces of metal. It's a hobby. He makes them for the church fair, and he sent me one. Of course, now he and Mom have a tradition of traveling on a church trip every Christmas. I think they're building homes in Puerto Rico right now."

"Your father is much different than mine," Beck said, shaking his head. "My dad didn't even know when or where he was half the time."

"Are you up for talking about him?"

Beck glanced at her, wary. "Maybe."

"How did he become an addict?" Allie asked.

"Does it really matter?" Beck shrugged, and for a second she thought he'd do what he usually did when questions turned to his personal life and deflect. But then he met her gaze and seemed to reconsider. "My dad was a trick skier, before that was even a thing," Beck said, staring at the flames in the fireplace as he seemed to sink into those distant memories. "He never medaled, since back in his prime they didn't have medals for the things he did. Twists and flips down the mountain. He was my hero. I idolized that fool. It was no accident that I'm good at going fast." Beck laughed at this a little. Shook his head. Allie heard real love in his voice. "But one day, he was just doing his normal thing. Jumping. Spinning. But he landed a trick wrong, that was all. A freak accident. He broke two vertebrae in his back. Several back surgeries and many prescriptions later, and he was suddenly selling off everything we owned to get his fix."

"That's awful." Allie tried to imagine Beck as a little boy, struggling to understand what was happening.

"He cheated, too, on my mother. Slept around. Ran with women who had a supply of oxy, or who knew someone who did. He used his good looks and his charm there, too. He didn't care much about my mother and me at home." Beck frowned at the fire. "Mom eventually had enough of that and had an affair with someone she met at the grocery store, of all places. She divorced Dad, married this other guy and moved to Florida."

"Why didn't she take you with her?"

Beck glanced sharply at her, and Allie suddenly wished she hadn't asked that question. She feared he'd clam up now, just when she was starting to truly understand him. Or at least have some understanding of what made him tick. "I was fourteen then and didn't get along so well with the stepdad. I thought they were abandoning Dad, and I wasn't going to do that to him."

"You were loyal. That's admirable, Beck."

"Loyalty didn't get me anything but a lot of headaches." Beck shook his head. "I thought I could take care of Dad, but he was a mess."

"And you were basically just a kid yourself," Allie pointed out. "It shouldn't have fallen to you."

"There was no one else." Beck made it sound like the thing he had to do. "I went out to visit Mom once in Tampa on Christmas." He stared at the tree a beat, and Allie wondered if he were reliving the time. "It wasn't a great visit. I hadn't seen her in months, and I had a lot of anger."

"I don't blame you. You were taking care of your dad and trying to be a kid all at the same time, and your mom left, so, I get it. You felt abandoned."

"Maybe I did. I didn't think about it much." Beck glanced at her. She wanted to lean over and hug away all the sadness in his life. "Still, I said some pretty rotten things to her. She didn't deserve them." Beck ran a hand over the blond stubble coating his chin. "When she told me I was too much like my dad, I couldn't argue. And after that, I didn't get Christmas invites to Tampa anymore."

Allie felt the heavy weight of that sadness, of a kid stuck between two parents who weren't really parents at all.

"No wonder you hate Christmas," Allie said.

Beck chuckled a little.

"It just reminds me of the family I didn't have. Won't have."

"What makes you so sure you're going to be like your father?"

"My mother was right about me and him. There's something unpredictable in him…and me. That's what makes us able to do dangerous stunts on the mountain. You can't put that away and settle down, really. It always burns there. My way of dealing with it is…not dealing with it." Beck shrugged. "Plus, I know that with how fast I live, it's really only a matter of time before I have a serious injury."

"You could quit all the extreme stuff."

Beck laughed. "I can't quit. It's in my blood."

Allie considered this. "Or you could see someone. A counselor."

"Nah." Beck shook his head. "I don't like to talk to *you*. Why would I be more comfortable with a stranger?"

"We all have issues."

"Even you, raised by perfect accountants?" Firelight danced on his face.

"Even me," Allie said and laughed. "Hey, I had the opposite problem. I had helicopter parents who would wrap me in bubble wrap if they could."

"Probably explains why you can't get enough of me," Beck said. "I'm the bad boy you could never have." Beck pushed himself away from his chair and joined her on the floor by the fireplace. His knee touched hers as he sat down beside her. He reached over and tickled her a little.

She shrieked. "Hey! Stop it!"

"I'm bad! I can't stop it…"

Allie fought his fingers as she dissolved in giggles. He tickled her mercilessly until she begged him to stop.

"Fine, I'll let you go," Beck said, his strong fingers finally relenting. Her side hurt from laughing as she gulped in air. Being with Beck felt like the ground was always shifting—serious, white-hot sex, laughter, all in a flash. She liked it, the unpredictability. She was beginning to think she truly wasn't the conservative, by-the-book woman she'd always thought she was.

"Wait… I'm not done." Beck lunged once more and Allie squealed as he tickled her again. She tried valiantly to fight him off, but he was too big and too strong, and soon he was right on top of her, chest to chest.

"Beck! Stop!" She moved to defend herself, but he grabbed her wrist.

"I will. I'm sorry."

"You should be." Now they were eye to eye. Breathing heavy, their bodies pressed together. She fought the urge to kiss him. She glanced at his lips.

"I'm sorry, Allie." She realized that he wasn't talking about the tickling anymore. He'd grown serious. Too serious. "I'm so sorry for being a jerk this last month. I…I owe you so many apologies. This time of year, starting with Thanksgiving on…just messes with my head. I make bad decisions, and… I'm sorry."

"Do you think sleeping with me was a bad decision? Be honest." Allie steeled herself for his answer, fearing the worst.

"No." He rolled off her then. The cool air hit her chest, and she sat up, blinking. "No, I don't regret that."

"Good. I don't regret it, either." The truth floating between them felt stark, but real. Steady. Grounded.

"Look, I don't know what's happening here. Between us." He looked at her, a long, steady gaze. "But I know it's turned my world upside down."

Allie almost wanted to hold her breath. She put her hand on his shoulder. He grabbed that hand and held it.

"I want to be with you. I want to laugh with you. I want to take care of you." Beck's blue eyes clouded. "Even though you make that really hard sometimes."

Allie laughed. She did, she knew she did.

"I don't know what any of this means, but I think about you all the time. I think about you when I wake up, and when I'm skiing or giving tours to clients, or when I'm in the shower or when I go to sleep. You're in my brain all the time like a fever, Allie, and no matter what I do, I can't shake it. I don't even want to shake it."

Allie could feel her pulse in her wrist and wondered if Beck could feel it, too.

"I've been running scared since the lodge, Allie. I know that. I thought I was saving you somehow from me, but if I'm honest with you, I was just scared."

"Scared of what?" Allie felt confusion whirl in her brain as she tried to process everything Beck was saying.

"Scared of losing you. Scared of hurting you. Scared of what I was going to become." Beck ran a hand through his blond hair and sighed.

"I was scared I'd already lost you," she said. "When you didn't call."

She saw pain cross his face and knew then that he'd known how much he hurt her. And that he regretted it.

"I know. I've been a fool. Can you forgive me?" He searched her face for the answer she already felt in her heart.

She nodded, suddenly unsure of her voice. Allie leaned in then and kissed Beck. Kissed him as if her life depended on it, because in some ways she thought it did. It felt terrifying to tell him the truth. Terrifying to lay herself bare like that. And then he kissed her back, kissed her hard, his tongue in her mouth, his lips on hers. His hand wrapped around the back of her neck, and she forgot about anything she might want to say next, or anything she might want to hear him say. In that moment, they didn't need words. Their bodies spoke for them, as her lips parted and welcomed his tongue. The mere taste of him made her want more, it always did, but today, she felt a fearsome desire for him, a black hole of need that she finally acknowledged to herself.

Beck leaned her down and the next thing she felt was the softness of her plush shag rug against her back and Beck's delicious weight on top of her. His mouth was on hers, devouring her, and she consumed him right back. Her leg kicked out, and she hit the table with the small Christmas tree. An ornament flew off, hitting the ground with a plink. Beck pulled away to inspect the damage, but Allie put her hands on his face and pulled him back down to her mouth. She didn't care about any ornament, didn't care about the whole tree.

All she wanted was Beck. Only Beck. All of him. He managed to pull away once more, his breath coming fast, his pupils so big his eyes looked dark with desire.

"Al…" It was a question, so much uncertainty conveyed in a single word. But Allie didn't want to think about what would come after. All she wanted was to climb into his skin, lose herself entirely in his body. She wanted him to fill her in every way possible, and she didn't want to think about what it might mean later. She wanted to taste him again. Close her eyes and pretend everything was as it should be. She wanted to heal his scars, reach back into his past and show him that boy was loved. She wanted to make it all better. It was that simple, and the only way she knew how to do that was with her mouth and her hands and the rest of her body. He eased backward, and she sat up, whipping off her shirt. His eyes widened as they took in the black lace beneath. If she'd known Beck would be here tonight, she would've worn the garters he always loved so much. But the quirk of an appreciative smile on his face told her he liked the black lace she was wearing just fine. He dipped down and laid a trail of kisses down the round slope of her breast. She groaned, as he flicked the thin lacy fabric down and freed her nipple. He licked it, softly, playfully as she arched her back, wanting more of his mouth, and she could feel the heat of the fire on her bare skin. Her body felt as if it had turned into a molten river of lava, and the heat pooled between her legs. Beck expertly worked the clasp behind her bra, and then both breasts came free. He licked one pink nipple and then the other, as they rose to meet his command, his eyes never leaving her face.

"You're beautiful," he murmured into her chest, and she groaned in response. "I want you. All of you." She wanted him, too, more than she'd ever dare admit to him or herself. His mouth on her body felt so right, as if it was meant for her, had been all along. He dipped downward, tickling her belly with his nose as he moved ever south. He clasped the delicate lace of her waistband with his teeth and tugged downward, driving her near wild with anticipation. He moved slowly, deliberately, as if he meant to take his time, savor her, inch by inch. His hands pushed the soft fabric away, sliding it down her bottom and her legs, and then she was bare, completely vulnerable beneath him. He expertly spread her legs, and they quivered beneath his touch, his strong fingers pressed into her thighs. "I'm going to make you come," he promised.

It was a vow that she knew he'd keep, as he put his mouth on her, his warm, wet mouth finding all the nerve endings at her most delicate center. She came alive then, every pleasure circuit in her brain lighting up, like holiday lights on a tree. She squirmed, her legs spreading wider for him, her pelvis rising up to meet him, lick for lick, moving to his rhythm. He'd remembered everything she liked, the tempo, the pressure, the perfect places. He played her with his mouth, as if she were an instrument that responded instantly to his touch. She clutched the thick carpet beneath her hands and held on for dear life. The desire built in her, a flame he tended with his tongue that grew hotter with each stroke.

"Beck," she murmured, running her hands through his thick shock of blond hair, not quite believing he was between her knees, worshipping her. She wanted it to last forever, but her body had a different idea. "God, Beck." She wouldn't be able to stop what happened next if she tried. She was tumbling toward the cliff, unable to stop. And then she climaxed, everything falling away but Beck and his expert tongue. Her body went rigid, every muscle taut as the white-hot molten lava of pleasure ran through her whole body. She let out a shout, something guttural and primal that she couldn't contain if she tried. Her muscles relaxed once more as she sank backward, her body feeling like it had lost all its bones. Her breath came hard, and her heart thumped in her chest.

Beck kissed the inside of her thigh.

"I love it when you come. You're so beautiful," he said. She had needed that. In fact, the last time she'd come like that...she'd been on Beck's couch. She wondered if any man could make her come like Beck did: hard and fast, with the sudden, earth-shattering shock she felt through her whole body, the after tremors coming in waves. Beck was on the move, slinking up beside her on the floor as she lay, spent, wondering how she could ever want sex again after a climax like that. She rolled over to face him and then they were kissing as she snaked a hand behind his head and threw a leg over his side. She could taste herself on his tongue, and soon the desire began to rise again in her belly. She forgot how easily Beck could make her want more, how she seemed never to get enough of the man. He was all muscle and talented hands.

She tugged at the waistband of his jeans, blinded with the need for more, and as he fell heavy and hard against her stomach, her white-hot want grew. He tossed his jeans aside, along with his wallet and his phone, not that he seemed to care.

"Condom?" she asked, but he was already reaching for his wallet. He pulled a single condom out and in seconds had rolled it down his shaft, the firelight behind him as the wood cracked and popped in the hearth. Then she pushed him back down, his back on the rug now, and took control. She straddled him and slowly, ever so slowly, began to move, each millimeter a delight of new sensation, as he filled her in the way she'd longed to be filled these last two months. Firelight danced on his bare skin as he grabbed her hips and moved her himself, a little faster, a little deeper. Sweat trickled down the back of her neck, the heat of the fire warm, as she lifted her hair to cool herself, both hands in her hair, her eyes on Beck. His gaze never left hers. He moved his hands up her torso and then cupped her breasts, and she arched into his hands, eyes fluttering shut. Pleasure, building, beautiful pleasure, rolled through her body as she picked up the pace. He groaned and she opened her eyes once more, eager to see his need grow on his face. She missed that, the want in his eyes for her.

"God, Al," he groaned, his thrusts deeper now, more urgent.

"Do you want me?" she asked, as she took him harder, her hips moving faster, grinding against his. She wanted to hear him beg, she realized. She wanted him to need her as much as she needed him.

"Yes," he admitted.

"How bad do you want me?" She suddenly broke contact, lifting her hips away from him, and he slipped free. He groaned, clutching at her, seemingly desperate to be inside her once more.

"Bad, Al. I want you so bad." She could see the need in his eyes, see the want. It fueled her, drove her. This was what she needed, his want. His need for her. She took her hand and wrapped it around him, working him with furious, long strokes. He threw his head back on the rug. "I want to be in you."

"Do you?" She teased him more with her hand, working him from root to tip.

"Al…" His voice was a warning, as he suddenly flipped her over on the floor, and she lost her grip on him. He was inside her then, making her gasp with surprise, the shock of him, fully taking her, delicious. He wouldn't be denied as he raked his chest against hers.

"God, I love this body. You're amazing."

Her whole body shivered with the compliment, its pulse purring in her veins. She loved Beck's attention. She couldn't apologize for it, either. She loved making him hot, making him lose control. She loved how even now his eyes burned with pure want. She felt heady with that power, and for once, it didn't feel like she was the one so powerless after all.

She lifted her hands and tangled her fingers in his soft blond hair, as her legs wrapped around his waist as she invited him in deeper, ever deeper. He groaned as she squeezed him. He pushed himself up on his elbows, and then the palms of his hands, and he gazed at her as he slowed the rhythm. His amazing chest muscles worked, and she traced them with her fingertips, awed by the simple beauty of his body in motion. This body he'd taken and pushed to limits other men didn't dream of, and now it was here in front of her and she was exploring it in ways she could never imagine tiring of. She stroked his body as if it belonged to her, because for this moment, this one moment, it did. She met his stare and for a second was fixed by it.

"I want to feel you in every way possible," Beck said, and he withdrew, rolling her over on her belly. It was primal, rabid, raw, as he pushed himself against her, entering her from behind. She gasped as he pushed between her legs, again and again and again, her chest against the carpet, his mouth on her ear. She felt primal, base, driven by pure animal instinct. No rules. No words. Just what the bodies did best.

"I think you need to be teased," he said, as he withdrew himself from her.

"No," she murmured. She wanted him in her, more than she wanted to breathe.

He moved his fingers between her legs, stroking her, making her pant with heat and need. "God, you're so wet. So very, very wet."

"I'm wet for you," she managed, voice hoarse.

He grabbed her by the waist and raised her up. He wanted her on all fours, and she wanted to be there. She loved and hated that he had all the control. But there was something delicious about giving in, giving up to her desire for him. He grabbed her by the hips and entered her fast, hard, the way she wanted it. He worked her hard, and the muscles in her arms strained as she struggled to keep herself upright. She loved the sound of him against her, how it felt being on all fours for him. She was surprised by how much she liked it, by how she wanted more. By how she felt like a dog in heat, run by pure animal need. This was what she was made to do. This was what her body needed. He reached around then, finding her most tender spot, and began rubbing it, ever so softly.

"You're going to come like this," he promised her, and she believed him. And then it was all him: his hands, his very hard self, and she knew she'd come again. She was already at the edge, and all it took was a gentle flick of the pad of his finger against her clit, and then she was toppling over the edge, plummeting into the great abyss. She clenched him, hard, crying out in a voice she hardly recognized. Pure animal. Pure release.

He pumped again and again, and then drove even deeper still, until he let out a guttural shout, and then, he, too, came at a deep, hard thrust, which he held fast against her. She took it, loved taking it, and when he collapsed on her back, sweaty and spent, she felt a glowing sense of pure accomplishment. That was sex worthy of any god. They fell together on the floor, needs temporarily satiated, and Beck spooned her protectively from behind. She felt so warm, so safe, so happy. It was the happiest she'd been in two months. The persistent ache in her chest was gone for the first time in a long time. Words bubbled up in her throat, like fizzy champagne, unable to be contained. She felt them coming, felt them take flight, and this time, there was no stopping them.

"I love you."

CHAPTER ELEVEN

BECK FROZE, HIS ARMS around Allie. The L-word landed loud and heavy in the room, and as much as he wanted to say *I love you, too*, the words dried up on his tongue, the familiar fear dragging them downward, keeping them deep inside him. He hated the L-word, hated how people threw it around so carelessly, so effortlessly. He'd never been able to say it all that easily. Hadn't been raised in a family where they said it routinely, by rote. He told himself that was because when he said it, he meant it. Except that what ended up happening was that he never said it at all. Not to his mother. Not even to his father, who died of an overdose at the hospital days before Beck's eighteenth birthday.

He knew in his heart he felt more for Allie than he'd ever felt for anyone. Was that love? It could be. So why couldn't he say it? Why was he such a coward that the words couldn't come out of his mouth? So he hugged her tighter to his chest, because he knew, without a doubt, that he was about to ruin this moment, about to possibly lose the only thing that mattered to him. It was as if that inky blackness in him, his father's legacy, had taken control of his vocal cords. But he knew that was a cop-out. He glanced past Allie to the Christmas tree near her window and felt like one of its bright silver balls was lodged in his throat. "I…need you."

That was horrible. He knew it was horrible, but it was the best he could do. He could admit he needed her, so why couldn't he say out loud he loved her? Meanwhile, Allie was pulling away from him, moving out of his arms. He could feel the distance growing between them, and he knew he put it there. He'd made this happen. And he felt lousy about it. But wasn't this what Beck men did? Pushed away the people who loved them?

Allie was silent for a minute, and he could feel all the wheels whirling in her head. He knew she'd be poring over this conversation in her mind, worrying over each word, and he hated that he'd done that to her. Something shifted between them. A wall had gone up between them in the space of a few seconds, made of something even harder than concrete and steel. He knew it was all his fault. He'd do anything he could to make her happy again, except that he knew the one thing that he couldn't give. Something in him was broken. He'd known it for a long time. And now Allie did, too.

Allie felt like a fool. She'd thought maybe Beck *might* say "I love you, too." Honestly, she was kicking herself for even saying it in the first place. She might as well just open the door so he could run out as fast as he could. What was she thinking? She hadn't been thinking, and that was the whole damn problem. She'd let the moment sweep her away, delirious with the aftershocks of Beck's hands and his tongue. Anytime she thought of the long pause after she'd said those awful three little words, she felt herself inwardly cringe. Yet he'd said he *needed* her. Was that good enough?

Her heart told her no.

Her heart told her that wasn't good enough, not by a long shot, and that needing wasn't the same as loving. Part of her felt confident Beck would come around, maybe, but another part of her felt tired of waiting. He'd slept over, but he might as well have been a million miles away. He managed to fall asleep, but Allie had lain there most of the night with her eyes wide open, trying to figure out what she was going to do next. She decided in the dark of the night that there really was only one solution to her problem with Beck. Only one thing she could do.

She must've fallen asleep in the wee hours of the morning, because she woke to find Beck tugging up his jeans.

"Leaving?" she asked him, sitting up and rubbing the sleep from her eyes. A dull ache of a headache thudded in her temples, a clear sign of lack of sleep. Sunlight shone weakly through her window, so it must yet be early morning.

"Gonna hit the slopes," he said as he zipped up. "My Christmas Eve run down Pete's Peak." Allie suddenly had a vision of her life with Beck: of eternally chipping away at the emotional wall he'd built, of waiting, constantly waiting, for him to give her what she needed, but not quite meeting that want. While he wanted her, did he want to change himself? Did he want to heal himself? As much as she wanted to do it, she knew she couldn't. Only he could do that. She sat silently, waiting for…what? An invitation to go along? He wouldn't invite her. This was Christmas. The time he ran away from everyone he cared about, when he cocooned himself in bad memories. She realized she had to make a change. She needed to do it. For herself, and probably for Beck, too.

"I'm moving to Denver." The words came out easily, but they landed heavily in the room. She'd decided this overnight when it seemed the only answer.

Beck froze as he pulled his shirt over his head. Then he quickly pulled it down and turned, eyeing her.

"Why?"

"I've got a job offer. For an accounting firm. Pays better."

"I thought you loved being your own boss." Beck moved closer and sat on the bed. His weight bounced her a little as she tried to read his face. Why wasn't he talking about *them*? But then, she knew why. There was no them.

Was he disappointed? Did she even want him to be? Wouldn't it be easier if this was just a clean break?

"I think it's better this way, if I go." Because she knew she would always be holding on to him if she stayed in the same town; she'd always be hoping he'd change. She realized she'd been waiting for him to change for years, waiting for him to want to change, and she couldn't wait any longer. She'd waited first for him to be more than a friend, and that had taken years, and now, when they were so close to being more, he didn't seem to want to move, to bend, to change at all. Worse, Beck wasn't arguing with her. He wasn't saying anything at all. She was about to walk out of his life forever, but he kept silent. Maybe he wasn't even into the chase after all. Or maybe she'd finally figured out how to run far enough.

"When did you decide this?"

"I've been thinking about it awhile." She shifted and turned, propping herself on one elbow.

"But what about…us?" Beck looked crestfallen and she could feel his pain, a thin cut of a very sharp knife. A surprisingly deep wound.

"What are we doing? I know you're not going to give me what I want, and I won't be able to give you what you want." She sighed. "I can't stay away from you. And you're right. I can't do casual."

"Al." Beck's voice sounded heavy, sad.

"Whatever it is we're doing isn't working," she said. "And I'm not going to ask you to change who you are."

"Ask me, Al. Just ask me." There was desperation in his voice. But how could she ask him? He had to want to do it himself. She couldn't just ask him to love her. He needed to do that all on his own.

"I can't do that." She shook her head.

"This is about last night, isn't it. About me not saying…"

Allie almost laughed. He couldn't even say *I love you* now. In some ways, it just underscored the chasm between them, a gap that might never be bridged.

"Al, I just need time. Please." Beck took her hand in his. "Please, just give me a little time."

His pleading tugged at her heartstrings. She wanted to give him this and so much more. She wanted to wait forever. But she couldn't.

"I just want to be loved, Beck. That's all. Completely and fully," she said. "I don't think you're ready to do that. You might never be ready."

Beck didn't argue the point. "When are you leaving?"

"Don't know yet. Most likely the first or second week of January."

"Can I change your mind?" Beck asked.

"I don't know."

Beck fell silent a moment. "Will you come with me? Today?"

"I thought you always skied solo on Christmas Eve."

"I want you to come with me."

Allie thought for a moment.

"Okay," she said after a beat. Her time with Beck

was running out and she didn't have the heart to deny herself what time she had left.

Few skiers were on the mountain, which surprised Allie. But then, a storm was supposed to move in around lunchtime, and so most skiers had opted to stay in their condos. They were the smart ones, Allie thought, as the air had already dropped ten degrees by the time they'd made it to the ski lift, which would take them to one of Beck's favorite black-diamond runs. The backcountry he normal skied was closed for the weekend, due to avalanche alerts, and Allie was just fine with that. The idea of skiing unmarked trails was still a little terrifying. Allie shivered, even though she was wearing an extra layer, and the clouds seemed to hang low in the sky. It felt colder than any of the weather reports predicted. Her fingers tingled in her gloves and she gripped her ski poles a little tighter.

As they got on the ski lift, empty of all but them in line, the snow flurries started to fall.

"Are we going to have time to make this run before the storm comes?" she asked him.

"We should," he said, looking up at the sky and then at his phone. "Weather says the worst shouldn't hit until after two."

"That weather app has been wrong before." Allie remembered their time at the lodge and then felt a little heartsick about it. If they'd never gotten stuck there, would Allie be leaving for Denver? Probably not. She'd probably still be pining for Beck, waiting in the shadows of his friendship, hoping he'd take notice. Denver would be better than that, too, she thought. Denver offered the possibility of a fresh start.

They rode the ski lift to the top, the view breathtaking from the suspended metal bench. She wore her downhill skis and poles, a traditional skier, and Beck sat loosely, one foot out of his snowboard as it dangled. Beneath them, it was a long way down to the snowy ground, and up here, Allie felt like she could reach out and touch the treetops.

"I don't want you to go to Denver." Beck wouldn't look at her, as they both stared out into the cloud-covered mountain above them.

"I know. But I think I have to do it." She just didn't see a way forward where she and Beck worked, and she wasn't always running after him and he wasn't always running away, or vice versa.

"I told you I was trouble," Beck said. "I told you that you'd be better off without me. But now I'm in deep with you. I don't know how to let you go."

"That's why I need to leave. You've got things you need to deal with…your past…"

"Let's talk about something else," Beck said, his mood abruptly turning black.

For once, Allie obliged him. She had to, or she'd start crying on this damn lift, and that was not what she wanted to do. "So, no adventure tours today?"

"Gave my staff the rest of the week off," Beck said. "Willis, Gwen and Zach deserve it. We don't need to chase the holiday dollars. We've gotten a lot of good trips already this year."

Allie nodded, but then remembered something that had stuck out to her on the spreadsheets. "You just have three employees and yourself? No more?"

Beck nodded. "That's right. Why?"

"I have to go back and check the paperwork, but it seemed like you had much more in payroll this year. Did you hire more staff?" *Focus on the mundane, focus on the business*, Allie thought, as she watched his snowboard swing beneath the seat. She was pressed against him in the two-person lift, their shoulders square.

"Not that I know of. And I approve every hiring decision."

"You didn't hire contractors, maybe? Temp workers?" She rubbed her own skis together and watched the snow fall, mingling with the snowflakes already in the air, headed to the ground far below.

"No. Gwen handles the front office, and Zach helps Willis and me with the tours. I run a pretty lean operation."

"Did you give raises to Gwen or Zach or Willis? Or bonuses?" The wheels in Allie's mind were already turning. This was what bothered her about Willis's books. It seemed like he was paying *too* many people. But maybe he was just paying himself.

"No bonuses, and just the normal three-percent raise I give every year," Beck said.

"You're sure."

"Positive."

"Then I think there's something wrong with Willis's reports." She tried to tread carefully. She didn't want to throw around allegations, but she suspected he could be embezzling.

"Like what?" Beck frowned.

"I don't know. I went over the books. Payroll went up by thirty percent over last year. I thought you must've hired new people. Or given raises. Or both." Allie glanced at Beck's profile as he stared out into the cloud-covered mountain. "But if you didn't, then Willis's reports are off."

"Willis does payroll," Beck said, voice low. "I never wanted to mess with it. And whenever I suggested you could do it for us, he balked."

Allie felt a growing unease in her stomach. Willis was embezzling—she was becoming more and more sure of it by the second.

"Could he be stealing from you?" Allie almost hated to bring it up.

Beck seemed to shut down then. "No," he said. "He wouldn't do that to me. There's got to be another answer."

Allie knew she was right. She hated that Beck doubted her, but she also understood that his friendship with Willis went back years, longer than she'd known him. But it still irked that he wasn't taking her claims seriously. It just underlined the fact that Beck didn't really trust her, wasn't really letting her in his life. It couldn't be more crystal clear to her: moving to Denver was the right decision.

The ski lift spit them out at the top of the mountain, just as the wind kicked up and suddenly the snow started falling harder. Allie put down her goggles, protecting her eyes from the icy onslaught, and glanced down the mogul monstrosity before her, the double-black-diamond run that Beck had picked. She was a confident skier, but even her confidence was challenged by the icy drop. And the increasingly poor visibility on the mountain.

They seemed to be the only two skiers crazy enough to take on this mountain today. Allie was beginning to regret her decision to come out. She feared that in the back of her mind she'd somehow wanted to believe that the magic of Christmas on Christmas Eve would fix everything. Beck would say he loved her and they'd live happily ever after.

"Visibility sucks," Beck said. "This isn't going to be easy." He glanced at the sky. "We could try to wait it out a bit, or we could call ski patrol and take a ride down. They could take us down in the snowcat or by snowmobile."

"Since when do you let the ski patrol babysit you?" Allie shook her head. "There's no way Liam Beck would let a little snow get in the way of a good run."

"Yeah, but…" He paused, looking at her. He didn't think *she* could make it. That was what this was all about.

"I can do it," she said, lifting her chin and adjusting her goggles.

"You don't have to, though. The storm is worse than predicted and coming in faster than we thought." Beck's warnings felt like a challenge.

"The fastest way is down. Isn't that what you always say?" she said, and she pushed off with her poles. There was really just one way down, and the faster she got to the base of the mountain, the faster this day would be done. She cut small turns around the moguls, the bumps hitting her knees as the force of gravity pulled her ever faster down the slope. She was fast, but Beck, of course, was faster. In seconds he'd caught up with her, zigzagging down the slope in front of her, cutting a winding S in the snow with the edges of his snowboard. It took her a minute to realize he was leading the way, his bright yellow jacket visible in the growing fog of snow. She was reassured by seeing him, as the trees on each side of the trail became harder and harder to see as the wind kicked up, flinging pellets of hard, icy snow against her goggles' lens.

The snow was nothing but ice, too, and her skis kept slipping as she willed them together with all the strength she had in her knees. At some point, Allie started to realize that she could barely see Beck. He was still just about twenty feet in front of her, but the snow was closing in, blurring his brightly colored jacket. She'd need to go faster, need to catch up with him. She drilled down, turning less and focusing on getting down that mountain even faster. Her skis felt only barely in her control on the icy incline, as if one small slip would send her crashing. She hit a bump and sailed into the air, flinging her arms out, and then landed hard, but managed by some miracle to stay on her skis.

Beck came into view once more. He moved like liquid—languid, easy, and yet she knew the effort it took to make taking this run look effortless. Then he disappeared again in the whiteout. Without Beck's yellow jacket it was quickly becoming a white blizzard of snow and she could barely see the tip of her own skis as they dived in and out of the newly fallen snow. Allie caught up to Beck once more. She watched as he took a wide turn, hit a ramp of ice and flew into the air, grabbing his snowboard's edge. Magnificent, really, she thought. He was an amazing athlete, so graceful, it was like watching a kind of dance.

He flew over a snow-covered boulder. He soared high in the air, but beneath him, Allie saw a dart of green. What the hell was that? It looked like another snowboarder, who'd come from seemingly nowhere. Allie thought they were alone on this mountain, but she'd been wrong. The green-jacket skier seemed out of control and flailing, and Beck, midair, contorted himself to narrowly avoid hitting the man in the green jacket. But in the process, he caught his edge on an icy patch on landing and went flying. Head over feet, toppling into the snow in a massive wipeout. Allie's heart leaped in her chest. It looked horrible: he'd pin-wheeled, and now he was facedown in the snow. She skied to him and slid to a stop.

"Are you okay? Beck?" she cried, throwing down her poles and kneeling to unbuckle her skis.

"I'm fine," he groaned, as he got to his feet. He knocked the helmet he wore. "That's why I wear this," he said. "Damn that guy. Did you see him? Out of control."

Allie nodded. She stepped out in the snow. "Come on, then. I can help you."

He took her hand and got up on his feet, but then groaned in pain and toppled over. "Ah, dammit." He looked down at his ankle in the snow.

"I think I twisted it."

"Bad?"

Beck tried to put weight on it and nearly crumpled. He would have except he'd caught Allie's shoulder for support. She held him upright.

"Bad," Beck said. "Can't put weight on it." He pulled his phone from his pocket. "No service," he muttered. "Not on this side of the mountain." Allie checked her phone as well, but found the same problem.

"What are we going to do?" Allie's mind darted in a dozen different directions. The storm was coming. Pretty soon it would be impossible to find Beck at all, even if she did ski all the way down to the base of the ski lift so they could dial in for help. How would the snow patrol find him in the middle of this black diamond when visibility was next to zero? They'd have to wait for the storm to pass, and who knew when that would be.

"We need to get to one of the towers of the ski lift. It might have a direct line to the ski patrol, or we might get better cell reception there."

Allie took off her skis and stuck them in the ground in the shape of an X.

"Lean on me," she said, offering her arm. "We can both get over there. I don't want to leave you here."

She already felt the cold start to seep into her bones as the icy snow pelted her face. The temperature around them was dropping steadily. She needed to get him to help as soon as possible, and in this whiteout, she doubted she'd be able to find him again if she left him here in the middle of the slope. Even the trees at the edges were hard to see in the now nearly horizontal snow. The angle of the slope was about forty degrees, so walking across it would be tricky in the best of conditions, and these were far from those, but she was willing to try.

Beck leaned on her and they made it, limping, across the slope. "Are you sure the lift is this direction?" she asked him.

"Better be," he said. It wasn't like they could see more than ten feet in front of them.

Eventually, though, Allie thought she could make out something in the distance. A lift chair moving across the sky, the cables mostly obscured by the blowing snow.

"There," she said, as the two hobbled toward it. Beck's weight was heavy on her shoulder, his arm around her as he leaned, but she wasn't about to leave him in the blizzard. About halfway to one of the ski lift markers, she pulled out her phone and saw she had one bar. She hit the emergency call button on the screen and the phone connected with the ski patrol. In minutes, she'd told them their location, and a unit was dispatched to pick them up.

"You saved us," Beck said, gratitude lighting up his face. "What would I do without you?"

Beck was a horrible patient. He barely had the patience to lie still for the X-rays in the emergency room where he'd landed, after a quick trip to the first aid station at the ski patrol outpost proved that his injury was more serious than a sprain. It turned out he had an ankle broken in three places, and he'd be grounded from all outdoor sports for about six to nine weeks. Worse, he'd been admitted for surgery on the damn thing. He needed pins to stabilize it, and the sooner the better, so he'd be in the operating room first thing in the morning.

The doctors argued among themselves, too, about whether or not this injury would affect his snowboarding. One thought he'd recover with no issue, but another thought his ankle might very well never be the same. The news should've sent him into a tailspin. It should've made him fear he was finally following the path of his father: risky sport, injury and then his ultimate demise. But he didn't fear that. He didn't even really care so much about the ankle, about the worry of recovery. All he cared about was Allie. All he worried about was that she might leave for Denver and he'd never see her again.

Right now, she'd left the hospital and gone home to shower and change. She promised to come back with food, but he was kicking himself for letting her go without apologizing. For everything. For not saying "I love you," for insisting they ski on Christmas Eve instead of doing Christmassy things, for messing up her life so much that she felt the need to move hundreds of miles away to Denver.

Beck could not let Allie go to Denver. Especially when he knew she was moving *to get away from him*. If it was a job she couldn't refuse, that would be one thing, but he knew Allie better than anyone, and he knew she loved being her own boss, loved owning her own shop. It was one of the many things he admired about her. He was the same way. He loved owning his own business. He couldn't imagine working for someone else, and he didn't see Allie doing it, either.

Who would look after Allie in Denver? Hell, who would look after him? If the day on the mountain had shown him anything, it had shown him that she looked after him as much as he looked after her. That was what real partnership was all about. He had to think. He had to figure out how to keep Allie here, how to keep her in his life. He knew it wasn't fair to ask her to wait for him to battle his old demons, to finally and at long last grow up. Every adult thought about the future, but Beck realized he'd been using his past as a get-out-of-adulthood card, and that all needed to end and it needed to end now.

Maybe she was right. Maybe he wasn't his father. Maybe he could live a life free of his parents' mistakes. He would apologize and then he'd give her the Christmas present burning a hole in the pocket of his ski jacket. He planned to give her the gift…and ask her to stay. Permanently. And he just wanted to get it over with, because nerves were beginning to build in his stomach, and he wasn't used to feeling jittery. Very little made him nervous. He wasn't used to the feeling and he didn't like it.

But he was worried his request would be too little too late.

"Dude!" Beck looked up to see Willis standing at his door. "I heard the ski patrol took you down the mountain. You okay?"

"You sure you care about that, Willis?"

"Course I do, man." Willis stroked his long beard and edged into the room. He looked like he always did: worn jeans, hoodie sporting the logo of some craft beer Beck had never heard of. But he might as well have been a stranger.

"Why don't you want Allie to take over our payroll? Really." As he'd had a couple of hours lying around in this bed with his foot in traction, Beck had a little bit of time to think about everything Allie had said on the lift. And he'd used his cell phone to double-check all the payroll numbers in the business bank account, and he'd found that Allie had been absolutely right. Willis had been paying "overtime" to employees that never actually went to them, but had been diverted directly to his own account.

"She's all in your head, man. I don't think you see clearly when it comes to her. Don't know what you see in Greenie."

"What did you say?"

"You heard me."

Beck frowned. "Did you start those rumors about Allie? Give her that nickname?"

"Damn straight, I did." Willis almost seemed perversely proud of that accomplishment. As if tarnishing someone's reputation was a skill to be admired. "It was for your own good, Beck. She's too tame for you."

"Had nothing to do with you trying to break us up so you could save your own skin." Beck felt sick inside. He'd trusted Willis, and the betrayal ran deep. Insulting Allie was just salt in the wound.

He glanced up, eyes sharp. "What do you mean?"

"You want to explain the overtime? The overtime that went directly to your account?"

Willis shifted on his feet and stuffed his hands into the pocket of his hoodie. "I don't know what you mean, man."

"Yes, you do. I trusted you. And you betrayed me."

"Beck, please. I can explain."

Beck waited.

"I needed the money. I've been in trouble for a while."

"What kind of trouble?"

"Debt. Lots of it. I spend too much, got over my head with that house I bought last year and the new Jeep." Willis glanced away from Beck, ashamed.

"Why didn't you just come to me, then? I would've given you a loan."

Willis shook his head. "I didn't think you'd miss the money. You didn't care about it. You never really cared about it. You never once looked at the books. And, frankly, you haven't really given a shit about me, either. When was the last time we even *talked*, man? We used to grab beers all the time, but it's been months since we went out."

"So you steal from me?"

"I didn't know what else to do."

Beck shook his head. He wasn't going to take the blame for Willis's decisions. "I want you out of my sight. This partnership is dissolved."

"Beck, man. Please."

"No, Willis. How can I trust you now?"

A soft knock on the door took both men's attention. Allie stood there with a carryout bag filled with hamburgers and fries. "Come in, Al. Willis was just leaving."

Allie glanced uneasily at Willis, but he just brushed past her, muttering.

"Did you confront him?" Allie asked, when he'd gone.

"Yeah. You were right. He was stealing from me. I

can't really believe it." Beck shook his head. "I trusted him with everything." He glanced at Allie as she set down the bag of food at his bedside table. She looked beautiful in her skinny jeans and oversized sweater that showed both bare shoulders. She wore her auburn hair loose, and the fiery highlights shone even beneath the bright hospital fluorescent bulbs. He felt gratitude bloom in his chest. Allie had saved him on that mountain, showing the kind of resolve and courage that few people had. She deserved at least the same amount of courage from him. "I've got something for you."

Allie stopped unpacking food and glanced over her shoulder. "What?"

"Look in the right pocket of my ski jacket." She glanced at the jacket slung over a chair near the bed. She dug her hand in and pulled out the white box with the red ribbon.

"What's this?" Allie asked, surprise lighting her features.

"Merry Christmas," Beck said.

Allie looked shocked. "But…but I didn't get you anything."

"Open it."

She opened the box. A beautiful, delicate rose gold necklace shone there, with the simple word, *Al*.

"Beck." Her eyes filled with emotion. He saw tears in her lashes.

"Do you like it?"

"Like it?" She looked like pure joy. "I love it."

"Put it on."

Allie took it out of the wrapping and hung it around her neck. She latched the clasp and then it fell, right where he knew it would, in the small hollow of her neck. It gleamed in the light and looked perfect against her skin.

"It looks beautiful on you," he said. "Al. Come here." He reached out his hand and she took it. The contact felt so right.

"I love you."

"Beck." Emotion choked her voice. If she was going to cry, he would cry, too, he realized.

"I was an idiot for not saying it before. I love you. I've loved you since probably the first moment I met you. But I've been scared of what that means. All this time, I've been an idiot. I've been telling myself I'm protecting you, but I've just been protecting myself." He squeezed her hand and she squeezed it back. "But then, on the mountain, I broke my ankle and I thought…this is it. The injury that ends it all. I knew the injury would come one day and I used to think it would be the end of the world. I'd be like my dad. Lost, you know? But I wasn't. Because I had you. And I realized that if I have you, nothing else matters."

Allie seemed frozen to the spot, her eyes bright with emotion. He had to get the words out. He had to tell her how he felt. It was his only chance at making things right.

"Allie, I love you." The words flew out of his mouth, as if they were always intended for her. "I want whatever *this* is between us to be real. I'll do whatever it takes." He meant this, too. From the depths of his heart. "Allie, I don't want you to go to Denver. I know I have no right to ask you to stay, but I'm asking. I'll see a counselor. I'll get better. For you. Because I want to be the man you deserve. And if you decide to move to Denver anyway, then I'm going to open up an adventure company *there* and move right next door to you."

He held her hand tightly. Now the ball was in her court. She could still reject him. He prayed she wouldn't. Allie laughed a little as she swiped a tear from her eye. "So you are stalking me."

"I want to stalk you for the rest of your life, if you'll let me," Beck said. Allie leaned forward then and kissed him. "I never want to let you go again, Allie Connor."

"Is that a dare?" she asked him.

"One that I plan to keep," he said.

"Good," she said and took a deep breath. "Then I plan to stay and see that you do."

His heart filled with pure joy in that moment. Then he pulled her down to him and kissed her, tenderly, sweetly, with the promise of many more kisses to come.

EPILOGUE

One year later

THE SNOW JUST kept coming. Allie looked out the window of Beck's lodge, the one that had changed their lives forever, and watched as the snow poured down outside, falling in the crevices near the windows, coating the big pines outside, and the deep tread tracks left by the snowcat that dropped them here. The only way in was by snowcat or helicopter, but that was just fine by Allie. A cozy, no-fuss Christmas by the fire with Beck was exactly what she wanted.

"I guess we can always count on a blizzard when we come here," Beck said, laying a kiss on her bare shoulder as he came up behind her. She was barefoot, wearing only an oversized sweater, nothing underneath. Since they'd arrived, they'd taken off their clothes and had hardly put them back on. While not a traditional Christmas, it was surely the kind of celebration that Allie could quickly grow to love.

"I guess so. I'm glad you didn't sell it, though."

Beck nuzzled her neck and Allie leaned back into his touch.

"Me, too," he said. "We've christened every possible inch of this place, I think. We should call it the Sex Lodge."

Allie laughed. "I like it," she said. "Is this where we spend every Christmas?"

"I hope so."

Beck hit a button on the universal remote and the speaker system in the place turned on, playing a familiar Christmas song. Allie turned, eyes bright.

"I thought you hated Christmas carols."

"I do, but you love them. And anything for the love of my life." Beck grinned and Allie threw her arms around his neck. "You've changed my mind about Christmas, anyway. It might not be so bad, especially if we spend every year celebrating naked."

She broke the hug and then stood on her tiptoes to kiss him. She meant it as a quick peck, but with Beck there wasn't any such thing as he tightened his arms around her lower back and deepened the kiss. Allie wondered if the man would always leave her breathless like this, make her heart pound like she'd just run a sprint. It had been a year, and she still couldn't keep her hands off the man, still thought she was the luckiest woman in Aspen. No…the world. The last year had brought all kinds of amazing surprises, but most of all, the fact that Beck had mastered a complete one-eighty. Once he put his mind to something, it happened, and overnight, the partying and the playing around stopped. She had worried she'd be jealous, of all the women who came before and of all that flirted with him now, but in reality, he showed her every day that he picked her above them all, and made sure she felt that choice all the time. She'd been worried he'd grow bored, but as the days passed, he seemed to fall only deeper in love with her. He was a partner in the truest sense, and she was so, so very glad she hadn't moved to Denver.

He'd been seeing a counselor, too, to work through his childhood a bit, and the changes had been extraordinary. A year ago, Allie would've thought Beck would've never opened up to a stranger, a clinician, but the counselor had helped him work through some of his issues with his father and mother, and he'd been processing his anger toward them and his deep-seated fear of rejection that he carried from his childhood. She'd shown him that locking away emotions hurt him and Allie. Honestly, she was so proud of how far they'd come, and she was bursting with hope for the future.

"You've got a surprise under the tree," Beck said, nodding at the small real fir he'd brought into his house. The Christmas decorations were just a little sign of all the progress he'd made.

Allie glanced at the large bright box, wrapped in a bow.

"And so do you," she said. "I'm prepared this time." She fetched the silver bag from beneath the tree.

Beck raised his eyebrows in appreciation. "What's

this?" he asked, taking the bag and pretending to weigh it in his hands and then shake it.

"Well, if I tell you, that would spoil the surprise."

He dug into the bag and pulled out a silver ID bracelet with longitude and latitude measurements. "What's this?" he asked again.

"It's the location of this place," she said. "This place changed everything."

Beck took the bracelet out and immediately put it on. "It's beautiful. I love it." He looked at her and nodded. "Now...you."

Allie opened up the large box, trying to guess what it could be. The box was light, and she wondered if it might be that cashmere sweater she'd been eyeing in the boutique she loved on Main Street. Except when she opened the box, she found another wrapped one inside. And then another one inside of that, and then she pulled out a box about two inches square. She opened it, too, but inside, she found a brilliant dia-mond ring, a flat emerald cut, which looked almost completely clear, like glass. Her mouth fell open. And when she looked up, she saw Beck, kneeling before her.

"I love you, Allie. You've made me a better per-son, a better man, and I want to spend the rest of my life with you. Will you do me the honor of being my wife?"

"You're proposing?" A million thoughts invaded Allie's mind at once. Beck—the eternal commitment-phobe, the sex god, the man who'd vowed never to settle down—was settling down? Part of her was surprised, but, even more shocking, part of her wasn't. She realized, all this time that she'd been so sure of Beck's love, so sure of his commitment, that the proposal felt...completely natural. The next inevitable step in their relationship.

"Are you going to say yes?" Beck was starting to look nervous. And that was when Allie realized she'd just been staring, mouth open, at the beautiful ring. "Do I have to *dare* you to marry me? Is that it?"

Allie just laughed and jumped into his arms, wrapping her arms around his neck and letting out a monstrous squeal. Allie couldn't believe this. In no way had she seen this coming. But her heart filled with joy. She wanted nothing more than to live the rest of her days by Beck's side.

"Is that a yes?"

"Yes, yes, a thousand times, yes!" She kissed him, and he kissed her back, and Allie felt the whole world grow a little bit brighter. The frequency that ran between them seemed to grow stronger then, louder, and she loved it.

Beck plucked the ring from the box and slipped it over her finger. "Well, that was the most stressful game of double dare you I've ever played," he said, putting his hand over his heart and pretending to be winded.

"What are you? Scared of a little game? Scared of a dare?"

"I'll dare you to do something, all right. Come over here," he growled and pulled her into his arms.

"I dare you to love me," Allie said, looking up at him.

"I dare *you* to love me forever."

"Double dare?" Allie asked.

"Double dare you," he said and grabbed her by the waist, pulled her into his arms and kissed the life out of her. Allie knew in that moment in Beck's arms, she was exactly where she was meant to be.

* * * * *

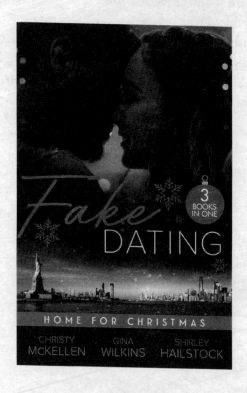

LET'S TALK
Romance

For exclusive extracts, competitions and special offers, find us online:

- **f** MillsandBoon
- **𝕏** @MillsandBoon
- **◉** @MillsandBoonUK
- **♪** @MillsandBoonUK

Get in touch on 01413 063 232

MILLS & BOON

THE HEART OF ROMANCE

A ROMANCE FOR EVERY READER

MODERN
Prepare to be swept off your feet by sophisticated, sexy and seductive heroes, in some of the world's most glamourous and romantic locations, where power and passion collide.

HISTORICAL
Escape with historical heroes from time gone by. Whether your passion is for wicked Regency Rakes, muscled Vikings or rugged Highlanders, awaken the romance of the past.

MEDICAL
Set your pulse racing with dedicated, delectable doctors in the high-pressure world of medicine, where emotions run high and passion, comfort and love are the best medicine.

True Love
Celebrate true love with tender stories of heartfelt romance from the rush of falling in love to the joy a new baby can bring, and a focus on the emotional heart of a relationship.

Desire
Indulge in secrets and scandal, intense drama and sizzling hot action with heroes who have it all: wealth, status, good looks…everything but the right woman.

HEROES
The excitement of a gripping thriller, with intense romance at its heart. Resourceful, true-to-life women and strong, fearless men face danger and desire - a killer combination!

To see which titles are coming soon, please visit

millsandboon.co.uk/nextmonth

MILLS & BOON
MODERN
Power and Passion

Prepare to be swept off your feet by sophisticated, sexy and seductive heroes, in some of the world's most glamourous and romantic locations, where power and passion collide.

Eight Modern stories published every month, find them all a

millsandboon.co.uk

MILLS & BOON
True Love
Romance from the Heart

Celebrate true love with tender stories of heartfelt romance, from the rush of falling in love to the joy a new baby can bring, and a focus on the emotional heart of a relationship.